Praise for the Montgomery Justice Novels

"The Montgomery Justice series satisfies on all levels, with plots that dovetail into one another and characters that aren't always what they seem."

—*RT Book Reviews* on *Behind the Lies*

"Robin Perini is synonymous with stellar romantic suspense."

—*USA Today* Happy Ever After Blog on *Behind the Lies*

"Perini refreshes romantic suspense."

—*Publishers Weekly* on *In Her Sights*

"This riveting book will keep readers on the edge of their seats and surprise them at the end. The tightly woven plot, quick pace and complex characters make for a remarkable read."

—*RT Book Reviews* on *In Her Sights*

"Robin Perini will keep you perched on the edge of your seat. Danger, excitement and romance...everything a reader craves!"

—*New York Times* bestselling author Brenda Novak, on *In Her Sights*

"Robin Perini delivers the goods—*Game of Fear* is an intelligent, fast-paced romantic thriller that kept my heart racing and the pages flying."

—Karen Rose, *New York Times* bestselling author

GAME OF FEAR

Also by Robin Perini

Finding Her Son

Cowboy in the Crossfire

Christmas Conspiracy

Undercover Texas

The Cradle Conspiracy

Secret Obsession

Christmas Justice

The Montgomery Justice Novels

In Her Sights (Luke's story)

Behind the Lies (Zach's story)

GAME OF FEAR

A Montgomery Justice Novel

Robin Perini

The characters and events portrayed in this book are fictitious. Any similarity to real persons, living or dead, is coincidental and not intended by the author.

Published by Montlake Romance, Seattle

www.apub.com

ISBN-13: 9781611098914
ISBN-10: 1611098912

Cover design by theBookDesigners

Library of Congress Control Number: 2014905351

Printed in the United States of America

To Claire Cavanaugh, the sister of my heart. For listening in times of trouble, for celebrating in times of joy, for crying with me in times of sorrow, and for carrying me when I couldn't walk on my own.

This book is for you, my friend.

PROLOGUE

Eight years ago

THREE IN THE MORNING CLOAKED TOO MANY SECRETS.

Seventeen-year-old Gabe Montgomery slipped around the side of the Denver bus terminal trying to stay out of sight. A blaring horn pierced the night and the hydraulic hiss of a bus door's opening snaked through the crowd.

A puff of warmth from an idling engine doused the November air in an eerie fog. Gabe shrank into the shadows. If he knew how to do anything, it was sneak. Tonight, for example, after partying at a club his father had forbidden, Gabe had stuck one leg into his bedroom window sight unseen—until he'd caught his father sneaking out of the house dressed like a stealth ninja.

Gabe couldn't resist. Maybe it was time for some payback. The last time he'd disappeared from his bed, his father had been waiting up when Gabe had crawled through the window. The memory of the scathing insults that followed still burned. The lecture about being smart in his choices or he'd never be good enough for the force still irked. Well, Gabe had his old man now, tailing him without being seen.

Except something was very wrong.

The smell of diesel clung to the air surrounding the fleet of buses. Gabe recognized the bulge beneath his dad's coat, just under his shoulder, packing heat where most wouldn't notice. His movements were too furtive to be answering a routine call from the sheriff's office. And Patrick Montgomery sure as hell wasn't wearing his official uniform.

His father glanced around, the guilty look on his face twisting Gabe's gut. He wanted to believe that one of his brothers had called, making a surprise visit home from the military, but he knew better.

Patrick Montgomery was hiding something, and Gabe's mission had changed. He vowed to discover his father's secret.

Gabe pressed against the bus terminal wall, his back digging against the brick, but the bite didn't faze him. His father stood in the shadows, nearly invisible in his black garb, surveying the area around him as if expecting an attack at any moment. Twice he'd checked his weapon and more than once peered into the darkness.

Gabe's father had decent radar, not as good as Mom with her Spidey sense, but decent. He could obviously feel Gabe watching.

"Damn right I'm watching, Dad." Big-man cop didn't even know his seventeen-year-old son had tailed him here.

Yeah, Dad. Your kid can outmaneuver you after all.

Gabe had wanted to be a cop since he was six. He knew what it took. But he'd been on the other side of the law, too, and had to admit sometimes walking off the straight and narrow path was more fun. He'd gotten into enough trouble this year to know the inside of the Jefferson County Sheriff's Office jail all too well. He hadn't spent as much time there as his older brother Zach, but Gabe figured he had a semester left to surpass the troublemaker of the Montgomery clan. Problem was, being the youngest of six hell-raising brothers, Gabe hadn't recognized that Patrick

Montgomery no longer possessed a whole lot of patience. Being grounded half of senior year sucked.

Pissed Gabe off. His father was a poster child for perfect. Perfect cop, perfect husband, perfect father.

To be honest, he'd never doubted that absolute truth. Until tonight.

Gabe squatted down and squinted through the night, out of his father's line of sight. The scent of gasoline burned Gabe's nose. The exhaust hit his lungs and he fought back a cough. Had to be quiet.

His dad was antsy, nervous. He fidgeted like Gabe had never seen, and Gabe had definitely never witnessed that particular expression on his father's face. What was his dad hiding? Had he gone over to the dark side? Gabe had heard his dad whisper over the phone about good cops going bad enough to know it happened.

His entire body stilled. Maybe he should just go. Did he even want to know the truth? He shoved the apprehension aside. He needed to know.

A bus pulled into the station, its headlights sweeping the parking lot and momentarily exposing an unexpected sadness on his father's face. Another emotion—anticipation—glittered in his eyes. Who was his dad waiting for?

The doors opened and, one after another, passengers disembarked. The excited, the down-and-out, the dead-tired . . .

Then a teenager with long, dark brown hair exited and scanned the terminal area suspiciously. Patrick straightened, his entire body going on alert.

Gabe took another look at the girl. A weird sense of déjà vu swept through him. She looked familiar, but Gabe knew he'd never seen her before.

She was gorgeous.

And scared.

She turned back to help the blonde girl behind her make it down the few stairs to the street. Ugly bruises marred the blonde's face and each step made her grimace and hug her arms to her body, as if her ribs ached.

Patrick Montgomery stepped out of the shadows and caught the girls' attentions, the relief on their faces obvious.

Idiot. Here he'd been suspecting his father was up to no good, yet obviously this was police business. He'd kick Gabe's butt for following him here. What if these teenagers were going into WITSEC or something? Maybe there was a U.S. Marshal around, too.

Gabe shrank farther into the shadows. If he got out now, his dad would never know he'd followed—

"Mr. Montgomery? You really came?"

The tremulous whisper stopped Gabe. He turned back to see his father sweep the brunette into his arms for a crushing hug.

"Yes, honey." Patrick's voice broke. "And it's . . . Dad."

Gabe stilled. No. It couldn't be.

Her hair. Her eyes.

His father's eyes.

And he knew.

"What the—" Gabe exploded out of the darkness and yanked his father away from the girl. The guilt and shock on his father's face ramped up Gabe's fury. "'*Dad*'? Is this some kind of sick joke? 'Cause I'm sure not laughing!"

"Gabe, I—" Patrick stopped and cursed. "Yes, Whitney is my—"

Gabe punched his father hard, knuckles cracking against his father's chin. He pummeled his father's chest. Gabe's vision blurred, not with tears but with fury. The man did nothing to defend himself.

"You bastard! How could you have cheated on Mom? On all of us?"

His so-called sister grabbed Gabe's arm with both hands and yanked him back. "Look, I'm sorry I screwed up your perfect life, but this is a crisis. We have to get my friend to safety. Someone's trying to—"

Bullets strafed the side of the bus, decimating anyone in the way. An elderly woman reaching for her suitcase sprawled to the ground. Panicked screams and cries of agony filled the night. Patrick homed in on where the shots had come from and ran that way, his gun at the ready. "Gabe, get the girls inside and call 9-1-1."

Gabe turned to grab them, then slipped on the blood oozing from the wounded. Before him lay the blood-spattered, bullet-ridden body of the blonde teenager. His sister futilely pressed her hands against the pulsing wound in the girl's chest.

"Don't die, Shannon. Oh God, please."

Gabe bolted to them, tipping over a large metal trash can to act as a temporary shield. He pulled off his shirt and stuffed it against the chest wound.

The girl moaned, "Need my book . . . the game . . ." A gurgling sound came from her throat and crimson rivulets ran from the side of her mouth. "Stop them—"

"Shannon!"

His sister's tearful cry twisted everything inside him. This was his fault. He'd kept them outside so some lunatic could take them out. "Get inside. I'll carry her."

Gabe picked Shannon up gently, even though he knew it no longer mattered. Her eyes stared sightlessly up and her body had gone completely limp. Crouching as low as he could, he ran for the door, his sister clearing the way. She'd grabbed the bags they'd brought with them.

Sirens wailed in the distance, but everyone stayed hunkered behind concrete walls until the police cleared the area. Gabe stared at his sister cradling the lifeless body of her friend. She rocked back and forth, tears streaming down her face. God, he'd screwed up. If he hadn't gone postal on his father, maybe Shannon would still be alive.

"Gabe?"

His father's frantic voice across the terminal broke through Gabe's shock and guilt. He waved his dad over, meeting him halfway.

Patrick Montgomery wove through the crowded area until he reached his son. "Is anyone hurt?"

Gabe glanced over his shoulder. "The shooter got Shannon and hit several other people, too. Looks like everyone else will make it."

A tic pulsed in his father's jaw. "And Whitney?"

"You mean your *daughter*?" Gabe couldn't keep the contempt from his voice. "A bullet grazed her arm, but she refused to go to the hospital unless you went with her."

Patrick's eyes flicked to the sobbing girl with obvious worry. "You okay, Gabe?"

Gabe laughed, the bitterness stinging his gut. "Oh, yeah, Dad.

Awesome. I find out my father's a cheater, meet my half sister, and witness a murder. Hell of a night. At least tell me you got the guy."

Patrick flushed. "The shooter was too far away. He had a long-range weapon. I didn't."

"Maybe you should have joined SWAT instead of Homicide. Not that you stopped anyone from dying tonight."

Patrick's shoulders slumped. "All I could find was the shooter's position. Maybe something will come from that. We'll talk later. I need to see to Whitney now."

Gabe crossed his arms, trying to stop the shaking that had settled deep in his core. He couldn't let his father see, though. "Yeah, I get it, but don't count on having that talk with me later. How can I believe anything you tell me after tonight?"

"What are you going to say at home?" Patrick asked quietly.

"Oh, don't worry. They won't find out from me what a bastard you are. I'd never hurt Mom like that."

Gabe walked away, his emotions running hot and wild. He couldn't leave the premises without giving a statement to the police, but nothing said he had to stay inside with that lying cheat. Gabe's eyes burned and he shoved his disillusionment inside. How could his dad do this to Mom? Another hero dead and buried. Patrick Montgomery was scum.

Gabe didn't know how long he waited through the chaos to be interviewed. Finally, they left him alone. The threatening tears had dried. When a black body bag wheeled out on a gurney past him, he stood, fists clenched at the injustice.

An hour ago Shannon had been alive. Now she was dead because of a coward shooting from the bushes. And because Gabe hadn't seen the danger coming; he hadn't moved fast enough.

A fire lit in Gabe's belly—a need for revenge, a need to make things right.

By the time he left two hours later, he'd made a decision. No matter what his dad said, Gabe was going to be a cop. A better one than his father. A SWAT cop, not a detective who investigated after the fact. Gabe would be on the front lines, kicking ass and taking names. If he could track down whoever had killed Shannon, even better. He never wanted to feel this helpless—or guilty—again.

CHAPTER ONE

Sammy's Bar hadn't changed much since Gabe Montgomery had turned legal almost five years ago. The clink of bottles on glass, the hearty laughter, the strike of a cue against the ball, cops and wannabes talking smack and reliving adventures over a few stiff drinks at the end of the day.

The door whipped open and the bite of the November air assaulted the room. "Shut that thing, would you?" he shouted to the new customer.

Winter had started off vicious this year. At least the warmth of the fire in the corner cut the ice lacing the air. This was exactly the place where Gabe had imagined himself after a shift—drinking a round with the deputies from the Jefferson County Sheriff's Office, easing the stress of the day before.

He sure as hell hadn't seen himself getting knifed, kicked off the SWAT team, and becoming the guy behind the bar pouring drinks, though. Even if he was deep into an undercover operation.

An op going nowhere at the moment.

This investigation had to move off point zero, and soon. With it stalled, his brother Luke would be retired before he and his family were truly safe.

Luke had poked at rumors surrounding corruption in the sheriff's office in a series of articles for the local paper, but he fought to remain low-key now, after nearly losing his wife because of his digging.

If Gabe's investigation could keep his brother's family out of danger, the deception would be worth it. But he needed a break in the case to walk through that door, and he needed it bad.

A couple of regulars pushed into the bar wearing blue and orange. *Sunday Night Football.* His bartender, Hawk, strode over to the television above the bar and flipped it on so they could check out the Broncos.

"Hey, Gabe. That show you've been waiting for is coming on."

At the bellow, Gabe glanced up at the muted screen over the bar. *America's Most Wanted* was covering an eight-year-old cold case.

Shannon Devlin's case.

Not that Gabe had forgotten a single minute of that night. Probably the worst night of his life, which was saying something considering in the last few months he'd nearly died at the hands of a gangbanger and was almost blown up by a traitor.

Some would call him charmed for surviving. Gabe knew better.

Images of the Denver bus terminal flashed onto the screen. Every few years, the show reran the episode near the anniversary of Shannon's death, the producers hoping this time a witness would grow some balls and step forward with information to solve her murder.

Gabe didn't intend to miss the show, even if it came at the dinner hour. Maybe this time he'd remember something more. Maybe this time there'd be some new lead he hadn't heard about. "Take over the bar for me, Hawk. I'll be back in a few."

"Got it, boss."

Gabe weaved his way through the kitchen, the scent of barbecue and frying oil permeating even the walls. He nodded at the dynamic duo throwing together sandwiches and prepping buffalo wings and potato skins for football night, grabbed his coat, and stuffed his arms in the sleeves before zipping it up. Bracing himself, he ducked his head down and stepped outside. The frigid wind howled, nipping his face with pricks of ice.

Yep, winter had definitely arrived.

He hurried past the basketball hoop behind the bar and across the small add-on parking lot to his house. Made going to work convenient. Especially now that he was the pseudo new owner of Sammy's Bar. At least for this op.

Gabe unlocked the door, strode into his kitchen, and flicked on the television sitting on the counter. The segment had already started. Within seconds, the sounds, the images, the words, threw him back to the night Shannon's life had ended.

The night Gabe's life had changed forever.

The shooter had never been caught.

He knew the segment by heart. A road between Angel Fire and Taos, New Mexico, five hours south of Denver. Shannon Devlin's car had broken down while she was driving to meet her teammates for a state math competition. She'd flagged a car down. The driver had brutally attacked her, nearly killing her. When another car had pulled up, the predator took off. The case might have been ignored as a teenager making a bad decision, except none of her other team members had made it to Taos, either. They'd never been found.

Shannon had survived the first attack, but not the second. The shooting that night played out across the television screen. Jumpy black-and-white footage from the bus terminal's surveillance system. The gunshots. The spattered blood. The screams. The broken bodies ripped apart by a long-range weapon.

Gabe eyed the reenactment. The more he watched, the more the base of his spine tingled. Even at seventeen he'd recognized Shannon was the target, but tonight he saw something new. Shots fired at exact intervals. And more. The shooter's hits were well placed, back and forth, clearing a path to Shannon, injuring but not killing those in the way. Why had he never seen it before? Gabe leaned forward and touched the screen. Each shot deliberate, accurate. Not random like the cops thought. Maximum chaos and only one dead.

Not murder. Assassination.

Like Patrick Montgomery.

Gabe reeled back. Also just like his father's death five years ago, there was no motive. No suspects.

With a sharp curse, Gabe hit the "Off" button on the remote. He should let the past go. His small flash of insight wouldn't change a thing. He was SWAT. He was no detective. When this job was over, he'd have to face reality. He wasn't a cop anymore, not the kind he'd wanted to be.

The phone rang and he grabbed it. "Yeah?"

"I got somethin'."

Gabe blew out a breath. Ernie the Rat. Slimy little guy who acted as one of Gabe's informants. "Hope it's better than last time."

"I'm tellin' ya, you wanted the scoop on cops in bed with Jeff Gasmerati. I got some news."

"Fine," Gabe muttered, still not convinced, but he refused to ignore a lead. He hadn't followed his gut when his best friend, Steve Paretti, had started acting strange. The guy had turned out to be the worst kind of cop. Gabe wouldn't let another dirty cop get away with it. "You know where."

"Got it. Usual time?"

"Yeah, make it good. I'm in no mood for crap tonight, Ernie. I'm warning you."

"I won't let you down, big guy."

Gabe hung up. He felt dirtier than pond scum, dealing with the likes of Ernie Rattori. But Gabe would stoop to any depth to do this job.

Hell, the assholes in Internal Affairs looked like choirboys next to him.

With Gabe's bum leg, undercover vermin catcher was the only help he could offer the sheriff's office anymore. Everyone thought he'd quit and bought the cop bar on a whim when the owner had retired. Captain Garrison was the only one who knew the truth—that this undercover op's sole purpose was to bring down the Gasmerati organization and its ties to the Jefferson County Sheriff's Office. *If* Gabe could find the proof.

He headed back to Sammy's to finish out his shift before meeting Ernie after the place closed. The sooner he got this investigation wrapped up, the sooner he could come clean with everyone—his old teammates, even his family.

Eight years ago he'd promised he wouldn't become his father, and here he was, lying to everyone he cared about.

Just like his dad.

The whirr of the circling Bell 212 helicopter rotors echoed through the cockpit. New Mexico's Wheeler Peak, barely visible in the dusk, loomed just east, its thirteen-thousand-foot summit laden with snow. Deborah Lansing leaned forward, the seat belt straps pulling at her shoulders.

Far, far to the west, the sun was just a sliver in the sky.

"It's almost dark, Deb. We have to land," Gene Russo, her local Search and Rescue contact, insisted.

"The moon is bright enough right now that I can still see a little, and we have the spotlight. Those kids have got to be here somewhere!"

Deb squinted against the setting sun; her eyes burned with fatigue. They'd been at it for hours, but she couldn't give up. Not yet.

"All the other choppers have landed, Deb. This is too dangerous. Besides, do you really think your spotlight's going to find a snow-covered bus on the side of the mountain with all these trees?"

"Five more minutes. That's all I'm asking."

A metallic glint pierced through a thick carpet of snow-packed spruce.

"There! I saw something." Deb's adrenaline raced as she shoved the steering bar to the right and down, using the foot pedals to maintain control.

"Holy crap, Lansing. What are you doing?" Gene shouted, holding on to his seat harness. "You trying to get us killed?"

He didn't understand. The bird knew exactly what Deb wanted, and she didn't leave people behind to die. Not after Afghanistan. She had enough ghosts on her conscience. She tilted the chopper forward and came around again, sidling near the road toward Taos Ski Valley where the church bus had been headed before it had vanished.

She dipped the chopper, scouring the terrain with the spotlight. A metallic flash pierced her gaze once again. “Gene, did you see that? Just south?”

The gray-faced spotter shook his head. “No, I’m too busy trying not to puke all over your windows.” He swallowed deeply and adjusted his microphone. “Could you fly this thing steady for a while?”

She sent him a grimace. “Sorry. I really think I spotted something. I had to go closer. I didn’t want to miss it. I need to swing by one more time. Really look this time, okay?”

Gene groaned. “Deb, I know you’re used to Denver terrain, but you can’t treat the Sangre de Cristo Mountains this way. These gullies and drafts can buffet a chopper, especially in some of the gorges. Your lift will disappear, and you’ll fly into the mountain.”

A peak rose toward them, and Deb pulled up on the collective control stick. The Bell followed her lead easily, but the sun was gone now. The near-total darkness made flying treacherous. The moon was the only thing making the deadly terrain remotely visible outside the spotlight’s range.

“At least there aren’t Stingers or RPGs shooting at us,” she said.

Gene shot her a look. “You were in the military?”

“Flew rescue missions,” Deb said. She shifted the steering bar. “I know I saw something down there, too. I’ve got that buzz. Come on, baby,” she urged the chopper.

Below, a blanket of snow covered a valley peppered with spruce, fir, and pines. The frigid temperatures, blowing snowdrifts, and icy roads had made the ground search difficult.

If Deb couldn’t find them tonight . . .

"Return to base, Search 10," the order crackled over the radio. "It's too dark. We'll continue tomorrow."

"Negative," Deb said. "I have a possible."

"This is Search Command. Give us the location. We'll add it to the coordinates to check first thing in the morning."

"By morning, those kids might freeze to death," Deb said. "If it's them, the least I can do is drop supplies." She flipped off the microphone.

"Uh, Deb," Gene pointed out, "they can pull your license for this."

She shifted in her seat. "I know. Keep an eye out. I'm going in as close as I can." She rounded another hill. "Come on, baby, come on," Deb begged the machine.

She skirted the tops of the trees directly next to the road, flying a lot closer than was sane. Suddenly, down the slope, a hint of dark blue appeared. She hovered, sweeping the area with the searchlight. The beam glinted off broken glass and chrome. Several figures stood on and near a big school bus, waving. Others lay on the ground, some suspiciously still.

"Damn it," Gene said. "You were right." He radioed in the location and stared at her, his expression awestruck. "You're good."

"Lucky is more like it," she said.

"No, that was dogged determination. You just wouldn't give up. You might be crazy, Deb Lansing, but you're a hell of a chopper pilot."

All-too-familiar guilt twisted inside her. "I have my moments."

She hovered over the downed bus and Gene dropped blankets, first-aid supplies, and food. Below, figures scrambled to the drop zone.

Banishing from her mind the haunting image of the desperate soldier she'd been forced to leave behind, Deb turned to Gene. "I can land in that valley we passed earlier. It'll be tight, but if there are any kids seriously injured, we may be able to transport some of them to the helicopter with the sled."

"What the hell. You've already pulled off one miracle tonight." Gene grinned. "Go for it."

Deb eased down the control stick and, with careful precision, guided the helicopter lower. Another glint of silver flashed in the spotlight, far enough away from the bus that it wasn't likely to be debris from that wreck.

"Do you see that reflection?" she asked. "Is it another vehicle?"

Gene peered through the windshield. "I don't know. I saw something, though. I'll call in the position for that, too. They can check it."

The chopper touched down, and Deb jumped to the snow-packed ground, ignoring the cold around her. For now, she had people to save. As Deb and Gene yanked out the sled to transport the wounded, two men ran toward her, one whose forehead was caked with dried blood.

"Please, we need help. Some of the kids are hurt bad. They need a hospital."

Deb scanned the inside of the chopper. How many could she fit and safely make it back? If she left equipment behind, she could carry someone extra. Her boss would be furious she'd taken the risk, but she'd worry about her job later.

Gabe cut a few limes and refilled the pretzels where some joker had upended a bowl, trying to prove he could balance them on his head after one too many. Gabe had called a cab and ushered the guy out. Hopefully the cop wasn't on duty tomorrow so he could sleep it off.

Gabe could understand. He'd faced the dark side of the city, but being here all day every day gave him a whole different perspective on his fellow cops. Once a drink or two stripped away their masks, men and women he thought he'd known well showed more than they realized.

Hopefully Gabe hadn't fallen into the trap. He had too much to lose. Giving away the investigation could get people hurt.

The thud of a pool stick and the clatter of balls falling in the pockets filtered through the chatter in the bar. Gabe checked the clock for the umpteenth time. Hawk shot him a knowing glance and poured two fingers of scotch. "Is your leg bothering you again . . . or is it that empty bar stool?"

Gabe scowled at Hawk. His bartender had reminded everyone of Gabe's cover story, part of the ex-spook's job. Fine, but Hawk hadn't been able to resist bringing up the vacant end of the bar. Shoving past the dig, Gabe pulled a draft. A deputy snagged his drink and sent Gabe a sympathetic grimace.

"You learn to deal with it," Gabe said with an exaggerated wince, just loudly enough for the cops nearby to hear.

He hated playing up the injured-in-the-line-of-duty card, a SWAT deputy driven from his job. So far he'd engendered pity, not suspicion, among the clientele. Every one of them knew it could have been them with a sliced-up leg. The gangbanger was doing time, but that didn't heal Gabe's nerve and muscle damage.

As to that empty bar stool at the end of the bar, he should focus on luring a couple of his prime suspects from the sheriff's office to it. Maybe pour a little liquid truth down their throats.

But it was Sunday night. She should be sitting right there. And he noticed when she wasn't.

Hawk caught Gabe's second glance. "Guess Deb and her gang from Search and Rescue aren't coming tonight. They hardly ever miss a Sunday football game."

Damn Hawk. The ex-spook could read minds.

Gabe shifted his focus to scrubbing down the surface of the bar and pretended he hadn't been completely obvious in his mooning over the gorgeous pilot. "It's getting close to dark. I hope they're not searching for some idiot driver who thought using chains was optional in the mountains."

"I hear you." Hawk delivered a couple burgers to a table, then rounded the bar. "That pileup at Loveland Pass during last weekend's storm sure was a mess. She had her chopper do things that shouldn't be possible, and she refused to leave until she could get everyone to the hospital. She must have nerves of steel."

"She's something all right." Gabe took another look at his watch. He hoped Deb wasn't doing anything crazy tonight. She didn't seem to care what chances she took. He didn't know what her demons were, but nobody flew like that without a monkey on their back—or something to prove.

Just like Gabe. Of course he knew exactly why he'd put himself in the potential crosshairs of organized crime. But why did Deb take those kinds of risks? If he had the freedom, he'd love to peel off those layers, but he couldn't do it. Not now.

Hawk pulled another couple of drafts. "Didn't Seth tell me she rescued you?"

"My brother talks too much." Gabe swiped some peanut shells from the counter. "She's probably rescued half of Denver since she arrived, but yeah. If not for her, I'd be dead."

"That's got to count for something." Hawk's grin was guileless. "Sounds like you owe her a date."

"Right. I'm sure that's what she's thinking." There was no doubt Gabe owed Deborah Lansing big-time. After the knife had sliced his femoral artery, she'd flown him to the ER in record time. The doctors couldn't believe he'd survived the blood loss, much less walked again given the leg's muscle and nerve damage.

When Gabe had taken over Sammy's, he'd offered her dinner and free drinks for life, along with his thanks. If not for her, he wouldn't be on the op, and he wouldn't have come to know her a bit, but she'd said his gratitude was enough. He wished all he felt for the pilot was gratitude, but he noticed a few too many little things about her. Like how she gave as good as she got with her Search and Rescue colleagues. Like how she was partial to the longneck bottle and potato skins. Or that occasionally she'd choose the chef salad and joke she needed a few veggies during the week. And once a month she'd go for a hot dog. All the trimmings. A woman who liked hot dogs—and ordered them—that was a woman Gabe could respect.

For months, whenever he brought her that plate, the urge to ask to join her grew stronger. Lately, though, she'd inspired more than just the desire for a meal and conversation. His subconscious had been working overtime, disturbing his dreams with some very interesting nighttime fantasies.

Yeah, Gabe was in trouble. He liked her too much. He noticed too much, and he really shouldn't be thinking about her. Not during the investigation.

"So, boss, when are you going to ask her out?"

Gabe whipped his head up and glared. "You know, they say that only the good die young, but in your case, an exception can be made."

"You wuss, Montgomery. Stop hiding behind your bar apron strings. Man up and ask her out."

Gabe wished he could, any other time he would have, but Hawk knew the risks. What was he thinking? Then again, his bartender didn't pretend to play it safe. Which was why he was behind this bar in the first place. Gabe didn't need Hawk needling him as it was. He couldn't get the auburn-haired helicopter pilot out of his head. Not during the day, and sure as hell not during the night.

Especially when she wasn't where she was supposed to be.

The woman worried him.

Gabe shouldn't care, but he did. For months he'd tried to pin down the answer. Was it that sexy-as-hell challenge in her eyes when she smiled? Or maybe the pensive look that she couldn't hide, that made him want to know more? Gabe fought not to rub at the scar tissue that still seized up his leg muscles, particularly after he'd been on his feet all day. Was it because she still lived the life he could no longer have? Did he seriously have thrill envy?

On cold nights like this, Gabe had to wonder. The painful limp was all too real. He could use an evening out of this bar, to stretch out on his couch with a double dose of ibuprofen, a hot dog with mustard, and a longneck bottle.

"Nothing to say? Oh, then you won't mind if I make a move on her?" Hawk's brow quirked.

Gabe slammed down a shot glass. "I see a firing in your immediate future, Hawk. I don't care if Seth got you this job or not."

Hawk just laughed, clearly not worried at all. "Have I ever mentioned that your brother is a whole lot nicer than you?"

Gabe shot him his best zip-it-or-die glare.

"Shutting up now, boss."

Gabe's gaze lingered on the bar stool once more. He'd made the right choice. Before long Ernie would be lurking nearby, hopefully waiting with some concrete intel on the Gasmerati crime syndicate, the group Gabe was convinced had engineered the threats against his brother.

A tin wind chime sounded outside the entryway and a group of laughing men pushed into the bar, followed by a woman with striking auburn hair. Deb Lansing.

Hawk elbowed Gabe. "She looks hot." When Gabe didn't respond, he leaned closer. "For the last few months you two have been sending signals a five-year-old would see. It's past time to make a move."

"Give it a rest. Now's not the time. You know that." Gabe knew the words to be true, but his heart rate picked up anyway when the group closed in on the bar.

Though her flight suit hid most of her curves, Deb's forthright smile and the spark of fire in her eyes kick-started Gabe's libido. Her bold gaze traveled down his body, then up, settling on his lips. Her no-nonsense stare fanned the embers into a full-fledged fire inside him.

"A shot of Cuervo for everyone, Gabe. On me."

"Oh, no." The head of the Search and Rescue crew shouldered in. "On me, Montgomery. We're celebrating."

"So, I'm not fired anymore?" Deb said, her brow arched.

Her boss frowned. "I haven't decided. After that stunt you pulled, you're grounded for a week. Then I may reinstate you.

You could have ended up splattering my chopper on the side of the mountain."

"What the hell happened?" Gabe swallowed back his fear. He knew Deb's rep, and he nearly leapt over the bar.

"The boss is overreacting," she said, sprinkling salt on her wrist, biting the lime. With a deep breath, she tossed back the tequila. Her face flinched as the drink went down.

"I don't think so." The guy turned to Gabe. "You were SWAT. You know about chain of command. Picture this. We're in the mountains of New Mexico. Snow everywhere. Cloudy day so the light sucked. Sun's going down. We call the flight crews in, but Annie Oakley here decides to disobey orders and fly several more passes. Practically gave her partner heart failure. Not to mention costing me at least ten years of life while I watched the air show."

"We found the kids, didn't we?" Deb countered. "I knew what I was doing. The risk was worth it."

"Look, Deb." Her boss snagged a peanut and popped it into his mouth. "You're a great flyer, but you can't save everyone. One of these days you're going to have to face that fact." He glanced at Gabe. "Get us two sampler platters." He downed a tequila in one shot. "And another round. I need it."

The rest of the group patted Deb on the shoulder before huddling at a table in the corner with their boss. "He'll get over it," one said. "That was some hellacious flying."

Gabe squeezed the bottle of tequila in his hand. How his grip hadn't shattered the bottle, he didn't know. "Deb, can I see you for a minute?" he asked through gritted teeth.

She'd taken a couple steps toward the S&R group but paused and turned toward him, her look quizzical. "Okay."

He clutched her hand and pulled her to his office, walked in and shut the door. He turned on her. "Are you crazy?"

Her mouth fell open and then a disbelieving expression that should have warned Gabe away crossed her face. "Excuse me?"

He clasped her shoulders. "You could have been killed." Gabe knew he was being unreasonable, knew he was out of line, but he couldn't stop himself.

Her arms thrust out to escape his hold, and she launched forward, pressing her hand against his chest. With the other hand she poked him, just below the collarbone. "I knew exactly what I was doing, Deputy. It's my job and I'm damn good at it. Or perhaps I should address you as ex-Deputy."

The barb didn't stop him. In fact, the flash in her green eyes only fed his desire to get closer.

"I know you're a great flyer, Deb. That's what terrifies me," he admitted. "I've gotten used to you sitting on that bar stool giving me a hard time. I'd hate to think I'd miss that because you decided to be a hero one too many times."

She stilled, the anger seeming to seep out of her, and her shoulders sagged. "You think that's what this is about. I want to be a hero?"

She dropped her hands. He didn't want to lose her nearness, but it was the disappointment in her voice that squeezed his heart.

"I didn't mean—"

"I don't leave anyone behind. Not ever," she said, her voice firm, but with just a hint of shaky desperation. "And especially not kids."

Her eyes flashed with pain, her expression haunted. He'd seen the same look in Luke's face after a particularly rough tour in Afghanistan before he'd turned journalist.

Gabe hooked her finger with his, the tentative touch cautious. He hated himself for bringing that inner ache to her eyes. He said nothing, but slowly he laced her fingers with his, staring at the connection. They fit together. Too well.

The outside world faded. In this small room, they were alone. He tugged her closer, unable to resist. He'd wanted to touch her this way for so long. Longer than he'd admitted. He wanted to know if his dreams were anything close to reality.

Her gaze rose to meet his, her cheeks flushed. She stared at his lips, then her tongue moistened her own.

Gabe didn't want to say a word. He didn't want to break the spell that had settled over them like a warm blanket. He leaned in, hovering closer, his lips just inches away. They tingled in anticipation.

Deb's phone blasted between them. Gabe sucked in a deep breath and straightened. With a last look, he let her hand drop. At his movement, Deb's eyes went from foggy to clear.

He'd almost stepped over that invisible line. And for a few seconds there, he hadn't cared.

But now, the moment was gone. Reality had intruded. For both of them.

The very girlie pop ring tone sounded again. She winced. "My little sister." She cleared her throat, reached into her pocket, and clicked on the phone. "Ashley? I didn't expect . . ."

The frown on Deb's lips made Gabe's brow furrow.

"I'll be there in twenty minutes," she said, ending the call. She looked up at him, her eyes full of regret. "I have to go. My sister needs me."

Gabe didn't try to stop her. Family came first. Always. He nodded.

She cocked her head. "I'll see you tomorrow night? The usual bar stool?"

"I'll bring a hot dog. On the house. No arguments." He paused, wanting to reach for her, to touch her again. He couldn't. The worst part of wanting Deb wasn't the need to touch her. It was wanting to dig into why she drove herself, why she took those chances. Why she'd risked her life tonight.

He didn't just want Deb physically; he wanted to know her, inside and out. A dangerous combination.

He sidled around her and opened the door.

"No gratitude, right?" She slowly brushed against him as she walked past.

At her touch, a long, slow breath escaped from him. "Agreed."

Halfway out the door, she looked over her shoulder, her expression pensive. "You surprised me tonight, Gabe Montgomery. It doesn't happen often."

She disappeared out the door and Gabe let out a long, slow breath. Too bad he liked Deb Lansing so much. Once he knew it was safe, he'd take Hawk's advice, because he knew one thing. Women like Deb Lansing didn't cross his path often, and he'd love to know if her bold spirit translated from the chopper to the bedroom.

But until he brought the sheriff and Gasmerati down, he had to find a way to keep his distance.

The solid wood desk dominated the office. Custom made in Italy, the finest money could buy, every item in this room let visitors know Jeff Gasmerati meant business. Deadly business. And no mistakes.

He leaned back in his chair and studied his latest acquisition. The Monet had disappeared during the Nazi's occupation of France. Jeff had paid a premier price. Something the world didn't even know existed.

He liked the feeling.

Just staring at the impressionist's masterpiece eased the tension at the base of his neck. He had one very big problem, but if his latest plans moved forward—as he fully expected them to—soon he'd make the syndicate his father had built look like a mom-and-pop shop.

Right now, though, his biggest headache was the cops and the press, particularly Luke Montgomery.

The phone rang and Jeff glanced at the caller's identity. Speaking of law enforcement. He gritted his teeth. "This line is off-limits to you."

"We have trouble. I just received news over the wire. A car's been found." Sheriff Tower's voice lowered to an urgent whisper. "Near Taos. A chopper pilot spotted it during a rescue. I recognized the location. It's them. The boys from . . . before."

Jeff drummed his fingertips on the mahogany desk. "We knew it would happen eventually. Eight years is a long time. People forget."

"What if someone puts it together with the girl's death? It's a risk. To both of us."

Jeff squeezed the phone. Tower was becoming a liability. "Make sure we have someone on the ground as they investigate. Let me know if concerns crop up."

"New Mexico's not my jurisdiction. I can't just—"

"It is now, *Sheriff* Tower. Figure it out. If evidence needs to disappear, make it happen. This is not the time for complications. Your son's poor judgment nearly cost us everything. You get me?"

The phone went silent. "I'll find a way," Tower finally groused.

"You've been given a cushy gig, Sheriff. Don't screw it up. I can take your position away as easily as I handed it to you. And your vices . . . well, let's just say you haven't learned from your son's death. A hundred grand in the last month comes to mind."

"I said I'll do it."

Jeff walked over to the antique Waterford decanter and poured himself a snifter of cognac. "I suggest checking on Gabe Montgomery and Whitney Blackstone as well. It's been eight years since that night. Neither of them is young and foolish anymore. They could cause problems if they recognize the connection with Shannon Devlin." He took a sip. Very smooth. "And, Tower, I won't tolerate further mistakes. There are plenty of men in your department who would step in if you met with an unfortunate accident."

CHAPTER TWO

DEB PULLED HER CAR UP TO HER APARTMENT BUILDING AND touched her lips. Gabe hadn't kissed her, but when he'd linked his fingers through hers, a shiver had traveled down her back, settling low in her gut. If Ashley hadn't called, Deb would be at the bar with Gabe right now, exploring feelings that made her very nervous. Which shocked her. If most men had tried to tell her how to do her job, she'd have kicked them hard enough to disable the guy's ability to pass on his genes. But then she'd recognized something in Gabe's eyes, an emotion she hadn't seen in a very long time. Concern. For her. In that instant, the high of finding those kids coupled with the months of ogling Gabe had cracked through defenses she'd built since her first day at boot camp.

She grabbed her bag from the car and trudged up the three flights of stairs. She should admit the truth, she wanted more than friendly flirting from Gabe. She got the physical attraction. That dark hair and those chocolate eyes made most of the women who came into Sammy's drool. That didn't touch Deb, though. What tempted her was that something extra she'd witnessed. Like how he made certain anyone who'd tied one on had a ride home. Or the times she'd caught him giving food out the back to someone in need. Or the easy camaraderie he shared with his brothers when they stopped in.

In her experience, more often than not the best-looking men were also the biggest jerks. Gabe seemed to be the exception. Which in itself scared the hell out of her.

Finally reaching the landing, Deb slipped her key into the lock. Ashley better have a good reason for being here and not at her Air Force Academy dorm where she belonged.

Deb shoved the door open. Her sister jumped up from the beige corduroy couch like a gun had exploded in her ear. The textbook vaulted from her hand landing five feet away.

"Easy, girl. It's just me."

"Thank God." Ashley shoved her blonde hair behind one ear, her movements edgy.

This wasn't like her sister. Deb hurried over to the sofa and tossed her rucksack into a corner. "What's going on? And please tell me you didn't take a bus from Colorado Springs."

"Of course not. I . . . just . . . I really needed to talk to you so I borrowed an upperclassman's car. He's flunking math. I traded tutoring time for the use of his ride for a few hours. I promised to get the car back before curfew. It's such a pain that first-year cadets can't have their own vehicles." Ashley relaxed a little. "Where were you?"

Okay, mentioning her celebratory foray to the bar wasn't happening. "Rescue flight. A church bus full of teenagers hit black ice going around a curve. Medevac choppers were called in from all over to find them, but it gets dark so early, we didn't have much daylight to look."

"You found them."

"Yeah," Deb sighed. "Finally."

"No, I mean you're the one who found them, aren't you?"

Deb shifted on the sofa. "It was a team effort."

Ashley crossed her arms in front of her and glared at Deb with that all-knowing teenage look.

"Okay, yeah, I spotted the bus first, and then everyone kicked into gear. We airlifted the worst of the wounded out to the ambulances standing by, and the ground troops had to take over due to the lack of light and rugged terrain."

"I don't know why you don't just take the credit. I bet you loved flying that mission," Ashley said.

"Okay, quit it." Deb threw a pillow at her sister's head. "Come on, Ashley, why are you here?"

Ashley snagged the pillow in midair, then hugged it close. "Something really weird's been going on. Someone's following me. Plus, I keep getting these strange phone calls and hang ups. I swear someone else is on the phone, listening, while I talk to my friends."

"*While* you're on the phone?"

Ashley frowned. "I hear these strange clicks and stuff. Sometimes there's an echo. Really faint, but enough to make me suspicious. God, listen to me. I sound as paranoid as Dad. Maybe it's the NSA skulking around again. Or the military. I realize that I'm attending the Air Force Academy, but would the school tap its students' phones like that?"

"Anything's possible, I guess. If the General had his way, he'd have bugged every room and phone line we ever went near." Deb tried to make light of the situation, but her stomach fluttered a bit at Ashley's words.

"Yeah, well, Dad's a psychotic, overprotective idiot. How they let him stay in the Army this long, I don't know. He's scary."

Deb laughed. "And that's exactly why they've kept him around so long. His paranoia has paid off too many times. Everyone hates him, but nobody bucks him . . . except you. You pissed him off royally by picking the Air Force."

"Big deal. So I didn't hold up the Lansing tradition of going into the Army, like you, Ben, and Rick. All following in Daddy's footsteps, like good little children."

"Brat. Respect your elders." Deb crossed her legs and faced her sister. "Besides, I'm a civilian now."

"Yeah, I know, and it's all my fault you're not out there flying those helicopters every day. I can't believe I need someone to act as my legal guardian here while I go to the Academy."

"Yeah, being a sixteen-and-a-half-year-old genius is tough. Imagine being tapped by the government for your code-breaking skills. You poor, deprived child."

"It was either that or go to jail after I hacked into the NSA to give them a taste of their own medicine."

"Don't remind me. I had the FBI at my door. And not for a security clearance interview." Deb sat up straight and stared down her sister. "You and your new buddies aren't screwing around with that stuff anymore, are you?"

"Would I do that?" Ashley batted her eyes, but Deb just shook her head in dismay. "Seriously, I'm legit. The only thing we're doing is hacking our way through *Point of Entry*, a video game that gives bored little brainiacs like us a legal way to hone our skills."

"Ashley, you're not still playing that stupid game, are you?"

"There's nothing stupid about P.O.E. We just broke through to Level 88, and it took more brain cells than all my Academy courses combined. Justin and Mylo were talking about going out to celebrate since they helped me break the last codes. It's fun working with a team instead of staring at the screen alone in my room."

Deb stood and walked into the kitchen. She poured a glass of orange juice and took a sip, studying her sister across the bar. She searched for the right words, but she just had to say it. "I'd still feel a lot better if you weren't doing anything that remotely resembled hacking. Especially with Justin. You two came too close to getting locked up."

"My advisor gave me the latest version of P.O.E.," Ashley protested. "He said, with my background, I might enjoy the challenge. Lighten up. It's only a video game, after all. Besides, I'm tired of being the too-smart-for-other-kids-to-do-normal-things-with geek. I want to be normal."

"It's a game where you pretend to break into banks, follow money trails, plant evidence on computers, and take down governments."

"And catch the bad guys," Ashley added. "It's harmless fun. The guys like the shoot-'em-up, and I like the math and computer stuff. Besides, if I go into Intelligence—like the Academy counselors seem to think I should—I'll need the practice. I have to be able to think like the bad guys."

Why couldn't her sister be like other kids? Deb placed her empty glass in the sink and foraged for a handful of granola. "Well, behave yourself. Your imagination is a little too creative sometimes, and the morals depicted in those games are questionable at best." Deb tempered her tone, knowing she'd get nowhere with Ashley. "I have enough to worry about with everyone in the family deployed to the Middle East right now. I don't need you in jail, too."

Ashley saluted. "Yes, ma'am. Orders duly noted. Pretend games only. Maintain my integrity. Got it covered, *Admiral* Lansing."

Deb laughed at the nickname Ashley had stuck her with. So she was bossy where her little sister was concerned. Ashley's moniker for her might have been General Lansing, but their father had already laid claim to that title. Deb hadn't stayed in the Army long enough to give him any real competition for the rank.

She took in the impish look on her sister's face. "You're lucky I love you, brat, because you are truly a wiseass. That mouth of yours is going to get you into trouble someday."

"That's not what Justin says." Ashley batted her eyelashes and smiled.

"Great. Now I have something else to worry about." Deb glanced at her watch. "You have school in the morning and I don't like you traveling the roads this late at night, even if it is interstate most of the way. Why don't you stay over and leave early in the morning? I'll call in for you."

Ashley shook her head with a sigh. "I promised the guy I'd get his car back before weekend curfew and I'm really going to have to push it to make it." She collected her books and slipped them into her backpack. "Besides, I've been trying to reach Justin by phone all day with no luck. His cell service is terrible. It's so spotty, half the time I can't get him unless he's in an empty field pointing his phone at the tower. I want to give him another call when I get back to school."

Deb walked Ashley to the door. "Are you sure?"

"I'll be fine. I . . . I needed to tell someone. Things feel a tad *off*, I guess."

"Let me know if you get any more hang ups or anything else weird happens. I worry about you. Justin and Mylo's info is in the address book in case you're off campus. Right?"

"Yes, *Admiral*, everything's there, along with all the school numbers, my roommate's cell, etcetera. Talk about an overreaction. You are so anal sometimes."

"Hey, pipsqueak. You're the one who got antsy. And you're not the easiest person to keep track of, you know. I like to have every contingency covered."

Ashley buttoned up her coat and arranged her scarf around her neck. "Look, the phone stuff is probably nothing. Besides, I'm almost seventeen. I'm invincible, remember?"

"The kids I transported to the hospital today thought so, too. Humor me and be careful."

"Yes, *mother.* I love you, too."

Deb rolled her eyes. "Go. You're driving me nuts. And be safe."

Ashley hugged her, and Deb held her sister tight. She was going to be an amazing woman someday. Scary amazing, actually. Emotion clogged Deb's throat. The truth was, she'd been a surrogate parent to Ashley ever since their mother had died of cancer when the little girl was only five, and the General had walled the whole family out in his grief. The protective maternal role was hard to give up.

Deb watched Ashley until she drove away, closed the door, and walked back into the empty apartment. A tremor of foreboding ripped through her. It almost felt like a premonition, like that feeling she got in Afghanistan when everything was about to go to hell. She raced to the door to tell her sister to come back, but the taillights had disappeared down the road.

She should call her sister's phone and insist she spend the night, despite the need to get the car back to her classmate—

No. Deb cursed and shut the door. She was being ridiculous. Nothing was going to happen. She'd text Ashley tomorrow and reassure herself that she'd worried all night for nothing.

No cars clogged the normally congested I-25 south toward Colorado Springs. The moon hung high overhead, the air cool and crisp. The smell of snow was in the air. Ashley couldn't wait for a school break so she could teach Justin to ski. He'd look so good in ski pants.

She turned up the radio and flicked through stations when an electronic beep sounded in the car. What the heck?

She looked down at the dashboard, her focus finally settling on the warning light. No way. A near-empty gas gauge? She'd filled up just before she went to Deb's apartment. Someone must have siphoned off most of the tank while she was visiting her sister. She gritted her teeth. Perfect ending to a screwed-up weekend.

It didn't help she'd had the creepy crawlies up and down her back throughout the whole drive. Talk about paranoid. She could have sworn someone was watching her, but she never even saw headlights in the rearview mirror most of the last ten miles.

Get a grip, Ashley, or you'll turn into Dad.

Her father thought she was a helpless idiot. She wasn't. Her sister had taught her how to handle herself in any situation. She had a 170 IQ, for heaven's sake. Even at sixteen, the workload at the Academy didn't challenge her that much. She glanced around, trying to place where she was. After so many trips to her sister's house, she'd memorized most every exit, and that dumpy all-night gas station was coming up soon. She'd have to stop even though they sold the equivalent of camel piss as high-octane fuel. Extremely high-priced camel piss, at that.

Over the next hill, she saw the sign for the service station, the lights a beacon in the dark. At least she wouldn't have to call Deb to tell her what an idiot she'd been not to have checked the gas gauge before leaving Denver.

Being a helicopter pilot, her sister obsessively checked everything, fuel and safety features alike, before moving an inch. She'd tried to teach Ashley to do the same. Apparently, the lesson hadn't taken very well.

Ashley flipped on the blinker and pulled off the highway, the car shuddering on its last fumes. That's all she needed, to seize the engine or something. The poor, beat-up sedan had seen better days. Now, Ashley prayed it would survive until she reached the Academy and gave it back to its owner.

She turned the ignition off and looked around. For an all-night station, the place sure looked deserted. The lights above her blinked, then flashed off, plunging the area into darkness.

Ashley froze, peering outside through the window.

Deb always told her to listen to her instincts. Right now, they were screaming that she should have stayed in town. She caught movement in her peripheral vision and slammed her hand down on the door lock, but it was too late. Someone had already ripped the door open.

The interior light flickered on. Screaming, she kicked out at the black-clad man trying to pull her from the car.

"Help! Please, someone help me!"

"Yell all you want, kid. No one around to hear you."

She screamed as massive arms pulled her body from the car and dragged her toward another vehicle. He tried to shove her into the back of a huge SUV, but she fought him. He slammed her head against the door frame, nearly knocking her unconscious.

With a final kick, she caught him in the crotch. He dropped her to the ground and she struggled to regain her footing. His backhand left her ears ringing and blood coursed down her split lip. The man grabbed a fistful of hair and yanked her head close. "Stay down or I'll hit you again, and this time I won't be gentle."

A blond man approached and her attacker said, "Grab her legs and watch out. She's a wild one."

The blond gripped her ankles and held her tight, grinning at her as they lifted her from the ground. She twisted and turned. She couldn't let them take her.

A third man opened the rear hatch further, and they threw her roughly into the vehicle. When she tried to rise, the blond backhanded her across the face. "What did we tell you?"

She sagged. Oh God. She was going to die. She couldn't keep a whimper from escaping.

The blond bent close, his voice no more than a whisper. "No use fighting. You're coming with us. Do as you're told, or you'll die."

"Please. Just let me go. I won't tell anyone—"

"Damn right about that." He chuckled and yanked out a few zip ties from his pocket and grabbed her wrists.

"Wait! You don't know what you're doing. My father is in the Army and he'll kick your ass if you don't let me go."

The man bound her wrists with the tie and bent closer, laughing. "Your father is in Kandahar and by the time Daddy Dearest gets here, Ashley, there won't be a trace of you left to follow."

Her eyes widened. "You know who I am?"

"Oh, yeah. Ashley Lansing, math prodigy, code breaker and Einstein-level genius. Accepted at the Air Force Academy at age sixteen, the youngest ever, even though teenagers your age aren't really allowed in the military. For you, they made an exception.

"Your father is Army General George Lansing, bastard extraordinaire. Your brothers are Richard and Benjamin Lansing, also serving overseas. One sister, Deborah, an ex-Army helicopter pilot, is now doing Flight for Life and Search and Rescue out of Denver, whatever allows her to fly the most. Mother deceased, probably to escape your father. Did I miss anything you needed to hear to believe me, or do you want me to start on your bra size and color of your panties next?"

A tear trickled down her cheek. She stopped fighting.

"We know everything about you, Miss Lansing. Move against us, and we'll retaliate against everyone you love. Starting with your adoring sister."

Ashley went limp. Oh God. Deb.

He placed zip ties on Ashley's ankles, then attached one loop to a hook in the floor. "That's better. You know, I was once in your place, but I was smart and I survived. Be smart and you might make it through this alive, too. Be stupid and . . . well, let's just say you won't be the first person I would have to get rid of for my boss. It's kind of my specialty. And I do love my work."

The metal tailgate slammed, closing Ashley in the cargo space of the SUV. Her phone was in the car. She had no way to contact Deb. Would her classmate report the car missing if she didn't show up? Would she be considered AWOL for not signing in before curfew? With luck, the police might start looking for her tonight.

Ashley scooted as far as she could, using her hands to feel her way around her. Nothing. Smooth steel. She pulled against the zip ties, but the hard plastic just bit into her wrists. She kicked the back door, hoping she could at least break the back taillight somehow.

The side door opened. The blond man looked behind. "Didn't I hit you hard enough to make my point? It's no use trying to escape. You belong to us now."

The guy with reddish hair, cut close to his scalp, bent down. "You owe me for that crotch kick, and I will collect."

He smiled at her, but his eyes were dead. He had no soul. None of them did.

Ashley sent up a prayer. Deb would look for her. Everyone would. They would find her. She had to believe that.

The third man approached on the passenger side and looked at the blond. "What do you want me to do?"

"We already went over this. After we're gone, clean up the situation," the leader replied. "Reset the videotape, then take her car to the bus terminal closest to the Academy and leave the note inside. The night clerk here will wake up on his own and think he fell asleep. Be sure to grab the spiked drink bottle so there'll be no evidence."

The blond slid behind the steering wheel. "Don't make any mistakes. You know what happens to employees who screw up." He paused. "I'd hate to lose you like we did Rogers."

The guy gulped, then nodded. "Sure, Niko. No mistakes."

The man's eyes flared, his tone harsh. "That was a mistake right there. Never say my name away from camp."

The guy panicked.

"Don't worry. This kid won't be telling anyone, but that's your last warning."

Niko turned the key in the ignition and the SUV rumbled to life. After shifting gears, he pulled the black Escalade out of the gas station. Ashley peered out the rear-tinted window and watched one of the station's dimmer lights flicker back on. The place still looked closed. No one would stop.

Her eyes burned as even that light was swallowed up by the darkness.

"Where are you taking me?" She wished her voice didn't sound so scared. Deb never showed fear. Ashley wouldn't, either. "What camp? A militia camp?"

"Try to think of it as computer camp for prodigies," Niko said, laughing at her question. "You've been a very bad girl, Miss Lansing. Your little foray into the NSA's computer has cost us. So, when we arrive, the Warden will want your assistance. I suggest you agree to do everything he says. For your sake, and the sake of your family."

He glanced over his shoulder, staring intently at her. "Otherwise, Ashley Lansing, you get to play with me. And I guarantee you won't like my kind of games."

CHAPTER THREE

Sammy's Bar showed its true colors as closing time drew near. Raucous laughter sounded from a corner, but it barely registered. He couldn't get Deb out of his mind, hadn't been able to stop thinking about her all evening long.

"It's showing on your face," Hawk said with a grin. "Did you at least get her phone number?"

Damn it. She'd scrambled his brains so much he didn't have any way to contact her. Was she listed? He'd find out once he got home. If not, he had a brother who could dig out practically any information on anyone. Family came in handy sometimes.

"Man, she must have rung your bell in your office." Hawk chuckled. "You looked shell-shocked coming out of there. I knew I should have gone after her myself."

Gabe grabbed Hawk's collar. "One more word, and you're fired. Not joking, Hawk."

The bartender's eyes narrowed to disturbing slits, then he blinked and the murderous gaze dissipated. "Interesting. You're serious about her. Guess I proved my point then."

Gabe released Hawk. "Was there a reason my brother didn't kill you when you two were overseas?"

"Sorry, I seem to be indestructible, unfortunately. Besides, you need me for your side job. Who else is going to watch your back?" Hawk stacked some clean glasses behind the bar. "Deb will probably be back. Maybe. If you didn't scare her off." He turned to the next customer.

Probably best if Gabe had, though he couldn't imagine anything intimidating Deb. Still, she'd never let her guard down with him that way before. He hadn't been ready for the intensity simmering between them, and now he regretted losing control. Trouble was, he was in no position to start a relationship. Even if his investigation hadn't gone anywhere yet, the whole thing could explode at any moment. If his brother Luke's investigation held any truth—and Gabe had no doubt it did—more than a few people had died trying to bring Jeff Gasmerati down, plus whoever in the Jefferson County Sheriff's Office had hitched a ride on the wrong side of the law.

Speaking of dirty cops, three deputies strode through the door. Bad news, but Gabe forced a smile anyway. "You're just in time for last call, gents. What can I get you?"

Within minutes, Gabe had pulled two beers on tap and sent a double shot of straight whiskey to the last cop. Menken downed it, then asked for another.

"Get a table," he growled at his companions.

Gabe didn't mention closing time again, even though he wanted to. His Jeffco captain, John Garrison, had told Gabe to watch these three specifically. John's suspicions ran deep with them. A few pieces of missing evidence in their key cases and a few too many closed-door meetings with Gabe's prime suspect, Sheriff Tower.

Everyone else in the office tried to avoid that slippery bastard, so the fact that the three musketeers, as Gabe had dubbed them, didn't, dinged his suspicion meter.

Tower's three deputies smelled of corruption. At one time, they'd been decent officers, but the scuttlebutt that went around the bar—and the informants who met Gabe—told a much uglier story.

Gabe didn't want to believe they'd turned, but he'd learned the hard way that betrayal by people you'd trusted came too damn easy.

Either he or Luke would get the proof. They had to. And soon.

Gabe rubbed the back of his neck. He hadn't found a lick of evidence against the sheriff. The guy was Teflon. Even when the sheriff's son, Brian, had been murdered last year amid swirling rumors about parties and meetings with Jeff Gasmerati, the local crime boss, they hadn't touched Tower's reelection.

Jeff Gasmerati was another matter. As a snitch, Ernie had become Gabe's window into the organization. Gasmerati owned half of Denver, with just enough legitimate business to insulate himself from the law.

Gabe hadn't been able to prove it, but if he were a betting man, he would say the sheriff was in bed with Gasmerati and had been since Tower was elected to fill the position vacated by the untimely death of a man who'd held the office for twenty years before him. Being sheriff in Jefferson County had turned into a lifetime job.

"Last call," Gabe announced, checking the time again.

Most of the cops in here tonight had come for a few beers, a game or two of pool, and were now packing up to go home to their wives or husbands. The honest cops, at least.

A few more of the Blue Brotherhood had shoved back a couple of shots, disappeared with a badge groupie for a quickie, then headed home to play the Good Daddy, tucking the kids into bed. Had Patrick Montgomery been one of those?

Gabe hadn't wanted to believe that about his father, but the longer he'd worked behind the bar, the more he'd seen what he hadn't wanted to know.

Dirtbags, like the three musketeers, made Gabe's stomach turn. They acted like saints in the bar, but Gabe knew better. His gaze moved from one face to the next, ticking them off his mental list. Maybe Ernie's info tonight would nail one and Gabe could feel like a real cop again.

He glanced at his watch. "Five minutes to stools up."

His announcement brought groans, but most finished their drinks and started bundling up to face the freezing temperatures outside.

Hawk cleared the dirty glasses and hauled them into the kitchen.

Soon the place would be empty.

Hawk's taillights headed down the street and away from the closed bar. Gabe watched from the shadows, making sure the ex-spy was well out of sight. He shoved his hands into the pockets of his down parka.

No birds chattered this time of year. A few engines sounded from the road, the occasional horn, but mostly the streets had gone quiet in this neck of Denver.

Shifting his stance to ease the ache in his leg, Gabe searched for movement. He tried to concentrate while he waited for Ernie, but his thoughts drifted to Deb Lansing. This attraction to Deb was crazy. Could a woman with a seeming death wish and a burned-out vermin catcher with a bum leg and no dreams left, find anything in common? Somehow, he doubted it.

He'd caught her watching him on occasion. She'd seen him limp across the floor, and her eyes had flashed with pity. He wanted to shed the role he played, but he couldn't. So he let her feel sorry for him even if it stuck in his craw.

To Gabe's right, a shadowy figure ducked behind the trash bin. Gabe tensed and eased sideways, adjusting his stance, his hand behind him, ready to draw his weapon.

"Psst. SWAT."

The nasal tone and familiar nickname had Gabe relaxing his fingers. Ernie.

"You're late and I'm freezing my ass off. Hope you have something decent this time. Your last tip led nowhere. I don't give second chances."

Ernie nosed out from behind the bin, dragging his right leg behind him. "I was . . . unavoidably detained."

"What happened?" Gabe asked.

The snitch shrugged. "Walked into a door . . . tripped down some stairs. Take your pick. They all work."

When the parking lot light hit Ernie's face, Gabe winced. The guy's skin was a rainbow of bruises, and one eye was swollen shut. "You need a doctor?"

"No, but a bag of ice and something to eat would be good. I missed dinner . . . and lunch, come to think of it," Ernie said, his expression full of hope. He climbed over a small snowbank, his limp obvious as he approached. "At least I can walk on this leg now. Thought I was gonna be on crutches."

Gabe shook his head. Ernie would do anything for a buck, but he'd come through a few times, so Gabe would humor him. He kept hoping Ernie would spill something big on Gasmerati or Tower and ask for protection. Poor guy was like the town punching bag for bad guys, and one of these times he wouldn't recover from their torment.

"Hold on. I'll be back in a minute. Stay hidden." Gabe retreated, making his way across the lot and into the bar's kitchen. He grabbed a baggie and filled it with ice, then snagged the sandwich he'd made for himself and stuffed it into a paper bag.

Ernie would never come inside the bar. Said he couldn't be seen in a cop hangout. This was already too close for the snitch's liking.

"Here you go." Gabe walked over to the log pile where Ernie had planted himself and handed him the ice and the dinner.

The snitch's onyx and gold ring flashed as he pressed the baggie to his swollen eye, the purple, green, and yellow mottling his skin evident in the faint light.

He opened the bag and rammed half the sandwich in his mouth. "Thanks," he muttered, his words garbled by the huge bite. He chewed some more, swallowed, and looked up at Gabe. "Got something good for you . . . if the price is right. This is the real deal, Montgomery."

Gabe lifted a brow. "You said that last time—"

"I know. I know, but even I get taken in by liars sometimes. This info's for real, from my own personal experience." Ernie looked around suddenly. "Hey, did you hear something?"

Gabe stilled, listening for a minute. "No."

"Maybe I shouldn't have come." Ernie's head whipped back and forth, sniffing the air, like a rodent trying to sense an approaching cat. He bit his lip. "Yeah. Maybe this whole thing was a bad idea."

Gabe went on full alert. His gut was telling him he needed this information, and he didn't want Ernie taking off. Then again, he didn't want Ernie dead, either. But, damn it, Gabe wanted to take down Tower and the mob bosses he ran with. "You staying or going?"

Ernie pulled a knife out of his pocket and passed it back and forth between jittery hands, his gaze still searching the shadows.

Gabe forced himself not to take the snitch down with a quick twist of an arm. Knives had that effect on him lately.

Finally, Ernie spoke again. "Guess I'm just getting jumpy. Look, I like you, Montgomery. You and your brother Zach saved my life when Tiny and his thugs came after me. I'd have been cougar food in the Rockies by now, so I figure I owe you."

"I'm listening," Gabe said.

Ernie scratched his nose. "You know sometimes, I . . . uh . . . courier a few specialty items for Gasmerati."

Gabe stiffened at the name he knew all too well. And not just because of his current op. Jeff Gasmerati had been cousin to Gabe's best friend and SWAT teammate, Steve Paretti. Gabe would love to beat the crap out of the traitor, but the guy was already dead.

Steve Paretti might have done the right thing in the end, but that didn't excuse the lies and treachery that almost cost Gabe half of his family.

Nothing did.

"Something big's going on," Ernie said. "Gasmerati's throwing around wads of cash like he grows it in his backyard."

"Is he expanding the business?" Gabe asked, shifting on his injured leg.

"I think he's going international, and he's keeping it very hush-hush." Ernie cocked his head. "Any of this worth something to you?"

"Could be." Gabe shrugged, but his heart sped up. International meant big risks. Big risks meant big rewards, but also a chance to make federal charges stick. With luck, Gabe could nail Gasmerati and maybe even rope in Sheriff Tower and his flunkies, too. "Okay. Tell me everything and we'll work out a price."

Ernie looked around again, obviously nervous. "I was at Gasmerati's building this afternoon, picking up a package to deliver. After I got it, I walked by Jeff's office. Heard something weird, like an argument. Lots of tension in Gasmerati's voice, so I slowed down and kind of took my time going past Jeff's door."

God bless the curious.

Ernie came closer, whispering the information so Gabe had to strain to hear. "Anyway, Gasmerati's having it out with somebody on the speakerphone, but there's another guy in the room with him. A translator, who keeps talking Russian, then repeating everything the guy on the phone says in English."

Gabe straightened. Russian? Could Gasmerati have tapped the Russian mob? "What did you hear?"

"Something about a transfer of cash. Soon." Ernie licked his lips. "They used the words *billion dollars.* Swear to God."

Gabe let out a low whistle. "What else?"

"The Russian guy seemed upset about a car accident. Jeff said not to worry. He had law enforcement connections. Just then someone came walking into the hallway, and I bolted. I've already been on the bad end of too many fists lately for screwing up, so I got the hell out of there."

And there was the first real proof—even if it was secondhand.

Gabe leaned forward. "Did anyone mention where this accident was?"

"Yeah, near Taos. Someone found a bus that went off the road yesterday, but also spotted a car that these guys apparently didn't want found."

A small gasp sounded from the side of the bar.

"Ernie, get out of here," Gabe said sharply.

The snitch's eyes widened. "Oh God. I'm dead." He scurried away as fast as he could on his injured leg.

Glock in hand, Gabe eased around the corner of the building.

A figure in a ski jacket hurried toward the street. Gabe raced after it. He had to know who'd overheard his conversation.

Within seconds, he caught up. Gabe spun the person around, slammed the intruder against the brick wall, then tore off the hood. Auburn hair spilled out over the jacket. "Deb? What are you doing back here at two in the morning?"

"Apparently, getting molested by you." The frigid wind whipped her hair across her face. She looked deathly pale, despite the fact her cheeks were red with cold.

"Hey, you're the one lurking outside the bar." He studied her face. "What's wrong?"

"I *thought* I wanted to talk to you. Now I'm not so sure."

"If you wanted to talk to me, why didn't you just use the phone?"

She scowled, shifting against him. His body went taut, suddenly aware of the soft curves pressed against him and the strength lying underneath that softness. He cleared his throat and stepped back. Her pupils dilated and his heart skipped a beat. He wanted to peel off his gloves and touch her skin, feel her pulse to see if his reaction was one-sided, but then her face turned to stone.

"I was on my way to the sheriff's office," she said. "When you crossed the parking lot . . . well, after all of your brother's newspaper articles about bad cops and deputies, I was worried about who to trust. I thought . . ." She rushed on, "Look, I know you're not a cop anymore. At least, I thought you weren't until that guy—"

Gabe cut her off. "'Until that guy' what?"

She hesitated, more wary now, but not backing down. "I didn't mean to overhear anything, but then he mentioned an accident on the way to Taos, in conjunction with a mobster. It shocked me. That's the rescue tonight that got me grounded. Do you think the church bus was sabotaged? And, why would a Russian care about any of this?"

Damn good questions. He had to back her off from this line of thinking. Fast.

"I don't know, but I'll make sure the police check into your suspicions." *Yeah, she'd be sure to fall for that line.* "It may be a different accident."

"Do I look like I just got off the bus from the country?"

Gabe swore again. "Okay, I said I'll look into it. Now, why were you heading to the station at this hour?"

At his question, all her bravado vanished. He'd never seen quite that expression on her face. She looked up at him, worry crinkling the corners of her eyes.

"My sixteen-year-old sister is missing. Ashley left my house about ten, planning to beat curfew, but never made it back to the dorm. The student who lent her his vehicle called me, freaking out that she hadn't brought the car back. We've both tried calling her, but there's no answer. This isn't like her. Something is terribly wrong."

Deb's face felt half-frozen, but the rest of her body was warm from Gabe pressing against her. For some stupid reason, she felt comforted by the pressure, instead of trapped by someone who might or might not be a bad guy. Despite what she'd seen, her instincts said to trust him.

She would, but only because she'd watched him for a long time. Over a year, in fact.

It had started the night she'd delivered him to the hospital. She'd given him a twenty-five percent chance when they'd loaded the stretcher into the chopper. She'd recognized the gray on his face, had seen it too many times in combat. Then his brother Luke had boarded. The reporter had clung to his brother and willed him back from the brink.

His odds had gone up to forty-sixty in her eyes. She'd still thought he had a better chance of dying than living.

She hadn't been able to keep things purely professional, though—or completely close off her heart. Those two Montgomery brothers had wriggled beneath her skin like a parasite. By the time she'd landed the chopper at the hospital, she hadn't been able to ignore them.

They didn't know, but she'd hung around, outside the waiting room. She'd seen Gabe's mother arrive, his brothers, an imp of a little girl, and even a sea of SWAT.

The connections she'd witnessed in their family had made her ache. She missed Rick and Ben. Now more than ever. If her brothers had been stateside, she could have picked up the phone and dialed them. They'd have been on the first flight to help her, but they were incommunicado and she was on her own to find Ashley.

"Your sister is missing?" he repeated. "If she's a student, couldn't she just have become tired and gone to a classmate's house and forgotten to call?"

Gabe still hadn't moved away from Deb, and for the moment, she didn't care—even though someone this much in her space usually made her skin crawl. "She wouldn't want the demerits. She's at the Air Force Academy."

He raised a brow. "Really? At sixteen? They don't take people that young."

"They made an exception for her. Lots of rules and red tape, but the bottom line is she's wicked smart. Too smart for her own good sometimes. They made her an offer she couldn't refuse. She and a friend hacked into the NSA for the hell of it. Guess it got the government's attention. They want her to be some kind of secret-weapon code breaker, I think." Deb bit her lip.

"Holy crap, she's one of the kids who hacked the NSA? It was all over the news."

Deb sighed. "Tell me about it. That's one of the reasons I'm so worried."

"So, you think someone found out where she is and something happened? It's not likely."

"Normally that's true, but she came by this weekend, worried." Deb filled Gabe in on her earlier conversation with Ashley. "I checked with the school. Neither she nor the car made it back. She never passed through the entrance gate or signed in on the dorm log-in sheet."

"Does Ashley have a boyfriend?" Gabe asked, gently.

"Yes," Deb admitted. "But I already tried calling Justin. I even woke up his parents. They're almost as crazed as I am, because they think he's missing, too. Justin sent his parents a text saying he'd decided to visit New Mexico Tech to see if he wanted to go there. He's graduating from high school this year."

Gabe relaxed a bit. "Then that's probably where Ashley is. Maybe he asked her to go with him?"

Deb shook her head and her chest tightened. The more she spoke aloud, the more the worry snaked through her insides, twisting her muscles into tension-filled knots. "I don't think so. According to Justin's parents he'd turned down New Mexico Tech earlier this week. So why would he text his parents that he was going there? And if Ashley was going there with him, why didn't she drop off the car she borrowed before she left?"

"You've got me." Gabe frowned. "So Justin hasn't been in touch with them since—"

"Saturday night. They've called him countless times since then. Last night, Ashley mentioned she'd been trying to reach him all day and was getting worried."

Gabe scratched his head. "Look, Deb. They're both kids—"

She shoved against his chest, pushing him away. "Montgomery, before you say one more word, let me tell you that I know my sister. She wouldn't take off without telling me. I opted out of my military career when my father was deployed so she could attend the Academy. In Ashley's mind, she owes me for that. Disappearing is the last thing she'd do to me."

He nodded his head, but Deb could see he had doubts. Thankful for the space between them, she crossed her arms. This had been a bad idea. Reaching out to him had been an impulse.

She should have known. Counting on anyone but herself was a mistake.

"Ashley has only been gone a few hours," he said, his weight shifting from one leg to the other. "Without more concrete evidence, I'm not even sure you can file a missing person's report yet."

"I know," she sighed. Gabe's leg was obviously bothering him tonight, but she couldn't let this go. "They're going to say the same thing at the sheriff's office. It's the other reason I wanted to talk to you. I thought maybe you could influence them. Convince one of the guys you know really well to help. Maybe at least ask the other officers to look out for the car."

Gabe tapped his chin. "If Neil Wexler is on, maybe I could talk him into a BOLO."

A small spark of hope kindled inside of her. "A BOLO? Is that the be-on-the-lookout-for thing?"

"Yeah."

"If you'd do that for me, Gabe, as soon as this is over, I promise I'll find a way to say thank you."

"Really?" He stepped forward and brushed the hair out of her eyes.

Her breath hitched. Now was not the time. Not with Ashley missing.

Gabe lingered for a moment, then dropped his hand. "Do you want to come inside the bar while I lock up? We may be at the station for a while."

"No. I'll wait here." A minute later, Deb regretted that decision. She huddled deeper into her coat. Was Ashley outside in this frigid cold? God, she should have made her sister stay. Why hadn't she gone with her gut?

Her instincts had kept her alive for her years in the Army. She knew better than to ignore them.

Seconds later, Gabe returned, his limp a bit more pronounced than it had been.

"You okay?" she asked.

His face tightened. "I'm fine. The cold weather makes me stiff." He flushed. "Uh, makes my leg stiff."

"Oh, really?" She couldn't stop the arch of her brow. Surely that wasn't a Freudian slip on his part? "We can drive to the station," she offered, "if you're in pain."

He scowled. "It's across the street."

"It's across four lanes of slippery, black-ice-covered street."

"*I'm fine*," he gritted out between clenched teeth.

"Does your jaw hurt when you get pissed like that?"

"Let's go," Gabe said.

"Lead on."

They walked down the small incline toward the street and made it onto the shoveled sidewalk with only a few near mishaps. The wind had picked up, blowing some of the snow around. The flakes glistened under the glow of the streetlamps, and the black ice shone like glass.

Gabe slowed down and took her arm. "Guess the street sanders haven't made it this far yet."

"Yeah," she agreed, "but it's prettier before they come." Her feet slipped and he caught her just before she hit the ground. She gripped his arm, the muscles hard beneath her hands.

"The snow may be prettier," Gabe added, a chuckle in his voice, "but it's tougher to walk on." He hauled her back to her feet. "You okay?"

She nodded, heat flaring her cheeks. Great. First, they were reduced to talking about the weather, then she almost lands on her butt. Way to impress a guy.

Not that she wanted or needed to. She'd always been better at being the buddy. Professional necessity. The few times she'd tried otherwise . . . well, it hadn't been pretty. Problem was, Gabe Montgomery could make any woman stupid. She shouldn't want more than a friend. She didn't.

Right, Deb. Talk about denial.

A few lights twinkled in the foothills of the mountains to the west and mounds of snow lined the walkways. Winter had come to the Rockies with a vengeance this year.

Oh, Ashley. Where are you?

When they reached the Jefferson County Sheriff's Office, Gabe held the door open for Deb. The renovated glass and metal building held every modern convenience, but it was still a cop shop at its heart.

Gabe waved to the desk jockey in the lobby, who glanced at the clock and raised his brow. "What happened that you're here at nearly three in the morning? Trouble at the bar?"

"No, Charlie. Sammy's is all closed up tight. My friend has a personal issue. Is Neil Wexler in tonight?"

Charlie smirked. "When isn't Wexler here? I swear he sleeps at the station whenever his wife's out of town." He signaled the detective's office. "So, what do you want him for?"

Gabe slid Deb a sidelong glance.

"My sister's missing," Deb said, her fear coming back full force.

Charlie's gaze flashed to Gabe. "Wexler is Homicide."

The word *homicide* crumbled something inside her. "Ashley's missing, not dead." Deb knew how the stories of missing girls ended. God, she prayed she was wrong. Maybe Ashley had had a brain meltdown and gone with Justin.

"Calm down," Gabe insisted. "Wexler was my boss while I was in rehab and on desk duty, so he knows me. He might be willing to do what we want him to do."

His gaze spoke volumes. *Don't mention the BOLO in front of Charlie. Don't rock the boat.*

The phone line lit up, and Charlie answered. After a quick conversation he hung up the receiver and waved them through. "Go on back. Wexler is waiting."

Deb sat in Wexler's cramped office, pausing to hear his reaction to her story.

Neil leaned back in his chair and sighed. "I'm sorry, Ms. Lansing. Without some sign of a crime being committed, my hands are tied. Your sister hasn't been missing long enough to even file a report."

Gabe tensed. "Deb knows that, Neil, but with the other kid missing, too, it seems like something is up."

"Yeah, they probably ran away together."

Deb burst from her chair. "Forget this. You don't believe me and I don't have time to mess around. I'm going to Colorado Springs and try the cops there. Maybe they'll listen to me."

Wexler pushed away from the desk. "They're going to say the same thing, but since you both seem so convinced, I'm willing to put out a BOLO on the car. That way, if any cop has a slow night, they can look around for it. Maybe we'll luck out. What's the make and model?"

Deb pulled a paper from her jacket pocket and placed it on the desk. "Here's all the information. Including color, VIN, and license plate number. The student she borrowed it from said there's a big dent in the right rear passenger door where another kid hit the car in the dorm parking lot. The upperclassmen's info is on there, too. Address, phone number, that kind of thing."

"This will help." Neil took the paper and scanned it. "I'll put the BOLO out tonight. If you have a picture of your sister, I can include that, too."

"I have one on my phone. Can I send it to your e-mail?"

"Send me a copy, too," Gabe said quickly.

After texting the photo, Deb waited while Gabe said goodbye to Wexler. Restless, she walked around his office. A black-and-white flyer on his bulletin board caught her attention. It showed the rear end of a banged-up car covered in snow. The plates read POE.

POE? Like Edgar Allan? Or like Ashley's game, *Point of Entry*?

"What's that?" Deb demanded, pointing to the flyer.

Wexler turned and checked out what she'd indicated. "Besides private, you mean?"

Gabe moved around the desk quickly and pulled the picture down. "Seriously, man, what's the story with this?"

The agitation in both their voices must have hit home because Neil snatched the paper and ran his gaze over it. "Came in an hour ago. A chopper pilot reported a vehicle in the same vicinity as another accident. One of the rescuers got a photo of the car. Looks like it's been out there a decade."

"I'm the pilot who reported that car," Deb said quietly. "I was doing S and R."

"Did anyone look inside the vehicle?" Gabe demanded, the words tense and startlingly urgent. "Did they find anything in it?"

Wexler's head snapped up, obviously thinking the same thing. "What the hell is going on, Montgomery? What do you know about this wreck?"

Gabe grimaced, a strange emotion haunting his expression. "I can't guarantee it's the same car, but POE is the license plate of a vehicle that disappeared eight years ago. I've seen the information about it in my father's cold case files. Three teenagers were driving to a math tournament in the mountains. They never made their destination and the car was never found."

"I guess it has been now. There were three skeletons inside and they'd all been shot."

CHAPTER FOUR

ASHLEY HUDDLED AS BEST SHE COULD IN THE BACK OF THE SUV. The frigid temperature outside made it so she could barely feel her fingers and toes anymore. Niko kept the heat down really low. She blew against her frozen hands; her warm breath made them sting.

She tugged at the zip ties binding her wrists, but she'd rubbed the skin raw. She bit back a small whimper. Even the smallest movement burned like fire licking her skin.

Her head dropped against the carpet. She didn't bother trying to sit up and look outside. They'd covered her with a blue, heavy-duty plastic tarp. She couldn't see anything.

And no one could see her. The vehicle sped down the road. The rhythmic thud of seams in the asphalt pounded into her brain. She had no idea how long they'd been driving. She'd lost all sense of time. It could have been two hours, five, or even eight.

She shifted her body and her calf muscles seized. She tried to stretch out her legs, but she had to make do with flexing her foot to ease the cramp. She had to go to the bathroom, and her jaw throbbed from her kidnapper's fists. She hadn't eaten or had anything to drink since Deb's and her stomach ached as much as her head.

Don't let it get to you. She could almost hear Deb's voice. *Fight.*

She moved her head toward the edge of the tarp, nudging it aside. Maybe she could tell if it was daylight.

Someone's fist smashed down on her back. "Smarten up, Lansing. We'll be there in a few hours. Don't blow it now."

A few more hours? Where the heck were they taking her?

The traffic pattern seemed to be more congested, more stop and go. Were they passing through a city? Would they stop to get gas?

She wished she dared to look out, try to attract attention. Signal for help. They'd have to stop again eventually.

That might be her last chance to get away. If they opened the back hatch, she had to be ready.

Snow crunched beneath Gabe's every step. Even the nonthreatening sound scraped across his edgy nerves the last few feet to Deb's car. One photo had provided Gabe with more new information than he'd gathered in years of searching. He needed to look at his father's old case files to confirm his suspicions—that the car contained the remains of Shannon Devlin's missing teammates—but he had little doubt.

Deb leaned against her car, silent and obviously distracted. Despite the frigid air, she didn't move. "I can't just go home. I've got to do something."

Her words broke through the eerily silent night.

Gabe studied her face under the streetlight, her rigid features, the shadows under her eyes. She jiggled her car keys in her hand and he tensed, her uncertainty disconcerting. He'd never seen her as anything but assured in her actions. Until tonight.

"You planning to head to Colorado Springs?" he asked.

"What else can I do? I have to find her."

He didn't blame her. If one of his brothers went missing, he'd be tearing the town apart.

"You're too tired to drive—"

She stiffened. "I know my body's limits."

He raised his hands. "Look, I know someone who might help, but he works days." He gestured to his house. "It's not that long until dawn. Want to come in?"

"Come in?" Suspicion laced her words and she stepped back.

"I know how it is when family's in trouble." He didn't try to touch her. "Let me help. I have some files to check out. Maybe Ashley will call and this will all be over. If not, have something to eat and drink until it makes sense for us to drive to Colorado Springs."

"Us?" The words were wary, like she had trouble believing all he wanted was to help and not take her into his arms.

Gabe led her across the parking lot. "Us. Seems like you could use an ally."

For a few seconds she didn't answer. Finally, Deb sighed, her face marked with worry. "Okay. Thanks. I'm jumping out of my skin. I can't believe this is happening. Last night, I was talking to her and now—"

"We'll find her, Deb." Gabe unlocked the front door and held it open.

She went inside, brushing against him—not as an invitation, though. His body thrummed at her nearness, but he'd received her message loud and clear.

"Do you really think Detective Wexler will do the BOLO?"

"He doesn't believe he needs to, but he promised. He keeps his word." Gabe entered, then closed and locked the door behind him. "Neil is a good guy. He's a natural skeptic, and not easily swayed by emotion, but we've got him curious."

"He could bury the request."

"He's a smart detective. He can't do much officially right now, but he'll keep an eye out for any related bulletins. Besides, we've laid the foundation for Ashley's case and, if I'm right, provided Neil a lead on a cold one."

His house's warmth took the edge off the cold. Deb headed through the living room and dropped her jacket on the back of the couch. "Why would Neil be so interested in three kids dying near Taos? Were they originally from Denver?"

"No, but their murder is probably related to an unsolved shooting here. I'm sure Neil's checking that information now. He'll look good for making the connection so fast."

"If only someone jumps on Ashley's BOLO that quickly."

Gabe shrugged out of his jacket, too, and tossed it next to Deb's. He kind of liked how they looked together, side by side, not alone. He shoved the romantic musings aside. The moment he'd dragged her into his office, things had changed between them. Yesterday, she might not have even come to him before trying to report her sister's disappearance. Somehow they'd gone from acquaintances to . . . he wasn't quite sure what.

He had to stop thinking this way. She didn't need a lover, she needed a cop. And despite what everyone believed, he was still a deputy with the Jefferson County Sheriff's Office. He turned to her. "Neil agreed to put your contact info on the bulletin, too. That should help a lot with credibility when you talk to the police in Colorado Springs."

"God, I hope so." She wrapped her arms around herself and looked around his house.

"Do you want a beer or any food?" he asked in an attempt to distract her as much as anything. He could imagine the horrors going through her mind. She'd seen more than most, but Search and Rescue was like being a cop in a lot of ways. It wasn't personal. Most of the time.

"My fridge is pretty bare since I usually eat at the bar, but I can nuke frozen dinners with the best of them or boil up some hot dogs."

"A beer would be great," she said with a sigh. "Maybe it will calm me down a little. My mind is racing." She hesitated. "Gabe, how do you know so much about the Taos case? That accident happened eight years ago. You would have only been in high school. When I was a teenager, I rarely watched the news, much less knew about anything happening an entire state away."

Gabe snagged two beers out of his refrigerator and walked into the living room, trying not to be pleased she'd checked him out enough to estimate his age. Even so, he dreaded the upcoming discussion. And how much to reveal. So many secrets. He chose his words carefully. "My father was in Homicide then. I have some of his old investigative files. One might tie to those kids."

After giving Deb her drink, Gabe set his bottle down, then walked to the wall-to-wall bookshelves across the room. He moved several large books on the history of flying. Behind them, he'd hidden the thick expandable folders containing Patrick Montgomery's final obsession. The notes and materials for Shannon Devlin's case.

"You keep all your old police files tucked away for a rainy day?" Deb asked.

"Nope." Gabe sat on the couch and set the five-inch bound collection of files on the coffee table. "This case was different for my father. It tortured him. The one he couldn't solve." *The one involving his daughter.* Gabe pulled out some of the folders he'd scoured over the years, whenever he could face the guilt, and opened the most worn manila file.

Despite Gabe's familiarity with the contents, the photo of the girl he hadn't been able to save still haunted him.

"She looks a lot like my sister, Ashley." Deb moved in close beside him. "That's kind of spooky. Who is she?"

"Shannon Devlin. She came to town eight years ago. Someone gunned her down in the bus station. My father and I . . . were there that night. I was standing next to her, but I couldn't save her. My father tried to catch the sniper, but he got away. "

Deb's gaze flew to Gabe's. "Oh my God. No wonder you reacted so intensely to that car bulletin in Neil's office. If that wreck is related to this case, maybe this is the break the police need to solve it."

"I hope so." Gabe pulled out a few more folders. The base of his neck throbbed, like it always did when he opened this file. These weren't sheriff's office files. They weren't even part of Patrick Montgomery's official investigations. Gabe's father had copied all of these materials in secret and continued to investigate on the side.

Then again, Patrick Montgomery had done a lot of secret things on the side.

Gabe shoved the bitter memories aside. If his mother ever learned that his father had conceived the daughter she'd always longed to bear with another woman, it would destroy his mom. She'd idolized the man. All Gabe's brothers did, too.

Concealing his anger all these years had made Gabe feel like an outsider sometimes, but he had enough guilt to atone for with Shannon's death. Tearing apart his family wasn't going to be one of his sins, so he kept his father's secret. No one would know from Gabe that the Montgomery brothers had a half sister born less than a year after Anna Montgomery gave birth to the final child she could carry.

Gabe spread out the manila folders, determined to concentrate on the job at hand. He flipped to the next page in the file. "Take a look at Shannon's bio. She sounds a lot like Ashley. Intellectually, Shannon was way ahead of her peers."

Deb scanned the page. "Wow, she was more than just a good student. Ranked number one in her class—a physics and math brain. Nearly perfect SAT math score. It says that MIT, Stanford, Harvard, and Yale were actively recruiting her."

"Shannon was set to graduate early. She'd been heading from her home in Angel Fire to the state math bowl in Taos, New Mexico, and was attacked on the way. The cops might have considered the attack random, except her three teammates didn't show up, either."

"The kids in the POE car?"

"Yeah." Gabe opened another folder and turned several pages, until he found the one he wanted. "Here's a picture of them with the car."

Deb leaned in closer, her breath warm on his cheek, her body pressing against him. "That looks a lot like the car on the bulletin. Why are they all wearing black?"

"They were geeks. According to their parents, they wore black long before Goth became a way of life. With POE on the vanity license plate, people speculated they were fans of Edgar Allan Poe, but the kids' parents didn't think so."

"You don't believe it, either." Deb sent him a side glance. "I can hear it in your voice."

"No, I don't." Gabe tried to focus, but Deb's proximity distracted him. His body tensed with awareness. He wanted to grab her hand. This was a story he hadn't been able to share with anyone since it had happened. He hadn't realized until this moment how much looking at this file over and over again had worn him down. "One of the boys' fathers thought it stood for a video game or one of the character avatars. Something like that. Shannon and the guys loved to play video games. She was especially good at it."

Deb's hand went to Gabe's leg, her nails digging into his jeans. "Like Ashley. Oh God. She plays P.O.E. It stands for *Point of Entry*. She plays with a team of other kids, too, and Justin was one of them."

A strange sense of déjà vu settled onto Gabe. "The POE license plate could be an acronym for *Point of Entry*. The game's been around a long time, and they keep putting out new versions every year." Gabe grabbed a small bound set of papers that had been assembled into a mock-up of a book. "This is a copy of Shannon's journal." He flipped a page, and gave up another memory that had been etched into his brain. "With her last words, Shannon mentioned a game and then she whispered something weird about stopping it." He turned a few more pages. "*Point of Entry* sounds familiar to me, too. It could be one of the games they played."

Deb grabbed his wrist. "Look!" She pointed at a notation in the lower corner of one of the pages.

Gabe looked down. Bingo. *Point of Entry.* His father had underlined it twice. "I knew I'd seen it somewhere."

"How could a girl who was killed years ago and three kids shot in the mountains of New Mexico tie into Ashley's disappearance? And Justin's?"

"I don't know, but there are too many similarities not to explore the possibilities if she doesn't call soon." He still hadn't told Deb about the other kids his father had been investigating. Kids who had never been found.

Deb stood up and paced the room, her energy frenetic. She whirled around. "Why did Shannon come to Denver after being attacked? What was she doing here?"

Gabe didn't like where these questions might lead, but she had a right to ask. He'd brought up the connection. "To get help from my father. He was a cop. He was supposed to protect her."

"Why not just go to the local New Mexico authorities?"

"She did, but they brushed her off. They thought the attack was random and her friends had skipped town."

"Like Justin."

Gabe nodded. "A . . . friend of hers . . . contacted my father and asked if they could come to Denver to hide. Shannon was gunned down when she arrived."

He could see the speculation in her gaze. No doubt the wheels whirred in Deb's head. She recognized there was more to the story. But in Gabe's mind, his sister, Whitney's, identity wasn't relevant. Not really.

Deb bent over and tapped the folder. "There's more in this accordion folder than just files on Shannon and her teammates. It's way too thick. What else was your father looking into?"

Gabe took a deep breath. He so didn't want to get into this now. He kept his gaze lowered. Deb saw too much.

"He identified a loose pattern of teenage disappearances, a few here and there, all across the country, over a period of several years. At first, I couldn't see the tie-in. After all, a lot of kids run away at that age, but it was obvious my father obsessively tracked certain ones." He sat back and sighed, shaking his head. "I always thought he was traveling down a rabbit hole. Until today."

Deb sagged onto the couch next to Gabe. "Why today specifically?"

"Because the few disappearances he starred in the files were all supersmart kids who supposedly ran away, often with an equally brilliant friend."

"Oh God. Ashley. Justin." Deb reached forward and grabbed Shannon's file. "I need to read these."

"Wait—"

She flipped open the folder and gasped. Spread out before her were the horrific crime scene photos from Shannon's shooting.

"Oh my God."

Gabe snatched the folder from Deb's shaking hand and closed it. "I didn't want you to see those."

"This can't be related to Ashley." Deb sat stiff, her entire body screaming *don't touch me.*

Gabe ignored the message. He put his arm around her, and even though she pulled away, he tugged her closer, stroking her back, cursing his stupidity. Even her tour in Afghanistan hadn't prepared her for the gruesome photo of someone who looked so much like her sister.

The problem was, if Patrick Montgomery was right, Ashley Lansing's chances did not look good.

Ernie clutched the latest package in his hands. His jaw throbbed and his eye had swollen shut. Gasmerati's thugs had given him another beating. Just for fun. He was tired of this life.

He limped down the narrow hallway as quickly as he could. He didn't want to give anyone else a chance to pummel him.

Wishing he could just get the hell out of Denver, but without so much as a twenty to his name, Ernie sighed. No one would give him a job, except doing this crap for Gasmerati. He hitched up his pants. He was so hungry they hung loose. The food Gabe had given him had been the only decent meal he'd had in days. He'd never collected on his tip, but he might have to. Going near the bar terrified him, though. He still didn't know who had been lurking in the shadows outside Sammy's.

"I knew we had a leak!" Gasmerati's bellow boomed in the hallway. "Why did it take this long to find out the traitor's name?"

Ernie froze, his swallow so loud the gulp echoed around him. God, did they know about him? He sent a furtive glance right, then left, and plastered himself against the wall. If Jeff meant Ernie, he was dead. He couldn't run far enough to escape the mobster's thugs.

"I want Grace O'Sullivan silenced," Gasmerati said. "I don't care if I've known her all my life. Luke Montgomery has run too many newspaper articles using inside information. I can't believe she's the one who betrayed us. Her husband is our damned hit man. Call him. We'll see if he's really loyal. Hell, I might throw in Montgomery, too."

Ernie tensed. Gasmerati was putting out a hit on Grace O'Sullivan—and possibly Luke, too? Gabe would pay big bucks for this.

"We should have known it was her," another voice chimed in. "She had the hots for Steve Paretti before she—"

"Don't speak that traitor's name in my presence, Sly," Gasmerati said.

Ernie shuddered. Sly made Gasmerati look like a choir boy. As Gasmerati's enforcer, Sly enjoyed his job too much. Ernie did all he could to avoid the muscle man. Everyone did.

Gasmerati's voice turned harsh. "Family doesn't betray family. Find out who she called at WITSEC," he ordered. "First the FBI looking into my business and now this. I want anyone involved silenced. I refuse to be brought down by a damn woman."

Footsteps thundered toward the door where Ernie listened. Panicking, he hurried out the side door. He quietly shut it, then limped away, praying no one had seen him.

The Montgomerys would want to know about this. If Grace was Luke's snitch, and the Montgomerys wanted to save her, they'd pay. Maybe enough to get him out of Denver.

For the first time in years, Ernie had hope that there was a way out of this mess after all.

Gabe stirred, his back, his leg, his whole body, sore and stiff. He opened his eyes, surprised to find he was still on the couch, the soft, warm body of Deborah Lansing tucked snugly against his side.

Outside, dawn was just breaking and the gray morning light filtered in through the blinds. Ice frosted the kitchen windows, so today would be another cold one. Gabe resettled the afghan his mother had knitted him for Christmas over his legs and Deb's, then leaned back in the softness of the couch.

She'd fallen asleep in his arms, worn out by anxiety, fatigue, and unshed tears. Even now, she wrestled inner demons that disturbed her slumber. She wouldn't like being this vulnerable to anyone. She prided herself in her strength. He'd learned that much about her.

And he found that spine of steel sexy as hell.

Gabe stroked her forehead gently and whispered soft words of comfort, like his mother had when he'd had a nightmare. Deb settled in and nestled closer, draping one arm around his waist.

Talk about sweet torture, and she didn't even know what she was doing to him. How many times had he fantasized about having her in his arms?

He had several choices. He could kiss her awake or move away from her so she wouldn't be embarrassed that she'd turned to him while she slept. He couldn't bring himself to do either. He just wanted to hold her a little longer.

Unmoving, he ran several investigative scenarios through his head and by the time he'd settled on a plan for the day, Deb's eyelids fluttered open.

First, her eyes widened, then she stared at him, then looked down at their entangled bodies.

"Oh, tell me I didn't do this . . ." She flushed crimson and pulled out of his embrace. "Gabe, I'm so sorry. I never meant to fall asleep." She brushed her hand across the front of his sweater.

He smiled gently, already missing the warm weight of her on top of him. "Actually I was thinking that the last hours were the best sleep I've had in a while."

She stilled, her eyes wary. "You can't be serious."

"When a beautiful woman falls asleep in my arms, I call myself damn lucky." The discomfort on her face told him he'd pushed his case enough.

"What time is it?" Urgency shoved her to her feet, her eyes searching for a clock.

"Too early to drive to Colorado Springs, but not too early for breakfast." He rose and went to the kitchen, yanking out a few microwavable entrées from the freezer. "What can I interest you in? Breakfast burritos or quesadillas? Oh, there's an ancient box of Pop-Tarts if you're the daring type."

He forced the conversation light. Today could be a really good day or a really bad day, but the foreboding in Gabe's gut made him suspect the latter.

Hesitant footsteps revealed her reservation. He forced himself to relax when everything in him longed to hold her and make it okay. Trouble was, he couldn't.

He threw the frozen entrées on the counter and grabbed the coffee pot. "I don't know about you, but I'm not fun to be around before coffee. Want some?"

He turned, empty pot in hand.

Deb stood a few feet away, a bit bemused. "Um, coffee would be great. Look, Gabe—"

"It's fine, Deb. I get the message."

Her cheeks flushed.

"Today, we're colleagues, right? Mixing business and pleasure breaks the rules."

Her eyes widened in shock.

"Don't look so surprised. I get it. I worked with a woman for years in SWAT. She was a sniper. She kept herself at a distance for a lot of reasons. That was one of them. Of course, now she's married to my brother." Gabe filled the pot with water and looked over his shoulder. Deb had given him the excuse he needed. As much as he could see himself seducing Deb Lansing, he liked her too much. It wouldn't be a one-night stand with Deb, and he had an investigation to run. He couldn't risk putting her in danger. "Business it is."

A few minutes later the smell of coffee filtered through his house. He handed Deb a cup and she sipped the dark liquid gratefully. Gabe nearly groaned.

Her eyes finally cleared, their haze from only a few hours' sleep vanishing. "When can we leave?"

"Nine is the earliest my contacts will be there. For now, eat up."

She sat down at the table, and he doled out breakfast, adding a bowl of salsa to hide the frozen-food aftertaste.

A few minutes later, Deb licked her lips. "Frozen or fresh, I don't care. I didn't realize how hungry I was." She glanced once more at the clock and leaned forward in her chair, her expression solemn. "Thank you . . . for your kindness last night. For being there."

Gabe ignored the small skip of his heart. "That's what colleagues do. Right?"

"Yes. Colleagues."

What an idiot. Gabe cursed his stupidity. Business was the least of the emotions he was feeling for Deb Lansing this morning and he'd given her the out. "Do you want the shower first?" he asked. "We have just enough time before we should go."

She shook her head. "More coffee." She poured a second cup.

Relieved, Gabe headed to the back of the house. His shower would be quick all right, and freezing cold.

Ten minutes later, he returned to the kitchen bearing fresh towels and a packaged toothbrush for her. Would she notice his lips were blue from the icy water he'd rained upon his overeager body?

Deb sat at the table, nursing her coffee. She looked more like herself now, alert, strong, and less vulnerable. More like the woman who could probably throw him onto his back and either stomp on him or have her way with him.

"Shower's yours if you want it." Gabe shifted. "I didn't know if you wanted to take the time to go home before heading to Colorado Springs. I left some long-sleeved shirts and sweaters on my bed if you want to change. I don't have any pants that would fit, though. Just sweats."

Deb faced him, her face fully cloaked in the iron curtain he'd come to recognize. "Thanks. I'd feel a lot better after a run through the shower. I want to get going as soon as possible."

By the time she returned, her damp auburn hair curling around her face and shoulders, Gabe truly wondered if he'd lost his mind. How could he have thought listening to a naked, wet Deborah Lansing taking a shower in his bathroom wouldn't require him to shove snowballs down the front of his pants?

Damn. She was loyal, sexy, witty, and—

She interrupted. "Thanks for the loan of the clothes, etcetera. I'll replace the toothbrush."

He moved toward her. "You don't have to. I have more."

"Oh." Her gaze lowered. "Yeah. Single guy. Who owns a bar. Of course you have guests."

He stepped closer. Close enough to inhale the scent of minty toothpaste, shampoo, and clean skin. Somehow his soap and shampoo smelled a lot sexier on her. He tilted her chin up. "Deb, you are the first woman I've had sleep the night at this house."

Her eyes rounded. "Really? Then why . . ."

"My mother." He brushed the hair back from Deb's face. "After raising six boys, my mother was used to buying for an army, so when I moved in she gave me a care package—or twenty. I could supply every person in the city of Denver with a toothbrush and still have some left over. Don't even get me started on how many boxes of condoms she threw in. Then she yells at me for not giving her grandchildren. I think she'd better make up her mind."

Deb laughed, a hearty, unexpected laugh that had him smiling like he never thought he would again. For a moment, the fear of the day went away.

"Well, I still thank you for the toothbrush and the clothes. I hope I can return the favor sometime."

Hell, he could think of a lot of things she could do, most involving a box of those condoms. Maybe all of them.

As if she could read his thoughts, her breath hitched and her eyes darkened.

For a minute, he feared he'd spoken those words aloud. Then her gaze dropped to his lips and she licked her own.

Screw being good. Self-control was highly overrated.

He stepped forward until their bodies were almost touching, then gently framed her face with his palms. She didn't move away. Instead, she closed her eyes and rose on her tiptoes to meet him halfway. He brushed his lips across hers. Once, twice, then took over the kiss and showed her some of the passion he'd been denying for so long.

"I thought we were colleagues."

"Shut up," she said.

He had no problem with that.

She wrapped her arms around his neck and pulled him against her, seeming to want everything he could give her and more. Blood rushed through his ears—and other places—and deep inside, some protective wall, brittle and unyielding, shattered. For the first time in a long time, a flicker of warmth reached the very heart of him as if her light had found its way into the darkness residing there.

A phone rang somewhere in the room, but Gabe didn't want to move. She was so warm, so alive in his arms.

On the second ring, Deb stiffened and looked over at her phone on the coffee table. "Ashley?" She bolted to the device, then fumbled with the buttons in her haste to answer. She pressed Speaker. "Lansing."

"Deborah Lansing?"

The tenor of the official-sounding voice made Deb collapse onto the couch. "Y-yes."

"This is the Colorado Springs Police Department. We found the car your sister was driving. It was abandoned at the bus station. You might want to meet us there."

CHAPTER FIVE

THE ROCKY MOUNTAINS LOOMED IN THE WEST, THE PEAKS even whiter than yesterday. Another dusting of snow had hit the higher elevations, but Gabe's tires hugged the roads despite the icy conditions.

Deb couldn't help but be glad she wasn't alone. She'd let herself lose control with Gabe, but she'd discovered, oddly enough, she didn't worry he'd take advantage. She couldn't remember the last time someone had just stepped up like he had. He hadn't asked questions, he hadn't balked, he'd thrown himself into her problems. Without asking for anything in return.

The frozen terrain outside the vehicle didn't appear inviting. Deb prayed her sister wasn't out there in that frigid landscape, hurt or unprotected. The image of Shannon's bullet-ridden body seared Deb's mind, and she fought to not react to the grief filling her. She'd failed her sister. She'd failed everyone in her family. "I was supposed to look out for Ashley. Keep her safe."

Gabe looked over from the driver's seat. "Hey, you don't know for sure that anything has happened to her."

"Ashley would never have abandoned someone's car at the bus station and not even let him know. She's pulled some stupid maneuvers, but in most ways, she's ultra-responsible. Part of me held out hope maybe she'd broken down and couldn't call. I was certain she'd be with the car." Deb turned toward Gabe. "What do I do if she's really been kidnapped?"

"Find her."

Simple words, but nothing felt simple anymore. Deb rubbed her hands over her arms to ward off the sudden chill that had nothing to do with the temperature.

Gabe adjusted the heater anyway, then his hand squeezed hers. He gave her a small smile of confidence, but didn't move his hand away. Surprised at how tightly she clung to the simple touch, Deb stared out the window, trying to shear the worst-case scenarios from her mind.

Seconds seemed to tick by like hours. Every mile Deb prayed for a phone call from Ashley. A text. A picture. A miracle.

"We're here." Gabe pulled into the entrance to the bus station. Snow piled in huge dirty drifts all around the edge of the lot, reminding her how bleak their prospects looked.

Several policemen and a cadet in uniform stood staring at an ancient green vehicle with a large dent on the passenger side. Typical student junkbox. Could Ashley have broken down on the way here, leaving herself open to predators? But why abandon the car here and not on the road?

Gabe pulled in next to the police cars, and Deb jumped out of the SUV before he'd even turned off the engine.

"Did you find my sister?" she begged the policemen. "Do you have any information at all?"

Gabe came up beside her. She longed to reach out and grab his hand for comfort, but she couldn't appear weak. She'd learned long ago that respect came from strength. Her father had taught her that, her brothers had taught her that, her Army unit had welded the truth to her core.

A rookie-looking cop spoke first. "She's not here and so far there's no location for her. We're hoping you can help us."

The cadet scowled at Deb. "I didn't think Ashley would do something like this to me. Guess that's what I get for trusting a kid." He turned toward the cops. "Can I take the car now?"

"Sure." The cop handed him the keys.

"What, you're not going to take fingerprints, or fiber samples, or even pretend to investigate?" Deb asked. "This car is a crime scene. My sister has been kidnapped."

"I highly doubt that," a second policeman said. "She left you a note saying she was taking off." The cop handed Deb a folded piece of paper.

Dear Deb,

Sorry. Things just got too hard for me at the Academy. I'm meeting Justin to look at other schools so we can be together.

I really am sorry.

Love,
Ashley

"My sister did not write this note."

The policeman sighed. "The kid said it was her writing. He could tell by the way she signed her name with the squiggly design she put under the *y*."

"It looks like her writing, but it's not," Deb insisted. "Besides, Ashley has straight As. It wasn't too hard for her. Did you even check that out with the school?"

"No." The cop glared at her. "It looks pretty cut and dried that she wants to be with this Justin character. And if you don't hold the attitude, I'll take *you* in for questioning."

Deb could barely quell the urge to show this guy exactly what kind of training she'd learned—not at boot camp, but at the hands of her two older brothers *before* she left for basic training.

As if reading her mind, Gabe gently clasped Deb's elbow and squeezed before stepping between her and the cop. "I've run police investigations before up at Jeffco. Did you at least look at the bus terminal security tapes to make sure that Ashley was the driver who left the car in the lot?"

"They're broken," the rookie snapped.

"All of them?"

"No," the second cop added. "Just the two on this side."

"Seriously?" Deb glowered at him. "Doesn't that seem a little convenient to you?"

The third police officer, who had remained silent until now, cleared his throat. "Lady, nothing about this case is convenient, except that note. It sounds like we're dealing with young love. She's sixteen."

"That boy is missing, too."

"We spoke to his parents and there is no proof these two kids aren't together. Your sister made the choice to go with the boy. We'll put out a bulletin on her, but not because she's the victim of a possible kidnapping. She's looking at grand theft auto charges for stealing the car."

"That's insane. She *borrowed* the car!" Deb planted herself inches from the cop. "Ashley is a good kid. She's missing and in trouble. Can't you see that?"

He ignored her and flipped through his notebook. "Yeah. She's good at breaking into the NSA. Good at pulling a few pranks in high school and giving everyone straight As in her graduating class. Your sister is in a lot of trouble, lady, and the district attorney will be in touch if the owner decides to press charges."

Deb whirled to the cadet. "You would do that? Even knowing this is completely out of character?"

"Hey," he protested, "I don't know her that well. It's not like we were best buds or anything. All she did was tutor me a bit. I took pity on her when she begged to borrow my car. I didn't psychoanalyze her first." The kid glowered at Deb. "And when Ashley comes back from her little jaunt, tell her not to bother asking me for another favor. I don't care how desperate she sounds. I don't need this kind of trouble."

The engine coughed to life and he screeched out of the parking lot. The policemen sauntered to their squad cars.

Deb rushed one of them, but Gabe held her back and snagged the note from her hands. He scanned it. "There's nothing they can do, Deb."

Her entire body shook with fury as the three cars pulled away. She jerked her arm from Gabe. "I thought you believed me."

"I do, but a note like this changes things."

"If Ashley was going to run away, she'd never leave me a vague note like this. She wouldn't hide her plans from me, either."

"Unless she knew you'd never go along with them," he said gently. "Her note—"

"If she was being defiant, she'd address the note to *Admiral Lansing*, just to get in my face about it. And that curlicue at the end of the *y* . . . that's not how she writes it. She's a geek. She draws a perfect spiral. Some craziness about ratios and math."

"I *do* believe you." Gabe let out an exasperated sigh. "I was *going* to say, her note looks a lot like some of the letters in my father's files."

"Why didn't you say anything in front of them?" Deb whirled around, her hands on her hips.

"Because I pick my battles. The police won't believe me. Not now. They've made up their minds. Every single case my father looked into was shoved aside by the police. Teens running away because parents put too much pressure on them, didn't care, needed to find themselves, whatever. A few of the parents haven't given up hope, but none of the disappearances are active cases anymore. I have no proof of any wrongdoing."

Deb could barely contain her frustration—and her disappointment. She wanted to punch something . . . or someone. "What about all the stuff we talked about after going to Detective Wexler? The POE plates, the video game, the possibility of a conspiracy?"

"Speculation, Deb. We can't prove any of it yet. Neil may be our best bet after all, since he's working Shannon's case."

"*If* they're connected. So, I just ignore the fact that my sister is missing? I let Neil traipse around investigating an eight-year-old murder while my sister could be fighting for her life? Great. At least you get *your* investigation solved."

"Low blow, Deb."

She let out a slow, deep breath and kneaded the back of her neck. She raised her gaze with a wince. "Sorry. I'm just—"

"Worried. Scared. Frustrated. I get it." Gabe's hands settled on her shoulders. He kneaded at the tension, the warmth of his hands easing the knots, his proximity at least making her not feel alone.

"I know how things work," he said. "We'll file a missing person's report at the Colorado Springs PD, even if they don't act on it. We can see if the cadet would sell us his car. But, unless the police do the forensic analysis, the chain of evidence will be compromised. Actually, the way the police and the kid were searching through the vehicle when we arrived, it probably wouldn't do any good. No one wore gloves, even when touching the note."

"Then where do we go from here?"

Gabe nodded toward the terminal. "Inside and show Ashley's picture around. Maybe we can find out if anyone saw her in the last twenty-four hours."

Deb fell in step with him. She studied his determined jawline. "You believe she's still alive?"

Gabe glanced over at her. "Yes," he lied. He had absolutely no clue. Not one of the missing prodigies whose names Patrick Montgomery starred had ever been found. Ashley fit that select victim profile like she'd written it herself.

Deb glared at the police station, the hairs on the back of her neck still standing up. She clenched her fist, her knuckles white.

"At least you didn't end up in jail," Gabe commented as he pulled the car out of the parking lot, his voice far too calm for her.

She glared at him. "They threatened to arrest me."

"You called the guy every synonym for idiot in the book. I had to look up some of the insults on my smart phone."

"Hardy har har. So, I can curse in several languages. Comes from being an Army brat." Deb shoved her hand through her hair. "He deserved it. He didn't take us—or Ashley's disappearance—seriously."

"We knew they wouldn't." Gabe let out a long, slow breath. "I swear, you remind me of my brother Zach. A hothead."

"When it comes to my family, you bet I am."

Gabe was right, damn him. Filing the missing person's police report went about as badly as they'd expected. But it was *Ashley*. Deb could handle most anything the world threw her way, but when it came to her baby sister . . . it was a hundred times worse.

"Deb, we knew filing that report wouldn't be easy. You let them get to you."

"I fought every day in the Army for respect. I'm not backing down in front of those yahoos."

"They were jerks, but you have to understand, ninety-nine times out of one hundred, those notes left behind are real."

"Don't confuse me with facts, Gabe."

"Hopefully we'll have better luck at the Academy."

She shifted forward in her seat as Gabe turned into the dormitory parking lot. The building rose high against the blue winter sky. Deb had been impressed with the campus the first time she saw it. Now, it brought only sadness and regret.

"This is where Ashley lived?" Gabe asked, ducking down to scan the building.

Deb nodded.

He drove past the dorm and turned toward the main campus.

"Why aren't you stopping?" Deb asked.

"We're meeting with Ashley's advisor first," he said. "I made a couple of calls while you were in the ladies' room after arguing with those cops. Caught a break with this guy. My brother knows him."

Gabe pulled into a visitor space and they headed up the steps to an administration building. Deb could already feel her heart pounding with the desperation of a mission gone wrong. She shoved the ingrained reaction aside. Ashley would be okay. She had to be.

He pulled a slip of paper from his pocket. "Room 190A."

They walked down the corridor against the sea of spit-and-polished Air Force cadets. Their light blue shirts and dark blue pants were perfectly ironed and creased. Their shoes were polished like mirrors. The boys had crew cuts, the girls all wore their hair short or pulled back.

"Ashley really fit in here?" Gabe asked quietly. "From the photos you showed me, uptight and regimented doesn't seem like her style. Why did she choose this place?"

"Don't kid yourself. These guys can get pretty wild, but the real reason she chose the Air Force was because she's addicted to flying. Got her pilot's license at fifteen," Deb said. "Ashley knew the Academy wanted her for her brain, but she wants to fly an F-22 Raptor, though she'd settle for any fighter. She's obsessed with the idea. Of course, it didn't hurt that choosing Air Force over Army drove my dad crazy."

"Does she get that wild streak from her sister?"

"No. From my dad. He was a fighter pilot in the Gulf Wars. I like the versatility of helicopters, but those two live for speed."

"Here we are." Gabe rapped on the door labeled Major Rappaport.

"Enter," a voice commanded.

Gabe swung the door open, standing aside for Deb.

A man who looked to be in his early thirties rose from the

utilitarian desk and walked around the table, holding out his left hand, since his right was missing. "Ms. Lansing."

After a brief shake, he turned to Gabe. "Deputy Montgomery. Your brother Seth just called to reinforce that you'd be coming by. Told me he'd kick my ass if I didn't help you." He shot Deb a sheepish look. "Sorry for the salty language, ma'am. Seth brings that out in me."

She smiled. "I'm ex-Army. Nothing I haven't heard before."

Rappaport studied her more closely. "I remember that now. Ashley thinks the world of you."

"And that's why we're here. This behavior isn't like her."

"Won't you both sit down?"

"Thank you for seeing us." Gabe shook Rappaport's hand, then waited until everyone was settled around the desk before taking a seat. "My brother speaks very highly of you."

"Your brother saved my life. He's a tough SOB. Carried me out of the fire zone. I owe him." The major's gaze rested on Deb. "Have you heard from Ashley? Did she say why she went AWOL? She had an active social life off campus, whenever possible, and she seemed happy here. I'm surprised she'd throw it all away."

Deb stiffened in the chair.

Ashley's advisor's expression was kind enough. He seemed perplexed, but he wasn't worried. None of them were. Everyone thought she'd just taken off for the fun of it. Deb didn't get it. Ashley deserved the benefit of the doubt.

Gabe squeezed her leg. "I'm working with Deb to find Ashley. What can you tell us about her school life? Was she having trouble with any courses? Or maybe difficulties fitting in due to her age? She's young for being here."

"The youngest we've ever admitted. As to difficulty with her classes," Rappaport chuckled, "hardly. She doesn't break a sweat in her computer-science and math coursework. English and history, not so much. She doesn't love to read and write, but she still pulled in solid As. She's something else."

"What makes her so special?" Gabe asked.

"Besides the fact she can hack government websites and databases with ease?" Rappaport asked. "Her innate intuition is phenomenal. I've worked in intelligence for years, and I've never seen anyone like her. That girl knows her way around code and computers like she's part of them. She could probably break any encryption ever invented, or come close. She'd be dangerous if she wasn't on our side."

Deb's brow furrowed. She'd known Ashley was gifted, obviously, but Rappaport was talking about another level entirely. "Does everyone on this campus know how smart she is?"

Rappaport smiled. "When a sixteen-year-old teenager can blow most of the faculty out of the water in intellect, you bet there's talk."

Gabe leaned forward. "Could she have made a student jealous, or even a teacher, because of her abilities? Did she inadvertently show someone up? Can you think of anyone who'd be jealous enough of her skills to do something about it?"

"What are you asking?" Rappaport frowned.

"Deb doesn't believe Ashley ran away. She thinks she was taken."

"As in kidnapped?" Rappaport stiffened. "But the police told us—"

"The police and I don't see eye to eye," Deb said.

Sympathy, then disbelief crossed his face. "I see. Then the note they found—"

"She didn't write it. I can tell. It's not her signature."

He raised his eyebrows. "Then who did?"

"We don't know." Deb wanted to shake him. "Why is it so difficult for you people to see Ashley would be a target? For almost anyone. Industrial or corporate espionage, security, investigators. God, even other countries." She could feel her temper ready to explode because acknowledging anything else scared the hell out of her.

"What did Ashley do with her free time?" Gabe said quickly, shooting her a warning glance. She knew he was right. She had to calm down. For Ashley's sake.

"First-year cadets don't get a lot of it," Rappaport said. "From what I gather, she hung out with a group of computer geeks from the local high school. I caught them trying to sneak in here one night to play a game I'd given her."

Deb gasped. It couldn't be. "A game? Was it *Point of Entry*?"

The major looked startled. "Yes. You know it?"

Deb met Gabe's shocked glance. "Why did you give her that particular game?" she asked.

"It wasn't just for her. Some politicians came through on a visit. One of the guests said he was associated with the game maker and asked if he could donate the latest version to the Academy Morale Fund materials. He'd donated to the other academies, too. I played a few levels, and it seemed like something the cadets would go for in their free time. The math was challenging, so the copies went in with the rest of the approved games."

"Holy sh—" Deb bit her tongue. "What was the name of this politician?"

Rappaport's brow furrowed. "Sorry, it's been a while. We get a lot of VIPs around here, but I can check."

"Please do," Gabe said, handing over a card with his contact information on it. "The information is critical to our investigation. It's important we get his name."

The major studied them both. Deb recognized the suspicion—and the skepticism. "This doesn't make sense. What's the real story? What could Ashley going AWOL possibly have to do with a video game?"

Deb opened her mouth to respond, but Gabe's face went cold and his jaw tightened. He stood. "She's not AWOL. She's missing, Major, and she could be in big trouble. We're certain of it. I suggest you pull the game off the shelves until we know what's going on."

Gabe pulled up to a large brownstone resembling the one the Unsinkable Molly Brown had inhabited in Denver. Big, brown, and expensive as hell. "This is it. One of Ashley's friends has big bucks."

Deb stared at the home and gripped her pants in her fists. "I should have been to this house before now, met his parents. Why haven't I? She spent a lot of time here."

"She's in college," Gabe said. "She has her own life, despite her age. You didn't do anything wrong."

"She's sixteen," Deb said, looking over at him, her gaze haunted. "Sometimes it's hard to remember that."

"You know who they are, though. They're high school kids? You met them?"

She bit her lip, distracted, then nodded. He could tell she was beating herself up.

"They used to be classmates before Ashley's early graduation," she said.

"She went to school in Colorado Springs?" Gabe looked over in surprise.

"My father was stationed nearby. When he was reassigned overseas, I left the service to act as her guardian. Denver was the closest place that I found a job. She lived . . . lives . . ." Deb faltered. "She's at the dorm during school, and has to stay on campus Monday through Friday, so it worked out. Or I thought it did."

Gabe had to stop this spiral. "Well, we might as well head in. Milo and Otis—"

Deb's lips quirked at the corners. "Just Mylo, actually. *Milo and Otis* is a dog and cat movie. Knowing that information does not go with your tough-guy image, Montgomery."

"What can I say? I'm Luke's daughter's favorite uncle. I'll watch anything with Joy, if it makes her happy."

Despite his smile, Gabe studied her closely. She'd backed off thinking of the horrors that could be happening to Ashley. She might have to deal with any one of those. But not yet.

"You're a surprising man."

He gave her a quick wink. "Hey, don't let my he-man sex appeal fool you. I can play Barbies and tea party with the best of them."

Deb's smile made him feel warm inside. It softened her features. He wished he hadn't waited so long to let her know he cared.

To Gabe's surprise, she leaned over and kissed him on the

cheek, letting her lips linger for just a moment. "I know you meant to distract me," she said quietly. "Thank you."

She exited the vehicle and Gabe followed. Well, okay then. He could mix a little beta with his alpha personality, if it garnered this kind of reaction. Good to know.

He hit the SUV's automatic locks. "You talked to Mylo, right? He knows we're coming?"

"Justin was supposed to be here, too."

The tension in her voice rose again. Would Ashley's boyfriend show? That could be good or bad news if he did. But he figured Deb would take Ashley going on a joyride over the alternative any day.

With a quick, experienced eye, Gabe scanned the surroundings. His gaze paused on the roof. "The house has satellite. These kids are set."

"According to Ashley, all of them have impressive computer setups. That's part of what initially drew them together."

They strode up the front steps and knocked on the door.

A woman about ten years older than them opened it. She gave them the once-over. "I don't do surveys, I've already been saved, and if you're trying to sell anything, I do my buying on Amazon."

She started to shove the door closed.

Gabe stuck his foot into the crack. "We are here to see Mylo, ma'am. This is Deb Lansing, Ashley's sister."

She didn't skip a beat. "Tell me he didn't get her pregnant." At their startled looks, she sighed. "He has a major crush on her. All those boys do."

"Uh, no. Pregnancy is not the problem and Mylo is not in trouble. I'm sorry he didn't tell you we were coming. Is he home?"

"He's on the computer. Where else would he be? He lives on that damned thing."

The woman whirled around. "Mylo! Some people here to see you."

Footsteps pounded up the stairs. A tall, thin, sandy-haired kid, all elbows and knees, stopped in the doorway. "Oh. Oh, yeah. Mom, they're coming to talk to me about Ashley. Is it okay if they come in?"

His mother gave him a look. "This time, but I've told you a hundred times to check with me before you invite people over."

Mylo blushed. "I know. I just got caught up in the game and forgot."

She shook her head in dismay. "Well, don't do it again."

The kid shrugged. "Okay, but Britney's coming, too. Remember? She's got red hair. You've met her before."

The mother huffed. "Fine." She gestured to Gabe and Deb. "You two might as well come in."

"Thank you, ma'am," Gabe said, stepping over the threshold after Deb.

"Watch that ma'am crap," Mylo's mom snapped. "I'm not much older than you, kiddo."

"O-k-a-y," Gabe drawled. "Consider it retracted."

Mylo had already started down the stairs to the basement. Deb and Gabe quickly followed.

"Sorry about my mom. She's a little weird sometimes. You can't pick your parents."

An image flashed in Gabe's mind of his father hugging Whitney at the bus terminal and the edge resurfaced. *Amen, brother.* He turned to Mylo. "You're a teenager. It's your job to feel like that."

His gaze was focused on an eighty-inch television that took up almost an entire wall, but a moment later, the screen went red with giant letters that read *Game over.*

Mylo glared at the screen. "I wish the others would get here. I can't do this alone." He looked up at Deb. "Is Ashley over her big exam phase? We missed her this weekend."

Deb stepped forward. "No. She visited me last night, but she didn't make it back to the dorms. I've been trying to find her. I hoped you could help."

"She's, like, missing? For real?" Mylo asked. "No way. We can't get past Level 88 again without Ashley."

"Level 88?" Gabe asked.

Mylo looked at Gabe like he was stupid. "Level 88? On *Point of Entry*. Duh. That's the magic level half the country is trying to get to. Hardly anyone makes it that far. It's wicked complicated. You have to break into banks and people's private computers. I hear on the next version, they're adding foreign governments, spy stuff, terrorist camps. This voice comes on the computer or TV and gives you a timed problem."

"A voice comes on?" Deb asked.

"Yeah, like a big all-knowing avatar. It's pretty cool. I can't believe we did it."

Gabe picked up a remote from the coffee table, toying with it. "This voice gives you a test on Level 88, but you said you couldn't get past it again. When did you make that level?"

"Friday, maybe?" Mylo said. "Early in the evening. We'd been really close last weekend on Justin's machine, but we had to wait for Ashley to get out of school to finish up. We're only on Level 80 on my setup. Justin, the douche bag, was supposed to be here today and another friend, Britney, said she'd be here a half hour ago. She used to go to high school with us and play the game a lot, but she moved to Toledo. Two hours later there, and her folks have a strict game curfew. It's a pain. She's in town for this week with her folks. She hit Level 88 with her new group, too. She's almost as smart as Ashley."

"So, you reached this high level on Justin's machine. What about Ashley's? I heard you guys snuck into the computer lab. Did you do it there, too?"

Mylo shrugged. "We got caught by Ashley's advisor and a couple of guards so we used Ashley's machine in her room instead. Her computer was superfast and she was one level away. We made it. Hit a record score." Mylo grinned, almost preening with pride. "We got the free upgrade of levels and everything. Ashley rocks at coming up with the passwords to break into the systems. I don't know how we'll break into the congressman's computer on the next level without her. How cool is it that the game has its own set of dirty politicians?"

Gabe sat on one of the four leather gaming chairs against the wall. "Tell me about *Point of Entry*. You said there are other teams across the country trying to do the same thing. Is it highly competitive?"

"Oh, yeah," Mylo enthused. "When our team knocked the Destroyers off the top of the leaderboard, they were so pissed. Sent us a ton of messages threatening us . . . especially Ashley."

"You keep the messages?" Gabe asked.

"You think they could be for real?" Mylo's eye twitched.

"Just show them to me."

Mylo logged in to the system. He accessed the message area

and scrolled up. He scrolled down, then up again. He frowned. "They're gone. The team's gone."

"What about their scores?" Gabe asked.

He punched a few more buttons and the leaderboard came up.

"You're the Eradicators?" Gabe asked, studying the screen. Sure enough, they'd blown away the high score.

"Yeah. Justin came up with that one 'cause we were wiping everyone off the boards. The Destroyers' scores are gone, too. Like they never existed. Weird."

"You know any of the real names of the other team members?" Deb asked.

"Yeah. I e-mailed with one guy. He asked me who broke the level." Mylo grinned sheepishly. "I told him I was the muscle of the team. I do the shooting, but that we had the smartest girl in the country—probably in the world—on our team. He asked about the rest of us and I told him Justin is almost as good as Ashley."

Gabe's instincts went haywire. He didn't need his mom's Spidey sense to know things had just hit the fan. "When did you start e-mailing with this guy, Mylo?"

The teen faltered. "I don't know, a couple weeks ago, maybe?" He switched screens and quickly checked his e-mail. "There's nothing here, but I had at least a dozen e-mails from him. That's . . . kind of freaky."

"Did you delete their posts?" Deb asked.

Mylo lifted troubled eyes. "No. Someone wiped all the messages on my computer clean."

The SUV shuddered as if driving over a cattle guard, then slowed to a stop.

Ashley caught her breath. As stiff as she was, it was now or never.

The back doors flew open, and Niko yanked off the tarp. Ashley blinked at the harsh sunlight beating into the SUV, its intensity blinding her.

"Bring her to the main floor," a disembodied voice called out.

Niko ducked into the back of the vehicle and untied her from the hook in the floor. Ashley waited for the right moment and kicked out. She scooted from the Escalade and jumped to the ground. Her legs nearly collapsed beneath her, but despite that and her near blindness she prepared to run.

Several metallic clicks sounded and she stopped, whirling around to see a dozen men with automatic weapons facing her.

A tall, bald-headed man stood in the center. He smiled. "I hear you are an unusually feisty one. You'll soon learn better, or we'll beat the stupidity out of you. I am known as the Warden. That should give you an accurate idea of your future accommodations."

He turned and went up the stairs.

Desperately, Ashley looked around, panic making it difficult to breathe.

A huge warehouse loomed in front of her, but when she gazed at the surrounding area, she saw no other signs of civilization. They were in the desert, no discernable landmarks beyond a few low hills. It was cold here, but not as cold as Colorado, and the air was dry. New Mexico? Arizona? Somehow neither of those seemed right. They'd driven too long.

Niko pushed her forward. "Don't bother memorizing the landscape. No one gets away from here. Ever."

She balked at the stairs; she didn't want to go into that building. What if she never came out?

He grabbed her arm and dragged her up the stairs and through the door. Once inside, she hesitated again and he shoved her hard. Unbalanced, she fell to her knees.

"Ashley?" a male voice called out.

Justin? She couldn't believe it. She pushed to a standing position and stopped, shocked and elated, but even more scared now. Justin stood across the room in shackles, one eye blackened, his jeans torn.

"What happened?" she asked, terrified for them both. "How did they get you?"

"Silence. This isn't social hour. You're here to work." The Warden walked between them. "You and Justin were brought here because you have shown an aptitude for *Point of Entry*."

"You kidnapped us because of *Point of Entry*?" she said, bemused. "A video game? Are you nuts?"

Horrified, Justin shuffled forward, but not in time to stop the vicious backhander the man gave her.

"Never cross me again. You are a convenience, not a necessity. I can replace you in a heartbeat."

Ashley held her palm to her throbbing cheek, but she refused to cry.

"As I said, you are here because of the game," the Warden repeated. "You were playing very well. You achieved Level 88, but, according to the searches of your computer, you were becoming too curious, delving into areas best left alone. You and your boyfriend's little digital sojourn into the NSA's database has resulted in an additional firewall and other problems for us that we expect you to solve. You're here now, Miss Lansing, to work. If you're smart, you will become an asset to our team rather than a liability."

"No way in hell," Ashley spat back.

"Niko?" The man gestured toward Justin. "If you would . . ."

The blow came so fast and hard. Justin hit the floor without crying out.

"Justin!"

Someone held her back, while Justin's unconscious body was carted away.

The Warden smiled. "Remember this little lesson, my dear. Everyone is expendable and your actions don't affect you alone. I only keep the ones alive who are useful to me."

CHAPTER SIX

GABE OPENED THE DOOR FOR DEB. SHE CLIMBED INTO THE SUV as he shut it and stared back at the house. And at Mylo. The kid raised his hand, and Gabe waved back.

"We spooked him," Gabe said when he slid behind the steering wheel.

"And we're no closer to finding Ashley," Deb whispered. He could see her struggle to control the panic. No matter what her experience, the stress of the last few days had taken its toll. Lack of sleep, worry. She'd break soon.

"A game. How can Ashley's disappearance be connected to a video game? It doesn't make sense."

"We're going to find out." Gabe dialed his brother Luke. This case was getting uglier and more confusing by the minute. He needed someone who could follow trails down rabbit holes.

"Montgomery here."

"Hey, bro. Can you get away to my house, or could Deb Lansing and I come to yours?"

"The helicopter pilot? She's the reason Zach's watching the bar, right? I had to crack up at that, little brother. Movie star, big, bad, super spy, reduced to being a bartender."

"He owes me after almost getting me blown up," Gabe said. "Besides, he's retired now, the bum." He twisted in the seat and took Deb's hand. "Deb Lansing's sister is missing. I'm helping her out. We're in Colorado Springs doing some investigating, but we have a cell phone video I want you to see."

"God, I'm sorry. What about the cops?"

"It's . . . complicated," Gabe said, stroking Deb's palm, knowing nothing he could do would comfort her, not until they found Ashley. "I have another request. Could you research the game *Point of Entry*? I have a copy with me and I need to know how to play."

"Don't have to research P.O.E., Gabe. I have the game set up on my system. I'm pretty good at it. You might as well come here."

"Thanks."

Luke hesitated. "You have any leads?"

Gabe met Deb's eyes and recognized the despair on the fringes of hope. He couldn't make it worse. "We're making progress." *If you called getting more questions than answers progress.* "If you talk to Zach, tell him I may need his help for another day or two."

"From what I hear, Hawk's taking care of Sammy's pretty well. Both Zach and Jenna went over to help. I guess having the Dark Avenger as a bouncer is keeping your rowdier clientele in line."

Gabe laughed, despite his crushing concerns. "I didn't even think of that when I asked Zach to fill in for me today. I may have to hire him permanently. What's Jenna doing there?"

"Keeping the flood of new female customers away from her handsome ex-movie star husband and cooking in the back. She sends the kitchen guys out to bus tables and stuff whenever possible."

"The cooks didn't give her a hard time about it?"

"No sane man messes with a hormonal pregnant woman. Especially one that far along."

Gabe didn't speak for a moment. "Have Zach keep her in the kitchen as much as he can."

Luke laughed. "Sexist much? Want her barefoot, too, since Jenna's already pregnant and in the kitchen?"

"No, you jerk. I want her safe. It would be better if she wasn't even there. I keep having that itchy target feeling on my back. Not sure what's causing it, but I know better than to ignore the warning. Ask everyone in the family to be extra careful. Okay?"

The phone went quiet. "What aren't you telling me, Gabe?"

A lot. "We'll talk later."

"Count on it," Luke said tightly. "I'll have more than a few probing questions of my own."

Gabe ended the call.

"This entire situation is insane," Deb said, leaning her head back against the seat.

Gabe pulled her into his arms. To his surprise, she immediately melted against him as if she'd been waiting for his touch.

She looked up at him. "I am so scared, Gabe. Ashley has been gone too long."

"I'm here to help." He kissed her forehead, then her lips, gently, giving comfort the only way he knew how. He was worried for her sister, too. "We'll find Ashley," he said, then sent up a silent prayer that if they did, she'd still be alive.

A sudden pounding on Deb's window had Gabe reaching for his weapon. He pulled the Glock. Mylo saw the gun and fell backward. He hadn't even stopped to put on a jacket, despite the frigid temperatures.

Deb slid down her window. "What's wrong?"

"Britney's mom just called to ask her a question, but I said she hadn't made it here yet." Mylo's voice cracked. "Her mom said Britney left two hours ago and their hotel is only ten minutes away."

Two stressful hours later, cold bit into Gabe's face. He shoved his hands into his pockets at the entrance to Luke's ranch-style house. Deb stood beside him, her hood up, her cheeks red from the icy wind.

Immediately the door flew open. Gabe couldn't miss the worry on his brother's face. He glanced at Deb, then relaxed his expression. "Took you long enough. What did you do? Take a detour to China on your way here?"

"We had to stop at the Colorado Springs Police Department again. There's another girl missing. I wanted to reinforce the unlikely coincidence of three teenagers disappearing from the same town in a matter of days."

Luke frowned, holding the door open for them to enter. "How long has she been gone?"

"At least four hours," Deb said, her voice cracking with emotion. "Justin disappeared Saturday. Ashley on Sunday. Now, Britney on Monday. Even the police have to act on this now. I wish they'd call in the FBI."

Luke closed the door behind them. "My wife and daughter will be home soon, so why don't we go into the den. We can view the video clip in private."

Gabe shrugged out of his coat, then helped Deb out of hers. They followed Luke into a wood-paneled room with a computer system and gaming equipment. Once everyone was inside, he shut and locked the door.

Gabe studied the impressive system. It wasn't as elaborate as Mylo's, but his brother was obviously no slouch at gaming, either. "Is this computer used for any of your newspaper work or investigations?"

"No, that's in my office. I try to keep the murder and mayhem files there, away from Joy's curious little eyes. As it is, I have to lock up any games not rated E for Everyone. She saw a few of the covers of M games I left out and was not happy she couldn't play them. She's all too eager to move past Hello Kitty and onto the big-kid games."

"That girl is four going on fourteen."

"Tell me about it. Have a seat."

Gabe dropped onto the brown leather couch across from the screen, pulling Deb down beside him. Luke arched his brow, but didn't say a word. He picked up a remote.

"Video first or the game?"

Gabe slipped his hand into Deb's. "How familiar are you with *Point of Entry*? You know about Level 88?"

"Who doesn't?"

Gabe and Deb exchanged a look.

Luke sighed. "Except you two. Level 88 is the Holy Grail in each version of P.O.E. I haven't made it past Level 60 yet, but then I do have a life and a family who wants to interact with me once in a while. When your wife is a sniper, it's a good idea not to piss her off."

"Better you than me," Gabe said. "Jazz can be damned scary when she's in a mood." He cleared his throat and pulled out his cell. "Let's look at the video first. The kids wanted to document reaching Level 88. Mylo sent it to my phone. It may be hard to see on the small screen, though."

"If you forward it to me, I can put it on the big screen."

Gabe looked at the phone for a minute and grimaced. He and technology didn't always get along. "I'm afraid I'll blow it away if I try it, and I want to show it to Neil, too."

"If you want, I can transfer it. I'm a tech guru, remember?"

Gabe found the video file, then handed his phone to Luke. "The one marked 'twelfth attempt.' It's dated Friday."

A minute later, the electronic magic was done.

"So what are we watching?" he asked, settling in next to Gabe.

"A mystery." Gabe flicked his phone to vibrate and shoved it back into the pocket of his jacket. He didn't want to be interrupted during the video. He had to stay focused.

"Sounds compelling. What do you mean by that?"

"Things happen in this video that I can't explain. The three kids in it are a team. They're about to hit Level 88 of *Point of Entry*. As soon as they do, it gets weird."

"Okay, let's do it." Luke hit a remote and the lights went off and the screen flickered to life.

Deb tensed and Gabe slid his arm around her. He knew how hard it was to see her sister on-screen and not know her fate. Deb clutched his other hand, her fingers tight on his. She'd been incredibly strong through all this. She'd fit in well with the other women in this family.

The idea shocked him, but not as much as it might have a few days ago. Still, it was a jump from being attracted to someone, dreaming of a few long, sweaty nights, to thinking of her as a prospective Montgomery woman. But he'd seen her face trouble with strength, her willingness to fight for her sister—just as he would for his brothers—without hesitation, without fail. She could very well be the first woman he'd wanted who really fit.

Luke turned to them. "If you think I should know something, jump in. I'll stop the video."

The clip started.

A pretty blonde sat next to a dark-haired boy on the couch, and their intimate smiles let everyone know the two teenagers were crushing on each other.

"Hold it," Deb interjected. "I guess I should give you some background. That's my sister, Ashley, and her boyfriend, Justin. They met in high school, when she and my dad first moved to Colorado. After she left for the Academy, Justin and two others formed a P.O.E. team. It wasn't long before he invited her to join them."

Luke frowned. "Why her?"

"She's a prodigy with computers and encryption," Gabe said. "She and Justin did the NSA hack job."

Luke's jaw dropped.

"Anyway," Deb added quickly, "Britney, the other girl who's now missing, had been the third member on Justin's P.O.E. team, but she'd moved away last spring. Ashley was thrilled to fill the opening. Soon, she was playing the game with them every weekend."

After Deb identified Mylo as the other frozen image in the background, Luke started the video again.

An expensive new gaming system held court front and center on the mahogany coffee table in the living room. Mylo handed out sodas and bags of popcorn, then flopped down into a gaming chair. Justin tugged open the bag and passed it over to Ashley. She grabbed a handful, then he dumped the entire contents into the bowl next to the four controllers.

"This is the coolest game ever," he said, grinning at her. "I can't believe you've picked it up so fast. You've got our levels going up faster than they were before. Being on Level 87 is awesome. It would have taken longer without you."

Ashley flushed and reached for a controller.

Mylo chugged back half his soda and grabbed a fist of popcorn. "Yeah, Blondie, you're not bad for a brainiac."

Justin scowled at him. "Back off, Romeo."

"I'm not hitting on her. Jeez," Mylo groused, turning to Ashley. "Seriously, it's a damn good thing you are a genius. Justin's smart, but these levels are getting too hard. Banks, spies, breaking codes and that kind of crap. Personally, I like the action-adventure stuff at the beginning of the game better. Guns, robots, and aliens are cool. These last ten levels have been frustrating."

"That's because Ashley is only here on weekends. She's the one that catches the weird numerical patterns and stuff. And she coded that killer password application," Justin said, pressing the power button and inserting the *Point of Entry* disk. After everything loaded, all extraneous talk stopped.

The three players concentrated on the game, following the clues, shooting the bad guys, and breaking through the various obstacles. Then they hit the safe. They tried several different password ideas, all without success.

Mylo threw down his controller. "I hate this. We're never going to break the last clue. A twelve-letter account code? Plus a three-digit number? No way. Give me the guns and ammo back." He fell back into his seat. "There better be something great behind that damn door."

"Would you shut up?" Justin growled, as the sequence he'd keyed in was rejected. "We can't concentrate with all your complaining."

Ashley suddenly shifted forward, studying the screen, her face alight. "Oh my God, I think I've got it. Justin, I think you were only off by one number. May I?" she asked, nodding at the screen. He handed her the remote and she entered the new sequence.

Nothing happened.

"Okay, that number blew it up, too. What a pain in the—" Mylo's voice trailed off as the large television screen showcasing the computer game went black.

"Did we do it?" Ashley asked.

Suddenly, a spinning sound echoed through all the speakers in the room. The noise seemed to explode around them.

"Congratulations, Eradicators!" a mechanized voice shouted. "You have reached Level 88 of *Point of Entry*. Please enter your individual e-mail addresses and contact information so you can receive your reward for attaining *Point of Entry*'s Secret Challenge. The world awaits your brilliance."

A cursor blinked on the screen.

"This is wicked!" Mylo wielded his remote in the air like a sword. "How do they do that? Talk through the TV and all the speakers like that. You didn't even have the surround sound on. He's like a MechWarrior, he's really in the room with us." Mylo keyed in his e-mail, then tossed the remote to Justin.

They each entered their e-mail addresses.

Luke paused the video. "Very easy to track them now. And people enter e-mail addresses on websites and games all the time, so they aren't suspicious." He pressed Play.

"Congratulations, Eradicators." The tone seemed a bit harsher than before. "You must take the oath. Swear to each other that whatever you do, whatever you see, from this level on, will never be revealed to anyone else. Swear it! The fate of the world depends on you."

Justin groaned and settled on one end of the couch, sidling up next to Ashley. "Okay, we are officially part of the geek patrol. I wonder if we get badges and have to do secret handshakes."

Ashley laughed and he leaned over to kiss her.

"Hey, quit fooling around, you two, and pay attention," Mylo insisted. "I heard we get upgrades and other cool stuff after hitting this level."

Ashley just sat there when he turned to her expectantly. "Oh my God, you're kidding. Right? We're swearing allegiance to a TV set? It's not like they can hear us."

Justin shrugged. "Well, um, it's part of the game."

"Oh, jeez. You guys really are geeks." Ashley shook her head, then finally raised her hand. "All right," she said with a sigh. "I swear."

Immediately the screen lit with a familiar icon indicating a new level.

"Okay, it's like the game heard us. That's too Big Brother for me," Ashley said with a slight shiver.

"For your first task, you will be asked to identify an access code with four related sets of numbers. They can only be retrieved by finding a way into your nemesis's secret database. He has stolen a substantial treasure and hidden it in his vault. The code numbers for entry are in the following sequence: first, there are twelve digits, then three digits, and finally five digits."

Mylo groaned. "Here we go again. More numbers crap. This will take weeks."

The mechanized voice continued, "As always, you will be given hints and prompts along the way, but you will have only thirty minutes to unlock the vault door and attain your prize. If you fail, the bonus round will lock you out of Level 88 for an extended period of time. If you succeed, however, more complex and exciting challenges await you."

"Man. We only have one chance?" Mylo protested. "That sucks."

"Everyone still in?" Justin asked.

At their nods, he took control of the computer again. The machine chimed, but the sound was nearly drowned out by the addictive music from the game's new level.

"If you are ready, enter the first four digits of pi to start the game."

Justin took up his control. "Am I crazy thinking that he didn't interrupt us when we were talking? Like he knew to wait."

Mylo whacked Justin on the head. "You are so paranoid. Maybe they're just timed blank sections. Or it's some weird new gaming technology. His voice sounds pretty robotic and there are tons of advances in that field," Mylo said. "Lighten up."

The television blinked an eerie green glow in the darkened room, showing Ashley's troubled face. "It is a little strange."

"Oh for God's sake," Justin said. "I'm sorry I brought it up. We only have a half hour. Let's just play."

Ashley grinned. "You're right. Besides, there aren't many games that actually require math and brains. I don't want to get locked out of the most challenging thing I've come across yet."

She gathered her calculator and other materials around her. "Let's do this!"

Everyone was on an adrenaline rush, but Ashley seemed euphoric. "This is so cool. Math, coding, encryption. All my favorite things."

"How come I'm not on the list?" Justin asked.

"I'm talking technological things, sweetie. Not people."

Mylo groaned. "Give me some guys with guns this time. Those I can handle."

Justin turned up the volume and looked over at Ashley. "Ready to play?

"Let's go, Eradicators." Ashley patted the controller and gave him a quick grin. "Concentrate hard. We're breaking into the nemesis's bank this time. I can't wait."

Luke's wall screen went black. The video clip was over.

Deb, Gabe, and Luke just sat there, staring at the blank expanse.

Finally, Gabe turned to Luke. "This was taken last Friday night. They hit Level 88 at Ashley's dorm, too. Justin disappeared the next day. Ashley, the following night. What do you think it all means?"

"Damned if I know, little brother, but we'll find out."

Cayman Islands—Tuesday Morning

Outside, the humidity hit ninety percent, the temperature nearing ninety-five, but that wasn't what made the account manager sweat. This couldn't be happening. He had to meet his client soon and the drinks he had last night must still be screwing up his head.

The bank was more crowded than usual due to the Monday holiday yesterday. Phones rang and conversations went on around him, but the manager's entire attention remained on the computer screen in front of him.

He must have keyed the numbers in wrong.

Throat tight, he pushed forward in his chair and carefully retyped the twelve-digit account number and the nine-digit code, made up of a zero, a three-digit bank code, and a five-digit branch/transit code.

Finally he reached the last digit. Hands sweating, he typed the number seven, sent up a small Hail Mary, and hit "Enter."

The screen went dark, flashed white, then black again. The account balance flashed on the screen, the white numbers showing him the same impossible figure.

His hand trembled. Panicked, he closed his eyes, then opened them again, and blinked twice.

"It can't be right." He reentered the numbers a third time, but nothing changed.

Oh, dear God in heaven. His chest ached, and he couldn't stop his panting breaths. He clutched the desk, fighting the urge to run.

"It's gotta be a glitch. It has to be." He paused and stared from the computer to the phone, and back at the monitor. Desperation choked off his breath. The moment he dialed the computer group, everyone would know.

His boss definitely wouldn't overlook this screwup.

The phone rang and he jumped. Quaking, he picked up the receiver. "Sir?"

"Well, what the hell is taking so long? Our client is waiting." The president of the bank's voice boomed through the receiver.

He swallowed, and his boss had to have heard the gulp. "Um. We might have a problem, sir. I'm missing one hundred twenty-five million US dollars."

The guards led Ashley to a new part of the complex down a long hallway. Huge mechanical doors slid open. She braced, ready to run, but a forklift deposited a large box, then a guard keyed in a code on the entry pad and the garagelike door slid closed, blocking out the sun.

"Wait here," Niko said. He walked down and met the guard several feet away. Too near to try to bolt, but too far to overhear their conversation.

She looked around quickly, trying to memorize the area for a possible future escape. She could break keypad entries. She hadn't noticed a palm print reader or anything more complex.

A boy was mopping the floor and sidled closer, but he didn't raise his head or pause in his task. "Don't bother," he said, his voice barely audible. "You won't find a way out. If there was one where they couldn't trace us, I'd be gone already."

"Have you been here long?"

He grimaced. "Do I look like I've been soaking up the rays lately?" His face was vanilla pale, his sandy hair shaved close to his head.

"Sorry," said Ashley. "I just got here."

"I know. Everyone's talking about it. How mad you made the Warden. Listen to me. Do what they tell you. Don't fight them. Don't question *anything*," he whispered as he passed by closer with the mop. "Anyone who causes trouble . . ."

A door creaked open and the kid stiffened.

"What?" Ashley insisted. "What happens?"

"They either tag you with a microchip or you disappear," he whispered and shuffled down the hall, adding, "I'm on my last warning."

Only then did Ashley see the shackles around his ankles.

CHAPTER SEVEN

DEB CLUTCHED THE ARMRESTS OF GABE'S SUV. THE VEHICLE slid through a street lined with snowdrifts toward her apartment building. The place couldn't have looked more unwelcoming. It wasn't a home, and her sister wouldn't be there. Might never . . .

No, Deb couldn't think that way. She had to focus on the leads. Ashley was a fighter. She was smart. She'd stay alive no matter what the situation.

She couldn't get over Ashley's expression while she played that game. Her sister had looked so happy, so excited, so alive. About the game, and about Justin.

A whole side of Ashley she hadn't recognized.

And that was all on her.

Ashley had everything to live for. Deb had to find her.

She sent a sidelong glance at Gabe as he pulled into a parking place. She didn't know what she would have done without him. She could maneuver a chopper with finesse—it followed her every movement—but she was out of her element now. She'd needed Gabe. More than he knew.

Gabe shoved the gear into "Park." "Neil will be able to justify Ashley's investigation to the brass with Britney's disappearance and the video connection. Let's get Ashley's things," Gabe said. "Maybe there's something in her stuff that will help since we know more of what we're looking for."

"I hope so. I've been through everything once, but maybe fresh eyes . . ."

Her voice trailed off as she stepped out of Gabe's SUV. A few minutes later, they reached her third-floor walk-up apartment.

Gabe was limping slightly by the time they reached the top. "You must have a blast hauling in groceries from the car," he said, a bit of strain in his voice.

Deb bit her lip and took in the tightness around his mouth. "Oh God, I'm sorry, Gabe. I forgot about your leg when I asked you to come up. I picked this place because, with my job, there's not much chance to exercise. My legs need to be strong to handle the helicopter and lifting gurneys and wounded people. That kind of thing."

Gabe's expression tightened, and she cursed under her breath.

How stupid could she be? He used to do that kind of thing all the time as a cop. She'd just reminded him that his leg was no longer strong enough for him to remain in SWAT.

Way to make the guy feel good, Deb. She sucked at this. She wanted to say something to him, like how much she appreciated him, how much she couldn't have survived the last days without him. Instead, she just unlocked the door. "Come on in. It's not much, but it's home. For now."

"You need to change your lock. Anyone with a credit card could break in."

Gabe followed her inside and she glanced around the sparse one-bedroom efficiency through his eyes. "The burglars would be disappointed. I don't spend a lot of time here, and it shows. Ashley didn't . . . doesn't . . . visit me that often anymore, since she had . . . has no car . . ." Deb's voice faltered. "I usually go to Colorado Springs to see her."

Deb wrapped her arms around her waist. Yeah, the place looked like hell. Empty shelves. Her gear stacked in a corner. The lumpy couch and the red torture chair were accompanied by cloth-covered packing boxes used as end tables and a coffee table. She hadn't put any personal touches in the apartment at all, except for one wall full of photos.

Gabe immediately walked over to the pictures. He studied one of a younger Ashley, complete with a silly beach hat and a sunburn on her nose. She sported a goofy face for the camera. "She's a really pretty girl."

Slowly Deb joined him, her heart aching as she took in the memories. "Ashley was so happy that day." Emotions choked off the words in Deb's throat. She put a hand to her mouth to stop the sob. "Oh God, Gabe, Ashley has to be okay."

Gabe gently pulled Deb back against his body, folding his arms around her. For a moment she sagged against him, then she turned in his arms, her fists gripping his shirt. "I can't . . . I need . . ." Her control was so close to shattering.

She stiffened. "Please. I need a minute."

He kissed her temple, then turned his attention to a photo of three men standing in military uniform, one a two-star general. Deb struggled to regain her composure. She didn't know how long it took, but finally she felt like she could speak without crying or screaming in frustration. She followed Gabe's focus and cleared her throat. "My father. He was at the Pentagon, then near Colorado Springs for two years. They sent him to Kandahar about six months ago. My other brothers are in the Middle East, too. None of them can really keep in touch very much. E-mail and social media sites help when they can get access to the Internet."

Gabe nodded. "My brother Seth is in the same business. Luke was in Afghanistan for a while, too. We almost lost him in an ambush. He was the only survivor and it still haunts him." Gabe glanced at her. "Not that he says anything."

"They can't. When I was over there, at least I had a bit more information on where they were. Now, being a civilian, I get nothing. I just have to believe they'll be okay."

She studied an older picture, one of a dignified soldier, a smiling woman, and four small children.

"That's your mom?"

Deb nodded, a wistful smile tugging at her lips. "She died of cancer when we were kids. A rare brain tumor. One minute she was there, the next she was just gone."

Gabe placed his hand on her shoulder and squeezed. "I'm sorry."

"Thanks. I guess we've both lost parents we loved."

She glanced at him over her shoulder, but a strange look crossed Gabe's face.

"You're right. It's hard to lose someone you love. No matter how it happens."

Odd choice of words, but Gabe didn't give her time to ask. "We should probably head out."

She nodded and walked over to the makeshift laundry basket Ashley used for storage. Deb's eyes burned. She touched one of the journals and flipped through it. Not like any other girl, her sister's books were filled with equations and numbers, not hopes and dreams and boys. God, this couldn't be all she had left of her sister. The protective wall enclosing her fears broke open wide and her heart shattered.

"How could I have let this happen to Ashley?" Deb tried blinking back the tears in her eyes, but they slid down her cheeks. "I knew something was wrong that night, and I didn't act on it. I failed her."

Without hesitation, Gabe strode over to her. "Don't push me away again, Deb," he said. "Let me be here for you." With that he wrapped her trembling body into his. He held her close, stroking her hair.

She shook her head against his shoulder. "This is stupid. I don't cry. I never cry."

He didn't say a word, just quietly held her, sturdy, secure, solid. Finally, Deb couldn't fight the battle to stay strong any longer. She collapsed against him, needing his comfort, accepting her vulnerability for one of the first times in her life. Somehow, despite all the horrible things happening around her, he made her feel safe.

With her head against his chest, she felt his heartbeat, its steady rhythm so calming to her battered psyche. His protectiveness soothed her spirit, made her feel less alone.

She loved that he towered over her. At five-nine, she'd been as tall as most of her colleagues in her unit, but Gabe was much taller than her. At least six-three.

She sighed, absently running her hand across his strong chest. His breath caught, his arms tensing around her. She stilled, a deep awareness rising within.

Was she wrong to want comfort? To escape, for a moment, from the grief that had been with her constantly since that phone call?

Being vulnerable scared her so. But right now, she needed whatever he could give her.

She needed his kiss and his touch.

She lifted her chin. He stared into her eyes, his own turning dark with passionate recognition. His fingertips drifted over her hair and he wiped away a tear from her cheek, his touch oh so gentle, as if afraid she'd pull away.

She couldn't move, couldn't breathe. His gaze held her prisoner. The world around her seemed to blur, as if the moment included only her standing in his arms.

Slowly, tenderly, Gabe lowered his mouth to hers. She closed her eyes. How long had it been since someone had touched her the way Gabe did?

She couldn't even remember.

Deb had kept herself apart from the men in her company. Fraternization only caused strife. She had to be one of the guys over there.

How long since she'd felt like this?

Or yearned for a sensitive caress, not hard and fast, but slow and . . . heartfelt?

With a sigh, she leaned in closer, her tongue edging out to taste him. A slight tang of coffee and something wonderfully male. A rumble started low in his chest and he deepened the kiss, exploring her mouth.

When he lifted his head, his hooded gaze met hers.

Dazed by the emotions rising within her, she simply stared at him.

"Wow," she said softly.

"Yeah," Gabe whispered. "I won't tell you how many nights I dreamed of what you would taste like. Better than I imagined."

Heat rose into her face and she bit her lip. She wasn't anything special. He didn't know it yet, but she'd made a lot of mistakes. She'd disappointed a lot of people. She hoped Gabe would never know.

She took a step back and cleared her throat. "Um, I'm not sure this was a good idea."

"Why? It felt like a really great one to me, and you weren't backing away." Gabe frowned and stroked her cheek. "It's not wrong to need someone."

She leaned into his touch. He made her feel too much—from the inside out. "It could complicate things. I need to stay focused on finding Ashley, no distractions."

He dragged a fingertip down her arm and the hairs on her skin stood on end. A shudder ran through her—the good kind.

"I know you're right," Gabe said, his brown eyes flashing, heated with unfulfilled passion. "This isn't the best time for either of us."

Reluctantly, he stepped back. "But I also know this, Deborah Lansing. If it weren't for your sister's disappearance and a few compelling commitments on my part, I'd be backing you into your bedroom and we wouldn't come out for a week."

She swallowed, wishing life could be so different.

"Can I take a rain check on that week?" she asked.

Gabe gave her a devilish grin and kissed her again. "You got it."

The tall expanse of the Jefferson County Sheriff's Office building loomed high near the foothills. Gabe hadn't entered Jeffco during business hours in months. Not since his very public exit because of his injury.

He let his limp grow more pronounced. Deb met his gaze and he recognized the comprehension in her eyes.

"You play the role well," she whispered. "I assume this is part of your . . . *compelling commitment*? I'll go along."

Damn. She knew exactly what he was doing. Part of him was furious at giving the truth away, the other part was glad. It lightened his heart to have one person besides John Garrison who knew.

He couldn't respond, though. Not here. He led her through the bullpen among curious stares. A couple of the musketeers were at their desks, and the heat of their glares followed Gabe the whole way. Crap. He should have done this over the phone.

Neil Wexler looked up from his desk, his eyes revealing his exhaustion.

"You look like hell, Detective," Gabe said. "Working round the clock now, buddy? That's dedication."

Neil stood slowly and nodded. "It's something, anyway."

Gabe started at the fleeting sadness he saw in his friend's eyes before Neil masked it. He hoped nothing was wrong on the home front. He and his wife should still be in honeymoon bliss.

"Have you heard something?" Gabe asked.

"About Ashley? No." Neil shook both their hands and he sank with a weary sigh into his chair. "But I understand you've been busy in Colorado Springs making new friends."

Deb winced, and Gabe shut the door without being asked. Neil was acting strange and, with the musketeers around, Gabe wasn't about to talk about anything like the video.

He held out a chair for Deb. "I let my temper get the best of me," she admitted, taking a seat.

Neil rubbed the bridge of his nose. "I understand, but you didn't help things. And I don't have any more information if that's why you're here. I did sign out the Shannon Devlin cold case file. I also talked with the police in Taos. Definite connection. They identified the car, but they're waiting on Forensics to identify the bodies. No one has any doubt, though."

Gabe leaned forward. "Something's here, Neil." He laid out the evidence. The video, the missing kids. P.O.E.

Neil's entire demeanor changed. He sat up straight. "Three kids in three days?" He grabbed a pen, snapped out questions, and started taking notes.

Gabe could feel some of the tension drain out of Deb at Neil's reaction. He had to admit to his own sense of relief. At least *someone* didn't think they'd taken a sanity detour.

When they were finished, Neil walked them to the door and opened it. "Keep in touch. I'll let you know if anything important comes up."

Deb hovered, and Gabe knew she wanted something more. Neil patted her arm. "I promise I won't ignore Ashley."

They nearly bumped into Sheriff Tower on the way out. He stood in the hall, staring at them, undisguised irritation on his face.

"Missing your old stomping grounds, Montgomery? I can't imagine what would bring you in here?" The underlying menace in the sheriff's voice couldn't be missed. "Anything I should know?"

Gabe's hand pressed into Deb's back, hoping to calm the frustration pulsing from both of them—her because Neil hadn't shown the urgency she'd hoped; him because Tower deserved a takedown. Smart and cool—that's what the situation called for.

At least for now.

"Not a thing," he said. "Checking in with an old colleague."

Tower frowned. "Detective Wexler is a very busy man. If you want to fraternize with him, do it when he's off duty. You are no longer one of my deputies. Remember that."

I won't be once you're in prison. Gabe didn't say the words aloud, but boy, he wished he could. This man had his hands dirty. Gabe couldn't wait to nail Tower. After he and Deb found Ashley.

So he simply gave the sheriff a terse nod and motioned to his leg. "It's kinda hard to forget."

Tower stepped closer, straightening to his full height, meeting Gabe's gaze eye to eye. "See that you don't, Montgomery. Your investigating days are over." The sheriff's attention snapped to Neil. "Detective, I think we should have a talk about your priorities. Now."

After Gabe climbed behind the wheel of his SUV, he sent Wexler a quick text. *Watch your back.*

A short while later came the response, *Watch yours, too.*

Followed up by a second one. *Seriously.*

"I expect good behavior," the Warden commented. He marched with two guards to the end of the hall. The line of teens stood silent in the white, spotless hallway. Every single one had a terrified expression on their face.

Ashley knew exactly how they felt.

She looked over at Justin and reached out a hand.

The sandy-haired-mop kid shook his head, giving her another warning, and glanced down at his shackles.

She withdrew her hand, but this was the first time she'd been near Justin. The Warden disappeared around the corner. Ashley peered up and down the hall carefully, then whispered to Justin. "They took us because of the NSA. They must want us to do it again."

"I know," he said, his voice low. "That's not all, though. You're not going to believe what I found out while I've been in here. Level 88 is real, Ashley. Everything we did in the game happened in real life. We broke into computers; we stole money; we stole user names and passwords. We did it all. And, once we downloaded the upgrade, they gained access to our computers."

Ashley's entire body went cold. "We hit Level 88 on my Air Force Academy computer. It's networked. Justin, they teach military strategies on that system," she hissed. "What have we done?"

"I don't know, but I don't intend to stay here," he said softly. "We have to find a way out."

"Damn it, shut up, you two," the mop boy snapped. "Don't you get it? Everything you do and say is monitored. This hallway has electronic surveillance. It's not a stretch that they have someone who can read lips watching your interaction."

The Warden and two guards finished their conversation and herded everyone toward a new corridor. A large letter *B* topped the doorway. Justin and Ashley exchanged glances. Time to take note of their surroundings and figure out an escape plan.

Ashley covered her mouth with her hand, pretending to cough. "How can we escape? Do you know anything?"

Justin ducked his head. "No, but a guy named Dave might," he whispered, his voice barely audible. "Just pay attention to the layout."

Ashley memorized their route as they trailed the Warden and guards down a few more lettered corridors. Each room they passed had a designation of either its purpose or a generic letter and number combination. She figured they had to be in the center of the warehouse by now. Room numbers were hitting the double digits. There were a lot more security cameras here as well.

Finally, at L8 they passed into a huge air-conditioned computer lab. Rows of mini cubicles with monitors and related paraphernalia took up a majority of the space. Most of the kids in the group headed to what must be their assigned stations, including Justin.

Ashley stood uncertainly near the Warden and one of the guards. The other had moved to the farthest part of the room and taken up a position there.

The steel door locked behind them, and Ashley jumped. "What the—"

She frowned as she recognized Niko holding the key. "Oh, it's you."

"Silence." The Warden turned around quickly. "I have not given you permission to speak. You are here to work. You are not to communicate with anyone except designated personnel—and, always, they are to address you first. If you have any questions, you will signal one of the attendants. You may receive answers only from them. Failure to comply carries dire consequences."

Ashley stood nervously. She'd never been good at following rules and keeping quiet. The Academy had helped with that, but this psychopath seemed to be taking control to a whole new level.

The Warden clasped his hands behind him. "Before you are assigned a workstation, understand this. You will have access to a computer system, but every keystroke will be monitored. The attendants will be walking around, watching you. In addition, surveillance videos are reviewed each night to ensure that no one is attempting anything devious."

Ashley nodded her head in compliance. Somehow she'd figure out a way around his system.

"Remember, Miss Lansing, your first job is to play the latest version of *Point of Entry* and win. Beat it, and you will be rewarded with more important work. Lose the game, however, and we will have no need of you."

"Speaking of which . . ." The Warden turned to Niko. "Who is the least successful gamer in the room?"

Everyone gasped.

"Or . . . who has broken one of my rules lately? We need a station."

Niko didn't flinch, but Ashley noted a slight tightening of his mouth. "Floyd has been seen talking to Miss Lansing on two occasions, though he is aware that he is on his last warning. In addition, his brother, Fletcher, did not achieve Level 88 after two weeks of trying. He failed again this morning."

Ashley's gaze flew to the mop boy. Floyd. The resignation and fear in his eyes nearly crippled her. Oh God. He'd warned her. Twice. She hadn't taken him seriously. What would they do?

"Ah, an interesting choice. Which brother?" the Warden purred. "Floyd or Fletcher."

The guards dragged them both forward.

"How sad for you both. Rebellion must run in the family. Floyd, we may have to check over all your surveillance video to determine what you've been up to. For now, I will keep you alive. Fletcher, it seems you have volunteered to free up your computer station." The Warden smiled. "Take him to the corner."

The room went deadly silent.

Floyd started to run after his brother, but Niko and another guard held the teen back.

"Don't hurt him! Take me instead." Tears ran down Floyd's face as Fletcher was walked to a padded corner with thick black walls and a grated floor. The corner contrasted starkly with the white walls and tile of the rest of the room.

The dark-haired guard left Fletcher there, walked a few feet, then turned and shot him through the heart.

No one said a word. A few choked sobs sounded as the boy slid lifelessly to the floor.

"Niko," said the Warden calmly. "Please show Miss Lansing to her new station and identify her duties. Someone escort Floyd to lockdown. I will deal with him later."

Niko came over and grabbed Ashley's arm. She stood there in shock, unable to move, unable to process what she'd just seen. Fletcher's death had been partly her fault. "Oh my God," she whispered. "How could he do that?

Niko shook her. "Shut the hell up, you idiot. His bloodlust may not be sated yet. Everyone's still at risk."

Tears filled her eyes and she staggered behind him, with a last, horrified look at Justin.

Niko thrust her down on the chair, the seat still warm from

Fletcher's body heat. Ashley couldn't stop her body from shaking. This couldn't be real.

"Don't do a thing," Niko hissed. "You're being watched."

"Niko," the Warden called again. "When you're finished, have someone wash down the walls and remove the body. It's proving distracting to some of our guests. I wouldn't want anyone else to fall behind."

CHAPTER EIGHT

GABE'S HANDS GRIPPED THE STEERING WHEEL, HIS KNUCKLES white with unchecked irritation. Tower was a piece of work.

His SUV sped through Denver, but the hair on Gabe's neck stood. He could feel Deb's focus on him.

"The sheriff doesn't know you're undercover, does he?" she asked.

What was he supposed to say? He couldn't reveal the details of his investigation.

"You might as well admit it, because the only other explanation of what I overheard behind the bar is that you've gone bad, and I don't believe that, Gabe. You're all hero."

The car pulled up to Luke's house and Gabe turned to her. "I can't talk about it. My operation has nothing to do with our investigation. And my family . . . well, I'm trying to protect them. Please, just leave it alone."

Deb touched his cheek. "I understand loving your family and wanting to protect them. They won't hear what you're doing from me."

He kissed her softly. "Thank you."

Gabe pulled his father's files from the backseat and together they walked up the pathway.

Jazz, his sister-in-law, answered their knock. "Gabe!" Her long, blonde braid swung at her hips.

She studied each step he took. She took his injury personally, since she'd been covering him when the gangbanger had knifed him. Gabe understood that, but someone else's sabotage wasn't her fault. Nor was the fact he'd lost his place on the SWAT team.

She still hadn't forgiven herself, though.

He kissed her cheek. "I hope you're keeping my brother in line."

A little blonde dynamo with crazy bouncing curls erupted from the house and grabbed him around the legs. "Uncle Gabe! I missed you last night."

"Missed you, too, short stuff." He passed the box to Jazz, then swung his niece into his arms. "How are you doing?"

"We went to the planet . . . the plant aquarium this morning." She scrunched up her face and sighed. "We saw a bunch of stars on the ceiling."

He laughed. "You mean the planetarium?"

Her face brightened. "Yeah. The planetquarium. It was so fun." She kissed his cheek with a loud, wet smack. "Did you come to play with me today?"

He kissed her back. Twice. "Sorry, kid. I have to talk to your daddy."

"Daddy? Why?" Joy stuck out her lower lip. "He doesn't play good as me. You're a doodoo head, Uncle Gabe."

"Joy! That's not nice," Jazz said, merriment dancing in her eyes.

Who couldn't just love Joy?

"A doodoo head!" Gabe gasped dramatically. "I thought I was your favorite uncle?"

Joy looked at him seriously. "Nope. Uncle Zach is now. He got me a cousin to play with who is just a little bigger than me. You haven't even bringed me babies. Aunt Jenna's got one in her tummy for me to play with soon."

Luke joined his wife at the door. "I guess she told you, little brother."

Gabe smiled. "She sounds eerily like Mom when she says stuff like that."

Deb shifted slightly, drawing Gabe's attention. "Oh, Deb. I'm sorry. I forgot to make introductions." Gabe hitched Joy onto one hip and drew Deb in closer. "Jazz, Joy. This is Deb Lansing."

Jazz's welcoming smile froze in shock. "Deb Lansing? Oh my God. You're the helicopter pilot who flew Gabe . . ."

Luke pulled Jazz toward him, his entire stance comforting and protective. She looked over at Deb and smiled. "You saved Gabe's life. Thank you."

Deb reddened. "I just flew the chopper. Your husband, Gabe, and the man upstairs did all the heavy lifting that night."

Gabe placed his hand on Deb's back. She glanced up at him, but he just gave her a wink and they followed Luke and Jazz inside.

His brother took the box from Jazz and peeked inside. "What's going on, Gabe? Is this more evidence? I haven't had much time to look into what we discussed last night."

"There have been a few new developments. Can we talk in your office?" Gabe said, giving Joy a meaningful look.

"Grown-up talk." Joy sighed. "I don't want to play in my room."

Jazz lifted the little girl in her arms and nuzzled Joy's neck till she squealed. "You lead such a rough life, kiddo. Your room looks like a toy store exploded in there. Whatever shall we find to do?"

"No, please." Joy pouted, her words turning into a sudden wail. "I don't want to go to my room! I want Uncle Gabe. It's not fair."

Jazz held tight onto the squirming little girl. "With that ungodly howl, the Prisoner of Zenda and I are off for a desperately needed nap." They disappeared down the hall, though it was obvious from their longing looks, both wanted to stay.

Luke chuckled. "God help me when she's a teenager." He nodded his head toward a hallway. "Come on back to my office."

He unlocked double mahogany doors. "To keep curious hands off the equipment," Luke said. He took a seat. Behind him four large computer monitors sat on a huge desk.

"More power to you, bro. That many LEDs would fry my brain." Gabe hated working on the laptop he had. He was more of a storm-the-castle guy. He'd leave the mousing to Luke.

Of course, his brother hadn't always spent quite so much time in front of a keyboard. Gabe studied a photo of Luke's Army Ranger squadron. The picture sat near his desk. All the men in that photo were dead, Luke being the only one to survive the massacre. Barely.

Physically, his injuries had mostly healed after he was discharged. Mentally? It had taken Jazz and Joy to patch the crater-sized hole in Luke's heart and soul.

Deb had obviously followed Gabe's gaze. She bent over and studied the picture. "Special Forces to investigative reporter. That's quite a jump."

"Not really," Luke said. "I just battle injustice with a keyboard nowadays, instead of an M-16."

"I've read some of your work," Deb said. "Impressive. You traveled all over the world for your stories."

"Not anymore. With my family, it's better to keep my investigations stateside."

"Probably a lot less dangerous, too."

"Not so you'd notice," Gabe interjected, giving his brother a pointed glare.

Deb looked at Luke in surprise.

"I have trouble ignoring tough issues and topics," Luke said. "I've learned the hard way that can mean that neither I, nor my family, are ever completely out of harm's way. I'm working on rectifying that."

"How?"

"Making sure the appropriate parties' collective asses are thrown in jail for a long, long time." He leaned back in his computer chair. "So, Gabe, what's going on that has you back here so soon? What's in the box?"

Gabe hesitated. "I need some research, Luke. Sensitive research, and I may need details that are not exactly legal to get. Are you okay with working around the system a little?"

Luke raised a brow. "This from a former cop?"

Gabe glanced at Deb. Her face didn't flinch. She gave nothing away. He shoved the box at Luke. "These are Dad's unofficial records of the Denver bus station rampage. We think Ashley's disappearance might be connected to what happened eight years ago."

Luke opened the box and sifted through it. "There's a lot more in here than just the bus station. Some of these dated files are later. What's with that?"

How much should Gabe tell his brother? He knew the answer. Enough for his brother to be on guard, not enough to give the biggest secret of all away. Their sister.

"Dad investigated well beyond the mediocre job then-Captain Tower did. Dad just couldn't let it go."

"That's not unusual. Lots of cops investigate cases for years, even after they retire." Luke tapped his fingers on his boot. "There's got to be more to this. How did you get this box?" Luke asked Gabe pointedly.

"Mom. After you discovered he hadn't told us the whole truth about his time in the military, I started looking into his past. And his death.

"Mom figured out what I was doing. I was still on the force so she gave me this huge accordion folder full of files that she'd found hidden. She recognized Dad's handwriting and saw the reference to Shannon Devlin. She said I should have them, that the night of the murder had changed me. That maybe someday I would be able to see things with fresh eyes. Whatever that means."

No new look would change the facts. His father had betrayed the woman who'd loved him her whole life. Still did. The kid inside Gabe would never get over it. The man found betrayal inevitable.

Deb laid a soft hand on his arm, cutting off his thoughts. She'd shown nothing but loyalty—to her sister, to her family. A small spark of hope flickered inside of him.

Luke pulled out a file and thumbed through it. "But Shannon Devlin was murdered eight years ago. Dad died five years ago. How could any of this be connected to your sister?" His questioning gaze focused on Deb.

"The game," she said, her tone certain. "Too many kids are missing, and they all played *Point of Entry*."

The Warden looked through the windows lining his office at the flurry of work. The faces of his charges held terror.

Good.

His newest acquisition, Ashley Lansing, had shown herself to be a troublemaker. But he couldn't deny her brilliance.

He had uses for her once he quashed her spirit. She was one of the few he might take with him once they completed the job here. He pulled out the plans of the bunker. The demolition would be total. There would be no trace of what had happened here.

The bodies would never be identified.

A knock came on the door.

"Enter." He folded the plans.

Niko entered, his face carefully masking any emotions. His protégé had been acting stranger than usual. That never sat well with the Warden. He tapped his fingers on the destruction plans, but didn't open them. Normally he would have given the task to Niko.

Not this time. A shame, really.

Niko approached the desk. "I finished the last job. The new recruit is here . . . in the infirmary. He put up a fight. Is there something further I can do for you?"

The Warden chewed on the offer for a moment, then smiled. Niko had been with him from the beginning. He understood more than most—which made him a risk he couldn't ignore. "Yes, I believe there is. We have a security issue, and I need your help."

Gabe and Luke pulled the remainder of their father's files out of the box and spread out the first half dozen. Luke looked at the headers of all the files, let out a low whistle, and rubbed his temple.

"Crap." Gabe flopped back in his chair. "It's as bad as I thought."

Deb turned to him in surprise.

"When my brother gets that tingle in his temple, it either means he's onto a big story or that something is terribly wrong. My mother passed some of her Irish intuition on to all of us. Not enough to divine the winning lottery numbers, but it's kept us all alive at one time or another."

Luke flipped open the most worn file and scanned the notes, reading the brief summary. "Shannon Devlin. The first victim Patrick knew of to investigate. Straight-A student. Math and physics whiz. Murdered at age sixteen. She escaped an attempted kidnapping and traveled on a bus to Denver, where she was killed. Case never solved."

Gabe gritted his teeth and Deb moved closer beside him, slipping her hand into his. He held her tighter than he should. Her fingers squeezed back. His racing heart slowed. Who knew a woman could drive him crazy with want, and at the same time, center him?

"Diego Morales," Luke read next. "Computer-science whiz. Straight-A student. Went missing the same year from Utah. Never found."

Another file. "Brandon Taylor. Regional Science Bowl champion. Missing in 2008 from West Virginia. Unsolved."

When Luke selected the file for Shannon's three friends, Gabe sighed. "We need to change missing to murdered. They were all shot."

Luke paused, then scratched the note beside each name.

A half hour later, even Luke was convinced the disappearances were no coincidence. "There is definitely a pattern here. Dad was on to something bad and it's not just a local phenomenon. These happen all over the country," Luke said grimly scanning the printouts and opened one of the files again. "Over two dozen kids over a few years. Just gone. Not troublemakers. Smart, good grades, mostly. All listed as runaways. Why?"

Deb crossed her arms in front of her and frowned. "Because the notes left for the parents are probably all forgeries. The one Ashley supposedly left me was close. Someone who didn't know her or her handwriting really well would think she wrote it. Some parents gave up; some police departments just didn't investigate."

Gabe touched her arm gently. "Well, we don't give up. The Montgomerys are a stubborn lot. Sometimes too stubborn."

Jazz walked into the room, carrying a tray of coffee and snacks. "Are you casting aspersions on my husband, best friend, and family members?"

"You caught me." Gabe laughed.

"Well, cut it out." She set the tray down, pulled up a chair next to Luke, then slid her arm through his. "Miracle of miracles, the pint-sized Energizer Bunny has worn herself out from her excursion and has fallen asleep in the middle of her princess collection. She didn't even wake when I picked her up and put her in bed."

She looked over the array of files on the coffee table and sent Deb a sympathetic glance. "Have you found anything yet that'll help?"

"Not enough," Luke said. "But this box of materials my father hid is full of potential. I can't believe he kept this investigation secret."

"Dad was good at keeping secrets." The words were out of Gabe's mouth before he realized, and he hadn't even attempted to block the anger in his voice.

Luke stared at Gabe. "Care to explain that?"

"No." He squirmed in his chair. "I'm just exhausted."

Damn. He'd thought he'd buried the disgust, but after reliving that night over and over again in the last days, all the frustration he'd pushed aside simmered beneath the surface, ready to explode. If he didn't leave now, he'd say something he regretted. He'd vowed eight years ago to never reveal his father's affair, or Whitney. Gabe refused to hurt his mom like that. He had to protect her—even from her own husband.

He rose, unwilling to give Luke a chance to push. "I've got to get over to the bar and see how they're doing."

The phone rang and Luke answered it. A minute later, after grunting agreement a few times, he hung up and threw Gabe a sympathetic look. "That was Mom. She's coming over. John's coming, too. She's been calling your phone all morning and you haven't answered. She said don't even think about leaving before she gets here. She's seriously angry with both you and John and she says you, especially, have some explaining to do."

Sammy's Bar had a full parking lot, but Gabe Montgomery wasn't inside. Ernie slouched against the wall, praying he was invisible. He'd watched and waited for hours. Gabe had to show soon. God, where was he? This was suicide to be waiting anywhere near here. If Gasmerati ever found out, Ernie would be cougar food.

He'd vowed never to put himself at risk by going in that cop bar, but now . . . maybe he should. He'd already called Gabe four times. Where was he? The guy hadn't left the place for any length of time in months. He wasn't home, either.

Ernie knew how to block his own number, but could someone find out he'd made that many calls to Gabe, even if he deleted them? Ernie didn't understand all this cyber-techno junk everyone was using today.

He was old school and if he wasn't careful, Ernie knew Grace O'Sullivan wouldn't be the only snitch with a hit out on her.

Luke Montgomery was already a target. With that kind of bait, Ernie was betting Gabe would help him stay alive. Ernie just hoped he was still in one piece when Gabe finally decided to get back to work.

The scent of pine filled each breath Gabe took. Luke's front porch was as close as he could get to being alone. He'd considered just grabbing Deb and heading back to her place to finish what they'd started. Now there was an idea.

If it weren't for everything around him hitting the proverbial fan. He sighed and pocketed his cell. He'd forgotten he'd shut off his phone before going in to see Wexler. He'd meant to turn it back on after, but Sheriff Tower's power play had distracted him.

A ton of missed calls greeted him, ranging from his mom to John Garrison, to his brother Zach. Then there was the series of blocked calls every ten minutes or so for an hour. Gabe even had a few from Mylo. He'd never been quite this popular. Unfortunately, he'd only made it through half his voice mails.

John's had him worried. If the captain had news he risked calling for, that meant something big was happening on the undercover op. Just what he didn't need, not with Deb's sister missing and his father's past swirling around him.

He needed to see his boss. On the other hand, it sounded like his mom knew something, and she was someone he couldn't look in the eyes right now.

He'd fought her intuition for years to hide the truth. Knots twisted the muscles on the back of his neck. He kneaded them and groaned when the tension didn't release.

The creak of the front door sounded. He stiffened, gripping the porch rail.

A flash of auburn hair in his peripheral vision made him relax a bit. Deb stepped out on the patio. "You're off the phone. Was there any news about . . ."

She couldn't even say the words.

He turned around. "Nothing about Ashley."

Her disappointment showed, but she, in turn, studied his expression. "Are you okay?"

"Yes. No. Who the hell knows? Things are . . . complicated right now, is all."

She looked into his eyes. "They love you," she said. "I can see that. Don't . . . don't take it for granted. Work it out."

He pulled her to him. He couldn't believe how much she'd engrained herself into his life in just days. How much she saw of the real him, and not the man everyone else assumed. The irony was, this wasn't how he'd envisioned spending time with Deb during all those long, lonely months in the bar.

"I don't know what to say to my mom, or John . . . Captain Garrison."

Deb looked at him, her gaze steady and knowing. "Sounds like she knows you're investigating out of the bar, doesn't it? You may not have to say anything to her." Deb's expression turned solemn. "My asking for help with Ashley's disappearance is screwing your job up."

He gripped her hand. "You're not the only one who needs answers. There are things I'm not prepared to talk about yet. Family situations that factor in, especially with my mother, but I want to help Ashley . . . and find justice for Shannon Devlin."

"You can't do it all, Gabe," Deb said. "You've already done enough. Detective Wexler is on the case—"

"I'm going to help you," Gabe said. "Look, my mother is almost here and it's going to get awkward. Just go with me on this one. Maybe your presence will keep her from reaming me too badly."

Deb shook her head. "Gabe Montgomery, are you asking to hide behind a woman's skirts?"

"You're wearing pants," he pointed out.

"Regardless. You're never going to make it to superhero status doing things like that."

Gabe sighed. "My family already has a superhero. My brother Zach was the Dark Avenger. I'm just trying to survive the next few minutes."

"Your mother can't be that bad," Deb insisted.

"You think so?" he responded. "Mom not only inherited the Irish Sight, she got the Irish temper, too. That red in her hair isn't just for looks. It's a warning sign for the unwary."

Deb raised her brow. "Mr. Montgomery, may I remind you that you're speaking to someone with auburn hair? Very, very reddish auburn hair."

"Yeah, and I'm not crazy enough to mess with you, Ms. Lansing. I've heard rumors. Those guys on your team would rather not spar with you, they say your knee should be registered as a deadly weapon."

"True." Deb smiled coyly. "If I get mad at you, though, I think I'll aim elsewhere. Wouldn't want to endanger an area I'm looking forward to exploring."

Gabe perked up, in more ways than one. She slid her gaze over him and grinned.

He groaned. "Whatever you're thinking, hold that thought."

Her eyes sparkled and he moved closer and put his arms around her. He lowered his mouth to hers, tasting her lips. She sighed and kissed him back, eager, hot, and wanting. Her hand eased down the front of his body, giving him a soft squeeze.

A grumble sounded in his chest.

He widened his stance, then lowered his hands down her back to her curves. Two could play at that game.

A whimper escaped and she nipped his lower lip.

A car's engine purred. Gabe groaned and opened one eye. Sure enough his mother and John Garrison pulled up in front.

Their timing sucked.

CHAPTER NINE

Gabe opened Luke's front door. "Mom's here," he announced.

"Grandma's coming?" A sleepy Joy padded over to her uncle from the hallway leading to her bedroom, dragging her blanket behind her.

He knelt down and smiled at the blonde-haired beauty. "Nap time over, short stuff? Maybe Grandma would like to look at your room when she gets here. I heard you have a pretty nice princess setup in there."

Luke raised his brow. "Wimping out, little brother? Man, what have you done?"

"Mom hasn't told me yet." Gabe felt bad for an instant about getting his niece to distract his mother, but he needed to talk to John alone.

"Maybe you could show Deb your room, as well?"

Deb's eyes widened. "You barely introduced us. Joy might not want my company."

"Are you Uncle Gabe's girlfriend?" Joy asked.

Deb's eyes widened and Gabe bit the inside of his cheek. Joy could charm anyone.

"You're almost as tall as my new mommy," the littler girl chatted. "You can see my room, too. Do you like princesses? My mommy has hair like Rapunzel."

Deb knelt down to speak with Joy and Gabe chanced a look at Jazz. She crossed her arms and glared at him. The jig was up. She knew him better than most. They'd been SWAT teammates for several years before his attack. "What's going on, Gabe?"

"Nothing." He picked up the phone. "Hey, why don't I order pizza for dinner?"

"Yay!" Joy ran around in circles. "Pizza, pizza, pizza."

He placed the order while Luke stood next to him, cursing. "You're digging yourself in deeper and deeper, and now it's not just with Mom."

"For heaven's sake," Jazz said, "your mother isn't scary. She raised six sons and not a bum in the lot. Don't let these guys fool you, Deb. She's amazing. She just doesn't let them get away with anything."

"Why thank you, Jasmine." Anna Montgomery stood at the front door. Gabe's boss—and her boyfriend—Captain John Garrison stood at her side. John shifted his feet, his eyes low, clearly uncomfortable.

She'd obviously torn into John already. Gabe swallowed. He was in for it.

"Grandma!" Joy raced toward her grandmother. "Come see my room. Uncle Gabe said you'd want to see my princesses."

Anna's brow arched, the movement identical to Luke's. "He did. Nice ploy," she said, staring down Gabe, before turning to Joy with a warm smile. "I'd love to see your room, honey. But first, I'd like to meet Gabe's friend." She looked pointedly at Deb.

Gabe tugged her forward. "Deb Lansing, Mom."

Anna's lips frowned. "I heard about your sister." She patted Deb's hand. "You'll find her."

"I have to," Deb said simply.

The two women's gazes met and Anna nodded. "You have the grit that will see you through this." She turned to the captain. "John, I'm sure you want to consult with Gabe since he's working undercover for you now. I want to see that princess room."

John winced and gave her a quick nod.

Gabe swallowed hard. "Oh, sh—"

Anna whirled on her youngest son. "Gabriel Francis Montgomery, do not say that word aloud. You are in enough trouble with me already. Swearing in front of my four-year-old granddaughter isn't going to win any points with me, and believe me, boyo, you need them."

Anna grabbed Joy's hand and she, in turn, latched on to Deb's hand and they walked away.

Luke blew out a breath. "You're working undercover and you haven't left the sheriff's office? No wonder she blasted you with all three names. She's pissed."

John rubbed his eyes. "I'm sleeping on the couch. We need to wrap this case up quickly." He nodded toward the porch. "Let's talk, Gabe." He turned back to Luke and Jazz. "Excuse us, please?"

Gabe didn't wait for a response. He walked outside. "How did she figure it out?"

"I needed to talk to you and tried to slip the calls in while she was painting. Unfortunately, she forgot something and came back in the room. I had put my phone down and it showed three calls to you this morning. She immediately knew something was wrong. A few pointed questions later, and she guessed. It wasn't pretty."

"Why did you call me?"

"Believe me, I wouldn't have if I'd had a choice." John paused. "The DA's case on that gun-running charge against Jeff Gasmerati is falling apart. The key witness disappeared. They found his body, minus a hand, in the landfill."

"You have his taped confession, right?" Gabe didn't like the look on his boss's face.

John slammed his fist against the railing. "We might be able to use it. If we could find it."

"What do you mean? It's in the evidence room. I heard the deputies talking about it under their breaths in the bar."

"That reassures me. Anyone could have overheard them."

"So what's missing?"

"Several confiscated files. Neil Wexler was the investigator in charge. He says he hasn't touched the evidence in months, but the log shows he signed it out at the same time he checked out the files from the bus terminal shooting. Now, everything has vanished."

"Shannon Devlin's case files, too?"

"Yes. It looks bad for Wexler, no matter what he claims, and Tower has a grin that turns my stomach. The fallout is going to be fierce."

Gabe studied his boss's grim expression. "What do you want me to do?"

"As your commanding officer, I want you to ratchet up the pressure on your contacts. We need someone to break, whether it's the cops you've been watching or a Gasmerati insider. I want this investigation closed. And not just for the criminal reasons." John rubbed his neck. "I feel like I've aged five years sleeping on that damn couch. If I want to salvage my relationship with your mother, I'd better get you out of the undercover business fast."

The knots in Gabe's shoulders tensed up. What he'd wanted for months, and now just what he didn't need.

He followed John back into the house to find everyone except Joy gathered in the living room. The sounds of her playing in her room echoed down the hall.

Deb stood against the wall, watching the byplay, her face curiously devoid of emotion. What had his mom said to her? What had Deb told his mom? A lump formed in the base of his gut.

Anna strode to Gabe and stared up at him, her green eyes flashing with an expression he'd seen all too often his senior year of high school.

"I'm tired of secrets, Gabriel. Secrets hurt. I'm tired of being hurt, too, by people who withhold information from me . . . for my own good."

And he'd been keeping secrets from his mother since he was eighteen.

She grabbed Gabe's hands in hers. "I get that you and John are cops and can't tell me everything. Your father was the same way, but this is different. I almost lost you more than once this last year. Consider me need-to-know, whenever you can, because I'm not letting silence destroy this family. I won't go through that heartache again."

She whirled on John. "Why is it that you sought out my son to be the one undercover?"

"I volunteered," Gabe hissed.

She turned to him in bewilderment. "But why, after everything that's happened this year?"

"Because it was the only way I could stay a cop."

Jazz gripped Luke's hand. "Oh, Gabe. If only I'd—"

Gabe whirled on her. "This isn't your fault, Jazz. Your weapon was sabotaged. I don't blame you for anything that happened, but . . . I. Am. A. Cop. It's all I ever wanted to do. I need to see this through. I need my family to be safe. Let me do my job."

"Oh, boyo," Anna whispered, her hand going to her mouth.

"Mom, stop." He sighed.

Luke approached and laid his hand on Gabe's shoulder. "Why didn't you come to me for help? My investigations cover a lot of the same ground."

Gabe turned to his family. "I couldn't make your position more dangerous. I may not be SWAT anymore, but I can end the threat of Gasmerati and Tower. I can protect my family this time and make up for not seeing that Steve Paretti was a traitor."

Ashley groaned when she saw the avatar she'd been assigned. Obviously a guy had been playing this game before her and designed this . . . supposedly erotic woman. She was clad in a football jersey, pads, and short-shorts. The woman turned and smiled seductively, her computer-generated breasts too big, her waist too small, and her hips too . . . something. Her fist pumped in the air, and all the loose lady parts jiggled enticingly.

Gag.

She glared at Niko. "I can't believe you're forcing me to play this bimbo."

"We don't have time to change anything. The Warden wants you to break Level 88 on this computer today. It's imperative."

Ashley tugged on the computer headset. "It's BS, that's what it is."

Forty-five minutes later, the screen went blank and an orchestra of music sounded through the system. Ashley waited, gazing at the screen. Had she made it?

A spinning sun exploded.

"Congratulations, warrior! You've reached the pinnacle of *Point of Entry VII.* Level 88! You've earned a chance at the bonus game." The voice dropped. "Now you must take the oath. Swear to each other what you do, what you see, will never be revealed. Swear it!"

Niko appeared at her side out of nowhere and keyed in a few strokes. "Skip all that. Go straight to the mission."

The screen darkened and the music ended. Moments later, the mechanized voice droned. "Let's begin your next challenge . . . there's a traitor in our midst. An important man is being blackmailed for inappropriate behavior and being forced to misuse his power. Your job is to find the evidence the blackmailers have hidden to use against him so he is safe. There are four hundred and thirty-five doors. You must find the evidence by unlocking several special keyed sequences. Are you up to the challenge? You have two hours. No longer. Unlock the right door. Break the code. Find the proof. Nail the blackmailer."

Niko pressed closer. "Ashley, succeeding at this mission is critical. Are you ready?"

"If I'm not, is the Warden going to shoot me, too?" she snapped.

Niko blanched. "I wouldn't doubt that outcome for a minute."

Washington, D.C.

The e-mail arrived just before 5:00 p.m. Congressman Raymond Reynolds, chair of the Armed Services Committee, clicked the icon from the familiar address.

A photo stared back at him.

Not just any photo.

"Oh my God. No."

His cell phone rang.

Hands shaking, he answered. "H-hello."

"Congressman, I see you received our message," a smooth voice commented.

"Where . . . how? That's private," he sputtered.

"Not anymore. Your every secret is ours, Reynolds. Every little sordid detail." There was a pause.

No. It couldn't be. He kept everything encrypted. He was careful. It was only a diversion. A hobby. No one else was ever supposed to know.

The voice chuckled. "I see you know what I'm talking about. Most constituents don't approve of their public officials being on the wrong end of a leather whip. You really don't have the figure for leather, Congressman. Neither does your . . . friend. I can see he enjoys being in charge." The voice lowered. "I especially like how much your wife gets off watching you take it up the . . ."

Reynolds sagged in his chair. "What do you want?" Resignation filled the room.

"Nothing. Yet. But you'll hear from us soon. When you do, we expect complete compliance. Do you understand?"

He didn't speak.

"I expect a response, pet. Isn't that the term he used?"

Reynolds swallowed deeply.

"Y-yes."

"Yes, what, pet. You know the rules."

Teeth grated. "Yes, sir," he spat.

"Actually, instead of 'sir,' I prefer the term you used with your friend, in that very interesting little room hidden behind your closet. What's my name?"

"Master." Reynolds bit the word out.

"Don't forget it. I have you by the balls. But then you like that. Don't you?"

"You can't—"

"Silence!"

Reynolds trembled, his whole world crumbling to dust.

"We'll have to work on your discipline, pet." A delighted laugh sounded at the other end of the phone. "You'd be punished if I were there. And I would bring a special someone to make sure you'd . . . enjoy . . . or at least remember your submission." There was a slight pause.

"Do exactly as we say, exactly when we tell you to, Congressman Reynolds, and these photos might not leak to the press. But say one word of this to anyone—Justice, Treasury, the Capitol guards—and the photos are on the Internet before you finish revealing this call."

A click sounded. Reynolds closed his eyes and thrust his fingers through his balding white hair.

This couldn't be happening.

God, what would they want?

He rose and walked to the window of his office, staring out across the Capitol Reflecting Pool. It didn't matter. He'd worked too damn hard to get here. He'd do whatever it took to stay. And damn them all to hell, they knew it.

CHAPTER TEN

THE AIR HAD TURNED FRIGID WITH A NIP OF SNOW SINCE GABE last stood on the porch with John. Driven by demons he'd yet to confront, Gabe needed the space. He didn't want to hurt his family anymore, which meant keeping his father's secret, and lying to his mother for the foreseeable future.

The past might be a nightmare, but the present was worse. He was torn between two promises. One to himself to bring down those who had threatened his family, and his promise to Deb to find her sister. Two vows that ripped him up inside. He couldn't give both everything.

He'd let *someone* down. There was no way around it.

The front door quietly closed and he gave a quiet sigh, recognizing Deb's clean scent.

"I'm sorry for leaving you in there. I just had to—" He turned and leaned against the banister. "You shouldn't have had to hear all that. Guess you didn't realize who you were signing on with when you picked me to help you. Pretty screwed up, huh?"

Deb studied his face, her own expression sympathetic and strangely resigned. "Your family cares about each other. A lot. Nothing to apologize for in that. But, Gabe, you can't afford to split your time. That's clear to everyone in that house. If you're already fighting Tower and his cronies, you're in enough danger without adding Ashley and me to it."

Gabe shifted slightly. She was right. The risks surrounding him were very real and it could spill onto her, too, just because she was nearby. Things were coming to a head on the undercover op case at the worst possible time.

"Ashley is in trouble, too."

Deb nodded and straightened. "I'm so grateful you believed in me, Gabe, when no one else would. I won't forget that, but Neil has bought into the case. We'll find my sister." She stepped back. "You should focus on bringing Tower down so that people like me can trust the sheriff's office when we need them. It's for the best."

"What are you saying?"

"That you have a duty to protect your family, and I won't be the cause of tragedy ruining your life. I've done that enough in my life."

"Deb—"

"Ashley is my responsibility. I've had to take care of my own for a long time. I'll take it from here." She rose up on her tiptoes and kissed his cheek. "You're a good man, Gabe Montgomery. Be safe."

Deb turned her back on him and started down the street.

What just happened? Gabe rushed after her. "I can help."

"I don't need it. I already called a cab." She pocketed her cell phone. "Look, things between us got out of control. I mixed up my desperation for . . . something else. Today was a reminder. You go back to your undercover investigation. And your family. As for me, I have to stop keeping secrets from mine and face up to my mistakes. Again."

He'd seen that look before. Just a few minutes ago on his mother's face. Deb wasn't going to budge. She'd given him an out, but he had a bad feeling everything he was trying to do was about to come crashing down around him. "Well, you're not standing out here alone." His jaw set.

"Fine. You have no coat on. Freeze." She rubbed her gloved hands together and looked over at him. "This gallant sticking-around bit is ruining my dramatic exit, you know. I thought I'd done quite well."

He laughed. "You did. It was Oscar-worthy."

A yellow cab turned the corner.

Gabe shoved his hand in his coat. "Your ride is here."

Her smile turned wistful. "I am going to miss you, Gabe, even though I shouldn't say it. Guess it wasn't meant to be."

His heart tripped in his chest. She was saying good-bye. She didn't need or want his help. The words hurt, because they were so very true.

Every time Niko walked Ashley to the computer lab, he took her a different route. Was he purposely trying to confuse her? Or something else? She hadn't been able to ask Justin if the maze treatment was standard operating procedure.

Whatever the case, Niko's attempts at obscuring the layout of this prison wouldn't work. Her innate sense of direction and memory logged every twist and turn. She'd learned several alternate routes to the lab. She'd spotted a few loading platforms and exits along with a seemingly endless series of white corridors and doors. She'd memorized corridor names and numbers.

At some point, she and Justin would have enough information to escape.

Niko shoved her forward. "Quit daydreaming," he growled.

The man confused her. Sometimes, he seemed so nasty and threatening. Other times, it was almost like he wanted to reach out to her. Physically and emotionally.

Yeah, girl. You're crazy. Niko softening? Not likely.

She touched her cheek, still bruised from where he'd back-handed her. Still, she wasn't as afraid of him as she was the other guards, especially that redheaded guard. She never wanted to be alone with him. Or the Warden.

"I need to stop and get some materials from the storeroom," Niko said. "Stay right beside me," he warned, "and don't touch anything."

He stopped in front of a door, a stylized bomb with erupting flames painted on it. Very P.O.E.-like. Niko keyed in a pass code on the control panel and they walked inside.

Holy crap, it was an armory. Ashley froze, staring at shelf upon shelf of weapons. Why would he bring her here and let her see all this? He had to know what she was capable of doing, of breaking into.

She could barely breathe as he grabbed some ammo clips off the shelves and shoved them into his pocket. Ashley wished she dared knock him out and try to run now. Deb could do it. She could take this guy down in a heartbeat.

Damn it, if she lived through this, she'd learn to protect herself better.

"Time to go." Niko took her arm and shoved her into the hall, then swiftly locked the door.

She scanned the surrounding area. C5. C6. C7. If the room they'd just left was a munitions room, what was in these other ones?

He walked her past a corridor that branched off to the side. Far down that hall, a reinforced door read C2. "Don't even think of trying to escape through that door *right now.* Remember what I've told you."

He held her gaze a moment too long, and a strange thrill coursed through her.

Was he saying don't try now? But maybe later?

He glanced up at the camera in the hallway and frowned. "Move it." He shoved her harder and didn't speak again until he'd sat her at her computer station. "Do what you're told and don't mess up," he said coldly. "Two more kids were replaced today."

He walked away.

His iciness had Jack Frost beat, but she still couldn't shake the sensation he was trying to tell her something. Maybe even help her. Was she succumbing to Stockholm syndrome, had she lost her mind, or was he playing games with her?

Gabe stood in front of Sammy's Bar, the mid-high sun in the sky above him. He shoved through the doorway determined to find a way to push this investigation forward. Until Tower and Gasmerati were behind bars, his family was at risk.

Hawk manned the bar, talking to a customer, his tone low. Zach and Jenna sat on two bar stools, while their son, Sam, had taken over a corner table, digging into an ice cream sundae. That wouldn't do. Once Gabe started poking at hornets in the sheriff's office, they could come back and sting.

Gabe forced a cheerful expression on his face and rubbed Sam's head. "Looks good, buddy. I may have to have one myself."

"It's awesome, Uncle Gabe." Sam gave him a trusting smile.

The knife in Gabe's heart twisted deeper. He had to protect them.

He knocked fists with his brother Zach and smiled at Jenna. "You keeping this joker under your thumb and out of trouble?"

Jenna turned on her bar stool, her pregnancy obvious, and a serene grin on her face. "Always."

Gabe laughed. "He's a lucky man."

"Ask him about the helicopter pilot who's got him turned inside out," Hawk piped up.

Jenna's eyes lit up. "Really?"

Gabe sent Hawk a quelling look. "Yeah, but we have to take a short break for a while."

Zach stepped closer. "Because of a certain problem of dirty cops on the payroll? I heard you might need some backup."

"And exactly how would you know that?" Gabe turned on Hawk. Damn it, for a secret op, he might as well have it announced by the town crier. Everyone seemed to know anyway.

"Don't yell at Hawk. Luke called," Zach said. "And before you say anything, little brother, he's worried about you. You've got circles under your eyes, you've lost weight, and you forgot to limp when you walked in here." Zach gave Gabe a knowing gaze. "That kind of oversight can get you killed."

Oh my God, he had. His leg hurt, but, against all odds, it was still improving. He needed to play the part of an injured failure in the bar. He obviously wasn't thinking straight anymore, if he'd forgotten.

Gabe glanced at Hawk. "Can you keep an eye on everything while I talk to my brother out back for a minute?"

"And me?" Jenna queried. "What do I do?"

"You get to distract Sam," Gabe said without a regret. No way was he putting her in danger.

Zach followed Gabe out the back. He turned to his brother. "I assume Luke told you that I'm still on the force?"

"Oh, yeah." Zach let out a low whistle. "Mom's pissed, and John's sleeping on the couch, but he should count himself lucky. She kicked Dad's ass out."

"What are you talking about?" Gabe asked.

Zach leaned against the brick wall. "That's right. You were a baby. Maybe not even born yet, when things were at their worst. I was in the first grade, I think. Dad was drinking. Mom was weepy. They fought all the time."

Gabe froze. This had to have been around the time Whitney was born. Did his mother know about his father's affair? Was that why she'd kicked him out? "How come I never heard of any of this?"

"Because, by the time you were old enough to know what was going on, they'd patched their marriage up. Things were rough for a while, but Dad never drank again after she kicked him out. Looking back, she probably had postpartum depression. Maybe Dad couldn't handle it." Zach glanced at the back door. "I gotta tell you, hormones aren't fun. Sometimes I just hold Jenna while she cries, and I take it on the chin when she gets upset, 'cause I can't do a thing about it."

Gabe kneaded his temple, the headache moving from the back of his head to the front. "Look, Zach. Keep Jenna and Sam away from this place. I've got a bad feeling."

"Already ahead of you," Zach said. "She'll ream me for putting her under house arrest, but with her pregnancy, I won't risk it."

"Who's going to guard her?"

"Seth. I contacted him last night. He just returned stateside. He's flying here tomorrow."

"It's a family reunion. Everyone's here but Caleb and Nick."

Zach grew serious. "And we can help. Don't be as stupid as I was and try to go it alone."

"Just keep your family safe," Gabe said, opening the door and striding into the kitchen. "I'm going to end this. And if Deb Lansing comes in, keep an eye on her. She's got it rough right now."

"She's the one you meant when you said that you'd met your match?"

"Maybe. Yes. No. Hell, I don't know." Gabe's cheeks flared with heat. "I just feel different around her. Like life isn't as dark and ugly as I thought. Which is weird considering what's going down."

They walked into the main bar.

"Yeah, I get that," Zach said, his warm gaze settling on his wife. "If the lady makes you feel that way, don't let her go."

Gabe frowned. "I'll do whatever it takes to protect her. Especially let her go."

The cab maneuvered through the snow-lined streets leading to the grocery store down from Deb's apartment. She needed the distraction. She didn't want to spend any more time than she had to thinking about the man she'd left standing in the street. He was the first man to comfort her since . . . she couldn't remember when. She'd stood alone and strong for so long, she'd almost forgotten . . .

Shoving the thoughts aside as quickly as she could, she filled a few bags and started her trek home. Her entire body was chilled, and not just from the November weather. She could be strong, she could fight, but sometimes, God, sometimes she just wanted to be loved.

She had no choice, though. She had to move forward and find Ashley on her own. If she'd asked, Gabe would have kept trying to help her. He was that kind of man.

Too risky, though. Distraction killed people.

Deb would go it alone. It's how her life had to be.

By the time she reached the third floor, her lungs ached from the strain. She was getting soft. Too much beer and too many fantasies. Time to get herself grounded and concentrate on finding Ashley.

She juggled the bags until she could shove her key into the lock. Before she could even turn the key, the door creaked open. *What the hell?*

Had she not pulled the door tight enough when she left? It stuck a lot in the summer, when the wood swelled, but this was November. That problem was basically gone. Still, it was hot in the corridor. She didn't want to call the police for a false alarm.

But she wasn't stupid, either.

She quietly put her bags down and reached for the gun in her purse. She didn't flaunt the fact that she had one, but her father had drummed it into her head that she had to be able to protect herself. Her brothers and the Army had, too. Her ass had been kicked enough times that she knew how to kick one back.

Not moving, she listened at the door for a long while.

The apartment was so quiet. Too quiet for Ashley to have miraculously returned.

She tapped 9-1-1 into her phone, but didn't hit "Send." Still, she kept the phone ready, then slowly, methodically searched room to room. The living room. The kitchen. The bedroom. The minuscule bathroom that probably couldn't fit a bad guy if he tried.

Just as she went back into the hall to check the final closet, her phone vibrated. She glanced down. Oh God, it was a direct message from her brother Rick from Afghanistan. She'd left e-mails and messages for all three male members of the family to get in touch as soon as possible.

Quickly, she opened the laptop she'd left on hibernate. The incoming video call flashed. Just when she thought she'd missed him, her brother's face appeared in front of her. God, he looked exhausted. She studied him more closely. He pretty much looked like she felt. "Hi, Rick."

"Hey, Admiral," he said, his voice jerky in the connection. "What's going on?"

Where was she supposed to begin? So much had happened. She didn't want to tell him, but she knew she had to. Deb took a deep breath. "Ashley's missing."

"What?" He sat up straight and swiped his hand across tired eyes. "Say that again. I don't think I heard you right. Communication is kind of garbled today."

"Ashley is missing. I think she's been kidnapped."

The sleepy look left his eyes, and they took on a deadly intensity that was new to him since going to the Middle East.

"What are you talking about, she might have been kidnapped? Why didn't you call?"

"I hoped I could find her before I had to tell you." She hesitated. "I know how much stress you and Ben have been under."

Rick nearly growled his anger. "Damn it, Red. She's my sister, too."

"I know. I'm sorry." Deb rubbed the back of her neck. "I'm really scared."

She gave him a rundown of the investigation. If he could have leapt through the screen, he would have.

"This Gabe Montgomery. Is he legit?"

Praying her cheeks hadn't turned pink, she nodded. "He helped when the cops wouldn't, but we uncovered enough to make them listen to me. I'm going to bring Ashley home."

Rick let out a frustrated groan. "I can't get leave right now. Things are too volatile in . . . Never mind." He leaned toward the monitor. "I'm sorry I jumped all over you. How are you holding up?"

She choked back the emotions that had been driving her crazy. "Alone. Like when Mom was sick."

He frowned, then his eyes glinted. "What's the motto?" He slapped his fist against his chest, his normal smile not reaching his eyes. " 'Never give up. Never surrender.' "

"You're comforting me with quotes from *Galaxy Quest*?"

"Nonstop fun like I'm having will do that to a person."

She smiled because he wanted her to, but they knew the truth. Things weren't good for the Lansings. "Can you get hold of Ben?"

Rick's eyes shifted left, just for a second, and Deb stilled, squeezing her nails into her palm to quell the foreboding rising within her. "What's wrong?"

"I'm getting chatter about some big moves. Ben's whole unit's gone quiet." Rick paused.

"What kind of chatter?"

"Sorry, Deb, you're not need-to-know. I shouldn't have said that much."

She stared at Rick through the screen, studying his features. Oh boy. She didn't like the looks. Something intense was going down. The worry for her brother that always bubbled under her skin poked through. But she knew asking more questions wouldn't help. "I understand. If you hear from him, contact me. Please?"

Her gaze met Rick's. He was scared for Ben. Deb shivered again. She couldn't bear the thought of Ben's black ops identity being discovered.

"I will, *Admiral*."

Shouting sounded from behind Rick.

"I've got to go." He faced the screen, his brown eyes determined, yet loving. "Find Ashley, Deb. I don't want Ben to come out of that hellhole he's in to find out she's dead."

Just as the screen went dead, a loud crash came from the back of the apartment. A man in a balaclava stood just outside her bedroom door.

The hall closet. She'd never checked it after Rick called. Fool. Her finger hit the button for 9-1-1, even though she knew no one would get here in time.

She was on her own. Like always.

Deb grabbed her gun. So be it.

CHAPTER ELEVEN

DEB GRASPED HER GUN IN BOTH HANDS. "ON THE FLOOR, NOW, or your brains decorate my apartment."

The guy didn't even hesitate. He whipped a heavy bag at her. It slammed against her hands, the shock knocking the gun from her grip to a spot under the sofa. He had the advantage, and the guy didn't hesitate, but charged, tugging an M1911 from his belt. No silencer.

If he'd wanted to shoot her, he would have done it, but he didn't even aim.

Then she realized the truth. He didn't want her dead. He wanted to escape.

Like hell, buddy. You're going down.

He swung the bag again and it smashed into Deb's chest. She grunted as her belongings scattered across the floor but didn't take her gaze off him. He charged at her, the ski mask hiding all but heavy eyebrows and eyes wild with anger. She backed up to give herself some clear space, and waited.

Time seemed to slow. Deb crouched, and he kept coming. With a yell, he lunged for her. Overweight and angry, he was like an enraged bull.

And she could use his momentum against him.

She ducked and swept her leg around, smashing him in the side of one knee. A loud pop sounded. He screamed, landing hard on the floor.

His gun spun across the vinyl. Deb leapt toward the weapon. She reached out a hand, her fingertips brushing the metal grip, but he recovered too quickly and grabbed her ankles, pulling her back.

She kicked out and connected with his face. He yowled. She twisted to her back. Blood poured from his nose, but he didn't stop. He fell on top of her, pinning her down with his weight.

"You're gonna be sorry, bitch," his sour breath whispered in her ear. He rose and backhanded her across the cheek. With both hands, he went for a choke hold.

Gasping for breath, she gouged his face with her fingernails, going for his eyes. When he leaned back to avoid her hands, he made himself vulnerable. She brought up her knee and rammed him hard in the crotch. With a pained groan, he curled up. She kidney-punched him in the back.

He huddled into a ball.

"Stay down, you son of a bitch," she ordered, her breath coming hard. Her focus on him, she turned to his weapon and picked it up.

Sirens sounded from down the street.

"You called the cops?" With a quick move for his size, he kicked out and caught her wrist. He connected, stunning her nerves. She dropped the weapon. He staggered to his feet and bolted for the door.

Deb grabbed a lamp and swung at his head, then tackled him from behind, knocking him to the ground.

She ripped off his balaclava, and he fought her again like a madman. Deb grabbed his hair in her fist and pounded his head into the floor.

He grunted a time or two, then stilled.

Her door burst open. "Sheriff's Office! Put your hands up."

Exhausted, Deb looked up, still sitting on his hips. "Nice of you to show up, guys. He's all yours."

Two uniformed deputies, weapons drawn, stared at her uncertainly. She recognized them from the bar.

"This man broke in," she said calmly and rose, her hands raised. "He stole a bunch of stuff in that bag that's now scattered all over the floor. When I confronted him, he attacked. I took him down. His gun is over there. Mine is under the couch.

The guy moaned on the floor and turned over.

"Menken? What the hell are you doing here?" one deputy said.

Deb looked closer. Now that he wasn't attacking her, even with a broken nose and bleeding head, she recognized him! Her robber was a cop.

The bell sounded on the swinging doors of Sammy's Bar. Gabe's attention whipped to the entrance.

A group of cops wandered in.

Would this be a break? He'd smiled and joked all day, trying to tease out a hint, a clue of someone who would break through Tower's wall of corruption.

"Hoping she'll show up?" Hawk asked, scooting past him to deliver a beer and burger.

"She won't," Gabe said. "She's headed straight to the real cops to find her sister. I'm here where I should be."

"He still mooning over her?" Zach asked Hawk, as he returned some of the menus to the stack.

"Pretending not to," Hawk said. "Your wife and kid make it home okay?"

Zach nodded, the relief clear on his face.

"You don't have to stay," Gabe said. "I can handle this."

Zach hitched onto a bar stool and met Gabe's gaze. "I think staying here is the right thing to do. From what I've heard, that woman is going to need help, and you won't be able to stay away, little brother. You care too much."

With a frustrated grimace at his brother, Gabe grabbed some menus. Trouble was, Zach was right. He couldn't get his mind off Deb. Was Neil taking her seriously? Had Tower cut off the investigation?

He approached a table of deputies, their heads bent together.

"Did you hear Internal Affairs is after Wexler?" one whispered, before looking around. He caught sight of Gabe and paled. "Just a plate of appetizers and a pitcher of beer," he rushed out, waving off the menus.

Gabe headed to the kitchen to put in the order. Been this way all day. Lots of whispering, lots of scanning other tables, lots of wary, somewhat fearful looks. It didn't take a genius to guess why. Stolen evidence, rumors about Neil Wexler, Internal Affairs on the prowl.

Not a fun time at the sheriff's office.

The entrance bell sounded again. Out of the corner of his eye, Gabe recognized two out of three of the musketeers. Where was Menken? Conversation hushed. They walked over and slid onto a couple of bar stools. Gabe gave Hawk a small nod, and he moved aside. This could be his chance. Menken was the leader. Without him there, the guys may have their guard down.

Gabe rounded the bar. "What'll it be, gentlemen?"

He took the order and had just started to pull a draft for them when a familiar head poked in through the kitchen door.

Ernie? In the bar? In the daytime?

Gabe nearly dropped the beer. Forcing himself to remain calm, he slid the foam-topped beverage to one of the cops. "Hawk, can you finish up?" he said quietly and walked toward the kitchen.

The snitch ducked behind the door. What the hell was he doing?

Gabe snagged his jacket from the hook beside the exit and stuffed his arms into the down coat. Even in the afternoon, the winter chill snapped in the air.

"Ernie? I thought you said you'd never come into a cop bar." Gabe's breath puffed with each word. Had he finally caught a break?

The guy had plastered himself against the building. "Things change." He turned to Gabe. "You gotta help me, Montgomery. I got information, but you have to get me out of Denver. Hide me or something." His gaze swept the area wildly. "Bad things are going down. I need out."

"Slow down, Ernie. What's going on?"

"Promise first. I give you this information, you'll help me disappear."

Gabe nodded. A guy this scared had to be telling the truth.

"You know Grace O'Sullivan?"

"Yeah." Gabe wasn't about to admit exactly how. Grace had

been Steve Paretti's high school sweetheart. She'd also been Luke's informant on the gritty exposé he'd done last year on the mob.

"Jeff Gasmerati knows about her. About her connection to Luke, and they just learned that she also contacted someone in Witness Protection," Ernie said beneath his breath. "They're going to kill her. Make an example out of her. Her husband has to do the hit to show his loyalty."

She could bring the whole organization down. Gabe let out a loud expletive. "Wait here."

He snagged his phone and called Luke.

"What's up, Gabe?" his brother asked. "I don't have anything more for you."

"Can you contact Grace?"

"Why would you ask?" His brother's voice grew cautious.

"Jeff Gasmerati put a hit out on her."

"Damn." Luke hung up.

Yep, Luke knew where Grace was. She must have been in contact again. Gabe turned to Ernie. "I'll get you some money to hide. Stay out of sight."

Gabe bypassed the kitchen to his small office and opened the safe. He pulled out some cash, then dialed another number.

"You shouldn't call me here," his brother Nick hissed. "You know that."

"I need help. I need to put a snitch in protective custody and I can't trust the sheriff's office."

"What's going on?"

When Gabe mentioned Grace, his brother's swearing made it clear he understood the severity of the crisis.

"Hole him up somewhere safe. I'll be in touch."

With the WITSEC process hopefully in motion, Gabe hurried outside. The asphalt was empty. As he walked the parking lot, Ernie shuffled out from behind the trash bin. "What took you so long?"

Gabe passed him a couple hundred. "Find yourself a motel out of the way, get a prepaid cell phone, and stay put. Call me with the number. We can help, but you're spilling everything. I want Gasmerati and Tower."

Ernie's entire body sagged and he clutched the bills. "Thank you, thank you. Um. You should tell your brother Luke to keep an eye out."

"What do you know?"

"Didn't hear a hit, just his name."

Gabe cursed. "Get out of sight. You know they've got ears everywhere."

The snitch nodded and scurried across the parking lot and into an alley. Gabe let out a slow breath. If he could tie the ordered hit on Grace O'Sullivan to Gasmerati, or maybe Tower, this whole mess could be over. He made a quick call to Luke, but his brother had already made arrangements for Jazz and Joy to go to a hotel. They were safe. For now.

Gabe had to find a way to put Gasmerati away, but he didn't know if the DA would risk Ernie as a witness. Still, people had turned state's evidence before with worse records than Ernie had racked up.

With a last glance at his disappearing figure, Gabe opened the door to the bar, removed his coat, and strode inside. He had to let Zach know the stakes had just ratcheted up. His gaze slid over the customers. Tower's goons had left. "They took off fast."

Hawk followed his line of sight. "The moment you walked out to meet Ernie," Hawk said, under his breath. "Don't know if they saw him, but immediately after you hit the back room, they threw a couple of twenties on the bar and hightailed it out of here."

Gabe's jaw tightened. Nick better come through fast. If those two had seen Ernie, the snitch might not live to check into his motel.

Ashley couldn't tell what time it was. The Warden and Niko had taken her watch, her phone, everything she had.

She now wore their clothes, ate by their schedule. If she wanted anything she had to ask—even down to a drink of water or a trek to the bathroom. She'd read about the psychology of breaking a prisoner's will. She understood what they were doing.

Well, screw them. She was her father's daughter and she wouldn't break.

Her fingers pounded the keyboard as her anger mounted. Finally, she relaxed in her chair staring at the code on the latest mission they'd given her. Those bastards. She knew what they wanted from her now. A back door to the NSA databases—and not just any databases. The databases that stored passwords to other databases, computers, and networks.

They wanted worldwide access.

Whoever had come up with the idea to use *Point of Entry* had been smart, much smarter than her—or maybe just more devious. Anyone reaching Level 88 gave these people a key to their local computers and home networks. How many had reached Level 88 over the years?

God knows she hadn't suspected anything at all. She'd downloaded the free upgrade to the game without hesitation. She hadn't checked for secret layers and invisible commands buried in the software.

The scary part was, if she was right, this updated version of P.O.E. looked like players wouldn't even have to hit Level 88 before the Warden took control.

Millions of computer systems worldwide would be compromised.

"Quit daydreaming, Lansing," Niko said, eyes narrow and suspicious. "You haven't touched your keyboard in the last four minutes."

"Do you have an aspirin?" Ashley asked, making a show of rubbing her temple and wincing. "I'm getting a wicked headache and it's hard to concentrate."

With an exasperated sigh, he stood. "Come on."

He led her past a bevy of kids hunkered down over their machines. They didn't look up as she passed. Until she reached Justin. She slowed a bit. He had headphones on. His screen showed the latest version of P.O.E. He'd reached Level 65. Still had a ways to go.

Justin took his eyes off the game and, on-screen, a gun took out his player. He turned white.

Niko smacked the side of Justin's head and yanked off his earphones. "You know the penalty for not passing a level, Mr. Connell. I suggest you focus on the game, instead of your girlfriend." Niko glanced at his watch. "You have twelve hours to reach Level 80."

"But . . . that took our entire team weeks."

"Then I suggest you get started."

Niko grabbed Ashley's arm and yanked her from the room, then dragged her down the hall. "You think you're so damn smart, don't you. Well, you're not. You have no clue what's about to happen here. Your IQ might be high, Lansing, higher than anyone since Shannon, but smart won't save you—" His voice trailed off. He cursed and stared at Ashley, a bleak look on his face.

"Something happened to her, didn't it?" she said.

Niko's jaw clenched. He led her through another door and into a new corridor she hadn't seen before.

Ashley's voice went low. "Like what happened to Fletcher?"

"Shannon asked too many questions. You're so damn like her, it's scary." He touched the side of Ashley's cheek, then dropped his hand. "Don't make her same mistakes. The Warden hates you because you won't bend to his will. You're very close to ending up like Shannon."

Ashley recoiled, from both his touch and the warning. God, she was scared. She'd only been here a short time, and it already felt like years. She had to find a way out for her and Justin.

Niko opened a door and the steel slam echoed, hurting her eardrums. The moment his footsteps thudded down the hall another door flew open. "Niko, the computer has a glitch. Everything is ready to go but the zip codes didn't print."

Ashley peeked into the room. Her eyes widened. Hundreds of express mail packages and printed labels littered several long tables, along with a stack of *Point of Entry Version VIII* games. It wasn't supposed to hit for a month.

"If you can't fix the problem, get a tech to come in and handle it. I don't have time now."

The man gestured to Ashley. "Can she do it?"

"No. She's new. She's not allowed to use that database."

The guy frowned.

"Look," Niko growled. "Tell the Warden I authorized you to use a senior tech. Then reprint the damn labels and get those games out today."

"Right." The man's voice lowered. "They pulled the explosives. We almost done?"

Niko's face paled, then he glanced at Ashley, giving the other guy a harsh look.

The man looked at Ashley with a sympathetic gaze. "Oh, right."

That didn't sound good. At all.

The man disappeared down the hall. Niko didn't move for a few moments, then his jaw tightened. "Son of a bitch."

He dragged her to another door marked Infirmary. He made her turn around so he could key a series of numbers into the panel. Once inside, he unlocked a large medicine cabinet full of grouped meds. He pulled out a small bottle of ibuprofen from among several similar-sized containers, opened it, and shook two tablets into Ashley's hand.

"If you need more, ask." He pocketed the bottle.

"Why can't I just take the bottle? It's small. With the headaches I get, I need more than two tablets, especially when I work on the computer."

Niko shook his head as he signed out the med. "We've had a couple of overdoses through the years. That's why the containers are so small. No one walks around carrying enough medicine to hurt themselves. If you need more ibuprofen, you come to me."

He thrust a water bottle into her hand. "Now swallow the meds and get back to work. The Warden wants you into that database by tomorrow."

"But . . . it could take weeks."

"You don't have weeks, Ashley. You have one, maybe two days. Time is nearly up. No more talk."

Niko led her back through the main room, past Justin, who tensed but kept his attention on the game.

Ashley longed to stop, but didn't dare after her last interruption.

Once she was seated, Niko bent close. "Don't think if you fall down on the job you'll be the only one to suffer. Justin. Your family. Everyone here will bear the consequences. I know how ruthless the Warden can be. Shannon was once a competitor and a close friend of mine. I don't take many risks anymore. No one does. I'm trusting you to do your part."

CHAPTER TWELVE

The bell on the bar's door jangled. Gabe sank onto a stool. "Give me a soda, Hawk. Lots of ice."

The place was deserted. Finally.

Zach wiped his forehead. "Your job sucks, Gabe. I'm going to check on my wife."

With a careless wave, Zach headed outside. Gabe grabbed his cell phone. He still had messages to retrieve.

He deleted the many repeats from his mother and finally started on his voice mail.

Mylo's voice filtered through the phone.

"*Been trying to reach you all morning, man. Britney texted me. Thought you and Deb should know. Brit's just pissed at her parents. She hates the place they moved. She wants to stay here. I'm meeting her, but it's all top secret.*"

Mylo sighed.

"*Um . . . anyway, I'm just telling you where I'm going. As a precaution, you know. Things have been a little too weird lately.*"

"Damn it." Gabe had a very bad feeling about this. He dialed Mylo. Straight to voice mail.

Cursing under his breath, he did a quick search and called Mylo's mother. The kid had told her he was going to meet a friend. He'd left a few hours ago and she didn't expect him back until later. Other than that, she didn't have any specifics.

He was a kid. That's probably exactly what happened.

Except Ashley's note had seemed perfectly legit, too. Had Britney's message to the boys been a lure? Or was she in trouble, too?

His phone rang. Wexler.

God, Gabe hoped he had some good news. "Montgomery."

"I'm on my way to see a dead body found in the hills outside Denver. Female. Small. Right size for a teenager."

Gabe's cut clenched. "Ashley?"

"No identification and it's going to be tough. The body has been decapitated. Hands are missing, too."

Gabe's gut heaved. This couldn't be happening. "I'll have to tell Deb."

"I hate to ask, but if it's Ashley, Deb can probably identify her. Can you bring her to the crime scene?"

"You don't ask for much, Wexler." Gabe kneaded the back of his neck. Once he told Deb, he wouldn't be able to keep her away. "We'll be there, I just have to call her."

Wexler gave Gabe the location. "You can probably catch Deb at the station. It was all over the radio. She was attacked in her apartment and she beat the crap out of the guy. Don't know all the details, but I heard it was one of Tower's three musketeers."

Gabe hung up without saying good-bye and raced across the street.

Ashley had a plan. Niko had warned her not to do anything stupid, but she wouldn't get an opportunity like this again. The moment she sat down at her computer and fired it up, she knew what she had to do.

If she was caught, the Warden would kill her for sure, but after what she'd seen so far, she didn't think many in this Godforsaken place would leave here alive anyway.

Pretending to bend closer to the screen to concentrate on the program before her, Ashley opened a new window in the bottom corner of her screen. Sweat trickled down her back, even with the air-conditioning in the room to keep the computers cool. If her keystrokes were still being recorded on this new machine . . . She'd just have to be smart about it. She had to take the risk.

They kept moving her around. Computer to computer. Sometimes they brought her to different rooms. Her tasks were always different, but Ashley could see how the program update was coming together.

They needed her to tunnel into the federal classified systems.

She looked around surreptitiously. No one was near.

She scanned the small box she'd pulled up. Lines and lines of code streamed past her. She typed furiously, then copied them.

Seconds later, she'd tunneled her way into the computer system. The camp's administrative network hadn't been that difficult to breach. It seemed too easy, but maybe they thought no one would care about mundane mail programs.

Maybe Ashley had found a vulnerability no one had considered.

Niko rose from his station.

Quickly, Ashley typed a few lines over those she'd copied. By the time he arrived, the box was closed and everything looked normal.

He walked over and studied her screen, one hand resting on her shoulder.

Ashley's breath caught. Did he know what she'd done?

He scanned the program, then nodded. "I like the approach you're taking. It might work."

His hand lingered on her shoulder and she fought not to shudder. He gave her such mixed messages. Was he trying to help her, or waiting for her to screw up?

The moment he turned his back, she flicked to the other window and typed in a very familiar address, then she said a small prayer and hit "Send."

She just prayed her sister understood.

Gabe plowed through the Jeffco Sheriff's Office doors. "Deb Lansing? Where is she?" he called out to the deputy on duty.

Before the guy could speak, Deb strode into the main lobby, anger and frustration on her face.

"I'm right here." She sported a nasty bruise on her cheek. She headed toward him, her tension visibly releasing with every step.

Gabe raced to her and hugged her tight. He couldn't care less who saw them. He could have lost her. She'd been in danger and he hadn't been there.

"Don't do that to me again," he whispered in her ear, then covered her mouth with his.

He pressed her close and she didn't pull away. Instead, she nestled in and wrapped her arms around his waist. She softened against him and his world went right. He couldn't resist, drinking in the sweetness of her. One taste, and he knew she was okay.

An awkward cough from a nearby deputy made Gabe raise his mouth.

Gabe looked into Deb's green eyes. He traced his thumb down her reddened cheek slowly.

"Who did this to you?" he growled. "I'll pound him into the ground."

Deb grinned, not moving from his arms. "It's okay, I pretty much took care of that. I used a few other street moves my brother Rick taught me before I went to Afghanistan. Menken's not going to be walking steadily anytime soon. Injured balls and aching kidneys will do that to a guy. The concussion from having his head bounced off the floor a few times probably doesn't help much, either."

"Menken?" Gabe repeated. "Deputy Menken did this to you?" So, it was one of Tower's henchmen. "What happened?"

She filled Gabe in quickly. "I don't know if I interrupted a burglary or what. Menken hid in my hall closet, then he came out of my bedroom fighting," Deb said. "He must've been all over the apartment. He tried to steal my underwear, jewelry, and a pair of red high-heel shoes."

"So this was a burglary? A stalking? What?"

"I'm not sure. At first, I figured it had something to do with our investigation, but I don't know. Menken is one sick puppy. The underwear proves that. The cops told me he put one pair in his pocket." She shuddered.

Gabe gave her another hug.

She winced. "Careful, I'm sore. We had a knock-down, drag-out battle over the guns. I'm going to be black and blue all over."

"Guns?" Gabe held her gently in his arms. "Remind me not to piss you off, Lansing."

She smiled up at him. "Consider it done."

She winced again, and his gut clenched. "I should have been there."

"I'm tougher than I look."

Gabe leaned down for another kiss. "You shouldn't have to be."

"Montgomery," Tower snapped. "What the hell are you doing sucking face in here? This is a sheriff's office, not a bedroom."

Gabe stiffened. Keeping his arm around Deb, he slowly turned around. "Sheriff Tower, you don't seem to have control of your staff. Is Menken just the next dirty cop to be revealed on your payroll? Like your son?"

Tower flushed. "Leave my son out of it. And nothing's been proven. It's her word against his. Now, get out of here, before I arrest your girlfriend for assaulting a sheriff's deputy."

Fighting with everything inside of him not to lay Tower out, Gabe stiffened his spine and faced the sheriff he would never respect. "Menken's the one who broke into her apartment."

"So she says. She could have invited him in. Seems to me she's not too picky if she lets you paw her like that in a public place. We have names for those kinds of women."

Deb grabbed Gabe's arm before he could lunge at the sheriff. "Leave it. He's not worth the fight he's trying to provoke."

As they turned and pushed open the door, Tower yelled, "Pussy-whipped, Montgomery? Guess being a gimp has made you chicken."

Deb's hands tightened on Gabe's arm and she yanked him outside. "It's not important."

"God, I hate that bastard."

Gabe stormed down the stairs, barely remembering to emphasize his limp. Deb raced to keep up.

"Forget him," she whispered. "He's blowing smoke. He just arrived a few minutes ago and doesn't know about the recording."

Gabe stopped. "What recording?"

"I called 9-1-1, then left the line open. The dispatcher has the whole thing recorded. I might take risks, but I'm not stupid."

Hmm. Evidence had been disappearing a lot from the sheriff's office lately. At least, if he nabbed it today, they couldn't blame it on Wexler. He wasn't there.

Crap. Wexler.

He turned her in his arms. "Deb?"

She met his gaze and her eyes widened. "I'm not going to like what you have to say, am I?"

Her entire body had gone taut with tension.

No way to soften the truth. "Neil called. A body was found off I-25 between here and Colorado Springs."

Her face went gray. She shoved him away and wrapped her arms around her body. She shook her head, again and again. "No. It's not Ashley. It can't be."

Gabe's eyelids burned as he pulled Deb's rigid body close. She didn't break down. She didn't cry. She was in shock.

He held her tight, knowing all he could do was be there for her.

"Is it her? Is it Ashley?" Her voice was barely a whisper.

"I don't know, Deb. I just don't know."

The Warden leaned back in his chair and looked across his wide expanse of desk at the man standing there, flanked by two guards. "Niko, it has come to my attention that you are spending an inordinate amount of time talking with Ashley Lansing. This disturbs me. I don't have reason to suspect your motives. Do I?"

"No, sir." Niko's face was like stone, giving nothing away. "I am trying to keep her on track. Whenever she seems to slow down, I remind her of the stakes. Her performance usually improves immediately after."

The Warden picked a piece of lint from his sleeve. "I see. So your undue interest in her has nothing to do with her striking resemblance to another girl who caught your attention eight years ago?"

The Warden watched and caught the momentary flicker in Niko's eyes. So the man had a weakness. It could not be allowed to interfere with the plans.

"No, sir. She does resemble Shannon, but I would simply prefer not to lose another valuable asset. You gave me the job of controlling her, and I'm doing it. She's a brilliant programmer. Her death would not help us right now."

The Warden considered that. The man had a point, but sentiment could not be permitted in his team. "I see myself as a fair man, Niko. Floyd was beaten for talking too much to Ashley Lansing. It only seems fitting for you to share that fate. As a reminder that you are here to guard and control, no more. Step out of line, and the rules apply to you."

The Warden stood. "Gentlemen, see that your colleague gets the message very clearly."

The guards grabbed Niko's arms. Hatred flared in his eyes, but not the fear the Warden had hoped to see. How unfortunate.

"Take him away." The Warden stroked his chin. "And watch the girl. Closely. She needs to learn exactly who holds the key to her living . . . or dying."

Gabe pressed on the gas, mentally urging the slow-moving traffic forward. They'd gotten caught up in rush hour, though at least they were moving south, away from downtown, instead of north on I-25. Horns honked around them.

Inside, the car was silent.

He glanced over at Deb. Her face was hard, determined, stoic. The muscle just below her jaw throbbed, and her eyes were rimmed red, not from crying but from holding back. Agitation seemed to pulse from every pore, and her legs bounced in an unconscious release of nerves.

"Almost there."

She gave him a quick nod, and he exited the freeway to the crime scene location. Up ahead, yellow tape marred the scenic foothills of the Rocky Mountains. Several vehicles surrounded the cordoned-off area, including a crime scene investigation vehicle, its white boxy silhouette obvious.

Deb's knuckles whitened as they pulled up. Neil met the car.

"Ms. Lansing," he said politely. "We still don't have an identification."

They ducked under the barrier and Neil led them toward an area where several technicians processed the scene, one taking photographs, the other collecting evidence.

Deb didn't hesitate. She rushed toward the shallow grave. "Please, God, don't be Ashley."

Neil grabbed Deb by the arm. "You can't go any closer. You'll contaminate the scene. They're still marking evidence and shooting stills. Not to mention taking molds of shoe and tire prints. This is a huge area to process."

The winter grass shifted in the wind, but it couldn't hide the coppery stench. Deb gagged, all color leaching from her cheeks. "Then why did I come?"

Wexler held out a photo. "To start with, can you identify your sister from this?"

Deb grabbed the picture and viewed the nude body. "Where's the face? Her hair? Why is the photo cropped just below her neck like that? Let me see down there. How am I supposed to know if it's Ashley?"

"You don't want to view the body if you don't have to, Ms. Lansing. We haven't found her head. Or her hands," Neil muttered, barely able to look at her.

Deb put a hand to her mouth, but her cry of anguish still escaped.

Gabe took the picture from her and peered at the truncated body, twisted, mangled, and partially wrapped in a dirty, bloodstained sheet. Contusions everywhere. Barely recognizable, except . . . He looked closer. "Is that a tattoo on her ankle?"

"Yes," Neil replied. "The number eighty-eight."

Deb let out a choked sob and fell to her knees. "Ashley doesn't have a tattoo. She's terrified of needles. It's not her." She buried her head in her hands. "It's not Ashley."

Gabe knelt on the ground and pulled Deb into his arms. He met Neil's gaze.

The detective patted Deb's back, then turned away. "Thank you for coming. I'm glad it's not your sister. We'll work on identifying the girl. Her family needs to know."

"Eighty-eight." Deb suddenly stiffened. "Oh, no."

Her knees shook, but she rose to her feet. "I just realized who it is," Deb said, her voice choked. "It's the girl Mylo and Justin played *Point of Entry* with. Her name is Britney Saunders. She disappeared, but Mylo sent Gabe a photo."

Gabe yanked out his cell phone and started pressing buttons.

Deb moved closer to look at the images. "I remember Ashley mentioning the tattoo. She thought it was cool, but she just couldn't work up the courage."

A smiling face stared at Gabe from the screen. The picture of Britney with her family. Sure enough, when he zoomed in, those eights peeked out above her shoes. He held up the phone to Neil. "This is how she looked the day she disappeared. Red sweater, blue jeans, black jacket, and running shoes."

Neil called over one of the forensics team to bring him the evidence bags. With gloved hands, the tech held each item open in turn, accounting for every clothing article that had been dumped several hundred feet away from the body.

"Looks like we've got our ID," Neil said, his expression solemn. "Colorado Springs PD will notify her parents."

Gabe shook his head. He'd met Britney's folks. Nice people. They didn't deserve this. No one did. He glanced over at the body bag that held what was left of Britney Saunders. Whoever had decapitated that young girl was either sadistic or they had no soul.

"Detective Wexler, we found something." The evidence tech ran down the hill, another bag in his gloved hand.

"What is it?" Neil demanded.

"A cell phone. The glass is cracked, but it still has power."

Gabe crowded in. Very carefully, the tech removed the phone and, using a tiny probe, pressed the keys to reveal the owner.

"It's Mylo's," Gabe said, swallowing the guilt choking his throat. He looked over at Deb. "He tried to call me. Left me a message he was meeting Britney, and I had the damned phone off."

"It's not your fault—"

"Then whose is it?" Gabe said. How was he going to look himself in the mirror? That kid had believed in him.

Gabe played Neil and her Mylo's message.

"Would he have set this up?" the detective asked. "Would Mylo have killed Britney?"

"No way. You heard him. He was scared. He's the dorky kid you saw in that video clip I gave you. Can you see him attacking anyone?"

"Then where is he?" Deb scanned the surroundings. "I don't see any sign of him or his car."

Neil frowned. "From the scuffle that took place around the grave, I think his name should be added to the list of other kids who are missing."

"Get inside."

Sly shoved Ernie into Jeff Gasmerati's office. Ernie pitched to the ground, his injured leg giving way. His nose hit the hard wood and he doubled over in pain. God, how had Sly found him so fast?

Ernie rolled onto his back and looked up into Jeff's cold expression.

"Ernie, Ernie, Ernie. I thought you were family."

Oh God. This was it. They'd found out. He couldn't stop shaking. "P-please—"

"Shut up." Sly grabbed him by the collar and lifted him off the ground.

Ernie choked and Sly slammed him into a wooden chair at the edge of the room. He secured his wrists and feet, and Ernie felt warm liquid flowing down his pants leg.

Sly gave him a grin. "I figured you for a coward." He turned to Jeff. "He's ready, boss."

Jeff strode across the room, his Gucci suit crisp. He bent toward Ernie and wrinkled his nose. "You been hiding in a garbage can, Rattori?"

Ernie nodded. "Yes, sir."

"That's where I found him," Sly said, "after he went out the window of the hotel trying to avoid this discussion."

"Not very cooperative, Ernie." Jeff pulled out his revolver. An old Colt .45.

The cold barrel slid up Ernie's cheek to his temple and pressed against his head.

"I hear you've been talking, Ernie. A lot."

Ernie squeezed his eyes shut. *Don't tell him anything. Don't tell him anything. He doesn't know the truth or you'd be dead.*

The pressure increased against the side of his head.

The hammer clicked.

The gun didn't go off.

Jeff chuckled and Ernie opened his eyes. "See, Ernie, I'm an honorable man. I'm willing to give you a chance to make it up to me. You know things. You've worked for me a long time."

Ernie nodded. "Y-yes, sir."

"Hand me the machete, Sly," Jeff said with a smile. "And bring the torch."

The man carried it over. Jeff ran his thumb across the blade. Blood pooled on his finger. He dabbed the cut with a crisp, white handkerchief, then stuffed it in his pocket. "I'll ask you again. What did you tell Montgomery?"

Ernie swallowed.

Jeff made a tsking sound.

With a swish, he brought down the machete.

Ernie's hand fell to the ground.

Pain sliced up Ernie's arm. He screamed. Blood poured from the wound.

Sly loosely wrapped the stump in a towel.

Ernie's entire body screeched with pain. He lifted his head.

"You betrayed me." Jeff pressed down on the open wound.

Spots of light dance in front of Ernie's eyes. He wanted to pass out. He prayed to pass out.

"Tell me."

"Grace O'Sullivan," Ernie panted through gritted teeth. "R-Russians."

"See, wasn't that easy?" Jeff turned his back. "Finish it."

Sly lit the torch and grabbed Ernie's arm, then shook off the towel.

Seconds later, Ernie's world went black.

Ashley stared at the computer monitor, but she couldn't think. She squirmed in her seat. She needed a bathroom, and she hated asking. She hated they controlled everything she did.

One quick glance and she eyed her guardian of the day.

The redheaded guy. If she could have avoided going to the bathroom she would have. Finally, she broke down and asked. He gave her a smarmy grin and told her to wait.

An hour later, he dragged her into the hall.

If he tried to come in the bathroom with her, she'd castrate him. Maybe she could break the mirror, grab a shard, and really do it?

"Move it, Lansing." He shoved her in the back, making her stagger.

She scowled at him. "I could walk faster if you took me to the restroom when I first asked you."

"Oh, is the little baby going to wet her pants?" he taunted.

Ashley clenched her teeth and turned back around. The mirror idea was looking better and better all the time.

Mop boy—Floyd—was cleaning out one of the bathroom stalls when they got there.

"Hey, pansy, get out of the ladies' room. She's got to use it."

Floyd poked his head out of the stall, looked up at the guard. "Sure. Give me a sec." He slammed the toilet seat down, rustled around a little, then walked out. "I'm not done cleaning the whole bathroom yet," he said, shoving his mop bucket in front of the second stall, leaving the one he'd just cleaned as the only one available. "I'll be outside."

The red-haired guy followed, glanced in the stall, then stood back.

As Floyd passed Ashley, his eyes flicked in the direction of the stall, then he winked. "There should be enough toilet paper. If not, you'll find an extra roll on the tank."

Ashley struggled to control her mystified expression. What was that all about? How many boys her age discussed toilet paper with girls?

"Hurry up, blondie. I haven't got all day to be parading you around. You have work to do. I ain't gettin' the crap beat outta me like Niko, so move it." He shoved past her, almost knocking her into the wall.

"You are such a gentleman."

He grabbed her chin and yanked her face to within inches of his. "Watch it, sweetheart, or I'll show you just how wrong you are." With that, he pushed her away and shut the bathroom door.

Shuddering, Ashley entered the stall and looked around. Okay, that was weird. There was plenty of paper left on the roll. Why had Floyd mentioned the one on the tank?

She stilled. The paper wrap on the roll set on the tank had been disturbed. She grabbed it. Floyd had tucked a note inside. She clutched the paper tight and sat down to read it.

> *Mainframe: Grid C shuts down that corridor and C2 exit. Set timer for 10:30 p.m. Security bypass lasts thirty min. Get out. Get help. Justin and Dave going, too. Tomorrow night. 10:45 p.m. Don't fail.*

The main bathroom door slammed open. "What's taking you so long? Do I need to come in there?"

"Sorry, my time of the month. Takes a little longer," she lied, praying they wouldn't check. Oh God, what if they did?

"That's disgusting." The guard slammed the door.

Ashley memorized the note, tore it into pieces, did her business, then flushed the toilet. They would escape and bring back help.

Thanks, Mop Boy Floyd. She soaped her hands and rinsed them. *You'll have your justice for Fletcher. These bastards will pay for everything they've done.*

CHAPTER THIRTEEN

DEB STARED OUT THE FRONT OF THE SUV WHILE GABE DROVE back to Denver. She couldn't block the images of Britney's body from her mind, couldn't stop the ache low in her gut at the thought of what her sister could be going through. But Ashley was a fighter. Like everyone else in their family. She'd do whatever it took to survive. Deb had to believe that.

Her phone buzzed, and just the sound caused her heart to lurch. She glanced at the number, then pressed her hand against her stomach. "Hello, Father."

"What the hell is this BS that Ashley is missing?" Her father's voice boomed out of the phone, no speakerphone needed. "I left her in your care. How can she be missing from a military academy? They barely let cadets off the grounds."

She was afraid. She wanted to see me.

The truth hurt, so Deb settled for the facts.

"She was on her way back to the Academy. The police found the car she borrowed abandoned at a bus station."

"Well, they damn well better find her, too." Her father sounded every inch the general. "Tell me what happened!"

Deb forced her voice to remain steady. She recognized his rage and didn't want to push it. She might be called the Admiral, but, because of his volatile temper, he was often referred to as *The Bastard General*, among other, less polite things. The name fit.

She gave her father the facts, just the facts, including the discovery of Britney's body.

"This girl played some stupid game with the same kids as Ashley and now she's dead?" he barked. "What the hell is going on over there?"

Deb held the phone away from her ear. "Gabe suspects all four members of Ashley's team are missing."

"Who's Gabe? He the Homicide detective?"

How did she explain Gabe? What he'd meant to her efforts. Without him, the police would still think Ashley had run away. She chanced a glance his way. His hands gripped the steering wheel, knuckles white. He met her gaze, offering with his eyes to step in. She shook her head and shifted away from him, staring out the passenger-side window.

"He's someone . . . helping me with the investigation."

"I caught that hesitation. You two shacking up or something?"

She wished. The thought whizzed through her head and she cleared her throat. "No."

"Good. I don't need you screwing around while your sister's missing. You find her. You hear me?" Disdain laced every word.

"I'm doing the best I can, Father."

"Yeah, well, we both know that your best isn't always good enough."

The pain came too swift, like a dagger buried deep. She didn't need the reminder. Memories of the soldier crying out to her to bring the helicopter back peppered her mind. His name. Tate Tinsley. He'd had a mother, a father, two sisters, and a brother. A wife and three kids.

She couldn't speak, just gripped the phone tighter.

Gabe reached across the seat and grabbed her free hand. He threaded his fingers through hers and squeezed. Half of her wanted to pull away and curl up in a tiny ball. The other half wanted to hand him the phone.

She resisted both.

"The Jefferson County Sheriff's Office has a detective on the case." She struggled with each word. "They're working with the Colorado Springs Police Department. They're doing everything they can."

"They could always do more. I'm stuck in Afghanistan, Deborah. Can't get leave."

Code for something big was going on—more important than his family.

"You keep your mind on your business. Stay after them. Stay in their face. And don't screw up again."

Her father ended the call.

Deb lowered the phone from her ear, the cell slipping from her shaking hand.

She looked over at Gabe, then down at their entwined hands. He squeezed hers tight, and she let him. She just prayed he didn't ask her to explain.

Even out the corner of his eye, Gabe could see her taking her father's words inside. He would love to reach through the phone and pound some sense into the SOB. The guy seemed to relish cutting Deb down—and somehow Gabe knew it wasn't because the General was worried about Ashley.

Gnawing on how to comfort her, Gabe turned the corner and headed the SUV back to his place. What could he say? "Your father—"

"Don't," Deb said quietly. "Don't say anything." She stared down at her hands and didn't say a word. "He is what he is."

"You know he's wrong."

"Is he?" Deb leaned back in the seat and closed her eyes. "It's my fault she's out there. She's my responsibility and no one else's."

"We're going to find her." Even to himself the words sounded too pat. They were far from locating Ashley.

They both knew it. And neither wanted to admit it.

She tilted her head to the side and opened bloodshot eyes. The bruise had worsened, but that wasn't what worried Gabe. Fatigue and something more frightening marred her expression. She looked . . . defeated.

"I want to believe you, but sometimes things just don't work out. Sometimes the good guys don't win. Britney Saunders didn't win. Those missing kids, none of them won."

He couldn't argue with her. He took the last turn onto his street.

He slammed on the brakes and let out a loud curse.

Deb jerked up. "What's going on?"

Flashing lights and squad cars surrounded his house and the back of Sammy's Bar. Cops milled around everywhere.

"It's obviously not good." Gabe pulled his vehicle into one of the few empty spots. He twisted in his seat to face Deb. "Look, I don't know what happened here, but you don't have to stay. Why don't you take the SUV home?"

She unbuckled her seat belt. "Sure, you've stood beside me and you think I'm walking away now. Don't even suggest it."

"Whatever happened here isn't about you or Ashley," Gabe said, searching the crowd for some sign. Where were his brothers? God, if anything happened to Zach or Luke, he'd never forgive himself. Where was Hawk? His arm rested on the back of the seat. "This is about a job I need to finish. I must have been careless, and I don't want to endanger you."

She met his gaze head-on. "I took down a pervert cop today on my own. I think I can handle whatever comes my way. You can argue with me some more, or we can just get out of the car and see for ourselves."

Certain they were making a mistake, but knowing Deb's picture would likely be in the dictionary next to the word *stubborn*, he stepped out of his SUV. When his bum leg hit the asphalt, he landed wrong and fought against a groan. Most of the time, the thing held him up, but occasionally it would buckle. Three flights of stairs and hiking the hills today hadn't helped.

With the audience, he let himself stumble to stay in character, but in reality he searched in desperation through the crowd for his brothers and Hawk. Face after face, and he couldn't find them. A stone settled in the bit of his stomach.

Finally a tall, brown-haired head caught his attention. Luke.

Thank God.

Hawk followed behind him.

Luke raised a hand and raced over. "Where have you been? We've been trying to contact you." He grabbed Gabe and hugged him tight and hard.

Confused at the intensity of his brother's embrace, Gabe patted his brother's back and met Jazz's gaze over his brother's shoulder. "Sorry. Detective Wexler put my cell phone into evidence.

Long story. I picked up a new one. Same number. It's charging. What's wrong?"

Hawk raised an eyebrow as if the guy could read much more into the story than that. There was, but Gabe was used to Hawk's skepticism. Hawk didn't trust anything or anyone.

"Next time you get rid of your phone, tell someone," Luke said, his voice a bit rough. "We couldn't keep the news from Mom, she heard it on John's police radio. She's freaking, worried it's your hand hanging from the porch."

"What?" Deb gasped. "Is it—"

"Britney's," Gabe finished. "I hope not."

Deb shifted her stance and a spotlight bathed her face in harsh light. Gabe winced at the discoloration.

"What the hell?" Luke said. "What happened?" He whipped around to Gabe. "What's going on?"

"Some men don't know how to stay down." Deb pressed gently at the bruise. "I'm fine."

She shrugged in that way Gabe had come to appreciate on the one hand and be irritated by on the other. She shoved aside what made her uncomfortable and moved on, never letting anything fester.

Except Ashley, of course.

"We have more important things to deal with than a little bruise. Can you take us to the . . . hand?"

"Sure," Luke said, and led the four of them through the crowd to the front stoop of Gabe's house.

A bloody hand dangled from a long string fastened to the underside of the porch roof. Someone had positioned it exactly right. Anyone walking past would see it.

"Who would have done something like this?" Deb asked. "It's barbaric."

Gasmerati was getting desperate. Gabe glanced over at Deb. Menken's attack. His connection to Tower. He had to get Deb away from this place.

Just as he opened his mouth to suggest she leave, the medical examiner's vehicle pulled into the lot. A woman dressed in black pants and a black jacket exited the van, her entire body stiff as she glanced around at the bunch of looky-loos. She dismissed them and pulled out a large case. She opened it, snapped on latex gloves, and grabbed a camera.

"Leah Hanson," Luke said quietly. "The new coroner. A bit of controversy when she won the election out of nowhere. Now she's in charge of a bunch of guys who've been at the ME's office a couple of decades. Went over real well."

Gabe noticed that Hawk's interest had certainly piqued with the new arrival. He checked her out a little more thoroughly as she contorted to take several photos of the porch.

"Stop gawking," Gabe snapped. "She's examining a severed hand. No lusting allowed. That's just sick."

Hawk just shrugged. "Different strokes. You've got this covered. I'll be in the bar. Zach can't handle it on his own much longer." He sent Deb a pointed look. "You be careful. And let me know if you need me to send a less-than-subtle message to the guy who did that to your face."

He crossed the parking lot and vanished into the back of the bar.

"I'm afraid to ask," Deb said.

"He wasn't kidding," Gabe said. "Hawk's got a thing about women and children getting hit."

"Just like I have a thing for people cutting off heads . . . and hands?" Deb took a step toward the gruesome scene, but a deputy stopped her. She scowled at him and the guy blanched at her expression. Gabe had to admit she really could be fierce when she wanted to.

After Dr. Hanson finally grabbed an evidence bag and moved over to cut down the hand, a small growl sounded from Deb.

Her gaze had narrowed in fury. "Is it Britney's?"

"I can't tell. It's not very big, though."

Luke's cell rang. He glanced at the screen and grimaced. "I should let you take this." He scowled at Gabe. With a deep breath, Luke answered the call. "He's okay, Mom. Promise." He placed his hand over the mouthpiece and glared at Gabe. "You didn't make any friends by disappearing for several hours," he whispered and handed Gabe the phone.

"Gabriel Francis, where have you been?" His mother's voice choked around the question.

"I'm okay, Mom. Promise."

He fielded her questions as best he could. The last thing he'd wanted to do was to hurt her, but he'd known Luke and Jazz would be at risk. He'd had to do something.

He finally got off the phone. "She's upset."

"You think?" Luke taunted. "Who wouldn't be? By the way, Ernie called me earlier. Also upset you weren't around. I was his last resort. He said he needed help. He also said something weird. He told me to tell you to look in Idaho."

"What the hell is in Idaho?"

"I don't know. He sounded pretty out of it, babbling a bit. He just kept asking where you were. He sounded frantic, but he wouldn't stay on the line. That's all I got."

Gabe looked at the forensics techs taking samples on the porch. A chill pierced his nerves. *Ernie had called. He needed help.*

Which meant he wasn't in hiding.

Please don't let that hand be his.

"You got a minute, Gabe?" Neil Wexler walked over, his notebook in his hand.

"Yeah. You get around, Detective."

"And you're at the center of too much chaos . . . not to mention severed limbs. Any ideas on this? It may not be a homicide yet, but I get nervous when body parts show up."

"The girl?"

Deb and Luke leaned in to listen.

Neil shook his head. "It's not Britney's hand. Definitely a male, but a small guy. According to Dr. Hanson, it's pretty bruised. Some of the fingers look like they may have been broken and not reset correctly."

Gabe swore under his breath. "I think I know. Check AFIS for fingerprints for Ernest Rattori, aka Ernie the Rat. He's from around here, and he definitely has a file."

"You know him, don't you?" Neil asked. "I've seen him lurking around outside the bar a time or two."

Gabe scanned his surroundings, then lowered his voice. Ernie had gotten careless if Neil had noticed him. "He's a snitch."

The detective drummed his fingers on his pad. "What's going on with you, Gabe? Dealing with snitches and Gasmerati? Not a good idea."

John Garrison walked over. "Detective, may I have a word with Mr. Montgomery? Alone, please?"

Neil stared at the captain curiously, then nodded. He turned to Gabe. "I'll check out those prints."

"Thanks, Neil."

As soon as the detective left, Garrison moved in.

"Get out of sight now," Garrison said sharply. "Take Deb. I haven't said anything, but we found a John Doe in the landfill, so this is the third body in the last week with Gasmerati's calling card. But this time it was left at your house. I don't like you standing out here, exposed, with all these people milling around. Too easy for a sniper to take you out. We'll secure the premises."

"You heard him," Luke piled on. "Move it. We have some talking to do."

Both Garrison and Luke were right. He had to get Deb out of sight. Too many people had seen them together. He should have forced her to return to her apartment.

Like he could force her to do anything. She was one stubborn woman.

And he liked that about her. Too much.

Gabe grabbed her hand and they quickly rounded his house to the side entrance, followed closely by Luke. "I'm sorry about this, Deb. I've put you in a bad position. They may have seen you."

With a quick survey, Gabe slipped the key into the lock, pushed it open, then sent his brother a sidelong glance. "Look, I'm fine. But I need you to keep everyone else safe."

Deb gasped and pulled a gun from the side pocket of her pants. "Don't move!" she said sharply, peering into the darkened room.

Gabe whirled around, gun drawn.

A ghost stood in front of him, barely visible in the dark.

Steve Paretti. Former SWAT teammate. Former best friend. Lying, traitorous son of a bitch.

"You bastard. You're dead."

Gabe lunged across the room and slugged the dead man in the jaw.

Paretti didn't fight back.

Luke grabbed his brother's arms. "I get to kill him first. He shot at Jazz. She almost died because of him."

Nick Montgomery, U.S. Marshal, stepped out from the shadows. "You can't kill him, Luke. Paretti's in protective custody."

The hubbub across the street drew all the officers away. They wanted to check out the garish display on Montgomery's porch.

Sheriff Tower smiled. Exactly as planned. All was still and quiet in the detention center, except for that idiot Menken.

Two of Tower's loyal deputies accompanied Menken down the hall and into the holding area. Lights-out was hours ago. Security cameras had been deactivated. The town drunks had been given the night off from arrest for DUIs in an unfamiliar surge of leniency from the sheriff's department.

Ernie Rattori's hand had done its job. He'd have to thank Gasmerati sometime for agreeing to the donation.

Tower wanted no outside witnesses for what was to happen next. He and the deputies snapped on latex gloves and made their way down the corridor.

Menken was still yelling in his cell when the sound of their footsteps finally broke through to him. The deputy's face had turned purple with rage, but Tower could see the panic as well. The man's behavior fit perfectly into his plans.

"Good evening, Menken."

The deputy lunged against the bars. "You've kept me locked up in this stinkin' jail cell for hours and haven't even let me call anyone. Didn't even spring me, after all I've done for you. You owe me, Tower, and don't you forget it. Now, get me out of here."

"Certainly." Tower unlocked the cell door, then tugged a belt from behind his back, holding it in his gloved hand. It was Menken's belt, complete with fingerprints, and was already looped to use as a noose. "Officers, I believe our prisoner is depressed. How could we have forgotten to remove his belt? We shouldn't be so careless. Bad things can happen when a man is suicidal."

Menken howled and charged Tower. The other two officers grabbed him.

"Remember," Tower said. "No unusual bruises."

Menken started yelling and fighting, but the deputies took care of the rest.

Ten minutes later Tower stared at the hanging figure in disgust. How could the man have been so stupid? Jeopardizing everything.

"You'll get out of jail all right, Menken," he told the lifeless man. "Unfortunately, it will be in a body bag. Deputies, make sure there is no evidence left behind, then disappear. I'll reestablish the security loop, then join the others at Montgomery's house across the street."

Without a last glance, Tower walked out.

Only a few stars twinkled in the frame of the small one-foot-by-four-inch window. Ashley huddled under the thin wool blanket and buried her head into the pillow. She could fight during the day, she could be like Deb. But at night—at night everything changed.

The moon had moved past her window. Lights-out.

A few coughs echoed through the corridors. A few sobs. Some male; some female. They were all in hell, and in the dark, there seemed to be no way out.

She couldn't let it get to her. She had a plan. If only . . .

A metal door slammed closed. Footsteps pounded down the concrete hallways. One after the other. Closer and closer.

The boots thudded with the precision of a metronome.

Her chest tightened. *Please, go on. Please don't find out.*

They didn't slow. They passed her room.

A tear squeezed out of the corner of her eye.

Then, the footsteps paused.

The clang of keys. A metal door creaked open.

"No. I didn't do anything!" The boy's high-pitched yell identified him at once. Geeky, tall kid with Buddy Holly glasses. Math genius. No name.

"Please, don't take me."

Ashley buried her head under her pillow. Was it her fault?

A loud, horrible scream sounded down the hall.

The large metal door opened again.

The footsteps came back.

Ashley's pulse pounded in her ears. She squeezed her eyes tight.

The keys jangled and clinked.

Her door opened.

"Lansing," a low voice whispered. "You've been a very bad girl."

CHAPTER FOURTEEN

Gabe crossed his arms and faced the man who at one time he would have trusted with his life.

"Maybe I'd better take off," Deb said, backing to the door.

"Don't leave, Ms. Lansing," Nick Montgomery said.

He wore a U.S. Marshal badge, and while he appeared calm, Gabe could see the regret in his eyes.

"You've been seen with my brother," Nick continued. "It's not safe for you to leave alone until this operation has been closed, no matter how well you can defend yourself. Hopefully, Steve has the nails for Gasmerati's coffin. He came out of hiding to help."

"And to save Grace," Paretti added. "I won't let her take the fall for me."

Gabe looked at his former friend. He couldn't believe the man he'd known since childhood was standing here alive. He should be happy, but the betrayal cut too deep. "Why should I believe anything you say? You lied to me for years."

"Steve had to in order to survive," Nick cut in.

Gabe whirled on his brother. "And why should I trust you, brother?" He paced back and forth, thrusting his fingers through his hair. "You knew his betrayal was tearing me apart, Nick, but you hid the fact Paretti was alive—even from me."

"Just like you hid the fact you're running an undercover op in the bar from the whole family," Nick snapped. "You can't have it both ways, Gabe. Your secrets are okay, but no one else can have them? Life isn't like that. Sometimes tough decisions have to be made."

"So, I'm just supposed to throw my arms around this traitor and welcome him back into the good-guy fold? Not happening, bro."

Nick bit out a curse. "Steve is in WITSEC and he's my responsibility. He threw the protection agreement away to come here, because he refuses to stay hidden while the people he loves are threatened. I could lose my whole damn case against Jeff Gasmerati if something happens to Steve, so back off."

"People he loves? Right." Gabe lunged at Paretti and fisted his shirt at the collar. He brought them face-to-face. "Tell me the truth, asshole, are you a cop or a criminal?"

Paretti shoved Gabe back. "I'm a cop. I've always been a cop." He clenched his fists, then suddenly, his shoulders sagged. "I hoped you'd understand eventually. The world isn't always black and white when you're undercover. Sometimes you have to do borderline things to stay alive and try to keep others that way, too."

He looked over at Luke. "I'm sorry. I tried to keep you and Jazz out of it. Jeff wanted me to kill you."

"You shot at us, Paretti. You almost killed Jazz."

"I knew where I was aiming, Luke. I might not be a SWAT sniper, but I'm a close second to Jazz. I missed on purpose. I tried to scare you, to get you both to run. Or at least hide until things were safer. But you didn't run."

Steve glared at Gabe. "And you're not running, either. Rumor has it that Jeff Gasmerati is dead set on taking you out." Paretti gestured around the room. "Maybe all of you. What is it about Montgomerys and sheer stubborn stupidity? Why can't you behave like a normal family and just leave."

"Instead of telling us what we already know," Gabe snapped, "tell us something that will help end this." He clenched his fists. He wanted to punch something, anything.

Deb moved to Gabe's side. She didn't take his hand or even touch him, but just her presence cooled his temper a bit, like spring rain dousing a fire.

Paretti let out a sigh and looked over at Nick. Gabe's brother nodded. "We've broken this many rules," he said. "Go ahead."

"I spent a couple months in a coma after getting shot," Steve said. "And then time in recovery before I could start to piece together my memory. I knew something big was in the works before I was forced to disappear, but it's hard to get info while you're supposedly dead, especially when your bodyguard won't let you so much as pee without watching." He glared at Nick.

"You're still alive, aren't you?" Nick said.

"If that's what you call hiding out like a coward."

"I'm not hearing anything that will help my investigation . . . or find Deb's sister," Gabe snapped.

"Before I was shot in the head and shoved into WITSEC, I overheard bits and pieces about a couple of hush-hush construction projects Jeff Gasmerati had his hands on. Most having to do with tech and selling video games. Probably pirated, but I don't know. My cousin was definitely part geek as a kid. He wanted to be the next computer whiz, but he never had the smarts."

Deb clutched Gabe's arm and leaned forward. "Did you hear any names mentioned? How about *Point of Entry*?"

An energy pulsed from Deb. Gabe studied his ex-friend. Could Jeff Gasmerati be involved with Ashley's disappearance?

Paretti tapped his forehead as if forcing his mind to work. "I like *Point of Entry*. Good game," Steve said, his brow furrowing. "But not that I remember. Most of the communication came in from some guy Jeff called the Warden. Right before things went south, there was a flurry of calls that he kept very private."

Deb sagged in disappointment.

"Where were the construction projects?" Gabe asked.

"Winslow, Arizona, got a lot of mention. Another was in southern Nevada. The only other one I could place was the last job. In Idaho, Ohio, Ontario, or something. I can't remember for sure."

"Idaho?" Gabe looked at Luke. "Ernie mentioned Idaho. It can't be a coincidence."

"I'll start following the money trail, looking for dummy companies or manufacturing sites Jeff may be connected with," Luke offered.

"The FBI and the Marshals are both checking for the same things," Nick said. "If I can find out anything, I'll let you know."

A loud, shrill sound split the night.

Everyone, including Deb, had a gun in their hands instantly.

"What the hell is that?" Nick yelled.

Gabe raced to the kitchen and yanked open the back door. "Alarm. Sammy's is on fire. Call 9-1-1. Zach—Hawk!"

Gabe sprinted outside. Deb ran after him, while Luke picked up the phone.

Out of the corner of his eye, Gabe saw Nick close the door, shutting Paretti out of sight.

Licks of flames showed through the bar's kitchen windows. The four of them raced across the icy parking lot. Just as they got within fifteen feet of the door, the bar exploded.

The other kids called it the punishment room. It was next to the infirmary. Not a good sign. Ashley stared around the plain gray walls and at the long metal table in the middle of the room, complete with stirrups and straps to bind someone, if needed.

They'd shoved her into one of two chairs in the room and left her there. Her feet were cold on the concrete floor. She rubbed her arms and shivered.

She'd never been taken here. She squeezed her eyes shut. God, had they found out what she'd done?

Her leg bounced, but she knew better than to get up.

Footsteps sounded down the hallway, this time, not the rubber of combat boots, but the click of dress shoes.

She remembered that from the latest version of the game.

A loud click of metal sounded and the solid door swung open. Ashley's heart thudded against her chest. *Don't pass out. Don't pass out.*

She blinked. Deb wouldn't let these guys see her even break a sweat. Her sister was the most in-control person Ashley knew.

The Warden walked in, along with another man who didn't look much older than her college friends. Both of them wore hospital clothes over street garb, evidently for protection.

From bloodstains? Ashley wondered.

Behind them came two guards who pushed Niko into the room in front of them. His left eye was swollen, his face bruised and bloody, but he didn't look cowed. He wore the marks like badges of honor as he stood at the foot of the table.

The Warden took a file out and smiled. The grin made Ashley shiver.

Could blue eyes really be so dead that there appeared to be nothing behind them?

"So, Ashley Lansing, it seems we have a problem with your attitude. You insist on breaking the rules, no matter who gets hurt."

"This time, Niko paid the price for talking to you too much. I have his word it won't happen again. It better not. He's out of chances. He was supposed to be monitoring your keystrokes, instead of giving you a guided tour of our facilities."

A loud gulp sounded from her throat, and the man's grin widened.

"So, you realize what you did." He shook his head and clicked his tongue. "I don't know why our most intelligent guests have to be taught the most difficult lessons. If you had just followed the rules . . ."

He slapped his hand against the door and a guard walked in with a tray of instruments.

Ashley's eyes widened. Oh God. She'd watched enough television to know a scalpel when she saw it.

She swayed in her chair.

"Prepare her," the man barked.

She jumped to her feet and headfirst barreled toward the open door. She shoved the cart out of her way, but Niko's muscular arm grabbed her around the waist. She kicked and screamed, twisting her body against him, but he held her fast. His eyes indicating no emotion.

Tears streamed down her face. "No. Please, no!"

She yelled until her voice cracked, but it was no use. They stuffed a gag in her mouth and she bit around the sour-smelling cloth, nearly choking on it.

Moments later they wrestled her flat on the table, shackled her legs and arms to the frame, and cinched a leather strap across her waist.

The Warden and his medical assistant donned latex gloves and snapped the material against their skin. From behind him, an assistant walked in with a surgical gown.

The man slipped it on and a mask was tied over his mouth.

His ice-blue eyes stared down at her.

"Cut her gown off," he barked.

They removed her top, leaving her breasts bare. He stared down at her nearly naked body. A tear squeezed out of the corner of her eye. Oh God. She wanted to curl up and die.

The assistant draped a blue cloth over her top half, a small hole cut in the side, then held up a syringe.

The Warden lifted his hand. "We won't be needing anesthesia."

He leaned over her, holding a scalpel that glittered under the lights. "You tried to leave the assigned area, Miss Lansing. You met with your little friend with the mop again. You thought you weren't seen. Had you planned to meet him there? You two think you're so very smart, but you're actually only arrogant. Don't you know we are always watching? Floyd didn't escape and neither will you."

He stabbed the scalpel into her side.

Ashley lurched up from the table, trying to get away from the knife, the searing pain. Blood ran down the side of her ribs. The gag muffled her screams, but tears ran down her cheeks.

"Hold her," the man muttered. "I don't want any mistakes. I want this buried deep."

He pulled a small chip from inside a vial.

She couldn't see what he did with it, but a moment later he held up a long pair of forceps.

No! She couldn't yell around the gag, couldn't get any air. In her panic, her breathing started to grow laborious.

Her eyes grew wide.

The Warden bent over her and jammed a probe into the gash.

Her chest heaved and bile rose in her throat.

They ignored her.

If she threw up, she was going to die.

The Warden poked and pulled. She couldn't stop the tears running down her face.

Sour burning erupted from her throat and she lurched again.

One last painful tug. "Oh for God's sake. Take the gag out before she asphyxiates."

The Warden rubbed something on her skin and placed a bandage on her wound. Then he tore off his mask and pulled out a file.

He held out photos in front of Ashley.

Deb. Walking into a bar. Going to work. Unlocking her apartment door.

"We'll know your location every minute of every day, Ashley. You make one move out of line, you try to escape or hack our system one more time, and your sister dies." He snapped off his gloves.

She lay there, panting. In too much pain to talk.

"Niko, do you have any words of advice for your friend?"

Niko's words were cold and hard. "Don't screw with us, Ashley. Do your job, and you might get out of here alive. One more mistake, and your sister will never know what happened to you, if she's alive to still wonder."

"Ahhh, it's nice to know the real Niko is back."

The Warden turned to the other guards. "Take her to her room. If she resists . . ." He smiled. "Actually, I don't think she's stupid enough to do that again."

Shrapnel flew toward them. Deb hit the ground as the fiery wood and metal sliced through the air. She lifted her head cautiously. Secondary explosions tore through both the front and back of Sammy's Bar. The back of the building was engulfed.

She ran around front, her feet slipping on ice and chunked piles of snow. She fought for balance and moved on. Smoke and flames billowed out some of the windows. Patrons, some burned and bleeding, staggered out the doors or used chairs to break through the windows to escape.

"We've got to get everyone out," Gabe yelled. He looked around. "Zach and Hawk are still in there!"

God.

She skidded to a halt. The main explosion had centered in the rear kitchen, but the front had suffered substantial damage as well. Cops and patrons helped drag the injured through the smoke, coughing and choking. A few people had collapsed on the ground.

A man with blood streaming down his face was kneeling on the asphalt, calling 9-1-1. Deb recognized him. He usually sat at the bar. She knelt beside him, amid the debris and broken glass. "Are there others left inside?"

The guy's eyes had glazed over in shock, but he nodded. He keeled over and Deb caught him and laid him down, shoving some chunks of debris under his legs to elevate them.

Gabe, his brothers, and a few cops started back inside, though. Fire engine sirens screamed in the distance, but with all the alcohol inside, the place could light up any second.

They had to get everyone out. Fast.

Deb ran in the bar. Soot burned her eyes as she peered into the roiling clouds of smoke. A fire blazed hot in the corner, near the kitchen door. Hawk and Gabe held fire extinguishers dousing the flames. Nick and Luke were dragging wounded people out the door.

Zach Montgomery—she recognized him from movies and late-night television—carried a female deputy out the door.

Deb searched the rubble for signs of the injured.

She caught a glimpse of a polished black shoe. She shoved aside a fallen table. Hidden behind it, a cop lay flat, facedown. She knelt beside him, then turned him over. A huge gash marred the side of his head, blood covered his face.

His chest didn't move. He wasn't breathing.

She felt for his pulse. No heartbeat, either.

No time for CPR here. Flames were licking closer to this section. Quickly, Deb shoved aside another table so she could grab him under the shoulders and pull him out.

Gabe passed the extinguisher to Nick and ran to help her.

"We've got to get him out of here," she wheezed, the smoke already affecting her lungs. "He's not breathing."

Gabe picked up the cop's feet, and they raced out of the building.

She knelt beside him, placed her hands on his chest, and started CPR. "Gabe, get an ambulance here! Fast."

He called a number. "They're already on the way. You need help with him?"

"No, I got this," she said, meeting his gaze. "Go save your bar."

"A life is more important."

"Then see if anyone else is in there." She tilted the victim's head back. "This is what I do. Go."

She focused on reviving the cop. When her arms had nearly given out, the paramedics arrived and whisked him off in an ambulance. She hoped he'd make it.

Deb sat back on her heels, then stood, her knees a bit wobbly. She scanned the horrific scene, too much like the aftermath of an insurgent attack. Cops and ambulances everywhere. Burned and bloody people being shoved onto gurneys and into squad cars for trips to the hospital. She wiped the perspiration from her brow. The front of the bar smoldered now, the smoke no longer hellish black.

Gabe came over and stood beside her, his stance stiff and unyielding.

"Are your brother and Hawk okay?"

"Yeah. A little singed, but fine."

"What happened?"

"Gas explosion in the kitchen. Both the cooks and several patrons are dead. A lot more are injured, everything from broken bones and third-degree burns to shrapnel and glass lacerations. Some of them aren't going to make it."

He rubbed his face with his hands. “God, I never meant for this to happen.”

“Was it an accident?”

His regret-filled gaze rose to meet hers. “No, I really pissed somebody off.”

CHAPTER FIFTEEN

THE BREAKFAST SMELLS OF THE CAFETERIA DIDN'T MAKE Ashley's mouth water. They just made her sick. She shuffled through the double doors to the lunchroom. With every step, pain pierced her side. She couldn't see the wound or get to it. The Warden had cut her just far enough back to be out of reach.

She wanted to dig the chip out, but she'd been warned. They'd know if she tampered with it. She was tethered to this place now.

In fighting, she'd created a prison with another set of bars.

The doors swished behind her, but instead of low conversations of kids pretending to be normal, she entered into an eerie silence.

The lunchroom was quiet except for the sound of spoons and the occasional plastic cup on the hard plastic tables.

No one had forks or knives.

Ashley slowly made her way across the room. She could feel the tension rise. Several teens glared at her. This place was bad enough. Ashley's troublemaking had brought the full fury of the Warden down on them.

Any whispers. *Punishment.*

Any note-passing. *Punishment.*

A failure on a level. *Punishment.*

And Ashley had somehow become the leader of the trouble-makers.

By the time she reached Justin's table, she thought she might pass out. She sat across from him. He lowered his gaze, then made a quick scissor motion with his fingers.

She nodded. Yeah, they'd cut her.

The muscles in his jaw pulsed. His gaze narrowed on the guards, skewering them with hatred. They both knew she couldn't leave with them as planned. The chip set off the sensors and then acted as a tracking device.

He frowned, then sat back, sadness lining his face. He didn't want to leave without her. She placed her hand on the table, inches away from his, for just a moment.

She needed him to leave. Needed him to get to Deb.

They'd never touched or kissed since they'd been here, but he still made her feel things she'd never felt before.

She just wished he could hold her, make her feel safe for a second. None of them were safe, though.

She flicked her gaze to Dave, snagging his attention, then back at Justin. Shielding her hand from view, she briefly made a walking motion on the table, then rested her hand on the table and gave a quick thumbs-up. They would leave through the C2 exit tonight.

As long as she did her part.

She'd already programmed the C grid to shut off. The timing had to be perfect. This was their one chance.

The redheaded guard slammed his hand down on the table between them. Then he grinned and gripped his baton. He slapped the wood against his palm and gave them all knowing glances.

He didn't have to say a word. He'd love to beat the crap out of them.

Everyone lowered their gazes.

The spoons stilled. The room had gone silent, the tension unbearable.

After several minutes, he walked back to his post. Utensils scraped against the plates again.

The moment the guy turned his back, Floyd, sitting at the table opposite Ashley, winked.

She had to wonder if, after his brother's murder, he'd gone a little crazy. Or if he just didn't care anymore.

Floyd had been here longer than almost anyone. He knew this place. He was the one who had warned her that the Warden had cops and FBI on the payroll, that once they got out, they had to find someone they trusted.

Justin had promised her he would find Deb—and no one else.

Ashley shifted in her chair. The movement pulled at her side and she winced. Floyd gave a slight cough. She looked at him, eyes wide. What was he doing?

He lowered his head and she followed the movement to his hands.

His finger barely stirred, but he tapped out a message in Morse code. *Mail sent yesterday.*

The package to her sister.

He knew? If Floyd knew, who else?

Panic made her cheeks flush.

OK, he tapped out.

But would her sister understand the message? Ashley could only pray. If Justin and Dave didn't make it . . . that package might be their only hope.

A few familiar guards entered the room, this time bearing automatic weapons.

The room went silent again.

Whispers had circulated since she'd arrived that something huge was going down. Guards with guns. It didn't look like it was going to be a lot of fun.

Ashley swallowed hard.

If the Warden was turning this place into an armed camp, maybe she'd been wrong. Maybe it would be better if her sister stayed away.

The charred shell of Sammy's Bar looked even worse in the light of day. The stench of soaking, burned debris filling the parking lot made Deb's stomach roil. This was Denver, Colorado, not a war zone, and yet, it looked like a drone had hit the place.

A shiver skittered down her back just before a warm hand touched her shoulder. "It's a mess, isn't it?" Gabe's warm breath teased her ear.

"You can rebuild," she said.

"Maybe."

She looked over her shoulder at him, at his fatigue-filled eyes, at the hurt just beneath the surface. She saw depths in Gabe that she hadn't expected. Especially after last night.

She faced him. "How are you doing?"

"No one ever asks me that." He touched her cheek. "Not bad, except I wish we hadn't fallen asleep in that hotel room. Not how I'd planned to spend our first night in the same bed."

She stared at the collar peeking over the neck of his sweater. "Me, either, but it was the best night's sleep I've had in a long time."

Gabe leaned close, his presence seducing her in the middle of disaster. "Too bad it took a fire and a break-in to force us into what we both want. Want to try again? Soon? Like tonight?"

God, he was charming. They hadn't spent the night in that hotel for a quick—or long—night of hot, wet, slow kisses. They went there because his place reeked of smoke; hers was a disaster, but more importantly, too many people knew where they lived.

He wouldn't take a chance with her safety. He'd been betrayed, but he still fought . . . for her sister and for his family. She knew if she needed this man he would be there. She couldn't say that about everyone.

Certainly not her father.

She couldn't even say that about herself. Not after what had happened in Afghanistan.

A comforting warmth emanated from him. Just a few more inches and he would kiss her. She placed her hand just over his heart. She wet her lips and a small groan purred in his chest.

"Am I interrupting?" Neil Wexler asked.

Deb started and sprang back.

"Great timing, Detective," Gabe muttered.

A small smile crossed the detective's exhausted face. Neil shook his head. "Just couldn't resist. Sorry."

He nodded at the arson investigator who knelt beside the gas line leading to the kitchen. "The fire department called it a very efficient attack. The perp used acid to eat through the gas lines, here and inside. As soon as the gas hit the air near the grill, the place went up. Simple, but effective."

"They knew exactly what they were doing," Deb said quietly. Gabe was in his own small war, and right now, the bad guys were winning.

"The explosion was definitely intentional," Neil said, thumbing through his notepad, "though it could have been chalked up to a gas leak if the section of pipe out back hadn't remained relatively intact. The regularity of the acid damage on the copper negates that." With a speculative look, Neil studied Gabe. "Exactly how many enemies do you have?"

Gabe let out a long, slow breath. "All former cops have enemies. Nature of the job, right?"

"You seem to have more than your share of people who want to kill you. Two incidents an hour apart. These are serious warnings, Gabe. We might want to put you into protective—"

"No way." Gabe ignored Neil and looked at Deb. "I'm not disappearing."

"Maybe you should . . ." Deb's voice trailed off when a car screeched into the parking lot. She tensed until John Garrison stepped out of the vehicle.

Anna Montgomery followed quickly. The wind whipped her coat open. She didn't seem to care, she just jumped out of the car and ran to Gabe.

She clasped him close, clinging to him, her arms firm and tight. Gabe hugged her back and closed his eyes for a moment.

Unconditional love. Deb could barely remember the feeling.

"I wanted to come last night, but John made me wait." She glared at the man to her side, then stepped back, looked Gabe over, then hugged him again. "I swear, the stress of mothering you boys is going to be the death of me. Can't you all settle down and be accountants or something? Work behind a desk and give me grandchildren to deal with instead of fear for your lives?"

Without hesitation she pulled Deb into a fierce hug. "You were wonderful last night, young lady. Saving that man who stopped breathing. Did you know he has two kids and a pregnant wife? She'd have been lost without him. You did a very good thing. You should be proud."

Anna touched Deb's face gently. "You're a hero."

Deb's heart constricted. Not having a mother much of her teen years, this kind of tenderness stunned her. This woman barely knew her and she'd just opened her heart.

A few blinks and Deb cleared her throat. "I'm glad he's all right. I wasn't sure when the ambulance took him away what would happen. It was relief when I called last night that he was being released today."

"You called." Anna grabbed her hands and squeezed them. "Do you know how rare that kind of caring is? Well I do."

She looked over at Gabe. "She's a keeper, Gabriel."

Anna threaded her arm through Deb's. "I was a law enforcement officer's wife for a long time, and now the new man in my life—not to mention my sons—risk their lives every day. That man's wife lived in dread of the phone call she received yesterday. You made sure she didn't have to accept that folded flag. That means a great deal to me. I won't forget it."

"I . . . I don't know what to say."

"Which makes me like you all the more." Anna grabbed one of Gabe's hands and squeezed. "This one can't seem to stay out of trouble. I'm glad you've been around to help. You know, I've never officially thanked you for getting Gabe to the hospital that night." A dark cloud fell across Anna's expression. "We almost lost him that day. Thank you for being there."

Anna hugged Deb again, and a lonely place inside her cracked open. Her defenses were almost gone. Gabe's mother had torn them apart and shredded them piece by piece.

Deb had missed this kind of caring since her mother died. She'd had to do the nurturing. For her little sister, and her brothers.

Her father had turned her away.

No one had ever just hugged her like Anna Montgomery.

Deb hardly knew what to say.

"Thank you," she whispered, just letting Anna hold her, the wall around her heart crumbling to rubble.

Ashley sat in front of the computer monitor, staring at several all-too-familiar algorithms. "Oh my God," she whispered.

The worst mistake she'd ever made, and she was seeing its results. She and Justin hadn't really been black hats, hacking into computers for crime and profit. They'd been more gray hats. Not quite altruistic in their breach of the NSA's database, but they hadn't exactly wanted to bring down the free world, either.

She recognized these algorithms. She knew the back doors and the traps, even though these were a bit more intricate. Cyber-geeks had their own signature. She had hers; the NSA security team had theirs.

P.O.E. was the means for the Warden and his cronies to break into the NSA computer system. God knew what else.

It had just become even more important than ever for Justin and Dave to escape. She just prayed they were both on track.

Hoping Niko didn't notice, she leaned forward and peered down the row of gamers until she saw Justin.

He sat at his station, twisting and turning the game controller in his hands, playing the newest version of P.O.E.

Version *VIII* was a huge leap. Graphics, story, challenges. And now, Ashley knew, once a player reached Level 88, the downloaded bonus game would provide a way for black hats to root through national security systems. All on the skills of those who had a gift for numbers and encryption.

Justin had those gifts. She couldn't take her eyes off the boy whose intelligence had seduced her and whose warm kisses made her feel special. She never wanted to forget those feelings.

He met her gaze, raised his fingers to his lips, and turned back to the monitor. A few minutes into his next mission, his joy dissolved into confusion, then flashed to fear as comprehension dawned.

Oh God. He'd recognized the truth behind the game. He dropped the controller to his lap and lowered his gaze.

He wasn't quick enough.

The red-haired guard strolled over. "Congratulations, Mr. Connell. Come with me. We're transferring you to the primary testing room to complete this mission."

Just as they'd planned, except now she and Justin both knew the real stakes of the escape. Billions of dollars, so many lives. This was bigger than three sixteen-year-old kids.

God, Deb, what have I gotten myself into?

It was more important than ever that Dave get past Level 88, too. He and Justin needed to be in the same location or their plan might fail.

She squinted at Dave. His brow was furrowed; his entire body tensed and he looked panicked.

This was not good. Maybe she could set another time bomb so the grid to this room would blink off as well. It was risky, but Ashley doubted she could hide what she'd done more than a few hours anyway.

Floyd had warned her of as much.

"They check the security logs and keystrokes every night. Anything unusual, they'll know it," he'd said.

With shaking hands, Ashley brought up a window and dove into the security codes. Fear drove her as she slid past one wall after another. Her layers ran deep. The timing had to be perfect.

"Ashley."

She jumped.

Not Niko. The sleazy voice of the red-haired man whispered in her ear. "This isn't the section of code the Warden assigned to you. What are you doing?" His voice was low, menacing, and horrifyingly pleased to have caught her.

She swallowed. She hit a button and the window disappeared, but she knew it was too late. She closed her eyes. Had she just killed them all?

"This is the section that came up," she protested. "I've had a few glitches on my computer today, but my assignment is nearly done. See?"

She pulled up the window she'd been working on as slowly as she could get away with.

The redheaded man turned off her monitor. "Go to the Warden's office. He'll deal with you." The man smiled, his eyes much too eager. "Or, maybe I'll be lucky and he'll turn you over to me."

The sheriff's official car screamed into the Sammy's parking lot and pulled up next to Garrison's. Great, just what they needed. Gabe had dealt more with the sheriff in the last few days than in his entire tenure as a deputy.

He preferred the latter.

Sheriff Tower threw open the door and slammed it behind him. He hitched his hands in his back pockets and a sneer creased his face. "Well, isn't this a nice cozy group? I have some questions for the bunch of you."

John Garrison stepped in front of Anna, and Gabe did the same with Deb.

Deb elbowed Gabe. "I don't need your protection," she hissed under her breath.

Anna pinched John's arm. "What she said." She winked at Deb.

"Sheriff Tower," Garrison said, by way of greeting, though his voice sounded cool. "What brings you here?"

The captain might be sleeping with Gabe's mother, but the guy was stand-up. He didn't back down from the sheriff. Gabe had to respect that. He'd just ignore that whole sleeping in the same bed idea.

"My town is going to hell and I want some answers, Captain." Tower's sharp gaze narrowed at Gabe. "Do you have any for me, *Deputy*?"

"No longer wear the badge, sir." Gabe tapped his leg.

"So the captain told me." Tower looked around at the destruction. "The ME's office identified Ernie Rattori as the former owner of the hand left on your front porch. Fingerprint match."

Gabe's stomach sank. He'd suspected, but he'd hoped the hand wasn't Ernie's.

"What have you got to say about that, Wexler? Why did I get a call from the press wanting a confirmation of the story when my own detective didn't see fit to inform me?"

"I've been working the explosion this morning, sir," Neil said through clenched teeth.

"Rattori was a snitch the vice squad used on occasion," Tower said, as if Wexler hadn't even spoken. "A known informer. You are no longer on the force, Montgomery, yet he showed up to talk to you several times. Wexler, you've been less than forthcoming with your investigations. If I were a suspicious man, I'd think you were working together. Now, do you want to tell me what's going on?"

Gabe shrugged. "I wish I could help, Sheriff. With the struggling economy, I've got beggars coming to the back of the bar all the time asking for handouts." Gabe shrugged. "I gave him a meal a few times."

"I thought you might deny any involvement. You've spared yourself an interrogation. For the moment."

Two more sheriff's cars pulled into the parking lot. Four deputies exited. Two with smiles, two looking as if they'd just downed a bad batch of wings.

Gabe's urge to slip his hand to his weapon nearly overcame him. "What's going on?"

One deputy pulled out his handcuffs. "Detective Wexler?"

The guy gulped. "I'm sorry, sir. I have to arrest you for conspiracy and theft of official evidence."

Neil stood, stoic, while the deputy's voice shook. The officer pulled Neil's hands behind his back. His jaw jerked, but he said nothing.

"This is crazy, Tower." Gabe stepped forward, but two of Tower's musketeers placed their hands on their weapons.

"Take him away."

The deputy read Neil his rights. He looked over at Gabe. "I didn't do this."

"I know." Gabe was certain, but innocent men went to jail. Especially when the brass wanted you to, and Tower looked much too confident.

"I'll call your rep," John promised.

"More important business first," Neil said. "Call my wife. Tell her I love her . . . and I miss her."

The deputy pushed Neil into the vehicle. Tower placed his hand on his weapon and faced Gabe. "If I discover you're in collusion with the detective, I won't hesitate to arrest you. I suggest you stay out of trouble, Montgomery."

The sheriff turned on John Garrison. "Meet me in my office first thing tomorrow morning, Captain. We'll be having a discussion about how you run your division . . . and exactly how little control you have over your staff . . . and ex-staff. I believe it's time for some changes."

Sheriff Tower sauntered away.

"He's a piece of work," Deb said. "What are you going to do?"

"Gabe's not doing a damn thing but continuing his investigation," John said. "I'll take care of Neil. Tower just overplayed his hand. I have friends, too. In the Justice Department."

"He's been planning this," Deb said.

"You're right." Gabe surveyed the scorched parking lot and what remained of the bar. "What I don't get is why, along with the Gasmerati evidence, they accused Neil of taking the information on Shannon Devlin's case. It doesn't make sense. Tower had plenty of cases to choose from."

"Unless he's planning to pull you into his web," Anna said, her eyes worried.

Gabe touched her cheek. "I'll be fine."

She shook her head. "No, you won't. Not until this is over."

His mother was right. As always. "We do know one thing," Gabe said. "It won't hold water in a court of law, but I think we just got our proof that Tower is in bed with Jeff Gasmerati."

The cold January air whipped from off the Rockies and sent a shiver through Deb. Gabe followed her up the stairs to her apartment, though this time they went more slowly in deference to his leg. "I'll just change clothes."

"Pack for more than one day," Gabe said, his hand hovering over the holster sitting under his jacket. "Until this is over, I don't want us staying in one place."

When she reached the landing, Deb paused. A package rested on her doorstep. "Weird. I didn't order anything. Especially overnight delivery. That's not in the budget."

"Step away from the package," Gabe ordered sharply. He set down the duffel he'd packed before leaving his house, unzipped it, pulled out a small leather kit and a cotton swab. Gently he swiped the outside of the package, then placed the swab into a test tube. He shook it.

The liquid turned green.

"No explosive residue. But that doesn't mean it's not rigged—"

"You always carry an explosive detection kit around with you?"

"After last night, I carry a lot of things on me that I never did before." He handed her the padded envelope.

"Oh my God!" Deb stared at the address label. "Ashley." Her knees shook. She threw her arms around Gabe. "She's alive!"

"How do you know?" He took the package from her and studied the address label. "From Intelligent Solutions?"

"No, no. Look who it's addressed to." Deb pointed to her name. *Admiral Deborah Lansing.* "No one but the family uses that nickname. She's alive."

Deb couldn't stop grinning. She unlocked the door, hurried across the room, and checked her answering machine. "No messages. Ashley didn't call." Deb scrubbed her hands over her face. "But, somehow, she sent me a message."

Her legs couldn't hold her any longer. She collapsed on the couch, nearly overwhelmed with relief.

"Hopefully there's a note or something telling us where she is." Gabe pulled out a pair of latex gloves from his duffel and sat down beside her. She leaned forward watching his every move. Her leg bounced with urgency. Was it almost over? Was this the key to finding Ashley?

Carefully, Gabe opened the flap and pulled out a box. "*Point of Entry.*"

"There's got to be more," Deb said.

Gabe opened the packing and peered inside. "Nothing."

"No note?" Deb's body sagged with disappointment, like she'd plummeted from a plane with no parachute. "There's got to be something."

For several minutes they carefully scanned every inch of the package. Deb shook her head. "Nothing on the outside or the inside."

Gabe flipped the case over. "Intelligent Interactive makes the game. But that's not who sent the game. What is your sister trying to tell us?" Gabe slipped his new phone from his pocket and hit the Speaker button.

"Hey, little brother, I'm still working on Dad's files," Luke said. "Any new crisis since last night?"

"Just another crazy mystery. Deb just received a package from Ashley."

"What the hell?" Luke asked. "Where is she? Where's she been?"

"It's not that obvious," Gabe said, handing Deb the phone. "You explain it, *Admiral.*"

Deb could barely speak, but she explained Ashley's hidden message.

"That's one smart sister you have," Luke said quietly.

He didn't add what Deb knew. That if Ashley had gone to these lengths and been unable to include a note, she was also in serious trouble. While part of Deb wanted to shout for joy that Ashley was alive, part of her heart twisted in agony.

No telling what her sister was going through, and they were no closer to finding her.

"She's special," Deb said, her voice choked. "We don't know why or how, but I'm looking at *Point of Entry VIII* right now."

Luke didn't speak for several seconds. "You can't be," he said. "*Point of Entry VIII* isn't even out for reviews yet. Super top secret."

"Which means Ashley is somewhere that has access to the game." Gabe fingered the box. "Should we try to play it or at least open it? See if she managed to send us any other message inside?"

"Has it been tampered with?" Luke asked.

"No. It's still sealed."

"Get Forensics to test it first. Unless you've already contaminated the evidence."

"I'm not a rookie." Gabe scowled at the phone. "I'm wearing gloves, but who am I supposed to trust?"

"Good point. I'll keep investigating things from my end," Luke said.

"And I'm phoning the FBI. I don't trust anyone local," Gabe said.

Deb gripped his arm. He gave her a tender smile and for the first time in what felt like forever, hope rekindled.

"Don't let anyone know you have that game," Luke warned. "Serious gamers are crazy. They'd kill to get hold of it ahead of release date."

"I hope you're exaggerating. I'm on enough hit lists now," Gabe said.

"Don't go crazy and do this alone, little brother. We can help."

"I know." Gabe clicked off the phone. He looked at the return address. "Intelligent Solutions. Reno, Nevada. It's not quite the same name as the company that creates P.O.E. Maybe a subsidiary?"

"Everything points back to that game," Deb said. "Even the first case with Shannon and her friends."

"There's some kind of connection. My father knew it." Bleakness filled his eyes. "We have to go back to the beginning. Start over with the first murder we know of—Shannon Devlin. She had a *Point of Entry, Version I* game case in her backpack when she died. Her teammate had the POE license plate on his car.

"What do you have in mind, Gabe?"

He started pressing buttons on his phone. "We need to talk to Shannon's parents in Angel Fire. I'm going to ask Zach to fly us there tomorrow."

"What about your investigation?"

"I have to trust Garrison to handle it. My family knows the danger. They're hunkered down. Your sister has called out for help. I'm not turning my back on her. Or you."

Tower hadn't met with Jeff Gasmerati one-on-one in the last eight years. The sheriff glanced at his holster and weapon lying on the table across the room. He didn't like standing in the room with a killer and no gun at his side.

The head of the crime family wore Gucci and his eyes penetrated like a dagger. Jeff drummed his perfectly trimmed nails on his desk until the door opened. A hulking man entered the room.

"The latest surveillance on Lansing's apartment. Menken pulled it off," Sly said.

"He served his purpose," Tower muttered.

Jeff scanned the paper. "Gabe Montgomery is getting too close." His gaze met Tower's. "They're headed to Angel Fire. To Shannon Devlin's parents' house. The one you shot in the bus terminal.

“I’m done with this,” Gasmerati growled to both Tower and Sly. “I want the whole thing to go away. Someone will take the fall. And it won’t be me.”

Tower shivered at the low, cold words, wishing he’d never heard them. “Neil Wexler will go to prison for the stolen evidence. Case closed.”

“It’s not enough. The Montgomerys won’t stop. The snitch’s hand didn’t work. Neither did the bomb. They just keep coming.”

“You’re lucky Patrick Montgomery died five years ago,” Tower said. “He’d have blown the business open.”

“True,” Jeff said. “Sometimes fate smiles. His death was a gift. Wish I knew who did it.” Jeff retrieved a Cuban cigar from its case and rolled it between his fingertips. “Now, what do we do about his sons?”

Tower shook his head. “You want me to take out the Montgomerys? All of them? They’re hard to kill.”

“A sniper’s bullet can rarely be stopped. Think about it, Tower.”

The sheriff blinked. It had been eight years since he’d picked up his rifle. His eyes were going, his reflexes weren’t what they used to be.

“You still have the stomach to be sheriff, don’t you?”

Tower stayed silent a moment too long.

“I see.” Jeff pressed a few buttons on his phone. “Take out your cell and check your messages. I’ve sent you a picture.”

A moment later, a message popped up on Tower’s phone. He tapped the screen and his knees shook. His daughter leaving her apartment building. Then a photo of her walking into her office. Another of her visiting the corner market.

She hadn’t spoken to him since she’d left home at eighteen.

She hated him. She'd sensed the change in him, when he'd thrown in with the mob. In her eyes, he'd fallen off his pedestal. But she was Tower's only remaining child and he still loved her.

Gasmerati knew it.

Tower was trapped.

"I understand," he said. "I'll make sure the Montgomerys are off the case. No matter what it takes."

CHAPTER SIXTEEN

DEB PULLED THE HOOD ACROSS HER FACE AND SKULKED JUST inside the entrance to the hotel behind a large decorative urn. She scanned the deserted lobby for anything out of the ordinary. They'd agreed not to stay in the same place two nights in a row.

This wasn't a bad spot to hole up.

After what seemed like forever, the sleepy clerk gave Gabe a key card. He ignored Deb and headed toward the elevator.

The clerk yawned and disappeared behind a door.

Deb hurried to the elevators, head bowed. Just in case.

Gabe waited for her. The elevator doors slipped open and they stepped inside.

A bit of her tension left her.

"Zach will have the plane ready at first light." He punched the fourth floor.

"I just hope they can give us a lead."

"Shannon was killed for a reason," Gabe said. "Maybe she wrote down a name or a place. Something we can trace."

Deb had to believe someone, somewhere knew where her sister was. She and Gabe just had to find it.

Once at their room, he slipped the card into the lock. The door creaked open to reveal a much different room from the motel last night. "Your brother knows how to pick them," Deb said, checking the sitting area, then pulling back the curtains. Denver's city lights twinkled in the darkness like a glowing carpet.

"Yeah, he came through. I don't want to know how." He thumbed through the IDs Zach had generated. His brother had simply handed over several sets without being asked. They could sign in as a different couple as the need came up—as long as they went someplace where they wouldn't be recognized. Having a wealthy ex-spy, ex-movie star around was coming in handy.

"Your family is . . ." She didn't know quite how to describe them. ". . . resourceful." Actually, they were amazing. Their own little commando unit. They might straddle the gray on occasion, but Deb would never doubt their loyalty . . . or their commitment to doing what was right.

Each member of Gabe's family seemed to have justice carved on their soul. More importantly, they really stuck together.

The Lansings had cracked some in adversity. Her heart ached.

"My brothers have their moments." Gabe scowled. "Except Nick. He gets a huge mark for the stunt he pulled."

"You probably don't want to hear this, but he was living up to the deal he made when he took his job. It requires secrecy. You did the same thing when you started pretending to be a broken-down ex-cop bartender." She walked over to the mini fridge and opened it, scanning the offerings. "Want a soda or a beer? Pretzels, maybe?"

"Don't confuse me with facts, Deb. And yeah. Pretzels and a beer would be great right now. Just one, though. Can't afford not to think."

He sank into the couch. "I still want to be pissed at Nick. For a while anyway."

She grabbed two cans, then sat beside Gabe and passed one over.

They cracked them open. While she ripped the pretzel bag, he took a long, slow swig from his beer. "What's this really about?"

"Nick hid the truth. Steve Paretti was my best friend. When I realized he'd played me all along, I started doubting myself. How was I supposed to be a cop if I could let someone fool me like that? All my life."

"This isn't just about Steve," Deb said. "I've been around you long enough to know there's something a lot bigger that happened the night Shannon Devlin died. You've kept it from your brothers, but it's slipping out, Gabe. They see it. So do I."

He didn't say a word for a few moments.

"It's not relevant to our investigation."

"Okay," she said lightly, "if you say so." She settled down in her seat and chewed on another pretzel.

Echoes of cars zooming past filtered through the hotel's windows. A siren screamed from several streets over.

Deb watched Gabe warring with himself.

She got that. When you said something aloud it became much more real.

Finally Gabe dropped his head back against the couch. "Why do you have to be so damned stubborn? Look, I hated my dad that night. Not the pissed-off-because-I-was-grounded-most-of-my-senior-year kind of hate, but unadulterated, gut-wrenching disgust. He'd always been my hero, and I'd just discovered he'd done something that could destroy my mom." Gabe looked at Deb. "You've met my mother. She's formidable, but devoted as the day is long. She loves unconditionally. How could he betray her?"

Deb shifted to the side to see Gabe more easily. "My relationship with my dad's not any better. That's not a secret from our phone conversation. Four-star Army general. As rigid as they come." She sighed. "Before my mother's death, he showed more affection. He adored her. He just assumed she'd always be there to take care of things while he saved the world. Her death rocked him to the core."

"He changed after that?" Gabe reached out and held Deb's hand. He stroked her palm and her heartbeat quickened in response.

"Oh, yeah. The transition was hard on all of us. My brothers and sister needed him. We were just kids. We wanted to cling to him, but it was like he hated to come home. The longer and more dangerous the deployment, the better. My aunt raised us most of the time when he was deployed, although I took responsibility for Ashley."

"How old were you?"

"Fourteen. She was five."

"You were awfully young."

"I was old enough to understand Ashley needed love. Love that my father wouldn't give. Besides, how could I complain? I saw the news. Saw the violence in the countries where he was stationed. To me, he was the bravest man on earth. He'd come home in his uniform, with that duffel bag slung over his back. I thought my father was a hero. We all thought it."

Gabe stared at her, his eyes questioning.

"He was the reason my brothers and I signed up."

"I hear a 'but' coming on . . ."

"I wanted to fly. I wanted to be a hero like my father. I loved helicopters, and doing search and rescue, but I didn't make a secret of the direction I wanted my career to go. I wanted to be a fighter pilot from the beginning."

"Jets? I could see you strapped in."

She sat the beer on the table and rubbed her eyes. "The speed scared me a little, but it was also exhilarating. Lansings aren't allowed to show fear . . . or cry . . . or wimp out on anything."

"I got that impression from your phone call. So what happened that you're now flying helicopters?"

Deb shook her head to dispel the memories. "I was home one Christmas. I thought for sure I'd made the cut for fighter training. I wanted to tell my father so I went toward his study. The General was on the phone talking to the detailer. He made sure I didn't get my shot at the jets. He *arranged* for me to get assigned to helicopter training. He manipulated the system, used his influence, called in favors . . . and changed my career."

Gabe looked over at her. "Maybe he wanted to protect you?"

An old anger burned in Deb's belly. "I didn't need his protection. I needed his support. When my brother went into black ops, he didn't stop him. When the other decided on Special Forces, he was proud."

She couldn't sit still. The memories swirled inside of her. She rose from the sofa and paced. "He'd preached all my life that if you go for it, do the right thing, follow the credo—honor, country, faith, and hard work—you could achieve anything you wanted. My father scuttled my career with a few well-placed phone calls. I'd seen him do it to folks in his command he didn't deem worthy. But I thought family stuck together. I never believed he'd do that to me. Or that he'd lie. He betrayed me. And without remorse."

"I'm sorry," Gabe said.

Deb chugged down the rest of her beer. "He wasn't who I thought he was. That's what hurt the most."

"Yeah. It sucks when a hero turns into a flawed human being,"

Gabe said, his voice laced with some bitterness. "Did you ever forgive him?"

"I guess. Sort of." She sat again, sadness sweeping through her. "But I don't trust him anymore. Our relationship has never been the same since his betrayal."

"Yeah." Gabe stared at the ceiling. "I never forgave my old man for what he did, either. Not really. I lived with it, but I got out of the house as fast as I could. I couldn't stay there, knowing he'd deceived my mother."

Deb didn't ask him to explain what had happened. The situation was obvious. Gabe's father had cheated on his mother.

"Love doesn't feel very permanent sometimes, does it?"

"I thought so for a long time." Gabe set his empty can on the coffee table. "My brothers' marriages seem solid, though. Luke and Zach have found partners they can trust. If I asked either one, they'd have no doubts in Jazz or in Jenna."

"But how can they be sure?" Deb studied her hands. "In war I watched the worst people can do to each other. Our supposed informants smiling at a soldier one moment, blowing them up the next. A complete disregard for life. No empathy for anyone. Between my career and my father, I don't know if I can ever completely trust someone else."

"Maybe you can't." Gabe scowled at her. "Hey, you're supposed to be making me feel better, not depressed. We're drinking buddies now. You have to have my back."

He smiled and she wanted to smile back, but couldn't. Her heart did a flip. She was about to say something really, really stupid.

"Is that all we are to each other, Gabe?" she asked, searching his expression. "Drinking buddies?"

Desire flared in his eyes and he leaned forward to pull her into his arms. "God, I hope not."

Seconds later, she was lost in his kiss.

Congressman Reynolds stared out the window of his home office. He could see the Capitol dome from here. His wife entered the room and wrapped her arms around his waist. She bit his ear. "You've been distracted lately. Maybe you need some . . . stimulation? Some centering?"

His body pulsed to life, but he moved across the room. "Not now."

She wrinkled her forehead and sashayed toward him. His groin throbbed at the sway of her hips. His body tightened as she ran her hand over him and then bit his shoulder. Hard. Where the bruises wouldn't show.

He knew what she wanted. He could tell she'd be good. Make him beg for the pain she'd give him . . . and the release.

Damn it, he wanted it, too.

Needed it.

"What's wrong, pet? You're looking so down. We're due for an adventure. It's been days." Her eyes sparkled with excitement. "Maybe we could play out a new scene? Or I could call—"

"No!"

She stilled, her entire demeanor shift. "You yelled at me. You don't do that. What's wrong, Raymond?"

He swallowed, then walked over to his computer and pulled up his e-mail. He stood back to give her a better view.

She stared at the photos and gasped. "Oh my God. Where did they get these?"

"Someone decrypted my files. They have all the videos, too. They could have everything." His voice grew panicked. "I mean *everything*. Do you understand?"

His wife gripped the desk, her knuckles white. "What do they want?"

"I don't know." He rubbed his eyes. "They'll call, though. I know they will."

"We have to make plans. We'll have to come up with a strategy."

"It won't work, Carla. If this ever comes out, I'm finished. Hell, we're both finished. I ran on a platform of family values. If these pictures ever see the light of day, it's over. No apology is going to explain that I get off on . . ."

He couldn't bear to say it.

He sat down at his desk and buried his head in his hands. Carla slumped on the sofa, her look stunned and mortified.

The cell phone rang. He stiffened when he saw the number.

"Reynolds."

"Congressman. I see you told your wife about us."

His eyes widened. "Your computer has a built-in camera." Raymond studied the small lens. He placed his finger over it. "Oh, don't bother covering it up. We got what we needed."

He didn't respond.

The voice chuckled. "You were expecting our call, I believe."

Richard said nothing, still reeling from the truth. He didn't know how long they'd been able to view what happened in his office. His unusual preferences aside, he'd had more than one candid discussion with his colleagues in this room.

He almost never closed his laptop.

"I see you understand the implications. A little added leverage. So, now's your chance to convince me that you really don't want this information to leak. I need some sensitive information about Special Forces movement in the Middle East, and you're just the man to get it for me."

Hotel sofas weren't meant for sleep. Gabe shifted his head; his neck protested. His muscles were in knots, but he didn't care if he didn't move. Deb was draped over him, sound asleep.

After kissing and snuggling for a while on the couch, they'd both fallen asleep. If his brothers heard about this, he'd never live it down.

Some Don Juan he was.

He didn't know how much time had passed since they'd showered and crashed on the couch. He shifted uncomfortably. At six-three, he hated short sofas. He liked being able to sit down and not have his head flop back.

But last night had been worth it.

She snuggled closer to him, her warmth seeping into his skin like a hot-water bottle. The citrus scent of her shampoo filled his lungs, relaxing him even more. He toyed with the auburn strands of hair. The silky locks slipped through his fingers.

He wasn't used to feelings like this. He usually went for nice, quiet girls. Maybe they'd just been too nice. Maybe he'd needed the fire and light and craziness Deb had brought into his life, though he wouldn't mind skipping the explosions.

But she was so damned brave, and so determined. He had no doubt she'd walk through hell to find the sister she loved.

No matter what she'd said the night before, he knew something else about Deb Lansing. When she loved, she loved hard and deep and true.

Could she love him like that?

Did he even want her to?

He stared at her face, peaceful in repose, and his heart swelled. It was crazy. She wasn't exactly beautiful; her features held more determination than that. Her jaw was too strong, her eyes too wide, and right now, the shadows beneath them pulled at Gabe. But put each feature together and he couldn't look away from her.

Had his brothers felt like this?

She shifted closer, her hand clenching on his thigh.

He'd give anything for her to wake up and look into his eyes.

As if she read his mind, those emerald beauties blinked, and she stared up at him.

She looked down at her hand, which lay perilously close to his lap. He couldn't hide his physical response.

She bit her lip, the vulnerable expression so different from what he'd seen since they met.

She pulled her hand back, but he covered it and held it closer. "Don't. I like it there," Gabe said, his voice husky, not so much from nonuse, but from the stranglehold she had on his heart.

"Would you like it better here?" She slid her palm over his crotch, her hesitancy still clear.

"Oh, yeah," he groaned, pushing up against her hand. With the stealth of a SWAT team she'd crept under his defenses and hit with a direct shot.

"Are we making a mistake?" she asked in a whisper, even as her body pressed closer to his.

"Probably, but I don't care. I've wanted you for months." He brushed his fingers across her cheek, then slid his hand to cup her head and lowered his mouth to hers. Unlike their other kisses, this one exploded in heat from the first second.

No question, he would make love to her tonight.

Nothing would stop him.

He settled her on top of him. Her hips pressed into his. She shifted against him, rubbing every sensitive nerve. He gasped, his body hard, wanting, and unwilling to wait. Her hair fell into a curtain around them, and she hovered above him, her lips just out of reach. He clasped the back of her head, pulling her closer.

"There's a perfectly good bed a few feet away."

"Too far," he gasped, then possessed her mouth, and his lips ground into hers. She moaned low in her throat and opened for him, returning kiss for kiss, her tongue sparring with his. He pulled her body even closer; his hands rubbed down her strong shoulders to her trim waist and settled on her hips. He cupped her curves and thrust up against her. His body strained against his zipper, but the pain kept him sane. Otherwise, he might lose himself in her kiss, in her touch.

Panting, she sat up and looked down at him.

"This is probably a really bad idea but I don't care, either." Then, in a fluid motion, she pulled off the sweatshirt, revealing a turquoise camisole underneath. A spaghetti strap dangled on her arm. The color made her hair appear as a sunset halo.

Gabe simply stared. In all his fantasies, he hadn't pictured her in silky lingerie. Would she ever stop surprising him? God, he hoped not.

His hands trembled slightly and tugged at the fabric at her waist, slipping underneath. Her skin, smooth and taut across her abdomen, shivered under his fingertips. He slid his hands up to brush the underside of her breasts.

She licked her lips and moved her own hands to the front of his shirt. She made quick work of the buttons, then pushed the shirt open. Slowly she lowered her body onto him, rubbing against his warm skin, like a cat. She nipped at his neck and arched her hips against him, her low moan of pleasure spiking his desire.

Gabe couldn't deny how much he wanted her. He knew it was wrong, knew that they were in danger, knew that his investigation might put her in even more peril. In fact, he couldn't be certain who was out to get them from one moment to the next, but, damn, he needed her.

More than he'd ever needed anyone in his life.

She skirted her lips across his jawline.

"You're thinking too much," she whispered. "I need you inside me."

He grabbed the bottom of her camisole and slid it up over her head, revealing her milky curves. He cupped them tenderly, reverently, awed by the longing inside him.

His hips shifted in a sensual rhythm, losing himself to all thought. She groaned, arching into him. He drew her down to taste her nipple and her hands clenched on his shoulders, her soft cries signaling her growing need.

Dazed, she struggled to undo the button of his jeans. In seconds she had the zipper down. She raised herself so he could push his jeans down to his thighs.

"We're going to get tangled up," Gabe said with a laugh.

Without letting him fully undress, she shoved her pants down her toned legs, lowered herself until there was nothing between them, then slowly moved her body sinuously back and forth.

He responded and he nearly sank into her. God, how he wanted to. He longed to make love to her and feel every sensation he could. Feel himself spilling into her.

That would be insane.

"Wait," he groaned finally, and felt into his pants for his wallet and a condom. He slipped it on, then plunged into her waiting heat, straining up against her as he drank in her cry of ecstasy. For a single moment he stilled and she pulsed around him. She gripped his arms, panting, dazed, desperate.

"More," she whispered. "Make me forget. Make me—"

His hard thrust cut off her words, and with each successive surge, his body sang in triumph. She reared back as he drove deep inside her, clutching at his arms as he kneaded her swollen breasts. He felt her tremors begin, her body clenching around him.

Skin damp with exertion, he drove her up and over and she shuddered to completion. Holding her hip, he thrust deeper and deeper, then shouted out her name, stunned by his explosive release.

Panting, she sank down on top of him, her heart pounding against his chest, but she didn't move.

Finally, she rested her chin on her hands, looked up, and smiled at him. "If this is what you do on a couch, I can't wait to try the bed."

His fingers ran through her hair. "Damn straight, lady. After what I intend to do to you on that bed, you're going to wonder why we waited so long."

She kissed him gently. "I already do."

CHAPTER SEVENTEEN

Ashley stood in the Warden's office, hovering near a window that overlooked the primary testing room. Justin sat in a chair close to the corner. A new recruit had just been brought in for that first fun-filled tour. Whoever it was had no idea what was about to—

Oh God. No!

Ashley closed her eyes, praying she'd been imagining things. She squinted. Sure enough, two guards shoved Mylo forward. He fell to his knees. Mottled bruises covered his face. She recognized that terrified look.

She hated this. A new recruit meant the guards were distracted. The perfect time for the escape. Why did Justin and Dave's one chance mean Mylo had to be imprisoned?

Then she realized the truth. They'd been brought here to die.

Now even more depended on Justin making it through. She didn't know if Dave had cleared the last level, but he was very smart. She hoped he'd reached Level 88. She didn't want Justin to have to try to survive and get help all alone.

She squinted at the new computer they'd put Dave on. He was attempting Level 88 again, one of the many missions from the new game.

She prayed it was just a simulation. With the upgraded code and the right knowledge, anyone from homegrown terrorists to an enemy country could access classified information.

Her heart skipped a beat as she realized how blithely she'd hacked into NSA with Justin. Everything had been fun and daring. She'd never considered the damage—even though she and Justin had never intended to use the information. They'd screwed up big-time.

If Justin and Dave didn't get the information to Deb and her father, people could die. A lot of people.

The door behind her squeaked open. "Well, Ms. Lansing. I see you've been causing trouble again."

She hated that voice. She straightened and slowly turned. "I haven't done anything you haven't already punished me for."

The Warden stood, his bearing stiff and military-straight, his expression very much like her father. She recognized the cold, aloof attitude well.

"Somehow, Ms. Lansing, I highly doubt that." He walked over to stand before her, too close. "You're the brightest, most instinctive, and inventive code breaker I've ever seen. In fact, we haven't witnessed anything close to the likes of you since the first version of *Point of Entry* was released. That girl, too, was curious and unwilling to cooperate. Do you know what happened to her?"

He opened a desk drawer, lifted out a photo, and passed it to Ashley.

Reluctantly she took it.

A bus station. A blonde-haired girl, her body riddled with bullets. Blood everywhere. Other people lying on the ground, wounded.

The girl looked eerily like Ashley herself, and the similarity made her recoil. Suddenly, it dawned on her that the victim must be Shannon, the girl for whom Niko still grieved.

"Look at all those bullet holes," the Warden pointed out. "You wouldn't want something like that to happen to you. Or your sister. Would you?"

Ashley shook her head numbly.

"Or to your brother Rick. Or how about Ben? Isn't that the name of the one who's a black ops operative?"

She snapped her head up, fear slamming through her like bullets from a machine gun set on automatic.

"Oh yes, I know about your brothers. We've been doing our research. In fact, we know exactly where they are at this moment. What unit they've been assigned to, the coordinates where they're currently encamped. Everything."

He opened the door. "Come, Ashley. Let's join your boyfriend, shall we?"

He led her to Justin's station. He was completely focused, clicking the controller buttons in his hand faster than she'd ever seen.

"Mr. Connell, your friend, Ms. Lansing, is here to observe you."

Justin turned toward her, his eyes haunted. "Ashley?"

The Warden backhanded Justin. "How dare you speak to her? I did not give you permission."

Justin dropped his gaze immediately to the controller gripped tightly in his hands. His face was red, but whether the color was from the blow or his anger, Ashley couldn't tell.

The Warden leaned over Justin's shoulder, studying the screen. "Very nice. You've nearly completed Level 89, Justin. Well done."

He smiled up at Ashley. "You might find this level of special interest, Ms. Lansing. Insurgents are trying to overrun a top secret American Army outpost in the desert. Land mines and bombs have been set around the perimeter as a deterrent to the attack. They may or may not save the troops inside. Justin has uncovered the access code to detonate and destroy the attackers."

The Warden smiled. "Justin, finish the mission."

"No!" Ashley cried. "Don't do it!"

Justin swallowed, his hands froze over the keyboard.

"Hit the button, Mr. Connell."

Justin still stalled.

The Warden put his hand over Justin's and pressed the trigger.

A huge explosion filled the screen.

"Congratulations!" a mechanical voice bellowed. "You've successfully eliminated your target. All of the insurgents are dead."

Ashley swayed, ready to faint. "Oh my God, no."

The Warden turned to her. "I see that you've figured out what we're doing, haven't you, Ms. Lansing?"

"No." She shook her head, not wanting to believe her suspicions. "You wouldn't do something like that."

"Oh, but I would." He laughed with delight, then his face turned cruel. "Let me make something perfectly clear. Your little rebellion is over. You have bucked me for the last time. I told you what would happen if you didn't stop, so don't blame me for the consequences of your actions."

She grabbed his arm. "Who did you hurt?"

"Hurt?" He feigned shock. "What a quaint word for the devastation I just released." He pointed a remote to the monitor next to Justin's and pressed a button. Live video feed flickered on. A small military compound burned, flames roared into the sky.

"Your brother Ben, his black ops team, and their hidden military base camp have all been decimated, and the fault is entirely yours."

"No!" she sobbed, holding her belly. It couldn't be. Ben wasn't dead. This couldn't be happening.

The Warden grabbed her arm. "I warned you, Ms. Lansing. I can get to anyone, anywhere. Don't forget again."

Deb's body tingled all over. She couldn't believe she'd lost control like that, but Gabe Montgomery had just ripped away the emotional defensive wall she'd used to protect herself for so very long.

While in the military, it had been self-preservation to not get involved with the men in her unit. Work and relationships didn't mix, particularly when you were fighting an entire desert of men for respect.

Since then, she'd dated, but the truth was, Gabe Montgomery had captivated her from the moment she'd realized he'd survived after his injury. He possessed gut and grit, but more than that, he had heart.

Now, he'd also laid claim to hers. "We really should have done this a long time ago," she teased. "How come you never asked me out?"

Gabe's eyebrow arched. "I watched you torpedo most of the men in the bar for months. You didn't seem overly receptive to advances."

Deb sighed. "They weren't you."

He caressed her upper arm. "So, if you weren't looking for a relationship or a hookup, why did you come to Sammy's anyway?

Most of the women there are badge bunnies. It doesn't seem like it's your scene."

Deb averted her gaze. "I miss being a part of a unit. The Search and Rescue team helps. That's why I usually come in with them. I couldn't ever join in when it was just cops. That thin blue line, you know."

"There's definitely a wall when you're not a cop—even if you used to be a cop. Things have been different for me, too, since everyone thought I was just running the bar," Gabe said. His fingertips glided down her skin. "You miss the Army?"

She shivered and eased off of him. Without answering his question, she tugged a blanket from the bed and wrapped it around her shoulders. Then she tossed him one.

He rose onto one elbow. "Hit a nerve?"

"You ever look back on something you did and would give anything you have to change the choice you made?"

"Everyone has a past. Some with more regret than others, but yeah. Some days I don't think about it. The last few, I've been reliving that day every second. Well, except maybe the last half hour. This sexy woman kept distracting me."

She lifted her lashes and met his gaze. She saw the humor, but also the sympathy. He was leaving it up to her whether she wanted to tell him or not.

With a sigh, she wrapped her arms around her knees. "We were doing a rescue mission just outside Kandahar. A real Leroy Jenkins. Multiple casualties. At least two guys with amputations."

She stared at the wall, but instead of a nondescript print, a cloud of dust from her helicopter's rotors appeared in her mind. Tension vibrated around her. A warning from her commanding officer rang in her ears.

"We almost didn't sit down. The landing area wasn't secure. They were close to scrubbing the mission."

Gabe moved over to her, but she shrank away. He didn't press.

"I checked out the site. What a mess. A half dozen injured friendlies lined up on the ground. Three US soldiers. There were two choppers, but we couldn't take everyone. I got the two double amputees and fit in everyone else I could. The extra load was dangerous."

She blinked, her eyes blurring. "I'd just started to lift off when this soldier staggered out of the desert, begging us to stop. He lunged for the helicopter. The lieutenant radioed me to take off. We had to get the patients to base. The soldier fell to his knees." She shook her head. "God. He raised his hands up to me, his eyes pleading for me to come back, and then someone blew his head off."

Gabe let out a low curse.

"I found out later he'd been followed. The insurgents took out everyone there. His name was Tate Tinsley."

"You saved the other soldiers' lives."

"Yes, but it's not their thanks that I remember from that day. It's his eyes. They haunt me. His family haunts me."

"If you'd waited, no one might have made it."

"Maybe. But now, I don't leave *anyone* behind. Not unless I know they'll be safe," Deb said. "Not ever."

Gabe pulled her into his arms. "The guys talk about you in the bar, you know," he murmured, kissing her temple.

Deb gave him a cautious look. "Oh, yeah? What do they say?"

He tucked a strand of auburn hair behind her ear. "Several of the cops have been at locations where you've flown. Or they've heard Search and Rescue talk. You intimidate the hell out of most of the guys who have seen you in that chopper. They say you can make that bird sing and maneuver in ways no human being should. They say you'll take the jobs other pilots won't." He hesitated. "They say you take risks that are crazy."

"Maybe I do," she whispered.

He cupped her cheek. "Take it from someone who knows. Dying won't make the past go away."

He leaned forward to take her lips, but his cell phone rang. He reached over and snagged it off the table, his muscles rippling in a most enticing way.

Deb longed to explore his body again. This time more slowly.

"Hi, Luke. What's up?" Gabe's brow furrowed, then he shut his eyes. "Damn. Thanks for letting me know."

Eyes bleak, he turned to Deb. "Ernie's dead. They found his body in the landfill outside of town. He was missing one of his hands."

"Oh my God. How?"

"Someone blew his brains out, execution style, and carved *snitch* across his chest."

Ashley fell to her knees. "No. Please. Not my brother."

The Warden grabbed her by the arm and yanked her to her feet. "Come with me."

She couldn't think, couldn't feel. Her entire body had gone numb. She looked back at Justin. He sagged in his chair, then he bent over and vomited on the floor.

The Warden yelled to a guard. "Get Floyd to clean it up."

He dragged Ashley back to his office and locked them in. "Listen to me, Ms. Lansing. One more step out of line, and I hand you over to my guards. I guarantee you won't like what they do to you."

Someone from outside yelled for the Warden, panic in his voice.

"Don't move. I'll be right back." He stalked out.

Ashley blinked back the tears. Ben would hate for her to give in. Maybe it would be okay. Maybe they were lying. Everything else they did was a lie.

Except she knew it was the truth. She knew the game worked. She even knew how.

She glanced up at the clock, barely able to read the time through her blurred vision. She wanted to curl up and cry for her brother. She wanted to call Deb or her father or Rick. Someone. They had to find Ben.

Except she couldn't do anything. She was a prisoner. With only one way out.

She forced herself to try to read the clock again. This time the numbers stopped dancing. Almost time. Would Justin pull it together enough so he could escape, unseen, from the crowd of kids going to dinner?

Floyd planned to create a diversion by spilling his mop bucket. She hadn't figured out what she could do yet, but this was their only shot.

Justin and Dave had to be in place when those timed locks released.

She listened at the door. Nothing. No sound.

Would the Warden be gone long enough for her to access anything in here? She dreaded what he might do to her if he found her messing with his things.

Actually, she wondered why she was still alive after the trouble she'd caused already. There was only one possibility. They needed her. That's why Floyd was still alive. Did he realize getting to the bonus round of *Point of Entry* meant the game became real? He must. He was brilliant. He had to know every time a kid beat Level 88 they were, in reality, breaking into banking systems, private computer systems, the IRS, Justice Department, Secret Service, FBI, CIA. Even the NSA.

A shudder went through Ashley. The right program could identify the country's nuclear launch codes. God knew what they were planning to do with all this information.

She scanned the room, then started to yank open the drawers. Most were locked, but a few weren't. Did she dare grab the scissors? With her luck, they'd be used against her. She wasn't strong enough to overpower the guards with a stab or two.

She pulled out the top-left drawer and saw the Warden's tablet. She grabbed it. This she could use. She tried to use the location feature to force the tablet to pinpoint their location. If she could do that, she could tell Justin the best direction in which to go. Maybe forward information about the compound's location to Deb somehow.

She knew they were in the desert somewhere, but—

The door flew open. Niko stood there watching her clutch the Warden's tablet to her chest.

Silently, he walked straight to her, took the tablet, shut it down, and returned it to the drawer. Then he stared at her, his face expressionless.

Terror crippled her, and her entire body shook.

"Idaho," he said softly.

"What?"

"Where we are. Isn't that what you were looking for?"

The Warden strode in. "I told you to take her out of here."

The blond man smiled at his boss. "I was explaining to Ms. Lansing that you didn't feel comfortable with her being in your office without supervision, so I was to guard her until you returned, then accompany her to the cafeteria. Isn't that what you wanted?"

The Warden stared back and forth between them for a long moment, then scanned his office before relenting. "Get her out of here. I think she's learned her lesson for today."

"Yes," Niko said. "I think she has."

The alarm sounded at midnight and all the automatic door locks engaged. The bed check would start soon to identify who had escaped.

Ashley snuggled in closer to her tear-stained pillow, grateful that Justin and Dave had several hours' head start.

Tonight more rumors had started.

The guards called it cleanup.

The *Version VIII* final mission programming was almost complete.

The camp would be closed. The Warden would move on.

Within a few days, everyone they found expendable—all the recruits—would be dead.

"Please, God. Let them get away. Someone has to bring help to this hellhole, or we're all going to die."

Then she turned her face to the wall, waiting for the beating that was certain to come.

CHAPTER EIGHTEEN

Zach's plane touched down gently at the Angel Fire, New Mexico, airstrip. Gabe's brother could definitely handle the controls. The plane came to a stop at the end of the short runway and Gabe peered out at the quaint mountain town, nestled in the Sangre de Cristo range.

"Nice landing," Deb said, unbuckling her seat belt. "That's a difficult maneuver, especially with this wind-shear factor on the way in."

Zach gave her that famous movie-star grin. "I aim to please."

Gabe scowled at his brother. "Hey, tone down the wattage on that smile, Dark Avenger. This isn't a Hollywood set, and you're married now."

"Yeah, I am married now, and very happily, too, thank you." Zach unclicked his belt and exited the pilot's seat. "You know, in most movie scripts, jealousy is one of the first signs of the big fall."

Gabe threw a quick glance at Deb to see how she was handling his brother's teasing. Except for the slight flush of her cheeks that most wouldn't notice, she didn't blink.

He glared at Zach. "And not breathing is one of the early signs of imminent death, bro. Keep it up and you'll have firsthand experience."

"Nah, you need me to fly out of here."

"Not necessarily," Deb said, flashing her own grin. "I've got my pilot's license."

"Well, you two are a cheerful bunch." Zach huffed. "I thought I was here to watch your backs, not my own. Let's get a move on."

Gabe laughed, but the trepidation inside him was building. He'd never met Shannon's parents. He hated forcing them to revisit the night of the girl's murder, or reliving it themselves, but unless Luke came up with something in his research, Gabe didn't know what else to do to find a lead on Ashley's whereabouts. "How are we getting to the Devlins'?"

Zach rose and unlatched the side door. "I called ahead. The guy who runs the place said he keeps a car on standby for pilots. We can take it if we're not too long. Ski season is busy this time of year, so when the weather is clear, he has a lot of planes coming through."

Deb and Gabe gathered their belongings while Zach opened the door of the plane. A numbing draft of cold air blew through.

"I really hate winter right about now." Deb shoved her hands into the arms of her coat and zipped it up. "Ready."

Zach completed his postflight check and Gabe scanned the area. Even though the runway had been cleared of snow, Angel Fire resembled a winter wonderland, a valley draped with a carpet of white surrounded by snow-laced mountains. Several ski runs cut distinctive swaths between the trees.

"I'd love to take a run down that big slope," Zach said, his expression wistful. "A few of them look easy enough for Sam to handle."

"Sam?" Deb asked.

"My wife, Jenna's, son," Zach added. "I plan to legally adopt him as soon as the paperwork goes through. He's only six years old, but he's adapted to being a Montgomery like he's always belonged. Actually, Jenna has, too."

"Why don't you fly Jenna and Sam down here sometime?" Gabe suggested.

"You were reading my mind, little brother. Once they get home, we'll plan on a fun trip."

"Where are they now?" Deb asked.

"Luke made arrangements for Mom, Jenna, and the kids to stay at Caleb's cabin. That place is hidden so far out in the boonies that even the wildlife doesn't know it's there. They'll be safe. And Caleb can handle more weapons than most."

"Caleb? Yet another brother?" Deb asked. "That's six boys? Your poor mother."

Gabe met Zach's gaze and they burst out laughing.

"Feel sorry for *us*, Deb," Gabe said. "Not Mom. You've met her. We didn't get away with a thing."

Still chuckling, Zach went into the building and retrieved the keys to the car. "I'll bring the Jeep around. You know where we're going?"

"That's what GPS is for," Gabe said, pulling out the new satellite phone Zach had forced into his hand, one with an extra-long battery. *So the baby of the family can call home regularly*, Zach had taunted. His brother's expression held just enough concern, Gabe hadn't slugged him. He'd taken the phone. This one even worked in the mountains. Deb's calls were being forwarded to his phone, too, since reception was spotty.

Of course, Zach's phone could probably get a signal on Mars. Gabe was dying to know how much it cost.

He tapped several numbers. "Shannon Devlin's parents haven't moved from their original home. Be ready, though. Mr. Devlin told me last night when I called that they never updated her room. It's set up like a shrine."

"That's tough," Deb said, but her face looked tortured.

What would Deb do if Ashley's fate was not what they hoped? He gave Deb a sympathetic hug, then dialed the Devlins to let them know they were on the way.

"Hello?" a strange woman's voice answered. Younger than the woman he'd spoken to the night before.

"Is this the Devlin residence?"

"Yes, who may I ask is calling?"

"Gabe Montgomery."

The gasp at the other end of the phone twisted Gabe's gut. Only one other person he knew had also known Shannon Devlin.

"It's Whitney Blackstone. Why are you calling my parents?" she demanded. "This is a very difficult time for them. They don't need more trouble."

Her parents? Was he about to meet the woman with whom his father had the affair? Today was getting better and better.

"I have an appointment to see them. It's important."

"What's this about?" Suspicion laced her voice.

Knowing he was a half second from getting hung up on, he laid out the truth. "I need to talk to them about Shannon," he said. "Her death may be related to some missing kids in Colorado."

Deb looked over at him, worried. He gave her a confident smile, when he felt anything but. The last time he'd tangled with Whitney hadn't gone so well.

She cursed. "Come on then. I guess it's good that I'm here. They'll be a mess after you leave."

"What are you doing there?" he asked. "I heard you'd moved to the east coast." He was sure he'd read a notation like that somewhere in his father's notes. At least, she'd gone to school out there.

"Not that I'm not interested to know why you think you have a right to know where I live, but I've taken a few weeks' leave from my job." Whitney lowered her voice. "They found the bodies of some friends of mine and Shannon's on the side of the mountain. My parents took the news badly. I'm out here to stay with them until after the funerals, provided the coroner releases the remains soon."

"I'm sorry."

She paused. "How could Shannon's death eight years ago be related to a current case?"

"That's what I've been asking myself," Gabe admitted. "Over and over."

"Are you sure you need to come now?"

"Unfortunately, yes." Gabe groaned inwardly. How the hell was he supposed to keep Zach from recognizing Whitney as their half sister? With luck, she'd changed a lot over the years.

But that was not the way Gabe's luck had been running lately.

He and Deb walked to the four-wheel-drive Jeep that Zach had brought around. Before she got in, Gabe grabbed her and pulled her close, holding her tighter than he probably should, but needing her steadiness to stabilize his world in some way before seeing Whitney Blackstone totally blew it apart.

The stainless-steel table pressed into Ashley's back, the cold metal making her freeze. She twisted her wrists against the leather of the restraints, then her ankles. The lightweight pants and shirt looked a lot like hospital scrubs. They were two sizes two big and engulfed her, but at least it hid her shape. Not that the Warden cared.

She tried to bend and twist her hands enough for her fingers to reach the buckles. She had to get out of here.

Steel boots clanked on the concrete floor. He had to purposely wear those boots just to freak people out. Even though Ashley believed that, she couldn't stop her Pavlovian reaction. Her side still ached from the last time he took the scalpel to her.

Niko opened the door and the red-haired man entered the room. She couldn't stop the whimper from escaping. The Warden followed them in, plus another man who delivered a tray of medieval-looking instruments, then back out swiftly, his face a tad green.

Oh God. They knew.

She blinked. She really was dead.

Niko remained stone-faced, but the red-haired man looked down at her, a strange, sick smile on his lips. The Warden looked absolutely livid.

"What did you do?" he demanded. "Justin Connell is missing. So is Dave Weaver. How did you get past the system? You and Floyd are the only ones with enough skills and guts to pull this off."

Ashley tried to look innocent. "I . . . I don't—"

The red-haired man bent down, close to her ear, his cologne cloying. "Please lie," he said softly, his breath a whisper across her cheek and neck. "I want you to lie. Make the Warden mad enough to give you to me. There are so many things I want to do to you."

He stood back, laughing.

The Warden paced, watching her, his expression chillingly familiar. A moment flashed into her mind. The moment before he'd murdered Fletcher in cold blood.

Ashley bit her lip hard enough to wince and didn't say a word.

The Warden clutched her throat with his right hand, squeezing. "Tell me what you did."

She tried to suck in a breath, but he pressed harder on her windpipe.

"What's our system's vulnerability?"

He let up for a moment, but she refused to respond. Furious, he cut off her air supply again.

Spots circled Ashley's eyes. Oh God. She was going to die. Deb would never know this wasn't her fault. This was Ashley's fault. She'd hacked her way into dying.

A tear leaked out and ran down her temple.

Her vision grayed.

"Sir, are you certain you want her dead?" Niko said. "I might be able to convince her to tell us . . ." Niko's voice faded away.

Ashley fought to stay conscious, but it was no use.

God, she hoped Justin and Dave made it to safety. Someone needed to tell the world what these people were doing.

A knock interrupted, and the pressure on her throat eased a bit.

"Warden, we may have spotted them on a traffic light surveillance camera. They hitchhiked with a trucker a few hours ago. We're trying to locate the semi now."

"Find them. Kill them. Kill whoever is with them. Leave no witnesses, do you understand? No more loose ends.

"Your fault," the Warden rasped, tightening his grip on her throat even more.

Ashley's fist clenched and she tried to buck his hands free, but there was nothing she could do. The spots faded. The gray shifted. And then her world turned to nothing.

It didn't take Zach long to drive to the end of the valley and up into the foothills. The Jeep eked its way up the snow-packed road. Without the four-wheel-drive feature and the chains on the tires, they'd have plummeted into a ditch several times over.

When Zach stopped the vehicle, he turned in his seat. "Maybe I shouldn't go in. Too many unknown faces might upset them too much. You and Deb should be the ones to go in. I'll wait here."

Gabe breathed a sigh of relief and nodded. "Good plan." He held out his hand to Deb. "Let's go. This is going to be hard."

They picked their way across the rocky driveway to a multi-level log home.

Gabe knocked on the door.

An older woman answered, her face lined with sadness. Gabe couldn't see any resemblance to Whitney Blackstone.

"Mr. Montgomery?" the woman queried, her voice a bit shaky.

"Yes, ma'am, and this is a friend of mine, Deb Lansing. We'd hoped to speak with you about your daughter."

An older man stepped through from the kitchen. His gray hair had thinned at the top, but what he had stood on end. "Whitney says you're related to Patrick Montgomery. The cop who tried to save our Shannon?"

Gabe bristled a bit. "Yes, Patrick Montgomery was my father."

"We never did get a chance to thank him."

"He passed away five years ago," Gabe said, wanting nothing more than to shift the conversation.

"I'm sorry to hear that."

Whitney walked into the room, and the resemblance she bore to the rest of the Montgomery family hit Gabe like a slug to the gut.

Shannon's mother gestured. "This is our other daughter, Whitney. She and Shannon were best friends before she came to live with us after her mother died. She can probably tell you even more than we can. Whitney, this young man and his friend are here to talk about Shannon."

Whitney nodded to Gabe but didn't move near him. "Yes, Mom, Mr. Montgomery and I have met before." Then she extended her hand to Deb. "I just learned of your travails a moment ago, Ms. Lansing. I'm sorry about your sister's disappearance. I hope you locate her soon."

Gabe raised his brows. Whitney Blackstone had some serious connections if she'd learned about Ashley this fast. She'd obviously checked them out since his phone call. He should have kept closer tabs on his half sister over the years. Just who was she?

Mrs. Devlin looked at everyone in the room, as if uncertain what to say. Finally, she pointed to the fireplace. "These pictures may help familiarize you with my daughter Shannon. She was an amazing girl. Brilliant. Funny. Gentle. A mother couldn't ask for more." Her voice broke again.

Gabe stepped closer to look at the series of photos decorating the large mantel. Half were of a smiling blonde teenager who looked amazingly like Ashley Lansing.

He felt Deb stiffen in shock beside him. He couldn't imagine what she was feeling right now, knowing this girl might have been murdered by the same people who now had Ashley.

Gabe examined the photos. In several, she held blue ribbons. "She was beautiful, and she looked happy."

He couldn't keep his gaze away from the other photographs displayed, though. Whitney Blackstone. His half sister. Riding horses, rappelling down a mountain. Graduating from the FBI Academy at Quantico, Virginia. No wonder she had connections. She was a Feebie. Had Shannon's death dictated Whitney's career decisions, or were the Montgomery genes at work there, too?

For the first time, he reflected on the impact that night must have had on Whitney. He'd always been centered on his own emotions, his own pain.

She'd lost as much, if not more than him that night, but his anger hadn't let him see it. His mother wouldn't be proud of him right now.

Mrs. Devlin reached out and touched one of the pictures, then smiled. "Shannon was so proud of herself in this photo. She and her friends had just won the county math bowl. They were going to state the day she was . . ." Her voice trailed off.

Mr. Devlin walked over to his wife. She leaned against him and he put his arm around her. "They were all murdered, Mr. Montgomery. Shannon in Denver. The boys in the mountains nearby. Their cases are still unsolved."

Mrs. Devlin sank against her husband. "Getting that call from your father, telling me what happened to my precious daughter . . ." She sobbed. "It was the worst day of my life."

Whitney went over to her mother. "Mom, this is too much

for you. Why don't you let me handle it from here? Don't put yourself through any more."

Mrs. Devlin smiled through her tears and touched Whitney's cheek. "I thank God every day for bringing you into our lives. If He had to take Shannon, I'm so thankful He also blessed us with you."

Whitney's eyes filled and she kissed her mother's cheek before nodding to her dad to take the frail, heartbroken woman away from the living room.

As soon as they'd left, Whitney faced Gabe. "If you're here looking into Shannon's death again, then it appears your investigation and mine are intersecting. I don't have time for BS stalling and neither do you. I'll show you mine, if you show me yours, and we'll try to figure out what is going on before anyone else gets killed."

The snow crunched under Gabe's feet as he and Deb left the Devlins' house an hour later. He clutched Deb's hand as they made their way across the driveway to keep his head from reeling.

Zach got out of the car, blowing on his hands and cursing. "Remind me to go inside with you next time. Please tell me you found out something that made me freezing my butt off outside worthwhile?"

"You might as well get in the car," Deb said. "It will take the whole ride to the airport to fill you in. I'm sure the guy would like his Jeep back."

She squeezed Gabe's hand and he took comfort in her touch. They headed down the hill once more. Ice coated the roads now, making it even more treacherous.

Gabe didn't even know how to begin. It wasn't with Whitney's true identity, though. "The Devlins' daughter is with the FBI. I mentioned Intelligent Interactive, the makers of *Point of Entry*, and Intelligent Solutions, the company who sent Deb the game, hoping she could use her resources to get us more information than even Luke can. She made a call. You ready for this one? Intelligent Solutions has the same address as one of the Gasmerati's dummy corporations that just popped onto the FBI's radar because of huge transfers of money."

Zach let out a low whistle. "Jeff Gasmerati."

"And the game," Deb said. "It keeps popping up."

"So what do we do now?" Zach asked. "Visit the company headquarters and take 'em out?"

"I agree with you," Deb said, her hand on her weapon. "Go in, scare the crap out of them, and find Ashley."

"It's not that simple," Gabe said. "Luke did some backdoor digging to see if he could trace the package Deb received back to the Reno address. The location is a mailbox center. All fake. Which, of course, makes sense now, but it's a dead end."

Zach hauled the wheel to the left to avoid a huge chunk of snow in the road. "So did you find out anything that'll help?"

"Just that everyone Shannon knew who played that game well is either missing or dead. Whitney showed us Shannon's diary enshrined in her old bedroom. There were other names mentioned—Randy, Kelsey, Niko, and Liam—but Whitney's never been able to locate them. They played competitively against Shannon's P.O.E. team a lot, more for fun than anything else, but when Whitney started searching for them, they'd vanished. Like all the rest."

Zach let out a low whistle. "What can I do to help? Maybe I could—"

"No way. You're not taking any more chances. Not with your new family and that baby on the way. The bodies are piling up high in this investigation," Gabe said, glancing at his phone. He'd missed a call from Nick while talking to Whitney. Another number popped up as well. The caller ID indicated the Air Force Academy.

Gabe dialed back.

"Rappaport."

"This is Gabe Montgomery."

"I have the name you wanted of the politician who gave us *Point of Entry*," Rappaport said. "Congressman Raymond Reynolds. He was chair of the House Armed Services Committee. Until today."

Gabe didn't like the sound of the major's voice. "What do you mean *was*?"

"It just hit the news. The congressman and his wife were found in a submerged car in the Potomac. According to the report, they left a suicide note."

Gabe gripped the phone. Two more deaths. "Thank you, Major."

"Have you found Ashley?" he asked.

"Not yet, but we will."

Gabe ended the call just as a low-flying plane buzzed over the Jeep, distracting him. He turned around. It sure as hell wasn't crop dusting this time of year, but the damn thing flew low enough to handle the job. Nearly took off the car's roof.

The airfield was only a short distance. Maybe it was a student pilot. He'd never get his license at this rate.

The plane turned and came back. A door slid open.

The hair on the back of Gabe's neck stood on end.

"Hit the dirt! They're going to fire!" he yelled.

A spray of bullets ripped through the car, smashing the windshield. Gabe felt the burn through his jacket and knew he'd been hit. It felt like a graze. He couldn't believe the rest of the shots missed him.

"Is everyone okay?" Zach said, yanking the car off the road into the minimal shelter of the trees in a lot next to the fire station.

No one answered. They just all leapt from the vehicle, hauling their guns from their holsters. "What was that all about?" Gabe swore, the sting in his arm feeling worse as the frigid air froze the blood coming from his wound.

The plane curved around.

"They're coming back." Zach ran up beside Gabe, holding a damn scary-looking weapon.

The plane did another pass, strafing everything in its path. The metallic sound of bullets hitting metal filled the air. The spray hit the Jeep again, then tore across the fire station and raked the truck outside.

Firemen raced out the doors, shouting.

"Get down!"

The plane raced past, showering another slew of bullets, littering the fire truck with holes and decimating what was left of the Jeep. Bullets spit through the trees and branches around Gabe, Deb, and Zach, hitting the bark, but not their bodies, thankfully.

"The guy's not stopping. I'm gonna have to take him out." Zach pointed his weapon and shot.

The plane teetered. White smoke spewed from the gas tank.

It yawed, then turned over and dove into the ground, exploding into a fireball.

"What was that?" Deb asked.

"Piper Cub. Modified with a machine gun," Zach said. "Someone spent a lot of bucks on that baby."

Deb cursed. "And someone seriously tried to take us out."

Gabe pulled her close to his side. "Guess that means we're on the right track."

He grinned at his brother. "I like your new toy. Can I have one for Christmas?"

"At the rate you're getting attacked, I think I'll move up your gift to Thanksgiving." He looked down at the gun. "Uncle Sam probably won't like that I just shot up a civilian plane with their prototype."

Gabe's sat phone rang and he put it to his ear. "Hello?"

"Gabe? I just heard there were shots fired near the airport, and there's a huge plume of black smoke in the air," Whitney shouted through the phone. "What happened?"

"The cardinals in Rome didn't elect a new Pope?"

"You're a jerk. Was anyone hurt?"

"Everyone's alive. I got winged, but seeing as they wanted us dead, I'll settle for that."

Whitney was silent. "Wait for me at the airport. I'll help deal with the local authorities. I'm going to move my parents someplace safe, then I'm coming with you."

"To Denver?" Not good.

"Yes, but we're going via Winslow, Arizona. I've got information on a warehouse that might lead to Ashley. We'll talk more on the plane."

CHAPTER NINETEEN

THE HUGE TRACTOR-TRAILER LUMBERED DOWN THE HIGHWAY, the trucker recounting tales of the road to entertain them. Justin tried to laugh at the guy's jokes, but he couldn't stop looking out the windshield. Where were they? He hadn't thought southern Idaho was this desolate. He never figured they had desert, but he and Dave had trudged through it for hours before hitting this road.

He wanted to spill everything to the trucker and beg for help, but Ashley and Floyd had warned him about the corrupt cops. He didn't know who to trust. Still, he wished he could get on the trucker's CB and announce the camp's presence to the world and beg them to go in and rescue everyone.

Only the fear that the heavy-duty weapons the guards carried would be automatically turned on all the recruits, including Ashley, kept Justin silent. If the Warden perceived an imminent threat, he would massacre everyone.

Dave wheezed beside him.

"You okay, buddy?"

Dave nodded at Justin, but sweat beaded his brow. Each breath was a struggle. Dave's asthma had slowed them down but as soon as the cell phone Floyd had stolen got a signal, Justin would call Ashley's sister. He'd stick to the plan, then get Dave to a hospital.

Every few seconds he looked for the bars to appear. He was exhausted, running on adrenaline. Dave more so. Hitching with the trucker had been a risk, but they'd needed to put distance between them and the camp as quickly as possible. Some of the local cops were probably under the Warden's control.

"You should have cell service in a couple of miles. This area is pretty dead." The truck slowed and the driver put on his directional. "Weigh station coming up over this hill."

The truck slowed to the top and a rest stop appeared, followed by the weigh station.

"That's strange. This one is usually closed. Guess I gotta stop or the cops will be after me. If you need a bathroom break and a stretch, you can get out and walk around for a few minutes. I won't be long."

Justin and Dave froze. Could they trust these cops, or the fact that the weigh station was uncharacteristically manned today? How far did the Warden's power reach?

"Could you let us out at the rest stop?"

The trucker's brows rose. "It's a quarter mile. You sure?"

Justin looked at Dave, who nodded.

"Yeah, we need to loosen up a bit," Justin said. "The walk will help."

The guy shrugged and pulled over. "Okay, but I'm on a tight schedule. If you're not inside the truck when the weigh-in is over, you'll have to hitch yourself another ride."

"We understand."

The trucker slowed. Justin and Dave jumped down from the cab. They ran to the nearest bathroom and took care of business.

Dave's wheezing grew scarily loud. "Should we keep going with this guy or walk until we get a signal? I don't like the fact that this place is open when it's not supposed to be."

"I don't, either, but you sound really bad."

"Hey, I'm still alive. That's something I didn't expect to be able to say when we planned this escape."

Justin looked at the blue tinge on his friend's lips and decided they'd have to go back to the truck. "We'll walk around and meet him on the other side of the weigh station. You're not going to make it much farther on foot."

Dave nodded, his exhaustion obvious. "Okay, then we'd better head out. I'm not moving very fast."

As they left the bathroom, they heard the drone of a plane.

"Get back. We can't be seen. We don't know who the Warden has on payroll."

They quickly hid and waited, hoping they hadn't been spotted. A moment later, an explosion rocked the ground.

Dave's panic stole the rest of his breath. Justin peered out the door. It was an inferno. Flames roared into the sky where the weigh station had been.

"What—what happened?" Dave panted.

"I think that 'scout' plane just took out the weigh station and the truck. As soon as it leaves, we have to get out of here."

Dave's face blanched. "That wasn't a scout plane. There's a bombing range out here somewhere in the desert. I remember reading about it. If the Warden got someone from there to do this, we're screwed. He knows where we are."

"I know he runs the camp," Justin said, "but you really think he has enough clout to deviate a military bombing run?"

"All they have to do is claim it was a training accident. They'll pay someone off and it'll go away."

"Man, this is way bigger than even Floyd and Ashley thought." Justin thrust his hand through his hair.

Dave sucked in another shuddering breath and bent over.

Justin propped him up. "You don't sound good," Justin said, fear of his friend dying from this attack finally hitting home.

"Don't . . ." Dave stopped and gasped a few more times. "Don't worry about me. If I slow you down, go on without me. You're the only hope everyone has to get out of there alive. Whatever happens to me doesn't matter."

"Not an option, buddy. We go together and become heroes together. Another mile or two and we can call Ashley's sister. She'll know who to trust."

Ashley coughed and hacked and dragged in a gasping breath. Heaven wasn't supposed to hurt so much, so she mustn't be dead. Close, though. Her throat ached and her eyes felt like they'd been pumped up with oxygen. Her lungs hurt, too.

She lay on the metal table, panting, not wanting to open her eyes.

"She's breathing again, sir, but it was close. Are you certain you want to kill her?"

"She cost me two assets. That Justin kid was almost as good as she is. Now all I have is Floyd and I know I can't trust him."

Ashley's heart pounded wildly against her ribs. The anger in the Warden's voice roiled her stomach.

"Still," Niko said, "you may need her, or as bait. She's the best we've ever had here."

Ashley didn't move; she tried not to even breathe.

The Warden swore, stormed to the door, and yanked it open. "Make sure her chip works, then slap a cuff on her. Get her in front of a damn computer." He glared into the room. "Watch her this time, Niko. *Every stroke.* The moneymen have scheduled an unexpected demonstration for tomorrow. I'm not happy about it. At all. God, I can't wait to shut down this damned camp, raze it, and move on."

Gabe tensed as Whitney pulled up in a gray, nondescript rental vehicle. He still hadn't said anything to his brother, but Deb kept giving him sidelong looks as if waiting. Maybe Zach wouldn't recognize the family resemblance, even though her beautiful features matched Zach the most.

She walked up, carrying a duffel and a briefcase, her face wary but determined. Gabe had to respect her for that. This couldn't be easy to face yet another Montgomery brother on such short notice.

Which, he realized, meant Zach was going to kill him for not forewarning him at all.

"There were no witnesses," Zach said, filling them in. "We don't know who was in the plane. The NTSB will look it over, but they probably won't find anything. Not if they run true to bad guy form."

"Is that technical talk?" Deb teased.

"You bet. I can throw in the word *minions*, too, if you want." Zach grinned.

Gabe growled. There was that damned smile again. "So what did the guy at the airport say?"

"The Angel Fire airstrip owner said he had no record of the call sign on the plane. He also said that I owe him a car to replace the one I borrowed. His insurance doesn't cover aerial assault. Fortunately, my insurance company does, but they aren't going to like me anymore. Two cars, one helicopter, and a cabin in the woods all decimated within the last year. I'm not their favorite customer at the moment."

Whitney walked up to them.

Zach turned to greet her, then did a slight double take. "Have we met?"

"Whitney Blackstone, Federal Bureau of Investigation." She flashed her credentials, then held out her hand and he shook it, but he kept staring into her eyes.

"You look very familiar. Are you sure we haven't met?" Zach asked slowly.

"No, I think I'd remember meeting the Dark Avenger."

"Well, hell," he said, rubbing his well-past-five-o'clock shadow. "I was hoping my scruffy whisker disguise would work better than that."

"Don't worry. One of my specialties is face recognition and recall. Yours is rather memorable from your stints on the tabloid covers."

"Ouch. Haven't you heard I've reformed?"

"Congratulations." Whitney turned to Gabe. "Now could we get on with this? The police are waiting to take your statements."

Gabe couldn't believe this exchange. They were bickering like siblings. Holy crap. The fact that they were both Montgomerys was frickin' obvious. Zach had to know. Based on the speculation in his eyes, it was only a matter of time before he put Whitney's appearance together with her identity.

A long while, and many repetitive interviews later, they were released.

Whitney had one last conference with the cops before she walked back to the group, standing next to Deb. "We can go now." She tilted her head toward Zach. "Have you filed the flight plan to Winslow yet?"

"All taken care of, though I'd like to know why we're going there," he said, still studying her. "We were just waiting on you."

"Then let's go."

They climbed into the Learjet and buckled in. Gabe asked Deb to sit in the copilot's seat beside Zach. The gesture was probably futile, but he figured the less interaction Zach had with Whitney, the better.

After Zach finished his checklist, he slid in the pilot's seat and turned around to face his half sister. "So, are we distant cousins or something? My dad was an only child, but you have to be somewhere on his side of the family."

"You've figured it out already, haven't you, Zach?"

The excrement-flinging fan was winding up now.

"Spell it out for me. I'm feeling a little slow."

Whitney paled, then raised her chin. "Somehow I doubt that." She clicked her seat belt into place.

"I'm your half sister," she said, her tone professional. "And before you ask, I'll tell you everything I know. Your parents separated for a short while. Your father got drunk, took my mother to bed one time, and I'm the result. Now that that little turd has been dropped into the punch bowl, we have more important things to worry about. Can we talk about Winslow?"

The Warden gave Ashley a look of such utter hatred that she shivered. The red-haired man followed out the door and slammed it behind them. Ashley bent over and gripped her knees to steady them. Thank God they were gone.

She glanced up at Niko. She didn't know what to make of him, but he'd saved her butt twice now.

"You have a death wish, Lansing?"

"You and I both know that my having a death wish is not going to matter within a few days. Tell me I'm wrong."

Please, tell me I'm wrong.

He met her gaze. "You're not wrong. And it probably ends tomorrow."

Hearing her suspicions confirmed made everything more real. That they were happening so soon made her blanch.

"Will anyone survive?" she rasped.

He was silent for a long time, then, without answering, he slapped a bracelet cuff around her ankle. "No use trying to take it off," he said. "Every few feet there's a detector. We'll know where you are. It takes a special screwdriver to remove it without triggering an alarm."

Niko moved aside. "Let's go. You're almost out of time. Go to your computer desk and finish your assignment."

Ashley rose and stared at him, but didn't press further. She passed the tray of instruments on her way out.

"Don't make me regret helping you," Niko said softly, then opened the door. "He would have used them."

Several armed guards marched down the hall, on alert, their weapons at the ready.

Niko shoved her into the corridor, then glared down at her. "Don't try to remove that bracelet, Lansing. We've had enough of your tricks. It's an automatic death penalty if you're caught."

One guard snickered and Niko gave her yet another hard shove in the direction of the computer rooms. "Walk faster. You have a lot of work to do."

Ashley strode through the corridor beside Niko. Every third step, the bracelet around her ankle vibrated. Weird. It both tickled and hurt a little.

They finally reached the computer room and went inside.

No one spoke to her. In fact, a few even glared. She sat down at yet another new terminal. The monitor flickered on. She had to believe Justin and Dave would get to Deb. But could they do it soon enough? She had to have a backup plan. With a sigh, she straightened her crooked keyboard. An odd scraping sound followed the movement. One end of the unit tilted upward. A small piece of metal stuck out below the left edge.

Careful not to draw attention to herself, she placed her hand over the metal and grabbed it.

She fired up her computer and while it booted, she slid her hand to her lap and opened her fist. In her palm lay a tiny screwdriver with a very odd-shaped end. She didn't recognize the metal it was made from, but she guessed what it was. Had Niko done this? When?

Even more important . . . why?

She pretended to cough and while bringing her hand back down from her mouth, slid the small screwdriver into the top of her bra. Her heart beat wildly. She swallowed hard to calm herself, even though that hurt like hell. If this meant that there was a chance she could escape, then she knew what she had to do.

She clicked various keys and entered the appropriate program. The subroutine she'd been working on in the background flooded the screen. It had taken forever to complete it. With the Warden and guards reviewing keystrokes, she'd had to go back and forth between commands so no one could infer her intent.

If she simply added this code, the program would leave a trail for the cybersecurity experts to follow.

She typed in a few keystrokes.

Immediately a red box flashed on her screen. "Don't do it. They'll know."

She paled. Oh God. Someone knew. She closed her eyes. This was it. She deleted the keys and waited.

One minute. Two minutes. Five minutes passed.

Very carefully, she started back in. She had to be smarter. Yes. The administrative system. Just like before. Eat away at the program from the least likely point of failure. She burrowed in, keeping her regular program running on the surface. There had to be a way.

She half expected to be torn away from her terminal any second and dragged to the killing corner like Fletcher, but it didn't happen. Terrified, but resolute, she planted the virus. The problem was, she had to trigger it live.

She'd just have to pray she could time it correctly.

If the virus remained dormant, nothing could be done to stop the Warden's plans. Not unless Deb got here.

Eventually, they'd catch Ashley and she'd pay the price, but she no longer cared.

She was a Lansing, and maybe she couldn't fight physically, like the rest of her family, but she certainly wasn't defenseless.

She had a brain that worked differently than most people's. She'd always resented being so different. Right now, she was glad.

She, Ashley Lansing, sixteen-year-old brainiac geek, was going to take these suckers down or die trying. She would never regret being smart again.

She went back to her NSA program, knowing she'd have to give up the module tomorrow. Could she get word to Floyd about the virus in case they chose him instead?

The Warden had been keeping them far apart.

She'd have to play along until curfew. Then, maybe, Niko would tell her what the plan was and when she should take the ankle bracelet off. Two more kids had finished today . . . then disappeared. She didn't know where they'd gone, but she didn't think she'd see them again.

On a last-ditch prayer, she reset the security grids. The defenses they'd added to keep her out were laughable. But if she didn't trip the sensors, then no one would know that the barriers would come down again tomorrow.

She only prayed she could find a way out and take some people with her, because as much as she loved her sister, she didn't know if Deb could make it in time. Justin and Dave didn't know they were set to be eliminated tomorrow.

Of course, if her sister had taught her one thing it was to never give up, never surrender. Okay, maybe that was the mantra from *Galaxy Quest*, but same difference. She'd fight to the end.

Ashley had one person to count on to get out of this place. And that was herself.

CHAPTER TWENTY

THE LEARJET'S PASSENGERS HAD BEEN DEATHLY QUIET DURING takeoff.

Deb watched the others warily. Tension was so thick it was suffocating. The look Zach gave Gabe promised eventual retribution for keeping the existence of a half sister from him.

It wasn't until Zach leveled off the plane for the short flight to the Winslow-Lindbergh Regional Airport, that the spell seemed to break.

Whitney pulled out a thick bunch of folders from her briefcase. "Gabe, I made you copies of some files on my Gasmerati investigation. I shouldn't have." She looked him in the eye. "I *really* shouldn't have. Do you understand?"

Gabe nodded. "Then why are you doing this?"

"Because I want who killed Shannon to pay, and I think whoever did has killed a lot more. I thought there were a lot of victims, but I wasn't making the connection directly to the game company until I spoke with you at my parents' house today. I hypothesized that there was some serial killer who had met them online or something."

Deb turned white. "Serial killer? Is that what you believe is going on?"

Whitney's expression was sympathetic and Deb winced inside. Gabe's sister told the truth as she saw it. She wasn't about to pull punches.

Deb respected and feared that personality trait at the same time. With all her strength, Deb braced herself for Whitney's judgment.

"I didn't have any other explanation," Whitney said, her voice cautious. "When I entered the Bureau two years ago, I started a little side project. I wanted to understand why Shannon died. Why our friends had vanished and were never found. I was in shock when the news hit that the car was finally discovered and they were obviously murdered. Until now everyone had simply vanished. Except Shannon. I thought someone must have become obsessed with good players and taken them."

"Did you work with Dad?" Gabe asked. "From what we've learned he believed that the missing teens possessed unusually high IQs who were gifted in math and science."

Whitney shook her head. "I never saw your father again after the night Shannon was murdered."

"Hold on for one damn minute." Zach's voice boomed from the cockpit. "You were in Denver when Shannon Devlin got killed? That means you must have seen Gabe that night. What the hell, bro? How long have you known about her?"

"Leave him alone," Whitney snapped.

Deb had to admire Whitney. She refused to be intimated by anyone.

"We were teenagers," she said. "I was desperate so I contacted your father to help Shannon. When she was murdered, I was devastated. Gabe was, too, but not for the same reason. He stood up against your father. For your mother *and* your family."

Gabe looked at her, really looked at her, and realized that his brothers' lives had remained intact because of her keeping quiet all these years. Not just him.

"Why didn't you ever contact us?" Gabe asked. "You could have showed up, or called, or put in an appearance at his funeral, which I'm sure you knew about. You seem to know a lot about us."

"I couldn't." Her quiet voice filled the cabin. "You have to understand, Shannon's mother isn't my real mother." A bittersweet smile tugged Whitney's lips. "My mother's name was Mariah Blackstone. She was a great mom, but she never wanted me to intrude on your life. When I was old enough she told me everything. It's not like she and your father had a great romantic history together. A one-night stand that he regretted almost immediately does not a father make."

Gabe coughed to cover his surprise.

"To put it bluntly, my mother thought of him more as a sperm donor than a love interest. I tried to do the same. After my mother passed, the Devlins asked me to live with them. Shannon had been my best friend since kindergarten. I was wanted there. It was for the best."

Whitney turned to Gabe. "When I met you the night Shannon died, I knew you were shocked and angry about my existence. I understood. Your father never knew about me, but I had to try to save Shannon's life, so I contacted him. I knew he was in law enforcement. It didn't matter, though. She died anyway."

"So my father just walked away from you?" Zach threw in. "Like you didn't exist? Was he that big a bastard to ignore the only daughter he had?"

Whitney sighed. "Look, I don't know the details. It wasn't a frequent topic around the dinner table. I just know my mother never wanted me to be part of your lives."

"But you were alone after your mother died. Dad would have taken you in," Zach said.

"And he would have torn apart your family." Whitney sighed. "But more importantly, it would have killed the Devlins. They'd just lost one daughter to a killer. I couldn't tell the woman who'd become a mother to me that she might lose me, too, because I'd found my birth father. It would have devastated her. It just seemed better if Patrick never contacted me after that night, so I made him promise. I didn't want to ruin her life, your life, or anyone else's."

"He just walked away," Gabe said, barely able to take in the swarm of information. He didn't know what he thought anymore. He looked over at Deb, and she gave his a small smile of support.

"You don't know your father very well, do you?" Whitney said. "He kept his word about not being a part of my life, but he set up a small trust to help me get through school. I didn't need your family to survive, no offense. I have the Devlins, and they love me like a daughter. I'm Whitney Blackstone, FBI agent, and I'm fine on my own."

She pulled out a folder. "I'm here for Shannon, and for Ashley. I have an investigation to complete. If we can work together, that's fine. If not, tell me now and we'll end our association in Winslow."

Gabe brought out some notes. "Ashley is my top priority, and we want justice for Shannon."

Whitney nodded. "Okay then."

"What's in Winslow, sis?" He tacked on the moniker at the last minute. Damn if he didn't like and respect this woman more and more as he got to know her. There was a lot of hurt under that prickly exterior and he'd caused a good part of it.

"Look, I'm not an expert on how shell companies are created and used." Whitney's voice had thickened, revealing she wasn't as unaffected by their acceptance as she wanted them to believe. "But according to my contact, one has popped up on the radar recently at the FBI Organized Crime Program. Hundreds of millions of dollars have filtered through EOP."

"EOP?"

"The name of the company. The FBI has traced it back to the Gasmerati family. Here's the kicker. EOP has the exact same address as Intelligent Solutions, the company that sent Deb the game. EOP also owns a warehouse outside of Winslow, Arizona."

"Isn't Winslow, Arizona, one of the locations of Gasmerati's top secret construction projects?" Deb asked, her voice eager. "Could Ashley be in Winslow?"

"I can't be sure, but if my sister were missing, I'd want to know exactly what was going on in Winslow at EOP," Whitney said. "And I'd also be interested that EOP is P.O.E. spelled backward."

The flight hadn't lasted long, but by the time Zach touched down the plane with ease, Deb had nearly scratched a hole in her pants. Her leg bounced, nerves wound tight.

Gabe tugged her fingers apart from his seat next to her.

Thankful he'd pulled her to the back row for the flight, she glanced over at him.

"I'm okay," she muttered under her breath. "Is this almost over?" *Please God, let it be almost over. Let Ashley be safe.*

Deb wouldn't allow herself to consider the alternative.

"I hope so," he said.

When Zach brought the plane to a halt, Gabe rose from his seat and checked his holster and ammo supply. "We make this simple, people. Find Gasmerati's warehouse and get Ashley out."

Whitney pulled out a slip of paper. "I arranged for a car. We're looking for Rural Route 2, just south of the Navajo Reservation."

"We go in quiet," Gabe added, Deb standing at his side. "Whoever took Ashley doesn't want her found."

"What about the cops or Feds or something?" Deb asked.

Gabe shook his head. "We can't trust them. Not after what's happened in Denver with Tower." He looked over at Whitney. "How about you?"

Whitney shifted, her entire body uncomfortable for the first time since Deb had met her. "I'm on my own on this one. I owe one huge favor to the guy who gave me the Gasmerati information as it is. I don't have enough for a warrant."

They really were on their own. Deb palmed the weapon Gabe had given her. "I'm ready," she said. "Let's find my sister."

"I'm coming with," Zach said, his face intent. "And I'm bringing a few toys. You guys draw more small metallic objects than a magnet. I want to survive to see my baby born."

They exited the plane.

"How did Jenna take the fact that you weren't coming right back from Angel Fire like you said?" Gabe asked his brother.

"For a completely hormonal pregnant woman, I think she took it pretty well." Zach rubbed the nape of his neck. "As long as you guys bring me home safe, she'll forgive me. Eventually."

Gabe winced in sympathy. "You didn't tell her we were shot at in Angel Fire, did you?" He shifted his arm. Deb had insisted he get the graze treated. A little antibiotic ointment and a bandage worked wonders. He could barely feel it.

"Hell, no. I'm not stupid." Zach tugged out a high-tech gadget that looked like it came off a Hollywood futuristic set. Or at least out of the *Transformers* movie's prop room. "So, we need to find a warehouse? This baby could locate the space station."

Deb's brow peaked. "Where did you get that tracker? Those are . . . *rare*."

AKA classified.

"I know people." Zach shrugged. "Besides, I'm not holding one advantage back until we find Ashley."

"Thank you," Deb said.

Gabe squeezed her arm. "Well find her."

They piled into the waiting vehicle, stowing guns and ammunition in the back.

Gabe slipped into the driver's side. "Where to?"

"Head north," Whitney said from the passenger seat. She laid a map out on the dash. "It should be a large warehouse. Easy enough to spot."

Deb sat behind Gabe, peering intently right, then left. She leaned forward and placed her hands on the back of Gabe's seat. "How far?"

Five miles later, Whitney took another look at the map. "How could we miss it? It's a huge building."

Zach tapped the coordinates into his gadget again. "You sure about that address?"

Whitney double-checked her file. "That's what it says. They could be lying. A lot of shell corporations do." She looked back at Deb. "God, I'm sorry. I may have given you hope for nothing."

Deb could barely breathe. Disappointment smothered her like wet wool. Her throat closed off. She couldn't speak. She just gave Whitney a nod, pressing her lips together. She couldn't say it was okay, because it wasn't. If Ashley wasn't in Winslow, where was she?

"Don't give up yet," Zach said. "I'm pulling the exact coordinates. Maybe it's underground. Let's see what we can find."

Gabe made a U-turn. Deb rolled down the window. The cold air blew into the car, but she had a clearer view. It did nothing to quell the growing fear that this was a wasted trip.

"Less than a tenth of a mile," Zach said.

Deb squinted, finally spotting something dark and square on the ground, far in the distance. "Stop," she shouted. "There's a concrete slab or something man-made out there."

Gabe slammed on the brakes, backed up a few feet, and pulled off onto a barely visible dirt road, driving up within ten feet of the desolate site.

They piled out of the car.

A huge, cleared area lay before them. The concrete—charred, pitted, and cracked—was slowly being reclaimed by the desert. There had been a warehouse here all right. They strode over to the remains of the manufacturing site.

Gabe knelt down. "Fire decimated whatever was here, and it burned hot."

"Military grade," Deb said. "I've seen it before in Afghanistan." The truth that Ashley wasn't here pierced Deb's heart. She bent over, her hands propped on her quaking knees. "God, Ashley."

Gabe tucked his arm around her. At least he didn't say anything. God, where did they go from here?

"Oh man," Whitney whispered from the center of the slab. She crouched down.

Deb stood up. She and Gabe started toward Whitney.

"Don't move," she said, her face grim. "We're on a crime scene."

Deb looked down at the ashes.

A small whitish bone poked out. Deb stumbled back, her body quaking. She shook her head. "It can't be." She fell against Gabe. "Ashley!"

The park down the road from the sheriff's office was deserted. Tower slammed his door closed and stalked to the waiting man near a Rolls-Royce SUV.

"Sheriff Tower, so glad you could make it." Jeff Gasmerati smiled, his expression much too friendly.

"We agreed not to meet again until Luke Montgomery ended his investigation. Or he was eliminated."

Gasmerati pulled off his leather gloves. "Your job was to divert Montgomery's attention, Sheriff. You have failed. Rather spectacularly, I might add."

Tower stiffened. "What do you want from me?"

"I want you to retire. You've gone soft. The eager sniper who took out that girl in the bus terminal eight years ago is dead. You don't see the betrayal of those around you. Even in your own command. You've outgrown your usefulness."

A chill emanated from Tower's core and spread to his limbs. His hand eased closer to his weapon. "I can retire, if that's what you think needs to happen. I can even disappear if you want."

"Oh, you'll most definitely be going away." The crack of a single gunshot split the air.

Sheriff Tower fell back, blood pouring from the wound to his chest.

"Guess he forgot about the last sheriff's retirement plan," Jeff said to Sly. "Dump the body in Montgomery's parking lot. That should give the Jefferson County Sheriff's Office and the FBI something else to stew about. It's time to clean house."

Gabe paced beside the rental car while Whitney contacted the Phoenix field office. His half sister was something pretty special. Tough, smart. Hell if he didn't like her. Zach seemed to, as well. But how would their brothers react to her existence? Or his mother?

At least he and Zach had seen her in action and her professionalism warranted respect.

He walked over to Deb and put his arms around her. "Are you okay?"

She shook her head, but didn't speak, just burrowed in closer to his chest. He enveloped her protectively. "I thought she was dead. I thought those bones . . ." Deb's voice trailed off.

"Whitney's sure they're at least five years old, maybe ten." Gabe rubbed her back. He had to stop getting caught up in his own drama and remember what Deb was going through. She was so strong that it was sometimes easy to forget she needed him—even if she didn't admit it. They'd all hoped to find Ashley here, or at least a lead. No one had expected bone fragments.

Whitney walked over to the two of them. "The Phoenix office is bringing a forensics team out. We'll figure out what happened."

"Can you tell how many?" Deb asked, her voice thin.

Whitney shook her head. "I'm not a forensics expert and the bone shards are small. But . . . too many. There were a lot of people killed there. The fact that a massacre happened in secret and no one knew . . ." Whitney didn't finish the sentence.

Gabe tightened his hold on Deb.

"We're nowhere closer to finding Ashley, are we?" she said, despair dripping from every word. Deb straightened. "There has to be some kind of lead out of this."

"If our suspicion is right about the Gasmerati family and the game people working together, maybe there's another location we can search."

"Our . . . informant . . . mentioned other construction sites. One in Nevada, right? One somewhere else. Idaho or Ohio. He wasn't sure."

A possibility stewed in Gabe's mind if Steve Paretti was telling the truth. "*Version VIII* is close to being released and Ashley has vanished. Shannon disappeared just prior to *Version II* releasing." He raced to the vehicle and pulled out a list. He ran his finger down the dates of the missing kids. "There are clusters of kidnappings. I need the release dates of *Point of Entry*."

"You got it." Whitney pulled out a tablet and tapped for a few moments. She strode over to him and they compared the list. "Not bad, Gabe. You'd make a decent detective."

"What are you saying?" Deb asked.

"Except for Ashley and Justin, there's been a distinct pattern. Approximately six months before each issue of *Point of Entry*, several high-IQ teens have gone missing."

Deb gripped Gabe's arm. "They just take them? And they're never found."

Gabe didn't know how to answer. He could imagine exactly what happened to them if the bone fragments here were any indication. The idea was too horrific to imagine.

A siren sounded off in the distance. Several vehicles sped toward them.

Whitney stepped back. "The local police are here to cordon off the crime scene. This is going to take a while. The FBI is on the way. State and federal forensics, too. I have to follow up, there's nothing you can do here. See if your informant can identify any other locations. We have to narrow down where she might be."

"I have access to equipment that will handle that," Zach said. "We can find a penny on the ground from outer space, if we need to."

Gabe nodded. "Okay, we'll head back to Denver."

Zach and Deb started toward the car. As he unlocked it, he yelled, "I'll leave it at the airport for you, Whitney. Keys will be at the rental's registration desk."

Gabe hung back, feeling awkward. Should he hug her? Man, this was messed up.

Whitney shifted her feet and looked at him. She nearly held out her hand, but she didn't. There was an awkward silence. "I'll be in touch if I learn more," she offered.

"Right. Same here."

He started back to the car when the sat phone rang. He looked down at the number but didn't recognize it. "Hello?"

"Uh, hi. I'm, uh, trying to reach Deborah Lansing. This is supposed to be her phone."

"Hold on. I'll get her." Gabe bolted to the car, pulled open the door, and hit the Speaker button. He indicated the call was for her and Deb grabbed it.

"Hello, this is Deborah Lansing."

The voice on the other end broke. "This is Ashley's boyfriend, Justin Connell. We were kidnapped. You have to help me rescue her or she's going to die."

CHAPTER TWENTY-ONE

Deb gripped the phone in her shaking hand. "Justin! Oh God, Justin, do you know where Ashley is?"

Zach and Whitney came running.

Staring into the phone as if she could see Ashley through the device, Deb gripped it tight with two hands. "Where are you, Justin? Where's Ashley?"

"Idaho." Justin's voice had gone urgent.

Gabe met Deb's gaze. Ernie had been right. So had Steve.

"D-desert somewhere in southern Idaho. There's a bombing range nearby."

Zach immediately began searching his phone and Whitney her tablet.

"What's the nearest town?" Deb demanded.

Gabe tightened his hold. "Keep it together," he whispered. "Get as much detail as you can."

Deb nodded.

"I don't know. But a couple of miles from here is a weigh station. It got hit with a bomb and exploded. They tried to kill us. They won't stop."

Bombs, explosions, what the hell was going on? "What are you talking about, Justin?"

"Just let me talk. I don't know how long this phone will last."

Justin took a deep, shuddering breath. "Ashley's in trouble. I tried to convince her to come with us, but they put a tracking chip in her and someone had to disarm the security system. She's the best—"

A sob escaped him, then an urgent whisper sounded in the background.

"Shut up, Dave," Justin hissed. "I know. I'm trying to be quiet. We hitched a ride, but they found us. The truck driver is dead, his rig exploded. We barely got away. We had to run. We're still in the desert somewhere near there, but I saw a sign advertising Reno. Black Rock City, too, though I don't know how far away they are. I don't think we're near the Nevada border yet."

He cursed. "My battery is on red and blinking."

Deb could barely talk around her fear. "Where's Ashley?"

"Still at the compound with the others. A huge gray warehouse kind of building, but it's filled with electronics. They had us working on computers. Look for power usage. Has to be huge. But the place is fortified like a prison. Guards. Guns. Sensors. The works."

Deb heard a wheezing sound in the background. "Are you hurt?"

The phone started cracking.

"Dave . . . bad. Hospital."

Justin's voice could barely be heard now. "No police. Can't trust them . . . hiding . . . men searching . . ."

"Justin!" Oh God, she was losing him. Her only connection to her sister.

". . . scared . . . help . . . Ashley."

The phone went dead.

"We've got to find them." Deb held the phone tight. "He's our only link to Ashley."

"We know about where they are," Zach said. "There can't be too many exploding weigh stations in southern Idaho."

"With the cell phone dead, we can't track their signal." Gabe frowned.

"I can search for them from the air," Deb insisted. "They know I'm a helicopter pilot. Maybe they'll leave me a sign or come out when they see the chopper."

"That could work against them if the other search party has one, too."

"I don't know what else to do."

Zach pulled out his credit card and his phone. "I'll find a chopper to rent in Black Rock City until we get a better location."

"Since I have to stay here for now," Whitney offered, "I'll check for any possible dummy companies or warehouses near southern Idaho and toward Reno. That will narrow down the possibilities."

"Thank you," Deb said.

Gabe tugged her in his arms. "We'll find that weigh station and those kids before they get shot or freeze to death. This damn game won't claim another life if we can help it."

Ashley lay in her brick-hard bed and checked to make sure the screwdriver tool was still tucked in her bra. Boots stomped up and down the hallway outside her room half the night and all this morning. The compound was on lockdown while the place was inspected before the big event tomorrow.

The Warden wanted nothing to go wrong. His threats had half the kids in tears. He pretended that if the presentation went well, they'd all be free. Ashley knew better. They were all dead anyway. No matter what happened tomorrow.

She'd always thought she'd do so many things. Finish college. See the world. Maybe get married and have kids eventually. She never thought she'd be looking at less than twenty-four hours to live when she was only sixteen.

She wished she'd told her family that she loved them more often. And that she'd accepted those kisses from Justin sooner than she had. She wrapped her arms about herself, rubbing up and down to warm her body.

More guards had guns now. They walked the corridors in pairs, making sure no one else would escape. Still, she kept up hope.

She had the screwdriver; she'd planted the virus. Now all she needed to do was be the one chosen for the demo and all the work the Warden had done would be wiped clean. Her virus would erase all those trapdoors the game had been opening for weeks in computers and databases everywhere.

She was sixteen and she would die saving the world. Could be worse.

Never give up.

Never surrender.

Never let the suckers get you down . . . unless you get them first.

Ashley prayed Deb would show up to kick butt and take names, even if she was no longer around to see it.

Gabe checked his watch when Zach landed the Learjet in Black Rock City, Nevada. A couple of hours.

"The chopper should be waiting," Zach said.

Gabe looked at his brother. "You don't have to go, Zach. Your wife—"

"Not happening, little brother. Deb can fly the chopper. You and I can shoot, rescue people, or whatever else is needed. You're not running this op alone, Gabe. This one takes teamwork. Take it from someone who learned that concept the hard way." Zach exited the cockpit and faced Gabe, a scowl on his face. "Family is about the only thing you have to rely on when life gets tough. You blasted me for going it alone not six months ago. Now I'm throwing your words back at you."

Gabe raised his hands. "I got it."

Zach crossed his arms and Gabe had seen that look on his older brother's face just enough to know Zach was dead serious. "We need the rest of the family to go up against these people, right? If this place is as fortified as the kid says, if the law can't be trusted—and after Tower, God knows I believe Justin on that—we need everyone we can get." Zach paused. "Even Nick and Steve Paretti."

"Not Paretti," Gabe snapped, shaking his head. "We can't trust him. Look what he did to Luke and Jazz."

Zach's jaw clenched, but Gabe could tell the conversation wasn't over.

What was Zach thinking? They had enough to go up against without worrying about one of their own team.

"Let's get the chopper," Deb said.

Gabe nodded. This wasn't over. Paretti had proven untrustworthy. They needed to be able to rely on everyone if they were going to save Justin and then get Ashley out of that hellhole alive.

Together, Deb and Gabe entered the lobby of the helicopter company.

"Oh yes. Mr. Montgomery. Everything's ready." The owner's grin nearly split his face.

"Guess that's what a hefty donation will do," Gabe whispered while the man finalized the paperwork.

Within moments they stood beside a Bell chopper.

"This okay?" he asked Deb.

With rushed movements, she inspected the helicopter. "It'll do."

While Deb completed her preflight, Gabe watched her closely. She was running on empty, they all were, having flown across a half dozen Western states since this morning. Winslow had been a blow, but for the first time since he'd recognized Ashley had been taken and wasn't on the run, Gabe had to admit he had hope they might actually find Deb's sister.

If they could find Justin.

Zach sidled up beside Gabe. "She's something else." A helicopter pilot himself, Zach studied her inspection. "She's good at what she does. Doesn't have to think about the next step," he said. "How is she holding up, Gabe? Really?"

"She's strong. She'll do what it takes to find Ashley," Gabe said. "Later, she might fall apart, but not until the job's done. She's a lot like us that way."

"God knows I'm not one to lecture—" Zach started.

"I wouldn't say that."

"Much," Zach continued. "But you need to rethink Steve. Nick vouched for Paretti. We haven't heard the whole story on his undercover status, but I know from you the guy is a good shot.

Not as good as Jazz, but good. We could use two positions if the building is as large as the footprint at Winslow." Zach placed his hand on Gabe's shoulder. "I know what he's done, but we need him, Zach. And you need to trust Nick's judgment on this one."

With a scowl, Gabe shoved his hands through his hair. Anger still roiled inside him. It had barely lessened at all. "I'm not ready to trust him that much."

"I am," Deb said. "I'll beg him, if I have to. Because my sister's life is more important than hurt egos at the moment. Betrayal sucks. I know that firsthand. You know I do. But your brother vouched for him. In the time I've known you, you've bragged about Nick more than once. I'm willing to trust his judgment. It's *my* sister's life at stake. Bring him in." She crossed her arms. "Now, are you ready to find Justin?"

The truth of Deb's words slammed into Gabe. Man, what the hell was he thinking? Deb was right. Besides, he didn't have to trust Steve. He just had to let him shoot.

"I hear you, Deb. There's only one hitch." He looked back and forth between Zach and Deb. "What if Gasmerati shows up? Do you think Steve can actually kill his own cousin?"

A tinge of orange bathed the Nevada desert sky. Deb strapped in, her hands steady, even though her heart pounded with anticipation.

"Put on your headsets," she ordered Zach and Gabe, then slipped on her own. "All set?" she asked through the mic.

"Let's go," Gabe said. "We're running out of light."

The whirr of the rotors emitted a high-pitched squeal and, a few minutes later, Deb lifted the center control stick. The chopper rose in the air and started north.

Zach set out binoculars and opened a large duffel. A slew of weaponry overflowed. Semiautomatics, a couple of clubs, knives, rifles. God knew what else. "The owner didn't see your stash, did he?" Deb asked.

"Nah. We'd probably be under arrest if he did, but if we're in a firefight, we're going to need it. We're not leaving without those kids."

"Have an extra set of binoculars?" Gabe asked while he spread out the map.

"Yeah." Zach dug around in the bag. He found the second pair and passed them over.

The sun had fallen even lower in the sky. "Maybe an hour or so of daylight left," Deb said, peering at the ground.

She pushed the steering bar and the bird headed north, veering down slightly. "What are the coordinates for that weigh station? If the trucker they hitched with is dead, the kidnappers aren't far behind. When they learn Justin and his friend weren't killed, they'll call out the troops, en masse."

Gabe studied the map and circled an area. "Luke's looking into the weigh station. We'll have to guess until he calls. From what Justin said, the camp is probably near Saylor Creek Bombing Range. It's south of Mountain Home Air Force Base. That's a good eighty miles as the crow flies to the Nevada border." He shifted the map. "If I were them, I'd head for an area that's not totally flat. They'd want someplace to take cover, if they need to, though even this area doesn't offer much."

"Good eye," Deb said. "That's where I would have headed, too. Let's hope it's as obvious to Justin and Dave on the ground."

"Nick is arranging a safe house and guards for the boys to go into as soon as we find them," Gabe said smoothly. "Plus, I called Caleb and gave him a heads-up. He's got everyone in our family in Denver packing."

"So what's the plan?" Zach asked, all the while scanning the desert surface with the binoculars.

Gabe did the same on the other side of the chopper. "Luke is gathering the troops. As soon as we know where to go, we'll finalize plans."

The sat phone rang. God, she hoped Luke had come through with the location.

"See you there," Gabe shouted. He twisted in his seat. "A local news report said the police found a truck and weigh station blown to smithereens off of Highway 93. Not a whole lot to identify, but enough of the driver remained to determine that he had been shot through the temple. Before the bomb hit," Luke said.

Zach cursed. "Any mention of the kids?"

"Nothing. If they haven't been recaptured, then they're still out there somewhere."

"What are the coordinates?" Deb asked.

Gabe relayed them.

She adjusted course.

"The other kid sounded sick or hurt," Gabe said. "They won't be moving fast. If we start the search pattern near the truck explosion and go systematically from there, we may luck out."

Deb scanned the horizon, looking for anything out of place. They had to be there. Had to be. She pushed the chopper to its limits. "We should be nearing the explosion area soon," she said, following the ribbon of highway that dissected the desert landscape. "You see any unfriendlies?"

"Nothing," Zach said. "Makes me nervous."

"You got that right." Gabe smoothed the map over his lap, growing more impatient by the minute. A half hour later, there was still no sign, and the sun had gone down lower in the sky. Shadows started falling over the mountains.

Gabe's gaze swept across the barren vista.

"Anything?" Deb asked, the pit of her stomach twisting in knots. Flying missions overseas, facing gunfire, was nothing compared to searching for her little sister. Deb couldn't remember ever feeling quite so much terror as this moment. So close and panicked, they might end up being too late.

"Not yet. Maybe they didn't get as far as they thought."

Each minute seemed to inch the sun lower in the sky. "Wait!" Gabe shouted. "Blue fabric came winging out from behind that mound."

Deb turned the helicopter and moved very low very fast. Gabe caught his breath, but Deb's hand didn't waiver.

A blue T-shirt lay on the ground. "Smart kids," Deb said. "That's something Ashley would do."

She circled the area. One of the boys crawled out and yanked the shirt behind the rock. "They know we're here."

"I'll set her down," Deb said. "Be ready to grab them so we can take off immediately."

"Two ATVs approaching fast from behind," Zach yelled. "They're armed."

Deb pushed the chopper to cover the distance. She cursed. She couldn't land between the boys and the ATVs. She quickly landed on the packed earth. She hated this part. Waiting, wanting to help. She sat at the controls, ready to pull up as soon as the boys were inside.

Gabe palmed his weapon and opened the door. "You call out, Deb," he said. "They don't know me."

She cupped her hands. "Justin! It's Deb Lansing."

The boys ran toward them, sprinting as the ATV roared closer and closer.

Zach and Gabe bounded out of the helicopter, guns at the ready.

"Run, Dave!" Justin yelled. "Faster."

Dave fell. Justin hauled him back to his feet.

"They found us!" Justin sprinted out into the open first, heading right toward them.

Dave followed, but it was easy to see how much he struggled. She wanted to get out and run, but she had to stay ready.

The helicopter's rotors whirred, buffeting them. The ATVs pulled within range, spewing dirt in the air, then split off.

Taking advantage of the dust cloud, Gabe raced toward the kids, firing as he ran. Zach veered toward the second ATV.

Deb leaned forward, straining to see the murky view. Shots rang out. Dave stumbled.

The ATV quickly gained on the boy. He couldn't seem to get back on his feet.

"South!" Deb shouted.

Gabe shifted, aimed at the gunman pointing his weapon at the boy. Direct hit. The man slumped over. The driver pulled out a pistol and shot Dave where he lay.

"No!"

"Get down, Justin!" Gabe yelled.

Justin dove.

Zach hit the second ATV's gunman in the head.

The vehicle swerved. Zach's shot missed the driver's heart. He turned the steering wheel toward Justin. Gabe and Zach both fired, killing the driver instantly, but the vehicle's trajectory was set.

The ATV smashed into Justin, knocking him down and running over him.

Deb's fists clenched the controls. There was nothing anyone could do. God, she hated this part of her job. Useless. Waiting.

Gabe ran to Justin and knelt beside him. Zach ran to Dave. They returned quickly to the chopper, each man holding a boy in his arms.

Zach loaded Dave onto the floor. "He's bad. You have medical training. Watch him and I'll fly."

Deb nodded, slipping into the back beside the unconscious boy. Within seconds Zach lifted off.

While she settled Dave, Gabe checked Justin. One side of his head bore a long cut and a huge bruise.

He tested his pulse. "It's weak, but there." He ran his hands over Justin's arms and legs. "He's in bad shape. I think there are cracked ribs and probably internal injuries. We have to get him to a hospital immediately."

"I don't know about Dave," Deb said. The boy's lips were blue, his chest covered with blood. Gabe removed his shirt and thrust it into Deb's hands. She tried to stanch the bleeding. "Look for a medical kit. See what they have." Wheezes sounded from the boy's chest.

"After I get the coordinates for the nearest hospital, I'll tell them to stand by," Zach yelled.

Deb had no time to answer, no time to think. She and Gabe worked side by side. Her best leads to her sister now lay unconscious. Deb prayed they made it through, so they could tell her where Ashley was, before it was too late.

As Zach flew them through the ever-increasing darkness, Deb shivered.

What if it was already too late?

CHAPTER TWENTY-TWO

DEB PACED IN THE WAITING ROOM WHILE GABE SPOKE TO HIS brother Nick in low tones.

The small town had only one surgeon, and Dave had needed the OR first. The bullet had come close to his heart. He was in a coma on a ventilator. They didn't know if he'd wake up.

Justin had gone into surgery to repair his spleen. The kid was banged up, but alive. Gabe had gotten hold of both sets of parents. They'd probably be here soon.

If only they could've found Justin and Dave sooner. Maybe if she'd flown faster, made better choices.

Deb rubbed her hands over her face. Southwestern Idaho was a huge area. So was the bombing range. How could they find Ashley in time if they didn't know where?

A surgeon pushed through the double doors and mopped his face. Exhaustion tugged at his eyes.

"How is Justin?" Deb practically lunged in the guy's face. "When can I speak with him?"

"I should only be talking to his parents, but these are unusual circumstances. I can only give you a brief. He came through the surgery okay. I'm more concerned about his head wound. We're doing everything we can to keep the swelling down."

Deb's tension ratcheted higher, and Gabe joined her, his hand on her shoulder.

"As far as talking to him . . ." The doctor shrugged. "I have no idea when he'll wake up, or if he'll remember. In traumas like this, sometimes memories of what happened just before the accident never return. It can vary from losing minutes to days or more. He's going into recovery now. If you're the praying kind, you might want to start."

The surgeon turned around and headed back to his patients.

"Ashley can't wait." Deb rubbed her tired eyes.

"Nick is making some calls," Gabe said. "As soon as they're stable, we'll move them to a more secure location."

Deb nodded. She walked to the edge of the waiting room and looked out the window. The lights of Reno twinkled, but looming over them, a large, black monstrosity of a mountain shadowed the foothills.

Gabe moved in behind her and rested two hands on her shoulders. She leaned back into his warmth. She knew Gabe's touch, his scent. Over the last few days she'd become accustomed to him.

He kissed her hair gently. "What are you thinking?"

"That I'm so thankful you're safe, but Ashley's still out there." Deb closed her eyes. "She might be dead."

He squeezed the muscles and kneaded them slightly. "You can't give up. She got Justin and Dave out."

"Stupid girl didn't come with them. She played hero." Deb's voice cracked.

"She did what she had to do. She's a hero. Just like her big sister."

Gabe turned Deb around and drew her tightly into his arms. "Our cavalry rented a hotel room across the street to plan and brought some of Zach's best gadgets."

"We have to get out there looking." She could hear the slight hysteria tingeing her voice.

"I know you're beat, but my brothers have been working on a plan while we were here. They're close."

"How?" Deb insisted. "All we know is a warehouse in southwestern Idaho."

"That matches up with Ernie's cryptic Idaho message before he died. Steve Paretti spoke with Grace. After getting her and her son to safety, she had written down the name of the construction company in her notebook. I guess she's been trying to nail Jeff Gasmerati for a long time."

A spark of hope sparked within Deb. "Can we track that information?"

"Luke's researching a company that bought a big tract of land around here in the last several years. Whitney's matching it with the FBI's list of possible Gasmerati shell companies. They're close."

Deb glanced over at Nick, who had the cell phone to his ear. She lowered her voice. "Whitney is with your brothers? Do they know who she is?"

"Yeah, and she pretty much told them to man up. Zach's watching out for her."

Deb's phone rang. She looked down. "Oh, no. It's my father." She let out a slow breath and picked up. "Hello?"

The General didn't speak for a moment. "Deb? I . . . uh . . ."

She hadn't heard him stutter like that since . . . Fear clamped her gut. She braced herself. "What is it? What's wrong?"

"It's Ben." Her father's voice went thick with emotion. "There's been an explosion. The Army lost all communication with his unit."

He paused. She didn't want to hear it.

"Deb, they think Ben's dead."

She froze. No. Not true. Not possible.

With both hands, she clutched at Gabe, her mind strangely numb. She couldn't think, couldn't feel.

A fog fell over her. She could barely make out her father's words.

Something wet streamed down her face.

"Deb, what about Ashley?" Her father's voice was soft, hesitant. "Did you find her?"

He'd asked her a question.

Gabe's thumb wiped away her tears. She clung to him.

"Not yet."

He paused. "I see. I'd arranged to come stateside, but now I'll need to wait until I receive confirmation . . . of your brother's . . . status."

"I'll find Ashley," Deb said softly. "I promise."

She heard the hitch of her father's breath on the other end of the line. "I can't lose two of my kids, Deborah. Do whatever you can."

"I . . . I will."

Her father cleared his throat. "Stay safe, Deborah. I . . . I do love you."

He disconnected before she could respond.

He hadn't said those words since her mother died.

She clutched the phone, unable to move. She'd wanted to stay on the line with her father. This was the man she remembered from so long ago. She wanted him here. She wanted someone to count on.

Gabe stroked the side of her cheek with his knuckle. "You all right?"

She looked at Gabe. He's the one she could count on. He'd never let her down. He'd proved that already. No matter how tough things got, he was always there.

"You heard?"

"Enough," he said gently. Gabe's phone rang. "It's Zach," he said, then pressed Speaker.

"We found the warehouse. Wheels up in twenty minutes."

The wake-up alarm shrilled over the intercom and echoed down the hallways.

Ashley groaned and pulled herself up to a sitting position. Her room had no windows, but from the grit in her eyes, it had to be night. Why were they getting up now?

She'd heard the moneymen might be coming this afternoon or tomorrow. What was going on?

She dressed swiftly, not wanting to be caught unprepared should the Warden or one of the guards come in.

The Warden was still angry with her. He hated her so much, he would probably do the deed himself when it came time to kill everyone.

She had to stop thinking like that or she'd paralyze with fear. Bravery came and went with increasing irregularity.

Moving carefully, she slipped the tiny screwdriver back into her bra. Today would be the day she'd use it. Ashley couldn't avoid finishing the programming they'd assigned her the day before. She'd had to do it right. She couldn't fool them.

Niko was the best programmer among the bad guys, but even the Warden knew code. Enough to verify her subroutines did exactly what they were supposed to.

She'd embedded the grid commands deep, the virus even deeper. But after Justin and Dave's escape, they checked her computer thoroughly every night. Was she really that good, or had Niko just chosen not to see what she'd done?

The two kids down the hall had disappeared yesterday. Ashley closed her eyes. She'd watched Niko carefully last night. He'd come inside, his face almost gray with fatigue.

And she knew. The purge had started. The least talented went first, but no one was getting out alive. They'd outlived their usefulness.

She didn't hope to get out alive. She could stop what they planned, though. But only if she or Floyd did the demo. She definitely shouldn't tick anyone else off until then.

The Warden had engineered the creation of a pervasive piece of code that would make any computer on any network vulnerable. If the computer was connected, he and his people would have a back door into the system. Anywhere in the world. Military, government, financial. Ashley shivered. They had to be stopped.

Boots and shuffling sounded in the corridors. Guards were escorting people to the cafeteria, she assumed, before starting their unusually early day.

Tension made her fidgety. She sat on the bed and her ankle bracelet hit the metal bedstead with a clang.

She studied each corner of the room. No obvious cameras in the ceiling, but she'd seen enough to be careful. There were vents, and she couldn't risk being caught. This could be her last chance.

Lying on the bed, she huddled beneath the blanket, tucking her legs into a ball, feigning feeling ill. Niko said if she used the wrong tool on the cuff, she'd set it off and they'd know. She sent a little prayer upward, then pulled the small screwdriver from her bra.

Nerves had her fumbling as she felt around the bracelet. A small screw attached at the back.

God, what she wouldn't give for a flashlight.

The blanket clung like a suffocating hand around her throat. She caught the groove in the screw and turned. No alarm went off. Did it trigger a notification somewhere else? She was committed now.

Every few turns, she fumbled with the screw. Finally, the tiny piece of metal fell to the bed. After undoing the second screw, she pulled apart the ankle monitor and brought it up to her chest. She had to risk a bit of light to check it out. She lifted the blanket slightly. Inside the bracelet two small sets of marks were scraped into the inside rubber casing. *C2.*

That was the door Niko had pointed out when he'd led her to the armory, and again when he took her the long way back to her room tonight.

A door, metal, but no guard. Only the wall panel. She'd seen cameras . . . and yet . . .

God, could she trust him? If she was wrong . . .

She had to take a chance. There was no time left.

A loud knock sounded at her door.

"Get up," Niko's voice yelled. "You're on display."

Heart pounding, she tucked the tracking device into her pocket and made certain her pants covered her ankle. For a while, she'd let them think they knew where she was . . . and she prayed she'd know the right time to run out of door C2. She'd take whoever she could with her.

Niko slammed open the steel door. The clang echoed through the halls. The Warden stalked in, Niko and the red-haired guard behind him. "We're going to the main computer room. Our guests are coming earlier than expected." The Warden's eye twitched in irritation. "They want to see you play. You will perform brilliantly. Understood?"

She nodded.

"I'm serious, Ms. Lansing. No stalling. No purposeful mistakes. Nothing rebellious at all. You will do exactly what you are told to do or I will gun down Floyd and your friend Mylo. Right in front of you. Do I make myself clear?"

She nodded again, but she felt sick this time. Endangering herself was one thing, but her friends? She hadn't even been allowed to talk to Mylo since he'd been here. At least he was still alive and hadn't vanished like so many others.

She ducked her head, not wanting the Warden to see her hatred. No mistakes. No trouble. Not today.

"Good." The Warden gripped her chin and yanked it up so that she had to look him in the eyes. "You screw up even one thing, and I'll shoot you right in the chair after I dispose of your friends. A little blood on the machine may make the next person more receptive to commands."

Ashley clenched her teeth so she wouldn't spit in his face.

"Niko, pat her down. I'm heading to see our guests now." He addressed the red-haired guard. "Watch her carefully." The Warden paused. "In fact, watch them both."

She swallowed.

Niko patted her down, not even pausing as he felt the ankle bracelet in her pocket.

"Bring her," Niko ordered the guard, then stepped away, until he stood behind the red-haired guard. In a movement so fast she barely caught it, Niko formed his fingers into a *C*, then held down two fingers. "Today should be very interesting. Remember your lessons well."

Ashley walked through the doorway with them. She understood what Niko meant. Today was the day to escape through C2. He would do—or had done—whatever he could to help her.

CHAPTER TWENTY-THREE

Deb hunkered down behind a dune and settled into position overlooking the northwest corner of a huge square building. Darkness shielded them from view, but dawn wasn't that far away.

Gabe's family had come through. Zach and Whitney, of course. But Luke and his sniper wife, Jazz, the über-mysterious black ops brother Seth, and even Nick had flown in. They'd need the help.

Poor Gabe had even relented. Steve Paretti held a sniper location in sight of one of the building's corners.

"Is everyone in position?" Deb whispered to Gabe.

He swept the area with infrared binoculars. "Close."

Gabe clicked his mic. "Roll call, Mousketeers?"

Each member of the team sounded in through the communications system. "Affirmative," Seth responded last. "We have good coverage, but no obvious exits."

Nine against however many manned that huge building. The odds didn't look good. Even Zach and Luke, with their combined equipment and skills, hadn't been able to find a hole in the security.

She shivered, fighting a fear that threatened to overwhelm her resolve. Not for her, but for Ashley. Deb rubbed her temple. Did they have a chance?

About ten feet away, Jazz Montgomery had set up her Remington 700/40 to provide a clear view of two sides and two exits. Jazz must have noticed the sag in Deb's shoulders and crept over before flipping off her mic. "I can tell you one thing, Deb. When the chips are down, there's no one I'd want on my side more than the Montgomerys. They don't give up. They fight until the end. If Ashley is in there, they'll get her out."

Deb nodded. "Thanks."

Jazz gave her a small smile and resettled her Remington against her shoulder, returning to an eerily still, prone position.

"She's right."

Deb shifted closer to Gabe. "What's happening?"

"We're waiting." Gabe didn't waiver from sweeping the area with his binoculars. "We need to create a break in their security to gain access to the building. Zach and Luke will do the tech work. They have heat sensors and are looping the remote viewing cameras, shutting down what they can. If it doesn't work, we'll have to pull in reinforcements."

Deb swallowed hard. "Ashley may not have that kind of time."

"Believe me," Gabe said. "We're all aware of that. We'll do everything in our power to get into that warehouse as quickly as possible, but if we screw up, we could put every innocent life in that place in more danger."

"Is your family safe?" Deb asked. "Have you heard?"

"Yeah. Mom stewed for a while, until Caleb gave in. No secrets, about the op anyway. She's got her rosary out for us." His voice lowered. "We decided not to tell her about Whitney. Not yet. She'll kick our butts for keeping it from her, but we need to find the right way."

"Good luck with that. From what I've seen, your mother doesn't take any prisoners," Deb whispered.

"Yeah. I don't know what she'll do."

Deb could finish the sentence for him. *About me keeping a secret for all these years.* She moved her hand to stroke his arm with a comforting touch. "She loves you. She'll forgive you."

"Yeah. Probably. No matter how much we hurt her. She's like that."

His words said it all. The guilt ate at him, probably had been all these years. His back stiffened as he tried to shake off too many thoughts.

"At least Neil Wexler's been cleared," Deb said, a not-so-subtle attempt to change the subject and get him out of his head. There would be time for that. Later. "Tower kept good records and they were able to tie him to Menken's so-called suicide. They also arrested two more deputies. I'm so relieved for you."

"I'm just sorry I couldn't sit in a courtroom and watch Tower go down. The SOB is dead," Gabe informed her.

Deb couldn't stop her jaw from dropping in surprise. She'd thought they'd have another battle with the sheriff once they returned to Denver.

"Yeah, Nick just told me," Gabe said. "One shot. Assassinated. Hand cut off."

"Gasmerati."

"Once we find Ashley, we'll bring Gasmerati down. Luke and his family will be out of danger."

He didn't mention failure, as if he wouldn't entertain the notion. Deb prayed he was right. Because if Gasmerati was eliminated, Gabe would be safe, too.

"I've got bad news." Seth's voice sounded through their communication devices. "Really bad."

Deb's entire body tensed. She dug her fingers into Gabe's arm. "Tell us," he said. "We need to be prepared."

"Fresh digging on the east side of the building. Our radar shows human remains. At least a half dozen."

Deb couldn't move, or breathe. "Ashley?" she asked quietly.

"I don't know," Seth said. "We won't know until we dig."

Deb didn't fall apart. She couldn't. Gabe pulled her close to him and rubbed her arms. The chill taking over every fiber of her being begged for heat.

"It's probably not her."

Deb's jaw clenched and she nodded, but everything inside seemed to shatter. First Ben, now Ashley? God, none of it could be true.

Gabe turned her to face him. "Look at me, Deb."

She stared at his chest. She didn't want to look. She didn't know if she could hold her emotions back if she saw the least bit of sympathy in his eyes.

He lifted her chin. All she saw was determination and fury lighting his eyes.

"We'll find Ashley, honey."

Deb nodded again, unable to respond to the unexpected endearment. She looked back at the warehouse. She just prayed they found her sister alive, and not her body.

Step by step, Ashley closed in on the computer room. She couldn't stop her heart from slamming against her chest. Only a few more feet.

Niko slowed the pace as he and Ashley approached the corridor to the computer room. "Go check the rooms," he ordered the guard. "We want no mistakes."

The man nodded and methodically opened door after door. Once he'd moved far enough away so he couldn't hear their conversation, Niko drew her close to the wall.

"Shut up and listen. We're between cameras. Act like you feel nauseous in case the guard comes back."

Ashley clutched her stomach and bent a little at the waist, one hand on the wall as if she needed support.

Niko moved in closer. "It has to be today. They've planted gas canisters in the basement. They'll take everyone down there, then destroy the building. By tonight, this place will be gone."

Shocked, she stood again, though the pain cramping her stomach was now real. "Why are you telling me this?"

Niko stared at her in frustration. "You've got guts like I've never seen, Lansing. The worst part, you're who I used to be. Who I thought I could be before . . . You're like Shannon coming back to remind me—" He stopped. "Never mind."

"Are you coming with us?"

"I've done too much." Niko's voice was resigned. "I don't deserve to escape."

"You helped us. I could tell them . . ."

"There's no time. As soon as our important guests arrive, the Warden will be distracted. I'll disable as much of the security system as I can to help you and the others escape."

"Can we make it?" Ashley asked. "There are so many guards."

"Justin and Dave made it. The Feds have them. I've never seen the Warden so furious. I thought he might shoot someone just for fun." Niko shrugged. "He has before."

Relief flooded through her. "Then help could be on the way. Justin was going to contact my sister."

"The Admiral? The one you sent the game to?"

Ashley blinked in surprise. "You knew about that?"

"I told you. I followed every keystroke you made."

"Then I was lucky it was you watching me."

"You'd be dead right now if the Warden hadn't betrayed me and planned to get rid of me, too," Niko said bluntly. "If she shows up, how could I signal her? No way can I risk a phone call or text."

Boots sounded down the hallway. Ashley bent over even more, imitating some dry heaves. There had to be a way. "She taught me Morse code," Ashley said, her voice hesitant. Then she smiled. "No. Four stars," she said. "As in a four-star admiral. Like the address label. She'll get that it's from me."

The Warden's voice boomed down the hall. "Niko, where the hell have you been? Get her in here. She's late."

Niko grabbed her by the arm. "Yes, sir. She started to vomit, so we stopped for a moment."

Ashley wrapped her arms around her waist again, feigning sickness.

"She can throw up all over the damn computer lab for all I care. Just get her in here."

As they walked across the expanse, Ashley blanched. Mylo and Floyd stood in the black corner against the wall. Fletcher's blood still stained the grated floor. Her stomach lurched for real. She understood the warning.

Niko shoved her into her computer chair. "One screwup, one gunshot. You've got two friends. Two chances. Then you go to the corner."

"Nice performance, Niko, but a little too late for me to believe," the Warden hissed. "I'll deal with you later."

Faint light rose from the horizon. Dawn was approaching.

Gabe tensed. Their positions were more vulnerable than ever. "Status?" he hissed in the mic.

"These people have a military connection or someone in the government," Seth said, frustration piercing his voice. "Their equipment is military grade like I've only seen in black ops. Either black market or with major connections in D.C."

"When do we go?" Deb asked.

"Incoming!" Seth's voice boomed over the airwaves. "Everyone take cover. Binoculars down. Chopper coming in from the southeast, heading straight toward the helo landing pad."

Gabe hit the dirt next to Deb and lifted his gaze. A large, luxury helicopter flew to the edge of the compound, then, rocking slightly, settled to the ground.

"That's one damn expensive design," Deb said.

"The moneymen." He touched his earpiece. "Heads-up. Anyone in line of sight take a good look. See if you recognize them. Maybe we finally have proof of who's behind this place."

The high-pitched squeal of the rotors slowed, then stopped. "This isn't a drop-off," Deb muttered. "They're staying awhile."

"Good. That means we clean up this mess that much sooner." Gabe crawled to a position where he could view the helicopter.

Two men exited. Gabe would know one of them anywhere. "Jeff Gasmerati. We were right. That son of a bitch." He hesitated, then, not caring who heard, added, "Watch Paretti."

"I know you don't want to trust me," Steve said, his voice furious. "But that's low, Gabe."

"We'll see."

Paretti muttered a very succinct curse, then signed off.

Seth let out a low whistle. "Eight heavily armed guards showed up to escort these guys inside. At least two muscle men with Gasmerati. From the bulk, I'd say they're packing Kevlar, and carrying a lot of weapons."

"How do we get in?" Deb asked.

"Ask and ye shall receive," Seth said. "Zach's top-secret-sensors-we-should-forget-asap came through. Whitney and I just located a tunnel and a hatch. We'll have to crawl the last forty yards, but if it's open and we can bring down that surveillance, we may have a way in."

Niko stared at the camera feed, searching again for the small flash of movement he'd seen on one of the dunes when the helicopter pad lit up. Had he imagined it, or had Ashley's sister come through after all?

A quick scan of the monitors made him smile. There it was. A slight discrepancy in the light hitting the sand in some of the pictures. Very slight, but the change could only come from one source. Someone had looped the cameras. Only problem was they'd missed the Minicams on the second security line.

Niko picked up his AK-47 and touched his pocket to check on the symbols for the doors. If the Admiral had brought friends, it was time to invite them in.

He strode down the hall and met two guards. "The helo is here," he stated firmly, as if he was following orders from the Warden. "I'm going outside for a quick perimeter check. Make sure everything is ready for our guests. Their satisfaction takes precedence over anything else."

Deb crawled over the sand to study the imposing warehouse. Hope rose within her. The tunnel gave them an option.

Now, if only Gabe's techy brothers, Zach and Luke, could bring down the sensors, they could storm this castle of horrors and bring Ashley home.

"Heads-up," Jazz said through the comm device. "I've got movement at the main door. A blond guy attached a sign. He's carrying an AK-47. Damn. He looked straight at us."

"Our cover blown?" Gabe asked. "I don't want to take him out if we don't have to, we're not ready."

For several seconds only the whisper of winter wind sounded. "I don't think so," Jazz said finally. "After he put up the sign, he pointed to a small circle right above his head. Then he just walked back inside. No alarm, no nothing."

Luke erupted with a string of curses. "They can still see us. There are three Minicams on a backup system," Luke muttered. "I'm looping their input." After a few seconds, he sighed. "We're invisible again."

"How bad is the damage?"

No one could answer Gabe's question.

Deb palmed her weapon and lifted her binoculars. She had no doubt everyone else had done the same. Her entire body tense, she watched, awaiting a mass attack from the building.

It didn't come.

Instead, the blond man appeared at another entrance. "He's back," Deb said. "At the loading platform. He's attaching something to the small door beside it."

"What's this guy up to?" Gabe demanded.

"Steve," Jazz interrupted. "I don't have a good angle with my scope. What's he doing?"

Deb half expected Steve Paretti not to answer.

"Weird," Paretti muttered.

She arched an eyebrow. He shrugged that maybe-I-was-wrong-but-probably-not look.

"Four stars in a row with an arrow pointing down at the tunnel Seth mentioned," Paretti said.

Deb gasped. "It's a message for me. Ashley teases me about being a four-star admiral. Sometimes I'd sign notes to her that way—with four stars in a row."

"Want to hear more good news?" Luke said. "Zach confirmed sensors are down at all three of those entrances. The security grid is spotty all over."

Gabe smiled at Deb. "Looks like we have our insider."

The black corner of the computer room loomed with a terrifying threat. Armed guards stood a few feet away, assault weapons at the ready.

Ashley's fingers shook and she fumbled on the keys. She couldn't make any mistakes. Her friends' lives were in her hands.

Ashley leaned forward and blinked. The screen returned to focus. She typed in another command.

The Warden walked past her, then stopped. "Mr. Gasmerati, Mr. Petrov, this is one of our star programmers. Ashley hacked into the NSA."

"Impressive, but only if you can do it again. Here and now," Gasmerati said, tossing down the gauntlet.

Ashley studied the two men. Well dressed, with ten guards behind them. Who were these men?

The Warden gripped Ashley's shoulder, squeezing hard enough to bruise. "Show them. Bring up a list of CIA operatives located in Kazakhstan."

Ashley glanced at Floyd. He frowned, but he couldn't help her. No one could. Not unless Deb was out there.

She had no choice. She had to stay alive.

Praying that she wasn't putting anyone in danger, her fingers flew across the keyboard. Firewalls fell.

An irritating humming sounded over her right shoulder. "You're taking too long," he muttered.

The Warden pinched Ashley's skin just at the base of her neck. She winced and typed in an incorrect keystroke. The program beeped at her.

"I can't work if I'm in pain," she hissed, trying to hide her fear.

The Warden bent down, sweat beading on his upper lip. So the man had at least one emotion, and he feared these two. In fact, the Warden was terrified. Ashley's belly roiled at the realization.

"You have one minute," he said. "Or one bullet flies."

"I just need a few more seconds," she said softly, pressing the preset codes to release the virus before hacking through to the government site.

A file appeared. A list of names and locations. A slightly altered list. Just slightly, though.

The Warden chuckled. "She just needed a little encouragement."

"She needs to learn respect," Petrov said. He scowled at the screen, then pulled out a tablet and tapped a few times. "Several names match what we already know." Petrov grinned. "Excellent." He turned and reached out his hand. "Mr. Gasmerati. We have a deal."

All the guards lifted their weapons.

The Warden looked around nervously.

Gasmerati smiled. "You're a loose end, Warden. As is everyone here."

"You can't do this," the Warden sputtered.

"Oh, I can." Gasmerati gave a quick nod. His guard held a weapon to the Warden's head. "Have your men move everyone to the basement. You remember the basement?"

The Warden gulped and nodded.

"Then bring in your guards five at a time. If you follow instructions, I may change my mind. You never know."

The Warden lifted the phone and gave the order.

Ashley's knees shook. Oh God. They were going to die.

Petrov walked over to her and put his hand on her shoulder. "I know exactly who the brains are of this outfit, Warden. When we leave, this one comes with me."

CHAPTER TWENTY-FOUR

GABE SNAPPED HIS BINOCULARS TO HIS EYES FOR A FINAL check on the delivery doors and surrounding areas that he and Deb would infiltrate while the others created distractions and drew fire. With luck, they'd pick off personnel when they exited the building.

Something was going on, though. According to Zach and Luke, heat signatures had been fluctuating wildly on both floors in that corner, and some activity was going on in a stairwell or ramp between the two levels.

"Dawn hits in fifteen minutes and we'll lose all our cover," Gabe said, thankful for his SWAT training. "We move in five. Get ready."

Gabe muted his mic and adjusted Deb's Kevlar vest one last time. He looked at her. "I'll protect you in there," he said softly, and kissed her, allowing his lips to linger just long enough to remind himself he had a lot to live for.

She looked up at him, dazed. "What was that for?"

"For luck," he whispered.

"Then let's make love like sex-crazed rabbits later, because I could use some more luck."

He cracked up laughing and she smiled at him.

"You ready for this, Deb?" he asked gently.

"Yeah, let's do it. Let's bring Ashley home."

Feeling slightly less desperate than before, they made their way down the dune toward the landing doors.

Suddenly, one of the guards burst from the main entrance and raced to the helicopter.

They ducked. "We've got movement," Gabe relayed.

"I see him," Jazz said quietly. "Target acquired. Do I take the shot?"

"Hold off," Gabe said. "We can't reveal our position."

The guard pulled out a black rectangular box.

Zach swore. "Oh, man, this isn't good."

Seth followed with a harsh curse.

"What's not good?" Deb asked through the comm.

"Iceman bomb," Zach said. "It's the nickname for an explosive that burns extra hot and extra long."

"Only one reason for an iceman. They're going to destroy this facility."

"Like Winslow?" Deb said with horror.

"From what you've told me, worse," Seth said. "This bomb won't leave anything behind. It burns at over five thousand degrees Fahrenheit. Everything in that building will be ash. There won't be a bone left to find."

"No one will escape." Gabe sucked in a harsh breath. "We've only got one chance . . . and God only knows how much time."

The smell of blood and death wrinkled Jeff Gasmerati's nose. Distasteful.

He straightened his Gucci suit and watched the guards' bodies slide to the floor, joining the first fifteen.

With each murder, his smile grew larger in direct proportion to the Warden's gray pallor. He patted the removable drive in his pocket. The key to everything. The uncompiled code for the game. Billions of dollars. Once he moved the game production to Russia, with Petrov's network, all his problems would be solved.

From Russia, with the program and Ashley Lansing, he could do anything, control anyone.

No more FBI. No more Montgomerys. No more headaches.

Another group of five guards entered the room.

They gasped, seeing the pile of bodies. Before they could raise their weapons, a spray of gunfire mowed them down.

"That's everyone?" Gasmerati said.

The Warden nodded.

Gasmerati possessed the precise number of guards and flunkies the Warden employed. He walked over to the man who had come to him with a simple idea ten years ago. Despite everyone's skepticism, even laughter, Jeff understood technology. He'd made the Warden's idea bigger and better. He'd even killed his own father when the patriarch of the Gasmerati family resisted his ideas.

He tugged a knife from his coat and sliced the man's cheek open. "Where is your right-hand?"

The Warden clutched his arm.

Jeff chuckled. "I mean Niko."

The Warden blanched.

With a frown, Jeff glared at two guards. "Find him. Kill him."

"We will do well together," Petrov said.

Jeff smiled. It would be interesting to see how long Petrov

survived their association. He believed himself to have the upper hand. He knew nothing of Jeff's true connections.

A knock sounded at the door. Sly strode in. "The iceman has been set. We have twenty minutes."

Gabe gripped his Glock and inched along the side of the warehouse. Deb had his back. He could trust her. He had no doubts.

They slipped inside the loading platform entrance next to the huge roll-up metal door. No sounds of boots or clanging of alarms greeted them, but a long, empty corridor stretched in front of them and a staircase went down to the left.

Too quiet. He met Deb's worried gaze. She had a bad feeling.

"It's the blond man," Seth's voice filtered through the mic.

Chaos and gunfire blared through the communication devices.

A loud shout sounded. "They're killing everyone."

More gunfire. Gabe's jaw clenched. Deb clutched his arm. He had to trust his brothers. He did trust his brothers.

Two minutes later it was over.

Seth heaved a breath. "Gabe, listen to this."

"No time . . . I'm dead." A voice he didn't recognize. Had to be the blond man.

He sucked in more air, the sound wet. Gabe could just imagine the blood bubbling from the side of the man's mouth. "Bomb inside. Kids were taken to—" His words went garbled. "Save them . . ."

"He's gone, and we're out of time," Seth said. "Everyone, go."

Gabe motioned to Deb. They moved forward again.

Someone coughed nearby.

"Shhh . . ."

Whispers filtered through a set of double doors. It sounded like scared kids.

Ashley?

Gabe and Deb eased down the hallway then peeked through the small inserted window. It was some sort of cafeteria and two kids stood huddled inside.

He shoved into the room. Mylo and a sandy-haired kid spun around in a panic, fumbling with their M-16s. A horrifying stench came from the blood-spattered duo.

"Whoa, hold it!" Gabe lifted his hands. "Mylo, it's Gabe and Deb."

Angry fire blazed in Mylo's eyes, then cleared. "Oh, man, thank God it's you." His shoulders sagged. "I thought we were dead."

Deb raced to them. "What happened? Where's Ashley?"

"Some big shots that flew in today have her. I only caught one name. Petrov," the sandy-haired boy said, his face streaked with blood.

"Gasmerati's partner." Gabe frowned. They had a name.

"How did you get away?" Deb asked.

"When they announced we were all going to the basement, we were in the back corner." Mylo shuddered. "This is Floyd. He knows everything about this place."

Gabe ticked through his father's list. The name sounded familiar.

"You said the kids are in the basement?"

"It's where they execute those who are expendable," Floyd said. "No one likes to go there. We slipped under the grates and went to the armory on the other side of the complex like Niko told us to do. Can't believe that blond bastard helped us."

And paid for it. "What about Ashley?" Gabe asked.

"We saw her in the C corridor with those big shots and about six guards. She covered for us," Mylo said, his face painted with an awed look. "She's crazy brave. Threw a fit, screaming that she didn't want to go with them. Biting and scratching. Petrov backhanded her, and in the chaos, we managed to escape. I don't know where she is now, but the kids downstairs are probably being gassed right now."

"This can't be happening." Deb closed her eyes. A tear slid down her cheek. She clicked her earpiece. "Ashley last seen in C corridor near the armory with Gasmerati. Six guards. Please, find her. Gabe and I are heading to the basement for a rescue. Over."

She turned to the group. "We have to save those kids."

Gabe thought he'd never seen a woman more heartbreakingly beautiful or brave. "They'll find her," Gabe said. "Okay, where's the basement, Floyd?"

"Follow me," he said. "Keep your weapons ready. They shoot to kill here."

The group hurried as fast as they dared. They turned right near the door where Deb and Gabe had entered and started down the stairs.

A flurry of shots echoed from several places inside the building and more shots answered.

"Move it," Gabe urged.

"The basement is here," Floyd whispered, finally slowing as they neared the bottom. "There's a big room that I've never seen anyone go into before."

"Any idea what it's used for?"

"Yeah," Floyd said softly. "Mass murder."

Gabe raced down the stairs, followed by the teenagers. Deb brought up the rear. She must be champing to search this place for Ashley, but she'd put her faith in him and his brothers. He just prayed they didn't let her down.

She could have his back anytime, and if they lived through this, he intended to tell her that. Among other things.

A series of rapid-fire gunshots sounded again in the distance. Gabe knew his brothers could take care of themselves. But still . . . Damn, he couldn't help them now.

One last step and he entered the basement corridor. The others crowded around him.

Two compound guards lay dead on the floor.

A weak cry sounded from behind the door. Gabe grabbed one of Zach's toys, jammed it against the panel, and turned it on. The machine whirred and lights flashed and a few moments later, the tumblers clicked. He wrenched open the door.

Acrid gas spewed from the room, its sour odor nauseating. More than twenty kids lay on the floor gasping, vomiting, and writhing in desperation.

One boy rolled over and looked at Gabe. "Get out. Heard talking. Bomb," he said. "Today."

Gabe took a second to tap his communication device. "Heads-up. Confirmation of explosive device to detonate today. Get everybody out."

"Ashley! Are you in here?" Deb called out, even as she dragged the retching kids from the room.

Some could still walk a little and they helped others. Gabe, Deb, Mylo, and Floyd half dragged, half carried the weakest ones into the hallway.

One figure remained huddled in the corner.

Floyd hurried into the room to help. The man turned over, vomiting all over himself.

The boy stilled. "You killed my brother."

Green with sickness, the Warden looked up at Floyd.

He raised the gun.

"Floyd—" Gabe rushed toward him.

"This is for Fletcher."

Gabe was too late. Floyd peppered the Warden with bullets.

He emptied the magazine, then tossed the weapon next to the body.

Tears streaming down his face, Floyd doubled over. He threw up and stumbled out of the room. Gabe placed a hand on his shoulder and met Floyd's tortured gaze.

The boy swiped at his wet cheeks. "Why don't I feel better?" he asked in a small voice.

"Come on," Gabe said, knowing nothing would help but time.

In the hallway, the gas had dissipated; the teenagers started to revive.

"Let's clear this room fast and go after Ashley," he said to Deb.

Seth's voice interrupted on the comm line. "Just found the bomb. We have three minutes to get out."

"We have twenty kids. We can't make it," Deb shouted.

Zach's voice came through. "The tunnel is almost directly above you. One flight."

Gabe grabbed Floyd. "An escape tunnel? You know it?"

"Niko told me."

"Two minutes."

Thirty seconds and they were up the stairs. Floyd entered a code and they scrambled into the tunnel. Lights lit automatically.

Deb half dragged a couple of kids with her. Gabe followed up at the rear.

Another thirty seconds and they neared the end of the tunnel. He raced to the ladder and scooted past the kids. He and Deb looked up. A lock.

"Damn it. How do we open it?" she asked.

The dial turned and the hatch slammed open. Jazz looked down at them from the surface. "Come on!" she yelled.

One by one, Gabe and Deb shoved the kids out of the tunnel. Finally Deb scampered up. He followed.

They stumbled only a dozen feet when an explosion rocked the earth. Gabe shoved Deb to the ground. The high-tech weapon didn't work like any other. The explosion didn't burst out, it imploded.

Black smoke poured around them, along with an intensive heat that rendered the building—and everything inside it—ash.

The comm device in his ear squealed nonstop and he tore the ruined earpiece out just as Deb did the same with hers.

Gabe blinked through the soot. There was nothing left

unscathed in the building. No one within the blast zone could have survived.

His back burned and he staggered to his feet.

"Your jacket's smoking," Deb shouted.

He jerked it off, threw it to the ground, then stomped out the blaze. Panting, he looked down at her.

She met his gaze but then turned in the direction of the compound and let out a low cry. Black soot billowed from the shattered concrete slabs, half of which now filled the decimated basement. The smell of the gas still permeated the air.

Deb sank to the ground. "Oh, dear God. Ashley, I'm sorry." Deb bent her head to her knees and rocked back and forth, back and forth. "I failed her."

Gabe bit back a curse.

"No!" He knelt beside Deb and wrapped her in his arms.

Deep shudders of agony shook her body and she clung to him. "I didn't save her. We were so close."

Gabe rocked her in his arms and let her cry, uncertain what to do or say.

He squinted through the smoke. Where were his brothers? God, had he killed them, too?

Jazz rose slowly, tears in her own eyes. "I can't see Luke," she said.

Then, Gabe caught sight of Luke racing to Jazz through the black swirls.

Figures began to coalesce. Nick and Paretti showed next, coughing, stumbling through the chaos. Finally Zach held up his hand in tired acknowledgment.

Where was Seth? Whitney? Gabe's heart thundered as long moments passed.

Deb lifted her lashes. "What have we done?"

Gabe couldn't speak. He kissed her hair, his own grief splintering and shattering all the light and warmth inside him.

Then, through the smoke another figure stumbled toward them.

Seth? Whitney?

A familiar face took shape then coughed.

"Gasmerati!"

At Gabe's shout Deb shot to her feet.

"Where is my sister, you son of a bitch?"

In slow motion, Jeff Gasmerati aimed his weapon.

Gabe raced forward. His leg gave out, costing him a half step. In that moment the gun fired.

Deb flew back into Gabe's arms and a second shot rang out.

Gasmerati's head exploded.

Gabe sank to the sand, Deb cradled in his arms. Blood pooled at her shoulder. She looked up at him.

"Ashley?" she whispered, blinking, as if trying to focus on him. "It was her?"

"No," he said softly. "Don't talk. I've got you." God, how had this happened? He hadn't protected her.

Not only her, but Ashley as well. He stripped off his shirt and pressed the material against her shoulder.

"Who's that?" Luke shouted.

Someone was running toward the helipad, dragging a figure behind him. Gasmerati's partner, Petrov.

"Petrov. Stop him!" Gabe shouted.

A helicopter zoomed in from the east, its sleek, black shape like something out of a sci-fi movie. Maybe someone Seth had called in?

Petrov fired. The chopper stopped on a dime, then rotated in the air, following the Russian.

A barrage of bullets peppered him. He fell dead. The small figure at his side dropped to the ground. Gabe squinted. Could it be?

An RPG took out Gasmerati's chopper, blowing it to bits, then the chopper disappeared into the sky.

Two people raced toward the fallen girl. Whitney and Seth.

Thank God.

Seth knelt down and lifted the small figure in his arms.

"Is it her?" Gabe shouted.

The swell of blackness parted, and through the smoke, Seth strode toward them, propping up Whitney on one side, balancing a blonde-haired girl close to his chest.

Holy crap.

"Deb . . ."

She tried to open her eyes. "I don't care anymore, Gabe. Ashley's gone."

"Deb. Look."

She heard a familiar shout.

"Admiral!"

"Ashley?" Deb struggled to sit up in Gabe's hold, tears nearly blinding her. "Oh my God, Ashley! It's really you." A sob broke from her and she held out her arms. "Ashley!"

Ashley stumbled, then fell beside her sister, laughing and crying as Deb hugged her close. "Oh, Ashley."

Tears streamed down Ashley's battered, sooty face, but nothing could detract from the joy in her eyes. "I knew you'd come for me, Deb. I just knew it."

"Always," Deb whispered and held on tight.

CHAPTER TWENTY-FIVE

DEB COULDN'T BELIEVE SHE HELD ASHLEY IN HER ARMS. SHE winced, her shoulder throbbing, her head going woozy, but she didn't care. She gently pushed the hair away from her sister's bruised face. "Are you okay, pipsqueak?"

Ashley nodded. "I will be. For a while there, I didn't know if I'd make it through." She grinned. "I just kept running that stupid mantra through my head, 'Never give up . . .'"

"'Never surrender,'" Deb finished for her. "Oh, sweetheart, I love you so much. Nothing matters now that you're safe." She looked over her sister's shoulder at Gabe. He still held his shirt against her wound, an enigmatic look on his face. But he seemed quiet and serene amid all this chaos.

He'd been her rock through all this, and she didn't know what she'd have done without him. She certainly wouldn't have been holding her precious sister alive in her arms right now.

Zach stood by Gabe, using his voodoo magic gizmo phone to call the authorities to come in and help transport the kids and clean up. "Medevac units on the way. Ambulances will be here shortly thereafter."

"Who were those guys in the chopper that came from out of nowhere?" Zach asked.

Seth's face grew cold. "All I can tell you is they don't get involved, in any op, without extremely high authority. I don't know what the hell's going on, but I swear, I'll find out."

"Gabe," Deb whispered, blinking feverishly. "I think I need a doctor."

Deb blinked against the bright light and stared around the room. "Ashley."

"Ashley's in surgery to remove a chip those bastards implanted inside of her. She'll be out soon."

Gabe stroked Deb's forehead, and she relaxed.

"It wasn't a dream."

"More like a nightmare," he said.

She looked up at him. "Everyone's okay?"

"Nothing that's not recoverable. Most of them went home after they knew you'd be okay. Mom's planning a huge, celebratory Thanksgiving dinner."

"How long have I been unconscious?"

"Forty-eight hours." Gabe swallowed deeply, and for the first time Deb recognized the sallowness of his skin, the dark shadows beneath his eyes.

"You look terrible."

His mouth quirked. "Yeah, well, interviews with the Feds can do that to you. Not to mention you dying on the operating table. Twice."

He clutched her hand. "I've never been more scared."

"What happened?"

"You lost so much blood by the time the chopper got there, it was touch and go." He looked at her. "I'm sorry, Deb. I told you I'd protect you."

"It wasn't your fault. Did they get everyone?"

He nodded. "It'll be a while before they can piece together who died in that hellhole. Whitney will do it, though. She's got some chutzpah. Called in I don't know how many favors to make the legal problems disappear."

He sat in his chair for a moment. She longed for him to hold her, but he stared at her.

"What's wrong?"

"It's over," he said quietly. "You have your family back."

"Not everyone," she said, her heart breaking.

"No. Not everyone. I'm sorry about your brother. What are you going to do now?"

Then she understood. No *us*. No *we*. Only her.

"I guess I'll move down to Colorado Springs, take care of Ashley for a while. Not take so many risks. She needs me." Deb bit her lip and waited. Surely this wasn't it? After all they'd been through.

"I thought so."

"What about you?" Deb asked, the words barely forming. Perhaps it had all been a lie. Maybe he'd realized she wasn't good enough, that if she could let Ashley down like that, she'd eventually let him down, too.

He shrugged. "Rebuild the bar, see if I can buy it for real this time. I'm not sure I want to go back to being a cop."

"Their loss." She gave him a smile, all the while her heart breaking. "I guess this is it, then."

"It's for the best, Deb."

"Yeah. For the best."

He stood. "I'll go tell the doctor you're awake. I'm here until you're released."

She couldn't bear to see him again. Not like this.

"Don't worry about it. Ashley's here. I have my family, Gabe. Just like you have yours. I'll be okay."

He turned to the door, his shoulders slumped. "You're an amazing woman, Deb Lansing. It's been an honor knowing you."

"Ditto," she said softly.

He quietly walked out the door.

She didn't cry. She wouldn't cry, but inside she balled up. Gabe Montgomery hadn't stolen her heart, she'd given it away. She'd never get it back.

Gabe knelt in the middle of the scorched remains of Sammy's Bar. It had been one week since Deb had come home. His pants hung on his hips. He couldn't sleep. He couldn't eat. All because he'd been a fool and a coward.

But seeing her lying in that hospital bed . . . she'd nearly died. He'd failed her in every way a man could fail a woman. How could she love him after that? How could she ever put her faith in him again? In his fatigue-filled mind, he'd convinced himself she was better off without him.

Maybe he'd been right.

A knock sounded on the new frame going up near the front. "Anyone home?" Neil Wexler stuck his head between the two-by-fours where the wall would be. "Place looks good."

"Better than it did," Gabe said, standing. He shook Neil's hand. "You look good. Happy even."

"Yeah." Neil grinned. "My wife's pregnant. I'm going to be a daddy."

"Congratulations." A wave of remorse washed through Gabe. Right now he couldn't imagine having a family of his own. Not without Deb.

"Yeah, we're excited. I wanted to stop by to offer you a job. As a detective."

Gabe stilled. "Why?"

"Because you're damned good at it and we could use a couple of upstanding deputies in the sheriff's office. I could tear up your resignation paper today."

Gabe slowly shook his head. "No thanks, Neil. I'm moving." He bent over to clear the remains of a chair.

"Sorry to hear that, but it was worth a try. You'll be missed." Neil turned around to leave. "Deb."

"Hi, Neil."

Gabe's head whipped up from his job. He straightened. The wood dropped from his fingertips as he drank in Deb's presence.

The color was back in her cheeks, but tension pulled at her mouth and she looked liked she'd lost a few pounds.

Neil tipped his hat to her. "See you around. Maybe you can talk some sense into him. He'd be a great detective."

Deb didn't answer, but stepped into the remains of the bar. "This is where we started, isn't it?"

She was here. *She'd* come to *him*. Gabe couldn't form a thought. This wasn't how it was supposed to happen. He hadn't figured out how to apologize. "I guess so."

Deb walked across the charred floor. "You're moving?"

"I thought about it.

"I see." Deb rubbed the nape of her neck. "I guess I was wrong." She stepped back and then paused. "No, wait a minute." She strode to him, toe to toe, and pulled his head down to hers.

The moment her mouth touched his, he groaned.

She shoved him away. "I thought so. You *do* want me."

"Of course I want you," Gabe growled. "What do you think I'm doing?"

"Running away?"

"Hell no." Gabe shoved his hand through his hair. He couldn't let her think the worst. Deb's words were an attack, but the expression in her eyes—he'd hurt her. He'd known it at the hospital; he'd convinced himself he was doing the right thing. He should quit thinking. He blinked, hating the caution in her stance, in her gaze. She'd come here. It was so like her.

If he wanted to prove himself to her, he had to shove aside the doubts. He had to lay his heart on the line. She deserved no less. "I'm getting this place ready to rebuild, then moving to Colorado Springs. To be near you."

She froze.

"I knew it the moment I got home. I almost lost you," he said. "I don't ever want to feel that way again, but it was my fault. How could I ask you to forgive me? How can I now?"

She clutched his jacket. "You're an idiot, Gabe. There's nothing to forgive. I'm the one who should thank you. You saved Ashley's life. Without you and your family . . ." Deb shuddered. "I don't want to think about what could have happened to her, to all those kids."

"I don't want gratitude, Deb." His heart burst open, and he couldn't stop himself from saying the words that had been simmering inside of him for too long. She was so close. He tugged her into his arms. "I want more, so I'm going to say it out loud. I'm in love with you, Deb Lansing. I love that you never run from a fight. I love you for your bravery, even when you scare the hell out of me. I love you for your loyalty, because you never turn your back on the people counting on you. And I love how much you love your family." Gabe's heart stuttered for a moment. He'd never made himself so vulnerable to anyone. He breathed in deeply. "I've loved you since the first day you walked into the bar. I just didn't know it yet."

"Then we're even," she said, her voice husky with emotion. "I fell for you the night you were shot. Later, I figured I'd remind you of that night. I guess I was—"

"Afraid to take a chance?" Gabe finished.

She nodded.

"You know, for a couple of people who live on the edge most of the time, we sure don't take a lot of risks."

"Not with my heart," Deb said. "Not until you." She threaded her fingers through his. "I want to be with you, Gabe Montgomery, but I'm not as wonderful as you think I am."

"I've watched you, Deb Lansing. I know you."

She stroked his hair back, her gaze holding his captive. "I've let people down before, like that soldier in Afghanistan. They held an inquiry and I was cleared, but I knew I should have taken the chance and done something differently. I let down Ashley, too. I don't want to let you down. That's my biggest fear."

He simply smiled. "You can't. Because if you're starting to fall, I'll be there to catch you."

With those words, he pressed his lips against hers. She opened herself to him, and with a tenderness unlike any he'd ever experienced, he let himself get lost in her kiss.

When he finally lifted his head, his lips tingled with such a feeling of right. This was what his father had shared with his mother. This was the reason his father had stayed.

This was the reason his mother had forgiven his father.

"I might let you down, too, honey, though I'm going to try my damnedest not to." He nuzzled her cheek. "The thing is, if we really love each other, it doesn't matter. We'll pick each other right back up and try again. Because that's what you do. When you love someone."

Deb studied him for several seconds.

"This is the part when you say you love me, too."

"Oh, yeah." She looked at him with a bemused expression. "I love you, too."

He couldn't stop the smile. His heart lightened. Yeah. She was his. He was hers. "Thank God. Do you think you could get used to a new name?"

"What?"

"Well, I like the name Deborah Lansing, but the name Deb Montgomery sounds even better. Will you marry me? Be my heart, my family?"

She didn't answer. Gabe's heart lurched in his chest.

"Should I get down on one knee?"

"No," she laughed, pressing against him. "Of course not." She threw her arms around his neck. "Yes! Oh my God, yes!"

"Whew," he joked, wiping his brow in relief. "My leg is killing me after all the running around we've done. I could get down on one knee. I'm just not sure I could get back up."

"I'll always be there to help you," she whispered. She'd found her home, someone to love, and someone to love her. She hugged him close, determined to never, ever let him go again.

"How about our own family motto? 'Never give up. Never surrender.'" She kissed his lips. "It fits."

"Say what you want about the Montgomerys," Gabe said, cupping her face between his hands, "but we definitely don't give up. So you, Deb Lansing, soon-to-be Montgomery, will fit right in. But more than that, we never stop loving each other. No matter what."

"I love you, Gabe Montgomery," Deb whispered. "And that will never stop."

Acknowledgments

WRITING CAN BE SOLITARY, BUT CREATING THIS BOOK HASN'T been. I am blessed with an unparalleled support system.

Jill Marsal, literary agent extraordinaire—your belief in me and in this book means more than I can ever articulate. Thank you isn't enough, but suffice it to say, I wouldn't be here without you, Jill.

Kelli Martin, editor—your insights helped make this book what it is today. We found the soul of this book together! Thank you.

Tammy Baumann, Louise Bergin, and Sherri Buerkle—what can I say, the Golden Meanies strike again. This one needed all your skill and patience. Ladies, I couldn't do it without you!

Mom and Dad—no matter what life brings, your undying faith and support in each other and in your children inspires me to keep going. The Montgomery family's loyalty and devotion springs from you. I love you both. No matter what. Forever and always.

About the Author

Photo Credit: Kyle Zimmerman, 2013

RITA® Award finalist, national bestselling, and award-winning author Robin Perini is devoted to giving her readers fast-paced, high-stakes adventures with a love story sure to melt their hearts. Robin sold seven titles to publishers in one year after winning the prestigious Romance Writers of America® Golden Heart® Award in 2011. An analyst for an advanced technology corporation, she is also a nationally acclaimed writing instructor and enjoys competitive small-bore rifle silhouette shooting. She makes her home in the American Southwest and loves to hear from readers. Visit her website at http://www.robinperini.com.